OTHER TITLES BY EMMA HOLLY

The Prince With No Heart

The Assassins' Lover

Steaming Up Your Love Scenes (how-to)

The Billionaire Bad Boys Club

Djinn Series

Tales of the Djinn: The Guardian

Tales of the Djinn: The Double

Hidden Series

Hidden Talents

Hidden Depths

Date Night

Move Me

The Faerie's Honeymoon

Hidden Crimes

Winter's Tale

Hidden Dragons

Hidden Passions

TALES OF THE DJINN: THE DOUBLE

EMMA HOLLY

Tales of the Djinn: The Double

Emma Holly

Discover other exciting Emma Holly titles at: http://www.emmaholly.com

Tales of the Djinn: The Double is an approximately 103,000-word novel.

ISBN-10: 1502546841

ISBN-13: 978-1502546845

cover photos: istockphoto.com—Yuri
bigstockphoto.com—greatpapa, mazzur

CONTENTS

CHAPTER ONE

THE Guardian of the Glorious City gave up on trying to sleep and stared at the high ceiling. Glinting faintly in the dimness, a diamond chandelier worth a few sultans' ransoms hung directly above him. Cade was home in the djinn dimension for the first time in weeks. He lay in a luxurious bed, enjoying every comfort a being could wish. The sheets were silk, the huge mattress beneath his back the ideal blend of firm and soft. A beautiful woman slept beside him, breathing quietly and slow. Her cute little butt—of which he was very fond—bumped his hip reassuringly. Elyse was human and not the sort of female he was used to, but he loved her with every drop of his warrior's blood. Feeling this way seemed a miracle. In all his years as a soldier, he'd never imagined he'd fall in love. Having Elyse welcome his devotion humbled him.

If the city whose safety was in his hands weren't in danger, he'd have counted himself lucky.

The man who should have been sleeping in this bed, who should have been overseeing the city's return to order, was Cade's sultan. Though Iksander hadn't been aware of it at the time, he'd spurned a powerful sorceress. Fatefully, she was no ordinary mage but an empress with ambitions both romantic and political. In revenge for Iksander thwarting her aspirations, Luna had turned every one of the Glorious City's residents into stone. Her thirst for vengeance had known no bounds. She'd petrified herself in the process too.

By the skin of their teeth, Cade and the sultan's small inner circle escaped her curse—the four men the city's only hope of mounting a rescue. Special interdimensional portals allowed them to send duplicates of themselves to the human realm, where Cade and his servant Joseph met Elyse.

The trio's voyage back to the city demanded all their courage and cleverness. Compared to overcoming those obstacles, destroying the sorceress's statue had been a snap.

Unfortunately, it hadn't been the remedy they hoped. Empress Luna had aces of her own up her sleeve. She'd sent a portion her spirit through a portal, leaving the remainder here to anchor her terrible curse. Half the city had recovered when they smashed her form. The rest remained trapped in stone.

The logistics of getting a populace in that condition back on its feet were headache inducing.

To make matters more difficult, the whereabouts of Sultan Iksander and their artist friend Philip were unknown. Presumably the djinn had made it through the portals into the human world. Wherever they were, they hadn't contacted Cade or Joseph by their prearranged signal. Cade couldn't even search for them until the city's portals were re-charged, a process that might take months. He couldn't search for Luna either, which meant they couldn't completely break her curse.

Simply praying things would turn out didn't suit his compulsion to take action.

His hands were clenched. He was getting too wrought up. Sensing his tension in her sleep, Elyse let out a grumbling noise and rolled over to face him. Her slender arm fell across his abdomen, one smooth leg sliding over his. Her skin was cool, her naked breasts a pleasing softness against his side. Elyse had been through a lot in life. She'd lost her mother when she was a baby. Her father, mysteriously enough, had fallen into a volcano. Her husband, also recently deceased, had married her under false colors—a deception Cade had revealed to her. He couldn't wonder she didn't trust easily. She'd recently confessed she loved him . . . with the caveat that she doubted she was *in* love. Though he understood the reasons she might hold back, the distinction stung. Cade was totally gone on her, as the humans said: no ifs, ands, or buts about it.

At least she trusted him enough to turn to him in slumber.

Not wishing to disturb her, he forced his lungs to go in and out evenly. The issues he couldn't address this minute would have to wait. The issues he could address were more than sufficient to keep him occupied.

First on the list was his double's continued existence. Cade supposed this wasn't his worst challenge, but it was frustrating. According to his understanding of the doubling process, Cade and the other him should have recombined as soon as they were face to face in the same dimension. That hadn't happened. His time with Elyse had changed him—broadened him too much, probably. Despite being animated by a lesser portion of their shared spirit, his original stayed stubbornly separate.

Cade snorted quietly. *Stubborn* might be his former self's defining trait, followed in close order by *narrow-minded ass.*

"You're thinking too loudly," Elyse grumbled sleepily.

She didn't mean she could hear his thoughts. Humans could do magic if they learned the proper formulas and disciplined their minds. Djinn magic was subordinate to that of humans—hence King Solomon's famous success in wrangling them. Humans were God's pets, favored above all the races He'd created. Fortunately for djinn, few humans possessed the unswerving faith casting spells required. Djinn, on the other hand, were born with the right mindset.

They believed in God and His wonders whether they wanted to or not.

"Sorry," Arcadius said, realizing his thoughts had drifted. He stroked Elyse's thick dark curls—the bane of her existence, to hear her talk, though he adored them. Her hair betrayed her secret wildness like nothing else about her. To others like his double, Elyse seemed plain and a little shy. To him, she was gorgeous inside and out: a quick-witted, warm-hearted beauty with a Samson's mane. "I didn't mean to wake you."

"S'okay." She patted his ribcage and yawned. "Anything you want to talk out with me?"

They'd talked and more last night. She'd been comforting and sexy and as sensible about their circumstances as he wanted to be himself. The last thing he wished was for her to think she had to cosset him ceaselessly. He understood human females valued independence. Though it didn't come naturally to male djinn, he'd try to let her stand on her own two feet. What he wouldn't do was make it *her* job to bolster him.

He drew her hand from his chest for a gentle kiss. "I suspect the best medicine for my worries is work. There's a lot to do. I'm going to bathe and dress."

"It's not even dawn," Elyse groaned as he sat up.

"It will be soon." He gave her bare hip a rub. "You go back to sleep."

"I want a job too."

He was striding toward the bathing chamber. Her mumbled words made him stop and look back at her. Though she'd snuggled into the pillow, her soft green eyes were open.

The way her hip curved into her waist brought warmth flooding to his groin. He ground his molars together, ordering his body not to react more than that. He was naked too, every part of him on display. He didn't want her to feel she had to coddle him with constant sex either.

He wrested his attention back to her request.

"I mean it," she said, every bit as stubborn as the other him. "I don't care if the job is sweeping floors. We don't know how long I'll be stranded here until the portals come back online. I won't sit around nibbling dates like a harem girl."

His lips twitched at that image. He probably shouldn't admit how appealing he found the idea of her in filmy harem garments, obediently awaiting his pleasure. "You want to sweep floors."

"Well, I'd rather do something more interesting, but as it happens I'm good at mundane chores. I'm a landlady, if you recall."

He hadn't forgotten. While they were in New York, Joseph and he had lived in the basement of her brownstone. "Give me a chance to think of something appropriate."

"Urgh," was her response to that.

"You're in an unfamiliar culture. Being a little cautious isn't an awful thing."

She sighed gustily. Despite the reaction, Cade sensed she teetered near surrender. "What happened to the woman who always looked before she leaped?"

Elyse bit a sudden grin. "She ran away with a sexy genie."

"Then she got what she deserved, didn't she?"

He turned again toward his goal. She lobbed a throw pillow from the bed, her arm good enough for the little cushion to smack his ass.

"Careful," he teased over one shoulder. "You wouldn't want to injure something you're hoping to use later."

"You're just my sex toy," she said, sounding like she was burrowing deeper into the plush covers.

"Promises, promises," he tossed back.

She didn't answer, so maybe she'd dropped off to sleep again. As he stepped into the spacious bath, he told himself that was for the best.

~

Elyse smiled into the pillow she was hugging. Arcadius—or "Cade" as they'd decided to call him to distinguish him from his double—was fun to trade banter with. He was fun to do a lot of things with, actually. Considering how different their backgrounds and natures were, how well they got along was a miracle. She was a born New Yorker: interested in people from other places but in a feet-firmly-on-the-ground kind of way. Until the day Cade turned to smoke before her eyes, she hadn't believed in genies. She'd been perfectly happy to leave imagining multiverses to physicists. Discovering that a door to the world of the djinn was hiding in her cellar had been an eye opener.

Discovering both her dad and her deceased husband had known about it had pulled the proverbial rug out from under her.

That axis shift was behind her, thankfully. Her father, may he rest in peace, had concealed the truth to protect her. Access to the incredibly rich, incredibly magical djinn dimension was valuable. People would kill to get it, as her cousin Cara and her crazy tattooed gangster boyfriend proved. In the struggle to control the door, Mario had slaughtered Elyse's husband with an enchanted djinn artifact. He'd also shot Cara's father—Elyse's uncle—in front of her. Part of the reason he'd done it was because Cara had cast a spell to make Mario fall in love with her, the same spell David had used to get Elyse to marry him.

The business was enough to make a sane person run for a padded room.

Elyse had resisted that temptation, deciding she'd rather help Cade rescue his people. Her father, always a passionate traveler, would have approved the choice. Leo Solomon prized the djinn for being a fascinating culture. The others only wanted to exploit them. Elyse hadn't expected her decision to lead where it did. Her husband's loss had been devastating, but Cade restored her faith in her ability to love.

As to that, their dangerous journey here restored her faith in her own courage.

You're lucky, she thought, *no matter how far out of your comfort zone this adventure is.*

Of course, she probably shouldn't call it an adventure. The problems Cade's city faced were deadly serious. In his position as Guardian, Cade oversaw not just the army but the police as well. She knew he felt duty bound to heal the wounds the sorceress had inflicted—entirely on his own if required. Given how much there was to do, she thought he was fortunate there were two of him.

Given the way they'd instantly annoyed each other, Cade and his double didn't share her point of view.

Despite her awareness that neither would be amused, Elyse snickered into her pillow. The sound of distant splashing brought her head up. She and Cade were in the sultan's apartments, partly to keep Iksander's staff settled in his absence but also because the original Arcadius objected to sharing "his" rooms with someone he viewed as an inferior version of himself.

He'd left her in no doubt Cade's taste in lovers proved his opinion.

But to heck with him and his prejudice. Thanks to his snobbery, Elyse now wallowed in luxury. If the Palace at Versailles had smashed into the Taj Mahal and then got bedazzled with fist-sized gems, a person *might* begin to picture her surroundings. The bedroom was the size of basketball court. From her peek at it last night, the bathroom was just as grand. If Cade were in there swimming, as the sounds she heard implied, maybe another tour should take priority over her beauty rest.

She knew from experience that her lover naked was an eyeful.

She slipped from the cushy bed grinning. Cade might be too focused on the work ahead of him to play, but she could still enjoy ogling him.

When she reached the huge blue and white tiled room, Cade was cutting through a two-lane pool in a beautiful steady crawl. Last night, she'd assumed this was the bath. Now she spotted a smaller tub beyond it with even thicker steam swirling over its surface.

So it's soak then swim, she thought, lowering herself to sit on the coping of the larger reservoir. As her feet submerged, she sucked air between her teeth. The water was almost too hot to bear. She'd boil like a lobster if she got in the second tub.

Happy to sit for the time being, she observed the powerful motions of her djinn lover's limbs propelling him through the pool. He looked human with the water sheeting and gleaming on his broad back: two arms, two legs, no extra tail or anything like that. It was hard to believe he could transform his solidness to smoke—even harder that he could fit in something as compact as a brass oil lamp. She hadn't seen him do that, but she'd watched his faithful servant Joseph emerge from one. She'd also seen Cade turn into a black raven, the same raven that was tattooed across his back. Their missing artist friend Philip inked the design. All Cade needed to activate it was to think the spell silently.

Face it, Elyse thought as she swung her legs through the hot water. *You aren't in Manhattan anymore.*

The next time he reached her end of the pool, Cade stopped and held the edge. He swiped water off his face brusquely. "Why are you out there? You're free to come in. You swimming won't bother me."

She smiled. He'd been extra careful not to offend her since she'd admitted she loved him too: his special brand of morning after awkwardness, she guessed. "The view is better here. I've been admiring your excellent form."

"My form."

"Swimming and otherwise," she clarified.

He was a naturally serious man. She loved the wide grin he broke into. Still hanging on the rim, he shifted over to face her more directly. "Otherwise, huh?"

"I don't think I can use the soaking tub," she added. "This pool is almost too hot for me."

Dismay flashed across his face, which she hadn't intended. "Forgive me. I didn't think of that. I'll change the settings immediately." He began to push up on his muscular arms.

"Stop," she said, laughing a little bit. "It'll wait till later. If the settings aren't magic, maybe I can figure them out myself."

He subsided and looked at her, his gorgeous blue green eyes probing hers. "I asked the staff to stay away this morning. Usually they wait in here to soap up and massage the sultan. I wasn't sure you'd be comfortable with that."

Elyse's eyes widened. "Well, I might like it, once I got used to it . . . though I probably wouldn't have waltzed in naked if I'd known."

"There's a special alcove for female guests. And only another woman would rub you down. When Iksander's *kadin* was alive, she'd have entered in a robe."

"I see." Getting used to the modesty requirements for djinn women, particularly the stricter ones for the upper class, was going to take some doing.

Cade put gentle hands on her knees. "If you bend a little," he said carefully, "you'll get on more smoothly. Especially if, as you say, you'd like a job."

Elyse stroked the side of his handsome face. His skin was smoother than a human's, his cheekbones as high as a movie star's.

"I can bend," she said, the tenderness she felt for him welling up in her voice. "I'll probably put my foot wrong here or there, but I don't want to embarrass you—or insult your people."

He looked relieved and then a teensy bit guilty. Elyse couldn't help grinning. If he thought she was going to start some feminist rampage through his home city, he didn't know her well enough to be in love with her.

That realization sobered her. It was nice to hear someone loved you but, really, only time could prove that kind of thing.

Sensing the bobble in her emotions, Cade kissed her left kneecap. "You okay?"

"I'm nervous about fitting in."

He chafed her calves reassuringly. His touch had a predictable effect on her libido. The sensitive folds between her legs heated and swelled. She shifted her butt on the warm poolside.

"Do you really have to go straight to work?" she asked wistfully.

"If I don't, the other me will take charge of everything."

She laughed. "He'll probably race you to get to your desk chair first."

"He's already trying to convince Joseph to work for him."

"It's too bad Joseph's original didn't wake from statue form. You both could have had an assistant."

"Maybe," Cade said. "I suppose Joseph's time in your world changed him too. We don't know if any of us who sent doubles through the portals will be able to recombine."

He looked grim, which was more his usual expression. Sorry she'd darkened his mood, Elyse petted the sides of his wet face. Cade's eyes rose to hers. Her body tingled from no more than that. That a man like this loved and wanted her was erotically inspiring.

Because he was very much a man, no matter what his origins, his attention drifted to her breasts. He licked his lips at the sight of her taut nipples.

"Maybe," he said, "letting Arcadius beat me into the office would be worth it just this once."

"Just this once?"

Her tone was husky. Cade's gaze returned to her expression. He slid his hands up her naked thighs. "Just this once for now. We can let tomorrow settle itself."

He stood, revealing that the water hit him at chest level. Elyse was considerably shorter. She might not be able to touch the pool's bottom. He rubbed her thighs in a way that turned her sex liquid.

"Come in with me?" he invited, the timbre of his voice lower than before.

"I think you'll have to hold me."

"That was the plan," he said.

He smiled as she put her hands on his broad shoulders. She supposed he felt the tentative nature of her grip. Giving her time to know he had her, he pulled her off the edge into the hot water. "You can swim, yes?"

"Not as well as you, but yes."

She was in his arms, her body buoyed by the water but brushing his. According to the stories he and Joseph told her, the Creator formed angels from air, humans from clay, and djinn from smokeless fire. She guessed heat didn't affect him the way it did human men. In truth, the temperature seemed to help his arousal on. His erection nudged her thigh, making her aware how thick he already was. His cock was big enough that she was grateful for his skill in handling her. Recalling the previous times he'd established this, Elyse's insides melted.

He noticed the reaction. One of his hands slid down her to grip her bottom. He squeezed her glutes with relish, reminding her he had a bit of a thing for her ass. Sometimes Elyse wished she had more curves in other places, but at least she had them there. Cade's breath came flatteringly faster. Their mouths were inches from each other.

"I'll be careful not to drown you," he promised.

"That would be good," she responded breathlessly.

His eyes seemed to glow in the second before his lips molded over hers.

She clutched him and kissed him back, abruptly desperate to flatten her slight breasts against his chest. His other hand came up to encompass the curving weight of one. He knew just how much pressure to exert. Her nipple ached deliciously as he pushed his palm over it. When his hold twisted slightly, a soft sound broke in her throat. Their tongues had been stroking each other hungrily, but at the little noise he broke free.

"God, I need you," he said.

He made her wild. Forgetting shyness, she dragged her hand down his side underneath the water and pushed it between their bodies. He groaned when her fingers caught and wrapped his erection.

"Put me inside," he said. "Take me while I take you."

She held the pounding length and shifted, placing the rounded head at her eager gate.

"There?" he asked.

"There," she said, and he pushed slowly in.

Her head fell back. He always felt so good doing that: smooth, thick, all his power and vitality seeming to concentrate in the rigid length. A growl rumbled in his chest as he reached her limit.

The way his fingers tightened on her rear was so exciting she nearly came.

"I love you," she said.

His pupils swelled darker, his face flushed with arousal and emotion. "Elyse," he rasped. "Hook your ankles behind me."

She hooked them, knowing he was about to let the reins off of his desires. He didn't disappoint. His grip was steel for the first downward draw and thrust.

"God," he said and repeated it.

Elyse's fingers dug into his big shoulders. He went faster, deeper. Nerves rooted deep within her pussy reverbed with enjoyment. He was a perfect mallet swinging against an erotic gong. None of his thrusts came all the way out of her, the closeness of his fit ensuring that the fluid of her excitement stayed where they needed it. More welled from her walls as he grunted, his animal side coming out. A moan of pleasure tore from her.

"That's not too hard," she gasped when he hesitated. "That's exactly what I like."

"Me too," he said, working even faster, swearing at the heightening sensations.

She had his rhythm now. She met it, thumping back at him until he cried out for her. She felt his stance change for better balance—knees bending, feet planted wide. His open lips pressed her neck, his panting both audible and felt. His face tensed, his eyes creasing at the corners as he screwed them shut. Elyse's emotions soared past any limits she was familiar with. She wanted to destroy him with ecstasy, to push past all his barriers, past his lifelong self-discipline and control. The next time he pulled her pussy down him, she dug the heel of one foot between his cheeks, against the entrance to his asshole.

He sucked a breath, maybe thinking she'd stimulated the nerves there by accident. She twisted her head around until her mouth pressed his ear.

"I'm going to take you there some day," she warned. "Really fuck you in the ass."

He jerked back and looked at her. His eyes were startled, but his cock had just gone harder. She smiled, feeling like the sort of dirty girl she'd never been before.

"I'd show you no mercy," she promised angelically.

She ground her heel beneath his tailbone as she said it, letting him feel how the sensations the pressure triggered ran into his erection.

"Fuck," he said, shuddering inside her. A muscle flicked in his jaw.

"Finish me," she said. "You're the one in charge this time."

He didn't waste the permission. He worked her frenziedly up and down his shaft, controlling the movements of her pelvis with his iron hold on her hips. With a speed that amazed even as it thrilled, he thrust into her, cursing and gasping and causing her to come hard and tight around him. The sound of the churning water echoed off the vault, nearly drowning out her cries. Bolts of intense ecstasy shot through her pussy and clitoris. Even so, she didn't forget what she wanted to do to him. She made sure her heel kept up the slightly illicit pressure, using the strength of her other leg to increase it.

"*El*—," he said, jamming deep and desperate into her.

The rest of her name was lost. He came in a long convulsion, her butt clamped tight by his forearms, his face buried in her hair. He shot until he couldn't shoot anymore.

Then he relaxed his hold on her. His palms slid up to support her back, their size impressing her as much as their protectiveness.

He looked at her for a long moment.

"You're crazy," he said, still trying to catch his breath.

She gave him the same angelic smile as before.

"You didn't mean that. About . . ." He cleared his throat. "About fucking me in the ass."

"Is there a rule that says djinn can't?"

He blinked at her. "No."

"Then maybe I did mean it."

"Have you done it before?"

"Are you saying I can't try new things?"

He blinked again, then shook his head for good measure. Her actions might have taken him by surprise, but her instincts told her she hadn't disgusted him. Before he could think too hard about it, she pulled free of his gradually diminishing erection. The water's heated cradle felt amazing after that nice workout. Lying back, she let her pleasantly humming body float on the rippling waves. She almost didn't want to close her eyes. The vaulted ceiling mosaic was as beautiful as a mosque.

Cade remained standing where he was, staring at her like he'd been poleaxed.

"Weren't you going to work?" she asked, unable to resist twitting him.

"Yes," he said. There was a pause. "Are you coming with me?"

"Yes," she said, more gratified by the invitation than she let on. "I just need a minute to enjoy my afterglow."

~

Arcadius woke just as the other him had an orgasm. He'd been dreaming of Iksander's pool, of having energetic sex in it with the foreigner. The strong little human was wild for it. Her tight wet pussy bucked up and down his shaft like a rippling fist. Arcadius had never encountered such lack of inhibition in a female—or thought he could be that moved by sex. Drawn to the brink of madness, the other him exploded. Caught in the dream, Arcadius couldn't stop his own body from going over in sympathy. He gasped as he ejaculated into the tangled sheets, the climax hard and pleasurable. This had happened last night too, when the apparently sex-crazed human had fellated his double to completion. Arcadius had been asleep and had shared the experience.

More than a bit dismayed, he rolled onto his back panting. He guessed the phenomenon hadn't been a fluke. He and his copy truly were linked psychically.

Crap, he thought, shoving sleep-mussed hair from his forehead. He should have strangled Joseph before he let the magician put this crazy plan for replicating them in motion.

Of course, the plan had been necessary. Their people had been threatened. And to a considerable extent, the stratagem had worked. Half the rescue squad had survived for certain—and half the Glorious City had woken up. That was a result even a dour man like him could be thankful for.

A rap sounded on his bedroom door, less polite than he was accustomed to. He grimaced. Whoever it was had probably been knocking for a while.

"One moment," he called, getting up and grabbing the figured gray silk robe he'd thrown over a chair last night. He drew it around him and tied the belt, hopefully hiding the evidence of his recent loss of control. Dawn hadn't broken. The room was an assortment of sparse shadows. Along with everything else, half the furnishings in his apartments were absent. Joseph, his trusted servant and magician, had miniaturized and packed up the things to make "Cade's" stay in the human world homier.

The sneer was still on his lip as he yanked the door open.

Naturally, the djinni behind it shrank back at his expression.

"Sir," said the tall older man. Though Arcadius didn't interact with this particular servant often, his name snapped into his mind.

"Nechum?"

"Yes, commander. I'm very sorry to disturb you, but there's a problem in the harem."

"Can't the eunuchs handle it?" Like a growing number of males in the modern world of their race, Arcadius considered the tradition of occupational castration archaic. He did understand it was hard to do away with. The families whose sons were chosen for the honor earned prestige and good salaries.

"None of the eunuchs woke," Nechum answered. "All four remained statues."

That was unfortunate. The women of the harem observed the rules of seclusion more scrupulously than any in the city. Silly as it would seem to a westerner like Cade's human, they might have decided it would violate decorum to ask for help until a female checked on them.

Arcadius scratched his jaw stubble in concern. "Have they been brought food and drink? And given a chance to inquire after relatives?"

"Yes, sir. That's how the problem was discovered. One of the women's younger brothers seems to have gone missing."

"Actually missing?" Arcadius asked. "Not simply petrified and misplaced?"

"I'm afraid I don't know the details."

"Do you think the woman would speak to me?"

"Doubtful, sir," Nechum said. "My wife, who spoke to them, didn't know who to refer them to. The matter seems to require someone with authority. If the *kadin* were alive . . ."

The *kadin* had been Iksander's wife, his only lover while she was alive. Among other sins, Empress Luna had brutally murdered her. The *kadin's* example gave Arcadius an idea he initially discarded. Unfortunately, no better solution appeared to replace it. He sighed briefly.

"My double's consort has an air of initiative." An air of rudeness was more like it, but in a pinch that might not matter.

"I observed the young lady yesterday," Nechum said uncertainly. Arcadius concluded Elyse hadn't made a positive impression.

"If the harem requires an advocate, she won't be afraid to speak up."

"That's true," Nechum admitted. "Shall I speak to the . . . other you?"

Because Arcadius was tempted, he shook his head. "I'll handle it," he said.

No one but he should have to instruct Cade's woman in the minimum good manners that would be required of her.

CHAPTER TWO

"YOUR presence is required in the harem," Arcadius announced.

Fortunately, Elyse and Cade had dressed—she in a modest long-sleeved tunic and silk trousers, Cade in vaguely military pants and a loose white shirt. He'd shrugged on a bandolier-like harness that held knives rather than bullets. Two curving scimitars were holstered at either hip. The jewels that glinted from their twenty-four karat handles were bright and beautiful. Because djinn loved decoration, she didn't assume this meant the swords weren't deadly. To Elyse's very private amusement, Cade's original was garbed almost identically—as if two high schools girls had texted each other the night before to coordinate outfits.

Less amusingly, Arcadius had ambushed them in the palace corridor on their way to Cade's office. The double made no attempt not to look autocratic. He was actually sneering down his nose at her.

Because he was tall and she wasn't, this didn't take much effort.

"Look, you—" Cade began to retort hotly.

Elyse touched his tense forearm, the corded muscles bared by his rolled up cuff. "Let me try to handle this."

Arcadius's supercilious eyebrows indicated he thought this would be good.

"Okay," she said, fighting anger and nervousness. She told herself this was no different than facing down an irrationally aggrieved tenant. Staying calm and keeping her wits about her was generally a wise approach. "I know it's tradition for a lot of your females to live in a cloistered way, but that's not what I'm accustomed to. I need to be useful and contribute. I'll do what I can to avoid offending people's sensibilities, but I am not, for any reason, going to allow myself to be locked up."

"Are you finished?" Arcadius asked.

"I am," she confirmed.

"In that case, I wasn't suggesting you be 'locked up,' as you put it. Your presence is required because a problem has arisen in one the concubine's families. She needs to speak to a female who has the ear of someone important."

"What happened to the eunuchs?" Cade asked.

"As luck would have it, none of their statues woke. I believe the other harem staff have placed them in a pantry for safekeepin."

Elyse did her best to throw off her Alice-down-the-rabbit-hole reaction. "So the, um, concubine is okay with me as her go-between?"

Arcadius shrugged. "I assume she'll be fine with it."

Elyse wasn't ready to assume anything. She'd seen how some djinn viewed humans.

"You can handle it," Cade said. "Just remind yourself she needs your help."

He was right. "Okay," she said to Arcadius. "I guess I'm your volunteer."

Arcadius gave her a curt head bow. "Follow me," he said, already walking off.

"You take care of her," Cade warned.

"Don't be an idiot," Arcadius threw back without turning.

Elyse couldn't have said why, but the snapped retort reassured her she'd be perfectly safe with him.

~

When Arcadius said *follow*, he hadn't been kidding. Elyse couldn't have walked beside him even if she wanted to. She had to force her legs to move quickly to avoid being lost at forks in the corridors. As they passed various servants, all of them gaped at her.

It felt a bit degrading, to be truthful.

"Hey," she finally said as the pace he set caused her to lose her breath. "You've got to have noticed my legs are shorter than yours."

Arcadius halted and faced her. He looked her up and down, taking in her winded condition. It was strange to see her Cade's gorgeous blue green eyes staring out from that stone-cool face. Could the two men really have started out as the same person?

"Forgive me," he said in a way that didn't let her know if he was sincere. "Djinn women walk faster."

"Well, I'm not a djinni," she said and out of childishness added, "duh."

His lips might have twitched a fraction at one corner. "I apologize," he said more convincingly. "I shall endeavor to moderate my strides. Here—" He dug into one pocket of his military style trousers. "You'll draw fewer glances if you cover up that hair."

That hair—as if he thought her curls were as unattractive as she did.

He held out a length of gold-bordered leaf green silk. Elyse didn't like admitting it was beautiful.

"I can arrange it if you don't know how," he offered.

Elyse was from Manhattan, fashion capitol of the world. She might not look like a model, but she knew how to do a scarf. She snatched the gorgeous thing from his hand, whipping it around her head to drape it fetchingly. If Elyse's chichi cousin hadn't turned homicidal, Cara would have been proud of her.

Arcadius seemed startled by her performance. "That's fine." He cleared his throat. "The . . . color suits your eyes."

Elyse gave him an innocent smile.

Arcadius blinked. "Right. Once we cross the courtyard at the end of this corridor, we'll have reached the harem."

To herself, Elyse acknowledged she was curious to see it. The building appeared to be a palace within the palace. A double perimeter of white walls protected it, each with its own golden door. Arcadius was allowed to pass the first but not the second. A tea pavilion covered in pink bougainvillea supplied him a place to wait.

"From here you proceed alone," he said. "The less you speak and the more you listen the better you'll suit everyone's purposes. I'll need you to repeat what you heard afterwards."

"Can't I take notes?" she asked.

"It is not permitted to record the words of the sultan's women."

"Well, heck," she said.

To her surprise, Arcadius smiled at her. "Just relax, maintain your focus, and you'll be fine. I'm good at helping people to remember."

She guessed he'd have to be, if he debriefed soldiers and whatnot.

Okay, she thought, squaring up her taut shoulders. *Into the fray go I.*

The fray turned out to be a peaceful and very luxurious oasis. The main harem room was huge with lots of windows set high up on the mosaic walls. Crowned by a soaring dome, the predominant colors were pale gold and silvery sage. The women—nearly a hundred, by her count—seemed dressed to coordinate. Their pastel hued gowns were an opium smoker's dream, silk and velvet and lots of filmy, transparent stuff. The women's skirts were long but boobage abounded—most of it excellent. Jewels abounded too, their settings and stones so stunning Harry Winston's ghost would have wept with envy. Elyse supposed the women were allowed to show off among themselves. She saw a number of headscarves like her own but only a few veiled faces.

"Please wait," said the servant who'd led her to the entry arch.

Elyse waited while an important looking older woman rose from a heap of pillows and came forward. She was one of the females who covered everything but her eyes. They were outlined with kohl and slightly hard looking.

Not a person to mess with, Elyse thought.

"I am the *valide sultana*," the woman announced in a stately tone. "Mother to Iksander, our great sultan."

Since it seemed appropriate, Elyse bowed. "I'm Elyse." She hesitated. Probably she needed a title. "Friend to the Glorious City's guardian."

Elyse guessed that was okay. The sultan's mom bowed back—not very deeply, she noted.

"The girl who requested your assistance is in her quarters."

That was good. This salon or whatever they called it was too distracting for Elyse to concentrate.

The same female servant as before led her down a smaller hall. One of the many onion-arched doors that lined it stood open. With a graceful bow, the servant gestured for her to go inside.

If this were a prison, it was a lovely one. The room was a silk-lined jewel box. Decorated in spicy shades of red and orange, a single high window with an ornate grate provided natural light. Colored glass lanterns supplemented that, pushing the dimness back further. In the center of the room, a woman sat on her heels on a floor cushion. Her head was lowered, her palms resting calmly on her gowned thighs, like a very polite geisha. Her hair was draped with a length of silk.

Elyse couldn't see her face until she looked up.

She gasped out loud before she could stop herself. The djinni was the spitting image of a famous Bollywood actress. Framed by incredibly thick dark lashes, her doe eyes were gray and soft, her skin pure cream brushed generously with roses. Her mouth seemed naturally full and red. Elyse doubted many men could see it without wanting to kiss her.

"Sorry," Elyse said in response to the lift of the djinni's brows. "I don't think I've met anyone as beautiful as you in person."

The djinni smiled, and Elyse's heart actually skipped. With women like this in his harem, Iksander's faithfulness to his wife became impressive.

"I am ordinary, I assure you," the djinni said in a sweet soft voice. "You are the one whose features are interesting."

Elyse's cheeks grew a little hot. "I'm Elyse," she said. "I guess you've heard I'm the commander's friend?"

"I am Yasmin," the harem girl returned. "Please sit and share tea with me."

The tea was mint, steaming in little glasses with silver holders to let people drink without being burned. Elyse blew on hers and sipped.

"It's true then," Yasmin said. "Humans don't like heat as much as we do."

She seemed interested rather than judgmental.

"I like this tea," Elyse said, though she set hers down. "Please tell me what happened to your brother."

Yasmin's beautiful eyes welled up. "I have two brothers," she said. "One our family no longer knows. He killed a friend in anger and became ifrit. Balu is our baby, only seventeen. He is a good boy, though perhaps a little wild. He has reached the age where he wants to rebel a bit."

"Why do you think he's missing rather than run away?"

"Balu likes to slip away from his lessons to visit the view cafés. They are . . ." She pressed graceful fingers against her mouth, searching for words to explain. "They are places where our people can steal peeks at the human world. Amateur magicians band together to create them. For as long as the magic lasts, they make money selling drinks and snacks. Sometimes the spells catch signals from your TV, and sometimes they spy on activities that are captured by surveillance cameras. They're very popular, though not so much with good families like ours. The view cafés the kids are obsessed with aren't always careful what they broadcast. They show things many people believe should be private."

"I see," Elyse said, trying not to wince. "Did Balu go missing from one of these view cafés?"

"We think so. My mother writes me, you understand. When the sorceress's terrible curse struck the city, she believed him to be in one. My father also recovered when the commander set us free. Father searched Balu's favorite haunt, the one all his friends sneak to, but couldn't find any sign of him or his statue. Those of his friends who woke swear he was with them. The police claim Balu must have taken advantage of the confusion to wander off. I don't think my brother would do that. He loves my mother, and wouldn't worry her."

"Your father looked other places?"

"Everywhere he could think," she said.

There seemed to be more to this story. Yasmin wriggled uneasily on her cushion. Her pretty silk gown rustled.

"Please go on," Elyse prodded.

"You'll think I'm silly. Even my father does."

"I won't," Elyse promised. "Everything seems possible to me since I've discovered djinn exist."

"Very well," Yasmin said. "Recently, I've heard whispers that other young people have gone missing. These things happen occasionally. We are a magic city, and people run afoul of sorcerers or spells. Sometimes the disappeared turn up again and sometimes they don't."

"What makes you think this is different?"

Yasmin leaned forward earnestly. "Because the *same* sorts of djinn are missing. Six so far, by my count. All are around Balu's age, all beautiful, and—unlike my brother—they come from poor families or are orphans. It can't be coincidence that they are the very people no one would raise an outcry about."

She stopped speaking and sat back on her slippers. Elyse tried to take her measure. The harem girl was upset but not hysterical. She seemed intelligent and not as if she were seeking attention. Then again, if the missing were djinn the authorities wouldn't raise an alarm about, how had Yasmin discovered the pattern?

"Could I ask who you heard these rumors from?"

The harem girl looked uncomfortable, her fingers bunching nervously on her thighs as if she wished she could clutch something. "I'd rather not tell you that."

"It could be important," Elyse said as gently as she could. "And I expect Arcadius . . . the commander will want to know."

"I can't," Yasmin said primly. "I'd be breaking a confidence."

She appeared determined to say no more. Elyse was no master interrogator, only a competent landlady. "Do you know any more details that might help?"

"None I can think of, though I can supply a picture of my brother. And the names of the other young people."

Elyse realized she should have thought to ask for them. She stood again and waited while Yasmin wrote them down. As she handed the list to Elyse with a small portrait of her brother, she looked like she wanted to ask something.

"Yes?" Elyse asked.

Yasmin moistened her luscious lips. "Might I ask . . . We have heard that Joseph the Eunuch returned with the Guardian. He is a powerful sorcerer. Perhaps he could cast a spell on the portrait to find Balu?"

In the course of their adventures, Elyse had come to consider Cade's assistant a valued friend. She was a little surprised to hear Yasmin refer to him as Joseph the Eunuch rather than his more common designation of Joseph the Magician. She concluded the harem heard enough to gossip to know everyone's business.

"I can certainly speak to him," Elyse said. "I assume you heard his double remains locked in its statue. I can't swear that, at this precise moment, his power is equal to doing what you ask."

Yasmin inclined her head modestly. "For the Guardian's precious right hand to even consider coming to our assistance would do my humble self and my family immense honor."

Elyse wasn't accustomed to the djinn's flowery manner of speaking. To her human ears, Yasmin sounded like she had a fangirl interest in Cade's associate. Yasmin was reserved for the sultan's pleasure. Did she think it was okay to crush on Joseph because his original wasn't a whole man? Joseph had only recently confided to Elyse that his duplicate body, the one he now inhabited, did in fact have all its parts. Would Yasmin be more fascinated if she knew or would it ruin her fantasy? Maybe she'd feel too guilty to continue having it.

Elyse shook her head. This was pretty far off the purpose she'd come to accomplish.

"I'll do what I can," she said. "I'm sure if Joseph is able to help, he will. If you think of anything else, please send one of the servants to contact me."

~

Arcadius wanted to debrief Elyse while her memory was fresh. Though the setting was irregular for a male and female who weren't intimate, he gestured her to the cushion opposite his. The area beneath the tea pavilion was pretty, with roses and bees and a sunny sky outside. The grass was wilder than it should have been, but it was possible to believe no tragedy had struck anywhere near this place.

"Boy," Elyse breathed, lowering herself with little grace to the firm square pillow he'd pointed out. "I need practice sitting on the floor."

A round chased silver table stretched between them but didn't block his view. Elyse crossed her legs like a tailor, the position drawing her silk trousers snug around her oddly fascinating calves. Though it had only been a dream, he remembered those muscles tightening behind his back as he plunged his cock into her. This was inappropriate to be thinking about right then. To make matters worse, she pushed her headscarf off.

Arcadius's expression must have betrayed his dismay.

"Sorry," she said, fanning her soft flushed cheeks. Her curls were a mass of uncontrolled black corkscrews. "I don't usually wear this much when it's hot. Does uncovering my hair really bother you? I'll put the scarf back on if it does."

Arcadius was a grown man. He'd seen women unveiled before. "Do as you please," he said.

The words were stiff. Elyse pressed her lips together to squelch a smile. At least she didn't tease him, the way he'd seen her do with his double.

"Shall I tell you what Yasmin said?"

"Please do," he encouraged.

Her report wasn't linear, but it did seem thorough. She'd observed not only Yasmin's words but also her manner, the same as he'd have asked one of his men to do. When she would have pushed Yasmin's list of names across the low silver table, Arcadius stopped her.

"No man but the sultan may read the hand of one of his women."

"Really? Reading a simple note is considered improper?"

"It is," he said gravely. "Perhaps you could read the names to me."

She read them one at a time. Arcadius didn't recognize any except the brother's. Naturally, he performed background checks on harem residents.

"I notice some of these names are girls," Elyse said.

"Yes," Arcadius agreed.

"Six teenagers seems a lot to go missing in such a short span of time."

"Unless they aren't missing. The city is likely to be in turmoil for a while.

Even here, where we keep close watch on our children, teenagers aren't always easy to pin down."

Elyse rubbed one finger across her cushy lips. Her mouth was one of her nicer features. Though he didn't wish to, Arcadius recalled how kissing it had felt. "Yasmin wouldn't say how she knew, but she seemed pretty sure."

"Servants go in and out of the harem. Perhaps she heard it from one of them."

"Maybe, but I could have sworn she felt guilty about something."

Arcadius considered Elyse's face. She was as confident of her opinion as a man would have been.

And nearly as plain as one, he reminded his unwillingly interested sex organ.

"Maybe I could talk to Balu and Yasmin's mother," she suggested. "I mean, I totally understand the police are busy, but I have time to spare."

"You can't go alone. You're the—" He struggled with his reluctance to voice the words. "You're the sultan's commander's consort. Whatever your habits in your dimension, here you require escort."

"Could Joseph take me?"

Arcadius contemplated. There was only one of Joseph, and his skills were unique. "I think I must accompany you myself."

"You!"

"Yes." He forced himself to face her shock calmly. "Simple though it seems on the surface, my instincts tell me this business is important."

Instincts were important. He'd learned to trust their guidance. Nonetheless, he didn't relish leaving matters at the palace to his double.

~

"*You* want to accompany Elyse on these interviews."

Arcadius's announcement caught Cade flatfooted. Cade was in his spacious office at the palace, where he and Joseph had set up a command center. Dozens of parchment scrolls were pinned by their corners to a corkboard that rolled on wheels. Enhanced by magic, each sheet was networked to a different sector of the city and relayed current conditions. A second corkboard updated him on military matters. Those of Luna's troops who'd recovered from her spell were being forcibly deported. Those who were still statues were being inventoried and stored under lock and key. Diplomatic inquiries from other territories were trickling in, most sympathetic but some poorly disguised attempts at gauging whether they were vulnerable to invasion. The Glorious City's cabinet ministers came and went, each requiring Cade's attention for their areas of concern.

Scattered incidents of looting had been reported. Because only parts of the city woke, many households were left without their heads. The elderly needed to be checked on, and probably he ought to establish emergency soup kitchens and food pantries. Schools were closed, and that left a lot of young people unoccupied. Cade needed a system for putting idle hands to use.

Their people's emotional condition was on his mind as well. The curse and its aftermath were more than physical shocks. Perhaps he ought to reach out to religious leaders. They'd be best equipped to comfort their congregations —the leaders who had woken up, at least.

God, he'd need more corkboards to keep track of everything.

"Yes," his original said. "The situation seems important. Also, it will give me the opportunity to observe the city in person."

Cade had already forgotten what situation he was referring to.

Elyse stood beside Arcadius, no more than a foot distant, looking disconcertingly at home next to the other male. Cade guessed associating with strange men wasn't unusual for her. He didn't recognize her scarf, and kicked himself for not remembering she'd be more comfortable in one. Her mouth curved slightly in amusement. She'd noticed his distraction.

"Arcadius means the harem girl with the missing brother. We want to speak to his parents and also see what we can discover about the other kids."

Cade's mind clicked back into focus. "You wish to do this?"

"Yes," she said. "It seems like something I can handle."

Her eyes were hopeful. Cade shifted his gaze to Arcadius.

"Elyse is right about us needing to take advantage of there being two of us. As long as we present a united front, we each have equal authority. Working in concert doubles our influence. If, however, we lock horns over trifling issues, people will be uncertain whom they should listen to. That isn't efficient."

"You're saying I can't afford to gainsay you."

"I'm saying if you let me go, you'll have this office all to yourself."

Cade leaned back in his chair, pursing his mouth as he considered Arcadius's proposition for hidden traps.

"I don't really need your permission," his original reminded.

"Cade." Elyse's voice was gentle. She stepped around his desk and sat on its edge facing him. Her hand touched his forearm, her thumb riffling his hair. "Can't you trust yourself to use good judgment? He is who you used to be."

Cade smiled at her. His original was who he used to be before he met her. Who could blame him if that seemed inferior? He patted the hand that caressed him.

"If you trust him, I can too. Have Joseph give you a magic scroll. Then you can contact me if you need to."

Arcadius's eyes had rounded as he watched this exchange. Maybe it was childish, but Cade enjoyed shocking the other him with how much he valued his human's opinion.

Joseph returned with another in the endless queue of worried officials.

Elyse jumped and said "oh!" as she spotted him. She covered her mouth when everyone looked at her. "Forgive me. Joseph, if you get a moment, I'd be grateful to speak to you."

Seeming aware she'd stepped outside normal female boundaries, she slid off his desk and made an *I'm-sorry* face. Cade smiled enough to let her know he understood. The goggling official tracked Elyse to Arcadius as if she were an exotic talking beast.

Ironically, she was more of a novelty than Cade's duplicate.

"Do have a seat," Joseph said, pulling out a chair to distract the official. "You can tell the commander everything you told me."

Cade suppressed a grimace. Hopefully *everything* wouldn't be as longwinded as he feared.

~

Because they seemed to have gotten the go ahead, Elyse followed Arcadius out into the anteroom. Seated and standing, a crowd of men waited their turn with Cade. Their vibrant silk robes fell to sparkly slippers in every hue imaginable. Since Elyse loved pretty footwear she could walk in, she was a tad jealous.

As Arcadius stepped into their midst, the men perked up and leaned toward him in unison.

"Have you a moment?" inquired a plump gentleman in yellow.

"I'm afraid I'm otherwise engaged," Arcadius said politely. "I know the other me will hear your concerns as soon as he's able to."

"Of course, commander." The man in yellow inclined his head with respect. "May it please our merciful Creator to prosper your endeavors."

Arcadius returned the bow, then placed his hand beneath Elyse's elbow. With a determination that surprised her, he steered them swiftly into the outer corridor.

The glint of humor in his expression enlightened her.

"You *wanted* to dump that mess on Cade," she accused. "You only pretended to vie with him to be in charge."

"Perhaps I'm not utterly desolated at how our dispute turned out. Giving audiences never was my favorite duty, especially when I was had other things to do. Iksander was far better at it than me."

The mention of the sultan sent a shadow across his face.

"He'll make it back," Elyse said. "From the stories Cade and Joseph told me, Iksander had a lot of fire. With all he's been through already, a trip to my world won't finish him."

Arcadius tilted his head at her. Did he think she'd overstepped by making observations about his important friend? Elyse wasn't inclined to apologize. Luckily, after a pause, he spoke.

"I forget the other me knows Iksander too." Confession over, his face turned resolved again. "Whether the sultan returns or not, we must ensure this city recovers."

"Pardon," Joseph said, stepping into the empty corridor after them. "The commander desires that you have this scroll. If anything comes up, the spell embedded in it sends the equivalent of a text message straight to him."

Elyse accepted the small rolled parchment. She glanced at Arcadius. "You can teach me how to use this?"

He nodded that he could.

"You wished to speak to me?" Joseph said to her. His manner was formal, not giving away that they'd become fond of each other. Elyse wasn't sure why he wanted to keep that private, but she tried to respond in kind.

"Yes." She pulled the small, framed portrait of Yasmin's brother Balu from the pocket of her silk pants. "I apologize if asking this is silly, but can you get a magical bead on where this boy might be?"

Joseph took the picture, holding it in both hands. He considered it quietly for a few moments. "Hm," he said. "All I'm sensing from this is surprise."

"Not fear?" Arcadius asked.

"No," Joseph looked calmly up from the picture to meet his other master's eyes. "I'm afraid the likeness gives off no hint of location."

Elyse accepted it back from him. "Do you know a harem girl named Yasmin?"

"Should I?"

She supposed having been a eunuch didn't guarantee he would. "Just wondering," she said.

"We should go," Arcadius interrupted. "Why don't I keep this for both of us?"

Without asking, he took the scroll and tucked it away. "Joseph," he said by way of taking leave.

"Sir," Joseph responded.

Elyse couldn't help but notice Joseph and Cade were a lot friendlier.

~

Located to one side of the palace steps but inside the perimeter wall was a grassy tarmac for flying carpets. Many took off and landed, their movements coordinated by traffic controllers in dark blue robes. Four crisply uniformed djinn soldiers waited beside an empty rug, bent arms stiffly saluting Arcadius. The carpet's guard walls were already folded up. Arcadius lifted Elyse over before she could prepare herself.

He hopped in without assistance—like he was vaulting the driver's door to a convertible. He and Cade were both athletic, a fact she sometimes forgot due to the serious way they carried themselves.

The soldiers followed his example with similar panache. They very studiously didn't look at her. Maybe her headscarf wasn't enough modesty for them.

"They're coming with us?" she asked Arcadius.

"They are. The city is . . . unsettled at present. We'll take no chances with your safety." He gave the lead soldier a signal. The man held the metal staff carpet pilots used as control sticks. Planting the end firmly, he bowed his turbaned head and murmured one of the djinn's prayer-like spells. The rug rose upward without a bump.

As it did, Elyse realized the spots on her waist where Arcadius had lifted her were tingling. She tried to ignore that as their vehicle sailed over the palace wall.

"Do you wish to sit?" Arcadius inquired politely.

Elyse shook her head. She wanted to look around Cade's home probably as much as Arcadius did.

In some ways, the djinn's Glorious City could have been any old world European metropolis. No skyscrapers or telephone poles spoiled the time-traveling effect. Buildings were historic, beautiful, and quaint. The central avenues were broad like Paris, the farther streets narrow and twisty. The foliage was Mediterranean, with palms and flowers and other sun-loving greenery. Yasmin's family lived in a handsome villa on a hill. The soldiers set them near an attractive garden next to a sparkling pool.

Elyse braced herself for Arcadius to lift her out again.

"I'll speak to the father," he informed her, seeming not to notice anything amiss. "Please interview the mother and any female servants."

Cade would have squeezed her arm before they parted, in case she was nervous.

"Will do," Elyse said, pretending she wouldn't have liked that.

~

Aside from her daughter being the property of a sultan, Yasmin's mother struck Elyse as a normal concerned parent. According to her, Balu was a good boy. He wouldn't run away. He was just a little wild these days. She blamed the view cafés. All that human media put wrong ideas into the minds of their city's youth.

"Begging your pardon," she added, remembering whom she was speaking to.

"That's all right," Elyse said. "Sometimes human media puts wrong ideas into our youths' minds too."

Yasmin's mother smiled unsurely.

"I need to ask one more thing," Elyse said, "and I apologize if the topic is sensitive. Yasmin mentioned you had another son?"

"I have one son," Yasmin's mother averred hotly.

They sat on cushions in the women's quarters of the villa, opposite each other at the inevitable tea table. Sunshine flooded in from high windows, making it clear that Yasmin's mother had once been as beautiful as her daughter.

"Right," Elyse said, trying not to wriggle awkwardly on her folded legs. "Once upon a time, though, you had two."

Once upon a time seemed to be a phrase Yasmin's mother could accept. She sat straighter than before, her posture proud. "That one shamed us. We no longer speak his name."

"Yasmin said he killed someone?"

"Out of jealousy he knifed his best friend, the son of a close associate of his father. When Ramis turned ifrit, we could no longer shelter him in our family."

Elyse took note of the name without mentioning she'd heard it. "Do you think the incident might have anything to do with Balu's disappearance?"

"I don't see how," Yasmin's mother said. "We paid the dead boy's family their vengeance price years ago. They accepted the settlement in oath court. They wouldn't risk their souls by retaliating against Balu." Her lips pressed together more primly. "If you were a proper person, you'd know that."

O-kay, Elyse thought. So much for interspecies cooperation and respect.

~

Their next stop was the view café Balu was last seen in. According to his mother, it was located in the Glorious City's grand bazaar. Elyse was grateful for Arcadius's presence. She'd have gotten lost in two minutes among the covered warren of colorful shops.

Despite the city's recent tragedy, business in the bazaar was bustling. Proprietors hawked their wares with great energy, many calling Arcadius by his title to buy them.

"Not today," he said to all of them politely.

Between a brass emporium and a store piled temptingly high with slippers, they found the establishment they were looking for.

Two of the four soldiers who accompanied them took up positions outside the café's entrance. The other two preceded them inside, sending Arcadius small professional nods when they'd decided it was safe to go in. The armed escorts made Elyse feel strange, but the djinn who caught sight of them didn't appear alarmed.

Arcadius drew longer glances than the soldiers did. She concluded the sultan's commander was someone everyone recognized.

Leaving that aside, Elyse looked around. The café wasn't short of patrons, most twentyish or younger, including a couple girls. Customers sat around scattered tables on floor cushions, drinking tiny cups of Turkish coffee and seeming mesmerized by two immense curving TV screens. One showed a Korean soap opera, the other a loop of nothing but German commercials. Elyse saw no subtitles on either, but the audience was laughing, so presumably they understood the words. A moment later, her eardrums gave a funny pop. Suddenly, she also comprehended what the actors were saying.

She made a noise of surprise and rubbed her ears.

Arcadius placed one hand lightly behind her arm. He bent closer to speak to her. "Part of the magic spun around the café allows visitors to understand different languages."

"Kind of like me understanding djinn from hanging around the other you and Joseph?"

"Yes, kind of like that."

Elyse broke into a grin. "That is so cool!"

Arcadius smiled faintly. "Let's find the proprietors."

The proprietors were a pair of young male sorcerers—magic nerds, from the skinny pale look of them. They remembered seeing Balu in the café on the day the curse took effect. "We came to be with our friends," they said. "Balu was a regular. We played everybody's favorite: *America's Next Top Model, Cycle 10*. I think it cheered people up. Those catfights were off the hook."

"I see," Arcadius said, though Elyse wasn't sure he did.

"Didn't that show take place in New York?" she asked.

The sorcerers' eyes went round as soon as they heard her accent. "Oh, my God," one exclaimed with surprisingly human intonation. "You're *from* there. And you're human. Do you know Tyra Banks? That female is the bomb!"

"Snap, Miss Thang," the other said as he swung his hand.

Elyse confessed she didn't know the supermodel, which calmed them down a bit.

"Would you honor us by coming back here some night?" the taller of the two invited. His short spiked hair had blue and yellow tips. "We'd love to ask you about your life."

"The consort has other responsibilities," Arcadius said before she could respond. He said *consort* like it was an official title, and for all she knew it was.

"Sure," the spike-haired sorcerer said before turning back to her. "But, you know, if it turns out you have time, we'd treat you like a princess."

Elyse thanked them for their offer, not answering either way.

They spoke to a few more patrons, who had little new to add. Balu was a great guy. Balu would pay for other people's coffee if they were broke. No, they had no idea where he'd gotten to or who'd think of hurting him. As far as they knew, he didn't have an enemy in the world.

"Well, that was a waste of time," Arcadius sighed as they emerged back into the bazaar. Their soldier escort fell into ranks around them.

"Oh, you never know," Elyse said. "We might have learned something and not know what. Plus, it was kind of nice to be treated like being human was a good thing."

She'd made the comment without thinking. Arcadius glanced at her. "Has someone insulted you?"

Of the people who had, he'd been the worst offender.

"I'm sure they didn't mean to," she said sweetly.

~

They followed up their visit to the café with a stop at a place Arcadius referred to as a bottle house. It was near the city's port at the river mouth, up a narrow cobbled lane in a pale yellow three-story building. From the name, Elyse expected a wine shop. As soon as their carpet landed, she saw this wasn't the case.

Some sort of priest in a deep purple cassock walked out the street level door. The plaque bolted to the yellow stucco above his head declared the building a refuge for homeless youth.

"Commander!" he exclaimed, pressing his hands together and bowing. "Thank you so much for coming. I wasn't hoping for any more than a police sergeant."

Arcadius swung Elyse over the carpet's rail, the process more casual for him now. "You were expecting us?"

The priest seemed confused by his question. "I submitted an aid request. Asking what to do about the stone bottles."

Arcadius's face went graver than usual. "Perhaps you should show me."

They followed him into a shop lined with wooden shelves. Brass amphora filled them, stacked three deep lying on their sides. Labels tied with red cord dangled from the necks. Names and dates were written on each one.

Elyse found the look of them inexplicably ominous.

"What is this place?" she asked, unable to hold her tongue.

"We are a shelter," the priest explained. "A safe place for young people who have no homes."

Elyse didn't understand. She looked up at Arcadius.

"When djinn transform to smoke, they no longer require food or warmth. They can remain disembodied indefinitely. The danger is that, after a time without taking physical form, they lose mental acuity. The bottle house's magic protects them against degrading."

"We wake them when we have better situations available," the priest said. "Families who wish to adopt or employment capable of supporting them. Unfortunately, as you can see from some of the dates of entry on the tags, there aren't enough good options."

Elyse found herself blinking rapidly. Perhaps it was her culture that made her think so, but this seemed pretty horrible.

"I stacked the stone bottles over here," the priest said, indicating another shelf to Arcadius. "I suppose we're lucky. The sorceress's curse turned no more than a third of our vessels to marble."

Arcadius moved to examine the petrified amphora. His face showed little expression but his hands were gentle. "Tell me," he said. "When you woke and took inventory, were some of your vessels gone?"

"How did you know?" the priest asked. "Unless you read the police report I filed?"

"We received a tip," the commander said.

The priest bent behind a counter to lift out a thick ledger book. He opened it to a pair of facing pages near the back. "These are the two individuals I couldn't account for. As you can see, we store portraits of everyone who stays here, along with brief biographies. These two were recent arrivals and still received visits from former companions. While it's not our policy to release residents simply to socialize, street children sometimes form strong attachments to each other. They like to assure themselves their friends' urns are here. The friends of these two noticed they were missing before I did."

Arcadius made room for Elyse behind the counter to look at the pages too. Paintings of a teenage boy and girl accompanied the short records. The portraits were rougher than Balu's but appeared to be good likenesses. The missing djinn were thin but attractive, with similar wide-eyed looks of hopefulness. The boy's face was slightly older, with strong bones and a wide mouth. The girl's waving golden hair and blue eyes reminded Elyse of a Renaissance angel. Her name was Celia. She couldn't have been more than fifteen.

"I believe Celia and Patrizio were romantically involved," their caretaker said. "They grew tired of scrabbling for survival and asked to be woken up together when their fortunes had a chance of improving."

Elyse's throat was tight. She couldn't have asked more questions even if she'd known what would be helpful.

"No one else is gone?" Arcadius asked.

"No one," the priest answered. "I checked very carefully as soon as the friends of these two left. I have their names and a general idea of the areas they wander, if that would be helpful. I don't mean to press, but is there anything I should be doing for the bottles that turned to stone?"

"For the time being, please just keep them safe from damage. We have reason to believe everyone will recover once we've rooted out the rest of the power behind the curse."

"Do you know how long that will take?"

"We don't," Arcadius admitted. "Rest assured, however, that every member of the sultan's administration is devoting their minds and hearts to solving this problem. None of us will rest until all our people are restored."

He spoke quietly but with passion. Clearly moved, the priest bowed respectfully to him.

~

The sun had set by the time they left the bottle shop, and Arcadius had much to digest. Elyse was quiet too, sitting in the carpet's rear with her knees pulled up to her chest. As they headed to the palace, she watched the streets recede behind them without truly seeming to take note. She held her scarf wrapped close. The breeze that blew the edges of her curls was cooler, and Arcadius hoped the air wasn't chilling her. Their driver had activated the lamps on the carpet's corners, but the safety precaution was uncalled-for. They weren't passing other vehicles or even other people. Everyone who could had gone home as darkness fell.

That wasn't usual. The Glorious City had an enjoyable nightlife.

It was some minutes before Arcadius noticed Elyse wiping wetness from her cheeks. She was crying. His heart tilted uneasily. He'd promised the other him he'd take care of her. Probably he ought to find out what was wrong.

He'd been standing, but he moved to sit beside her.

"Are you well?" he asked.

She wiped her face again. "Sorry. I didn't mean to get weepy. Those kids' stories got to me."

"Patrizio and Celia?"

"All the homeless kids. Your city is so rich. I didn't expect to encounter poverty bad enough that people would resort to letting themselves be locked up in bottles."

She was a woman, and women were often more tenderhearted than practical. Then again, Arcadius didn't like the situation much himself.

"In the past," he said, "we had sultans who gave every coin away. Still the poor remained with us and, inevitably, other leaders with better-paid armies overthrew those sultans. I suppose it is a commentary on djinn nature that our race seems not to respect self-effacing rulers."

Elyse nodded. "I'm not sure it's different in New York. We're also a wealthy city, and we have plenty of poor there."

An unexpected twinge of envy touched him. The other him had been to her world. If their spirits had recombined the way they were supposed to, Cade's memories would have been his as well.

"Do you wish to do this again tomorrow?" he asked.

"Oh, yes," she said. "I hope you don't mind having me along."

"Not at all," he assured her, surprised to discover he was relieved. "You were helpful."

"For a human, you mean." Her little smile told him she was teasing.

"For anyone," he said firmly.

The exchange pleased him for no good reason. He supposed she'd earned his respect today. She'd navigated unfamiliar waters without complaint. She'd experienced compassion but hadn't let it hobble her. Her accounts of what she'd learned were thorough and no more distorted by sentiment than a man's would have been. All in all, she was a competent assistant.

They parted ways in the palace's grand reception hall. She looked at him, her face tilted upward to suit his height. Her lashes were dark as ink, her soft green eyes wide and innocent. Her pink lips were slightly parted, their cushy shape unnervingly appealing.

"Thank you for letting me help today," she said.

He hadn't planned to but he took her hand. It nestled small and smooth in his palm as he bent over it. Pressing his lips to her skin was more pleasurable than he was prepared for. Her fingers twitched. As he straightened, a noticeable tingle coursed down his spine.

"Thank *you*," he responded.

His voice wasn't quite normal. He could hear that himself. Seeming flustered, Elyse blushed and tugged her hand back from him. He watched her climb the ornate stairway toward the official offices, where his double was presumably still working. She lacked the tempting curves of a harem girl, but something about the muscles of her bottom and how they shifted beneath her tunic kept his gaze glued to them.

His stomach growled. They hadn't stopped to eat all day. Should he have invited her to dinner? He pictured himself offering her succulent morsels from a platter. Her lips would close around his fingers. Perhaps she'd lick juice from them. Perhaps she'd hum with pleasure and close her eyes.

Perhaps she'd shift on her little bottom as she creamed with arousal.

A rush of heat to his groin warned him to stop imagining this. He was painfully erect, his cock thrusting urgently against his clothes. He wanted to debauch her in the nearest shadowy alcove, hard and deep and maybe more than once in quick succession.

Damn it, he thought. The other him's lust for her was rubbing off on him again.

~

The crowd in Cade's anteroom was finally thinning out. He was deep in discussion with the Minister of Foreign Affairs when Joseph sent him a scroll message that Elyse had returned.

"Excuse me, minister," he said with no remorse whatsoever. "We'll continue this later. I need to take another report right now."

The minister bowed and retreated. After a decent pause for discretion, Joseph brought Elyse in. Aware that Cade wouldn't want to talk to him just then, the magician closed the door behind her.

"You're a sight for sore eyes," Cade said.

Elyse smiled a little shyly and came to him. "Joseph said it would all right to interrupt."

"More than all right." He stretched in his chair and groaned as his vertebrae realigned. "God, I hate sitting like that all day."

She perched on the edge of his desk facing him. "You look tired." She stroked the hollows beneath his eyes with her thumbs. The touch was gentle and wonderful.

"That's funny," he joked. "I was thinking about you a minute ago, and it gave me a second wind."

He caught her nearer leg, lifting and bending it so that her shin rested lengthwise along his groin. He hadn't lied about her being in his thoughts—or about becoming aroused because of it.

"Hm," she said, the swell of his erection pressing the embroidered silk of her trouser leg. "That *is* funny."

Holding her calf wasn't enough for him. He lifted her onto his lap, wrapped her slender waist in his arms, and kissed her thoroughly. This was the way a long day of work should end. She held him back, her breath coming faster with the kiss. Her head fell back as he trailed his mouth down her neck.

"Are you hungry?" she asked.

Cade slid one hand up her front to squeeze a sharp-tipped breast. His cock was painfully hard, his whole being aching to take her. "Starving," he growled at her.

"I meant for food." She pushed weakly at his chest.

He tipped her back onto the desk, propped above her with his hips positioned between her lolling thighs. She bit her lip, her cheeks flushed inspiringly. Then, just as he began to tug down her silk trousers, her stomach growled noisily.

"Damn it," he said, not knowing whether to cry or laugh. "Didn't the other me feed you?"

"We were busy. If you let me call for a meal, I can bring you up to date on what we found out."

"Fine." He subsided back into his chair, his groin pounding annoyingly. Chances seemed good he looked sullen.

"You'll have more energy once you've eaten," she pointed out.

"Will I need it?" he asked, intrigued by that idea.

Elyse smiled at him.

CHAPTER THREE

JOSEPH the Magician—formerly Joseph the Eunuch—knew he shouldn't resent Cade and Elyse's happiness. They weren't so wrapped in each other that they forgot the city needed them.

They'd simply forgotten him.

In sharing the challenges of their journey home, Joseph had come to consider Elyse a friend—his first female friend in life. He'd trusted her with his secret: that he'd unintentionally made his double a whole man. At the time, Elyse had reacted more understandingly than he could himself. By making his copy different, he'd jeopardized the chance that he and it would reunite. Considering this was necessary to restore his power to its former level, a power their city certainly could use, his mistake wasn't trivial. Ever since he'd discovered it, he'd been afraid to think sexual thoughts.

They didn't belong to the man he'd been.

He laid his hand on the outer door to his apartment. Though he served the commander closely, Arcadius had long ago granted his request not to reside in his house, allowing him to have separate rooms. Joseph liked privacy—creature comforts too. He had both here: his own bed, his own bath and sitting room, which he'd decorated to suit himself. This apartment was his island apart from the sea of life where other people swam. Here he didn't worry that he'd never have a wife, that he'd grow old alone without anyone loving him. Here he read his books and he honed his craft. Here he was safe from feeling inferior.

Tonight, for once, he was reluctant to enter.

The palace corridor where he stood was dim. The majority of its residents had retired, though the working day had unavoidably been lengthened. Joseph forced his fingers to grasp his door's flowery knob. It was no use. He couldn't compel his hand to turn.

Well, fine, he thought. He had another task to accomplish, one he'd been putting off.

He could have sped to his destination in smoke form. Unfortunately, a confrontation with a human sorcerer in Elyse's realm had jammed his ability to shift. Usually, djinn were spared being bossed around by the simple fact that humans rarely knew they had the potential to do spells. In this case, Joseph hadn't been so lucky. The human, a tattooed gangster named Mario, had forced Joseph's smoke into an oil lamp against his will, despite Joseph being the more skilled practitioner. Another human's aid—Elyse's—had been needed to free him.

For now, Joseph had to travel by other means. He signed out a personal flying carpet from the palace's vehicle stores. The sleepy clerk didn't challenge him. Everyone was aware of Joseph's role as the commander's aide. Joseph appreciated the deference this earned him. Djinn who knew he was a eunuch might whisper their pity behind his back. To his face, however, he was treated with respect.

The carpet he requisitioned was the size of a small prayer rug. Joseph flew it from the palace up the broad Avenue of Palms. The city seemed untouched from above. The red clay roofs were as picturesque as ever, the golden domes and spires gleaming fancifully beneath a quarter moon. When he landed on its topmost level, he had the Arch of Triumph to himself. Hidden within its structure was the nexus he and Cade had used to reach New York.

The door to the portal chamber was sealed with powerful spells. Because Joseph had set them in place himself, they were easy to undo.

The room inside reminded him of old subway stations in Elyse's home. The walls were tiled, the architectural detail lovely but very cool. The floor and the few plain benches were marble and not cement. Nonetheless, this was not a place where humans or djinn would enjoy lingering.

Joseph checked the portal first. Its power was drained from sending him and Cade to the human world, resembling a guttering candle instead of a robust sun. He'd already examined the portals in the treasure room at the palace and underneath the Church of Sighs. Their condition was identical.

Considering half the administration's mages had turned to stone, three portals were too much to recharge. Joseph had to prioritize. The treasure room's nexus was the portal Iksander had left from. Reasoning that tracking their missing sultan through the same door he'd used would be easiest, Joseph had tasked the remaining royal magic corps with restoring it.

The other doors would have to wait.

His decision reaffirmed, Joseph turned to the object he'd put off surveying.

A grout-spattered sheet draped the statue of his original. The highest hump, where the cloth fell across his head, wasn't far off the ground. His body knelt just as it had in the moment he projected the lion's share of his spirit through the portal and into his copy. Arcadius must have covered his stone remains when he woke up here alone. Joseph supposed this was a compassionate act on his master's part, like closing the eyes of deceased people—no matter that the dead saw nothing.

Taking a breath to steady himself, he pulled off the concealing cloth.

And there he was, eyes closed with concentration, butt on his heels, palms flat and serene on his folded thighs. Joseph sensed the tiniest spark anchored deep within the stone. Part of him was still in there, still revivable, though not by him.

Then again, maybe he didn't want to revive himself.

If that were true, all the more reason to make a sincere attempt.

Unnerved by the sight of his familiar yet strange face, he circled the marble form until he was behind it. He laid his palms on the waves of his original's frozen hair. Quieting his emotions, he willed the magic that remained to him to radiate down his arms.

The small spark within the statue didn't react at all.

Should he turn up the power and risk doing unknown damage? Joseph tried an incrementally stronger surge. Nothing happened. Like everyone else who hadn't recovered from the curse, Joseph's original stayed locked in its suspension.

He dropped his hands. He'd tried and failed and for now he could give up.

His mood lightened shamefully.

~

As soon as the carpet lifted off the commemorative arch, Joseph started questioning his actions. Had he tried hard enough? Should he turn back and try again?

"Stop," he said aloud to himself.

Confused by the order, the smoothly gliding rug juddered to a halt.

Clearly, he hadn't been paying attention to the route. He'd overshot the palace by at least eight blocks. Now he hung over the winding cobbled byways of Old Town, where—despite the hour—a few businesses displayed signs of life. Two taverns were lit up, plus an outpost of the always popular Temple of Aphrodite. Righteous djinn of the Glorious City were free to honor any aspect of the Creator that called to them. As in olden times, having sex with the priestesses of the goddess qualified as worship.

If some priestesses made their living from this worship, that was their concern.

Business was good, apparently. Handsome carvings decorated the narrow building's front. Dolphins leaped from foaming pale jade waves with ruby apples caught in their smiling mouths. Mother of pearl cased the lintels, and flourishing rose and lime trees spilled from pots by the door. Perfume trailed out the windows in heady whiffs, inviting both the reverent and the lonely to draw closer.

It was precisely the sort of place Joseph made a habit of avoiding.

When he was twenty-two, an evil sorcerer had ripped his scrotum from his body. Some djinn who'd been castrated at that age would have retained their ability to function sexually. Joseph didn't know if his former master had added magic to his violence, but he hadn't been one of them. His parents had apprenticed him to the sorcerer when he was just fifteen, after which he'd lived more as the sorcerer's prisoner than his student.

Joseph had kissed girls in his youth, but he'd never made love to one.

He drifted closer to the temple, his carpet still out of reach of the sanctuary's soft lighting. The nearest window was open, the decor inside vibrant blue and gold. One of the young priestesses sat at a vanity mirror, combing her long auburn hair. She was naked from the waist up—perhaps from the waist down as well; the upholstered chair and the angle hid that from him. As she ran her comb down her gleaming tresses, the curves of her breasts came into and out of view. They were very pretty, full and temptingly shaped. Joseph's heart beat faster, his breath catching in his throat. His fingers curled toward his palms, almost feeling the weight of those creamy globes. The priestess's eyes were drowsy, her head tilted to the side. She didn't know she had an audience. If she had, she wouldn't have slid one hand down her belly and tucked it between her legs.

Joseph's cock went so hard so fast that the pain of his lust jerked him out of his reverie.

He couldn't do this. Bad enough he was spying on this female without her leave. It was crucial he not walk any farther down the path of being an able man. His original was a eunuch. Joseph must act—and think—as if he were one too.

He moved his lips on a silent spell, hastily backing his carpet out of viewing range.

Then he flew to the palace like a djinni chased by demons.

~

Nine times out of ten, sultan's concubines were daughters of noble blood. Rulers exchanged them as diplomatic gifts. For the women, a lifetime spent in a harem, scheming side by side with their rivals to catch the sultan's eye, was a great privilege. When she was accepted into their ranks, Yasmin had been elated.

Sultan Iksander was so handsome he was called "the Golden," on top of which he was considered a wise ruler. Aware that she was attractive, Yasmin had looked forward to rising in prestige by bearing a son to him. This would have been a coup. She was only a merchant's daughter, though her father was important. He'd pioneered a secret process for transporting goods across the perilous nonmaterial "in-betweens" that separated djinn territories with seas of mist. No other firm had her father's record of successful deliveries, or his reputation for honesty. When Iksander (or possibly his proxy) had consented to take Yasmin, the honor had been her family's too.

Yasmin hadn't expected to sleep with the great man exactly once.

Iksander had fallen for his wife Najat before reaching Yasmin in the rotation set by the chief eunuch. From that day until the one his beloved met her untimely death, Iksander was faithful. Following Najat's murder, the sultan went slightly mad. Night after night, he chose a different member of the harem to sleep with in his smoke form. This was an eccentric practice. Djinn generally made love to each other as solid beings. Yasmin found the experience pleasurable but ultimately disappointing. There'd been no connection between her and Iksander, no true intimacy or bonding. Like the other consorts, she'd been a vessel into which he exorcised his grief. When he'd slept with each female once, he turned that grief elsewhere.

To Yasmin's mind, she might as well have stayed a virgin.

On the bright side, the sultan's unconventional behavior had given her an idea. She could escape the harem the same way that he'd come in. Concubines weren't supposed to want to. Leaving their protected precinct was forbidden. Yasmin didn't care anymore. Her older brother had turned ifrit. Her younger had thrown off propriety to hang out at view cafés watching humans do silly things. What did it matter if she, her parents' middle child, rebelled?

A woman could die of boredom waiting for her neglectful master to visit her.

In the beginning, Yasmin was content to explore the palace in the invisible version of her smoke form. The sultan's complex was huge and there was a lot to see. Eventually, though, the wider world called to her. As a dutiful sheltered daughter, she'd seen little of the Glorious City before she was shut away. Reaching the metropolis was a challenge. Sophisticated spells kept intruders from smoking in or out of the palace. Fortunately, Yasmin's family had a knack for enchantments. With practice and determination, she perfected her ability to change into a solid form no one would look twice at.

Yasmin the concubine became a shy stray cat.

Delighting in the fiction, she gave herself a crooked black tail, three white socks, and a battle-scarred right ear. She looked a fright, perfectly safe from anyone falling in love with her feline form and wanting to adopt her.

Perhaps her lucky escape from being stuck in stone should have cured her of risk-taking. Instead, the very night her consciousness woke she slipped out again. She couldn't regret that now. If she hadn't been pit-patting around the city on her cat paws, she'd never have discovered other citizens besides her brother had disappeared. In truth, there might be more she hadn't heard about.

She hesitated at the irrigation pipe that was her usual exit from the harem into the palace grounds. Though she was eager to squeeze out, she was a God-loving djinni and didn't wish to be reckless. Sparing the moment she knew she should, she sat on her haunches, curled her crooked tail around her, and bowed her furry head.

Blessed Mother, she prayed silently. *Please protect me on my journeys as You protect the world. Guide my feet as You guide all Your children.*

She immediately felt more confident. Out the pipe she wriggled, into the soft night air. As always, her sense of freedom invigorated her. Accustomed by now to running on four legs, she bounded like a shadow through the shaggy grass of a dark courtyard.

Maybe she'd head to the market down near the port. Young people who had no homes often went there when it was closed, to scrounge for leftover food or sheltered places to curl up. Like anyone, rich or poor, they'd gossip with each other when they met up. Her cat form had learned a lot by eavesdropping.

A current of displaced air teased her sensitive whiskers. Yasmin turned to see where the draft came from.

A flying carpet was settling on the marble pavers that surrounded a small fountain. No lights announced the rug's arrival, nor was this an official landing site. If Yasmin's cat senses hadn't been so sharp, the vehicle might have slipped in unnoticed.

A tall man stepped off and began to roll up the rug like he meant to carry it. Was the pilot an assassin? Had Empress Luna's surviving allies come to finish what she'd begun? Yasmin's little heart thumped hard in her narrow chest. Should she run for help or should she attack? *Could* she attack, for that matter? Penetrating the palace's barriers required strong magic. She had some spell craft but probably not enough to combat a skilled practitioner.

Try, she thought. At the least, she could claw the intruder until he screamed.

She could also yowl herself, she thought a moment later. That would bring someone running, if only to shut her up.

Though she'd never made a noise in her animal form before, she drew in breath and forced out a terrible caterwaul. Despite the situation, she nearly laughed. No cat she'd ever heard sounded so ridiculous.

"In the name of God," swore the man with the rug tucked beneath his arm. "Quiet yourself right now."

His words had power. She shut her mouth and sat back on her rump, startled. The man who'd ordered her was Joseph the Magician, the very man she'd asked the commander's consort to turn to for help. Why was he flying in here so stealthily? *He* wouldn't act against the city. He was an honorable man.

Had he perhaps been using his magic to find Balu?

If he had, the commander's consort was unlikely to report to Yasmin until morning. Yasmin didn't think she could stand to wait that long. With no offense to her honorable parents, her younger brother was the closest person to her in the world. Losing their older brother Ramis in such a scandalous way had thrown the two of them together. Balu understood what it was to walk on eggshells in a fractured family.

With that to goad her, and possibly more besides, she trotted after the handsome magician into the main palace.

~

Joseph's guilt followed him to his rooms like a stubborn ghost. He did his best to shove it away. So he'd looked at a naked woman. His eunuch self might have done the same. The female form was lovely—no matter what a male did or didn't have the power to do with it. He'd admired the Almighty's creation. That shouldn't qualify as a sin.

He pushed his door shut behind him with extra emphasis.

He was alone, only the shadows keeping him company. His body seemed to vibrate with extra life, the pulse and thrum heaviest between his legs. He put his hand there and found his cock rigid.

He knew enough to recognize an erection when he felt one. Though those days seemed distant, he'd experienced the same swelling in his youth, before his parents sold him to the cruel sorcerer. He rubbed the ridge beneath his trousers testingly, sharp sensations washing out from the place he touched. Curious, he slid his fingers down the thick ridge to his testicles. Because massaging the hanging sac was enjoyable, he pulled his hand away. This caused his turgid penis to throb more intensely.

Why did denying oneself a pleasure make it twice as alluring?

The question was better suited to a philosopher. Ignoring his body's urges, he stepped to the sitting area of his rooms. Here, a line of windows opened into a small courtyard, one of many in the complex. Joseph's favorite armchair was positioned next to the view. He lowered his weight to the firm cushion, poured a glass of brandy from the decanter that sat nearby, and opened the heavy book he'd borrowed from the absent sultan's personal library.

The volume's title was *Creating Doubles with Magic.*

Everything he'd read thus far was useless.

The book contained spells to copy every item under the sun, including items invented by humans. It related stories of doubles throughout history. Humans who were the spitting image of djinn. Djinn who impersonated humans by imitating their appearance. Cloned works of art and mirror spaces. Incantations for playing back events on the basis of the vibrations they'd left behind.

In Arab countries, humans who were afflicted by their djinn twins were called *majnun* or crazy.

What the book didn't tell him was how to fix split duos who wouldn't reunite. Truth be told, Joseph couldn't remember precisely how he'd doubled himself and the others in the first place. He knew he'd put the spell into a design: twin overlapping suns their artist friend Philip had tattooed inside their right ankles. Joseph's current body no longer had ink there. Possibly reapplying the tattoo would help, but he couldn't say for sure—nor did it matter since Philip's whereabouts in the human world were unknown.

The question of why their souls had reacted the way they did to being split was another mystery. Cade's double, which had the smaller fraction of his spirit, seemed equally a person. But souls were special—ineffable even. If Joseph had to copy himself again, to breathe life into a replication of his body, he didn't think he could have done it.

His original, the him who was locked in stone, was the sole possessor of the secret.

That shamed him as deeply as his reaction to the priestess. Though he was whole in his sexual parts, in power he was less than he'd been before. His city was counting on him to solve this problem, and he seemed doomed to fail.

Overcome by despair, he leaned across the book with his hands covering his eyes.

A tiny *mrrp* jerked him up again.

It was the bloody cat from the garden, the one who'd yowled at him like an ifrit. Its silver eyes blinked at him from the shadows.

"How did you get in here?" he asked.

The cat ran to him and jumped into his lap.

"Stop that," he scolded, because the creature seemed likely to tear the valuable tome. He shoved the feline off, then closed the book and rose. Its footing swiftly recovered, the cat looked up at him from the floor as if he'd insulted it.

"Fine," he said, picking it up and draping it over his shoulder. Though small, the cat was heavy. As he petted its ruffled fur, it went limp and began to purr.

This was more endearing than he was prepared for.

"You should be chasing mice," he said, distrusting the appeal of the animal's languid warmth. Dumping the cat in the corridor, he shut his door again.

If only he could have shut the door on his other problems as easily.

Thunder rumbled outside his windows, a late spring storm rolling in. The electricity in the air tingled across his skin. Was the naked priestess gazing out her window too? Had she brought herself to climax? Was she, perhaps, interested in doing so again?

Joseph pulled the doors to the courtyard open, willing the cool damp air to buffet his body. Despite the drop in temperature, his erection didn't subside. Maybe it wouldn't until he saw to it. He pushed his hand down into his trousers, gripping his hardness within his palm and fingers. It seemed natural to pull his tight hold upward. Hadn't he done that as a boy?

Fuck, he thought, pleasure coursing through him even more strongly than before.

His penis was larger than when it was relaxed. It responded to his slow drag by hardening more. The head was pulsing, the veins engorged.

What he wouldn't give to thrust this stiff ache into a soft woman . . .

He reached the crest and pushed his thumb around on the silky skin. The slit at the center was leaking wetness, the hormones that stimulated its creation produced by his restored testicles. He was fully alive now: feeling, throbbing, capable of the act every djinni enjoyed. He bit his lip and let his head tip back.

Stop, he thought, but his thumb just kept going round and round.

It was like rubbing an itch that got worse as you saw to it.

He craved release more than his next breath.

Realizing the danger, he pulled his hand from his pants, fisting it hard enough to prick his palm with his fingernails. Surely he had the self-control to refrain from doing this.

He breathed in and out, his chest going up and down, his pulsing cock strafing its coverings with each movement. The air around his hips seemed hot, as if an invisible fire were wrapped around him. The fire licked at him like smoke, teasing his overexcited nerves. He started to rock his pelvis, the subtle motion instinctive. His scrotum ached, beginning to draw up with arousal. Within the sac, his testicles felt swollen. A little more sensation would bring him off. The tip of his penis tingled, moisture welling faster from the hole, sticking him to his light trousers. He could almost swear he felt a woman's mouth closing around him there . . .

Air hissed between his teeth as his scrotum jerked. The bliss of imminent orgasm—or what he assumed that was—tried to streak up his nerves.

"Damn it." Panting, he gripped and wrenched his balls so hard the pressure couldn't be anything but painful.

The sensation of being about to come ceased abruptly. His erection faded as well, subsiding into the quiescent state he was accustomed to. He closed his eyes with a mix of disappointment and relief.

I am Joseph the Eunuch, he told himself. *I put my city first.*

~

Yasmin felt like she'd been slapped twice over: first when Joseph dumped her cat form into the hall and then when he chose to hurt himself rather than let her pleasure him.

Not that he'd known she was doing that.

Mortally embarrassed and once again in her cat disguise, she streaked away down the corridor. If she'd been wearing her own face, she knew it would have blazed. She should have known better than to smoke back into the room after Joseph had thrown her out. She'd told herself she was worried for him, because he'd seemed disconsolate. That, however, was no excuse for her uninvited "help."

Yes, she'd been shocked to discover he was physically capable of desire. Every whisper she'd heard about the sultan's chief magician suggested the opposite. In her fascination with him, she'd collected quite a few stories. For that matter, she'd spied on him in smoke form before. Joseph was very handsome, but more than that, she found watching him peaceful. He was often up at night, studying his magic books or wandering the halls like her. He didn't give the impression that *he* was snooping, more that he was on patrol. He stood guardian to the palace even when others slept. His example had inspired her to keep an ear tuned for trouble when she ventured beyond its walls. She'd wanted to be more than a harem girl, sitting with her hands obediently folded in the hope that the sultan might someday return and notice her.

Yasmin longed to be useful, even if no one but she was aware of it. She'd thought it would make her and Joseph more alike—a secret bond she could cherish by herself.

That didn't justify forcing herself on him without permission. In the worst of his grief, Iksander hadn't forced himself on partners who were considered his property. The least Yasmin could have done was offer Joseph a choice.

Given his reaction, she couldn't doubt what the choice would have been.

Her claws scrabbled on the pipe as she squeezed back through the drain into the harem grounds. Per usual, no one noticed her. They didn't notice when she smoked back into her room either. The sultan's mother was a harridan, but Yasmin wasn't on her list of girls to keep a close eye on. Maybe this was surprising for a girl as attractive as Yasmin, but she was no troublemaker. She did as she was told.

She hadn't ever found that as depressing as she did now.

Back in her normal form, she flung into her luxurious bed and pulled the soft covers up. She thought of the many people who would be grateful to have that much.

You should be grateful, she told herself.

She tried to be—and maybe she succeeded. She relaxed enough to fall asleep, where her dreams were filled with images of Joseph the Magician writhing in ecstasy.

CHAPTER FOUR

ARCADIUS jerked awake at dawn and didn't know where he was. The shadowed room was too large, the mattress beneath him too comfortable. His heart was racing, his cock hard enough to pound nails.

That, at least, was familiar.

"Mmph," said a female voice. "Is it time to get up?"

Elyse pushed up on her elbow from the pillow next to him.

He gaped at her. What was Cade's human doing in bed with him?

"What?" she said, shoveling back her curls. "Has my hair gone crazy?"

She thought he was Cade. Belatedly, he recognized his surroundings as Iksander's grand bedchamber. Had his and Cade's spirits recombined while they were asleep? Maybe Joseph had stumbled upon a cure. Arcadius tried to force his brain to work logically. He could remember what he'd done the day before but not a thing his double had experienced. That suggested their consciousnesses were separate. Something else must be happening.

"Your hair is fine," he said cautiously to his accidental bed partner.

Elyse rolled her eyes and sighed. "You always think it's fine."

Was this cause for complaint? To him, it sounded like diplomacy.

Elyse shoved the covers down her body and sat up.

Arcadius's heart did a funny flip. He was a man, and seeing a naked woman was rarely a bad thing. That aside, he didn't expect to *like* Elyse without her clothes. She was lithe rather than lush, her breasts small but nicely shaped. Her nipples were relaxed, their color the same soft pink as her cushiony mouth. His morning erection pulsed, urging him to grab her and kiss them.

"Now *that's* a flattering look," she said.

His gaze jerked to hers. Her crooked smile was seduction personified. She lifted one eyebrow.

"Want to join me in the hot tub?" she invited. "I'll let you scrub my back."

It was a lovely back, from what he'd seen of it. He wet his lips as he hesitated. What were the rules of engagement in situations of this sort? Was it possible for her to cheat on him with him?

She laughed at his slowness and started strolling toward the bathing room. The sway of her hips suggested she was aware he watched. He couldn't stop watching, though he should have. His view of her ass and legs made his mouth go dry.

She had one deep dimple atop each cheek.

She tossed a tease over her bare shoulder. "Feel free to follow when you make up your mind."

Had a woman ever taunted him with this much confidence? Many females had flirted, but never so surely. He realized he didn't awe Elyse. For whatever reason, his arousal surged higher. His lust had been hot already. More than a little maddened, he threw off the covers before he could stop himself. Three bounding strides brought him close enough to catch her slender arm.

One quick tug spun her nakedness to him.

She made a startled noise, her hands bracing automatically on his chest as the tips of her breasts brushed him. She was where he wanted . . . or nearly. He slid his palms down the curvature of her spine to palm her bottom. The flesh there was so resilient he had to squeeze.

The pressure brought her satiny belly against his pounding prick.

"Well," she said, breathless and amused as he pulled her onto her toes. "I can tell which part of you woke up first."

She moved her hands, rubbing his back up and down before squeezing his butt like he was squeezing hers. Nerves jumped to life all over him, as if her touch turned his entire body into a sexual receptor.

The only thing more surprising was when her arms circled his torso. She pressed her cheek to his chest and hugged him.

"You are gorgeous," she praised. "And wonderful to see first thing in the morning."

She pulled back far enough to look into his eyes. Hers were warm, fondness and something deeper shining up at him. Evidently, she couldn't tell the difference between him and his copy. Arcadius's chest constricted. What would it be like to have her look at him with that expression?

"Elyse," he said, his hold shifting from her butt to her upper arms.

She laughed. "That's your work voice. And your work face. I assume you're going to tell me we don't have time to play around."

"I—" His vision flickered, disorienting him. For a split second, he felt her and simultaneously saw the sparse white walls of his dining room. Those walls weren't usually empty. Joseph had shrunk his favorite Sindbad tapestry to take to Elyse's world.

"Elyse," he repeated, but he and she were no longer together.

He was back in his proper body, in the dining room of his own residence.

He wore a brown silk robe he couldn't remember pulling on. His very large, very stubborn hard-on made it impossible not to notice he wore nothing under it.

He wasn't quite standing straight. His left hand braced his weight on the long table. His right held a quill with which he'd been scribbling a note.

You and I need to talk, the angry letters said. The final word was underlined, not once but three times.

Maybe he shouldn't have, but Arcadius smiled. It seemed his copy was a tad dramatic.

~

Elyse had figured out how to turn down the djinn-appropriate temperature in the soaking tub. She'd resigned herself to enjoying the jets alone when Arcadius slid into the seething water. His chalcedony eyes were lit from within by intensity, definitely not smiling. Covered to the waist by the churning waves, he stalked to her.

She wanted to ask if everything was okay, but her breath had caught in her throat. When he looked at her like that—so possessive and serious—she remembered he wasn't the same kind of being as her.

He gripped her under the arms and heaved her dripping up his big torso.

"Cade," she gasped. His hard-on pressed her right thigh. Her body went wet in a new way.

"That's right," he said, low and rough. "I'm the one you belong to."

She didn't know why he felt a need to say this but didn't get a chance to ask. Her weight went backward, her back lowered carefully to the tub's marble edge. Her thighs were already open around his legs. Sensing she'd better brace, she planted the sole of one foot on the side. Water droplets fell from him to her.

"Say my name again," Cade ordered, his eyes boring into hers.

"Cade," she repeated.

He fit his hips to the right position and plunged all the way into her.

She cried out. His entry was overwhelming but very good.

"Yes," she said, clutching his broad shoulders.

He didn't wait. He cradled her head with one hand, gripped her buttock securely with the other, and commenced pumping. She loved when he took control of her that way. In seconds, they were both groaning, his urgent movements exciting. She could tell this wasn't going to last long for either one of them. Their breath was choppy, their hold on each other tight. Cade shifted angles and worked his cock faster in and out. He had a gift for grinding her clitoris with every thrust, and his length and thickness pushing through her slick passage felt amazing. Sensation rose inside her, the nerves his shaft squeezed over coiling delightedly.

"Mine," he growled against her ear.

Only he could have made that claim a turn on for her.

"Yes," she panted, trying to beat her hips harder against his. She was so close she could have screamed. "I'm yours."

He grunted, going deep and triggering her. Her orgasm was as powerful as it was sudden. She arched, her sheath clamping around him. Despite the constriction, he drew back and shoved again—already spilling, she realized. He could go a long time, climaxes sometimes seeming to pile one on top of another. That happened now, his head flung back with shuddering ecstasy. She slid her hands up his chest and pinched his tight nipples.

She startled him but he liked it. He gasped for breath as his eyes squeezed shut. Slowly, they both relaxed.

"Elyse," he said throatily.

She rubbed his pectorals up and down. Cade's eyes opened. She smiled at him.

He didn't smile back at her. That would have been okay, except the expression he *did* have was sullen.

"Well," she said, unavoidably miffed by that. "You're in a mood."

He pulled out and away from her, leaving her wet body cool. "Sorry."

She wasn't sure he meant the apology. He stood and rubbed the back of his neck, gazing down at her with that same hint of suspicion or displeasure. Feeling exposed, Elyse sat up from her sprawl and pressed her knees together. "Why are you looking at me like that? Did I do something you didn't like?"

He appeared to force his face to clear. "Of course not. I'll call for breakfast. You finish washing up."

She watched him leave, unable to decide if she should challenge his denial. Men did get moody, especially when they were under pressure. Sometimes—at least in her experience—it was better not to know what they were thinking until they'd gained some perspective on whatever the problem was. Presumably djinn weren't so different from humans in that respect.

"Crap," she said softly to herself. At times like this she wished there were a handbook for dealing with males of all species.

~

Arcadius wasn't looking forward to the upcoming "talk" with his double, but he wasn't going to shy away from it. Deciding to avoid his usual work uniform—since his double would likely be dressed that way—he pulled a figured gray silk robe over brilliantly white trousers. Circling his waist with a wide azure sash satisfied his need for a splash of color. Because it wouldn't do to go unarmed, he strapped on a well-balanced but showy jeweled scimitar, plus tucked a handful of throwing daggers in hidden sheaths. He cursed when he couldn't find his favorite leather campaign boots. They seemed to have wandered from his closet, probably on his double's feet.

His annoyance over that made him snatch up a neatly wrapped package on his way out.

He must have resembled a thundercloud as he strode through the corridors of the palace and up the stairs to Iksander's apartments. Everyone who looked like they might want to speak to him ended up shrinking back.

As he arrived, he saw Iksander's staff had brought breakfast. They were rolling unloaded carts through the tall double doors back into the corridor.

"Commander," one of them exclaimed, offering a surprised bow as he caught sight of him. "Shall we bring an extra place setting?"

The question irritated Arcadius. It seemed to make him the outsider here. He hardly needed Iksander's level of luxury, but perhaps he'd miscalculated when he forced his copy and his lover to stay in the sultan's rooms. Rightly or wrongly, grand surroundings lent the people in them an air of importance.

"I'm sure I can manage," he said gruffly. "Please go on as you were."

This time, the whole crew of servers bowed and withdrew.

Arcadius rapped the decorated door but entered without waiting. He knew his way to the dining chamber. He'd eaten there many times with Iksander.

He never reached it. Cade, his copy, met him in the room of glass cabinets, where Iksander displayed the choicest part of his collection of diplomatic gifts. Cade wore the same thunderous expression Arcadius had displayed in the corridor.

"What the hell were you doing?" the other him demanded.

Arcadius presumed he referred to their brief body swap. He drew himself straighter. "I wasn't *doing* anything. My consciousness switched with yours by accident."

"And when you embraced Elyse while she was naked? Was that an accident too?" The other him bit out the words, his features flushed with rage.

"You sensed that?" Arcadius was taken aback by this information. "I couldn't tell what you were doing in my rooms."

"Perhaps what I was doing in 'your' rooms wasn't as exciting."

Perhaps it hadn't been, or perhaps the difference was due to Cade—allegedly—having the larger portion of their spirit. Arcadius didn't like that idea. It suggested he, the original, was inferior to his copy.

Whatever the truth, honor dictated that he give his double an apology. "I regret I was familiar with your human. Touching her was wrong of me."

Cade's face went dark with fury. "Damn right it was wrong of you! What's more, you'd better believe I won't tolerate another transgression. Elyse is *my* lover. You have no right to her."

Cade jabbed his finger into Arcadius's chest.

"Remove your hand," Arcadius warned coolly.

"I mean it," the double said. "I won't have you manhandling her."

Arcadius felt his eyebrows rise. "Are you forbidding me?"

"Don't you dare take that as a challenge. We got over that childish crap when we were fifteen."

Arcadius tipped his head to the side and smiled. "So we did. I'm simply intrigued by the notion that you view me as a threat."

The other him's breath huffed out. "Elyse has better taste than to fall for you."

"Because we're so very different," Arcadius mocked.

"Because you're the same old asshat I used to be!"

Arcadius intuited what the insult meant. His expression shut down with anger, his face as stony as if he hadn't woken from statue form. He wasn't certain what he would have said next. Something rash, he expected.

"Everything okay in here?" Elyse interrupted from the display room door.

"*Yes*," Arcadius and Cade snapped at the same moment. The timing and the intonation of their response matched precisely. It truly sounded like they'd answered with one voice.

Elyse pressed her lips together to hide a smile. She came a step closer, her gaze sliding measuringly between them. Her reaction to their raised voices wasn't wholly humorous. Arcadius found himself hoping she hadn't heard the details of what they said. He actually was a bit ashamed of taking liberties with her.

"Breakfast is getting cold," she pointed out.

"I'll be there in a minute," Cade said gently.

"Perhaps Arcadius is hungry too," she said.

Arcadius amazed himself by having to fight a blush.

"You're welcome to join us," the other him said stiffly.

"I ate," he said, though he hadn't. "I came to inform Elyse that, if she's agreeable to continuing our investigation, I have another lead we can follow up. Perhaps we could meet at the bottom of the grand stairway in half an hour?"

"I won't keep you waiting," Elyse promised.

He nodded and began to leave, then realized his fingers still clamped the tissue-wrapped package he'd grabbed on his way here.

"This is for you," he said, turning back and handing it to her.

"For me?" She accepted it wide-eyed.

Inexplicably unable to depart, he watched her open the white wrapping. His heart jumped as her plain human face broke into a delighted grin. "The sparkly slippers from the shop in the Grand Bazaar! How did you know I wanted them?"

"I noticed you admiring the shoes the ministers were wearing. I sent one of the guards back to purchase them."

Elyse was dressed in a simple silk bed robe and bare feet. She bent to put the jeweled slippers on, probably not aware that the movement caused her slight breasts to sway. "They fit!" She wriggled her toes. "And they're so comfy. Thank you for getting them."

"You're welcome," he responded formally. "Though, as I said, my guards ran the errand."

He wondered if she'd hug him. Apparently not. She squeezed Cade's hand instead. "Half an hour," she said, repeating his instructions for meeting up. "Down by the grand stairway in the reception hall."

He didn't ask if that was sufficient time. From what he'd observed, his double's lover was a woman who knew her mind.

~

"What was that about?" Elyse asked once they'd returned to the meal spread out in the dining room. She forked a succulent bite of melon into her mouth, half her mind on strategizing what clothes she'd throw on today. She didn't want to be late for her appointment. She had the definite impression Cade's former self wasn't the patient type.

Seated next to her at the long table's end, Cade let out a weary sigh.

"Must I explain?" he asked.

He meant about the fight with his double. "I suppose not," she conceded, giving him her full attention.

He squirmed uncomfortably on his Western-style dining chair. "Arcadius and I will sort it out between us."

"Okay," she said.

He was still ill at ease. "I'm sorry I didn't think to give you a gift. I could have sent a guard to get something too."

"You mean because you don't have a zillion other things on your mind?"

"The other me was more thoughtful."

Elyse put her hand on his and rubbed it. "I don't need gifts. I just need you." She searched for words to express her emotions. "You're the best gift life ever threw at me."

Her eyes welled up and he cupped her cheek. His gaze was as full as hers.

"I'm glad you caught me," he said softly.

~

The flying carpet pilot landed Elyse and Arcadius on a hibiscus-shaded, slightly worn down street. Worn down anything was unusual for the Glorious City, but—to Elyse's eyes—the patina of oldness was romantic. They'd traveled to the city's edge this morning. The buildings weren't as close together as the Old Town section. The structure she and Arcadius stood before was constructed of dark gray stone and, counting its grounds, took up half the block. Three brightly colored bicycles, the first Elyse could recall seeing, were chained to the ground level windows' security grates.

"What is this place?" she asked.

"Bathhouse," Arcadius answered, currently scanning their surroundings. "One of the names Yasmin gave you was listed on the work rolls as being employed here."

"Commander," interrupted one of the soldier guards. He gestured toward the Roman style stone arch that overhung the main entrance. "Read the inscription."

Elyse tipped her head to look. It took a couple seconds, but thanks to the linguistic spell Cade and Joseph had worked on her, she deciphered the lettering as saying *Enter and Enjoy.*

"Hm," Arcadius said as he rubbed his strong chin.

"What's wrong with 'Enter and Enjoy?'"

"It's a code phrase. It means this isn't an ordinary bathhouse. It's also a brothel."

"Oh. Well, we still have to go in. I promise I won't faint if we bump into a prostitute."

Arcadius actually laughed. "All right." He took her elbow to guide her. "Just let me know if you're uncomfortable."

A trip down a short dark hall led them into a broad domed space. High above them, grimy stained glass windows admitted dim spokes of sun. The faded grandeur of the place charmed Elyse—no matter if it was a whorehouse. The air was steamy and smelled strongly but pleasantly of herbs. No one seemed to be around. Maybe this wasn't a busy hour.

"Hello," Arcadius called. His voice echoed off the dome.

A tall young man, with a stunning androgynous face, stepped through the surrounding arcade of columns. Despite his youth, the djinni had an air of knowing what was what in the establishment.

"Party of six," he called back over his shoulder to someone they couldn't see.

"No," Arcadius said. "These gentlemen are guards."

The young man's expression turned quizzical, his gaze traveling between the commander and Elyse. Arcadius's hand was still on her elbow. "Party of two?"

"No," Arcadius said more firmly. "I am Commander Arcadius. This woman and I are making inquiries about a bath girl who disappeared a few days ago."

The young man put one hand on his narrow hip, his attitude unmistakably skeptical. "The Guardian of the Glorious City wants to know what happened to Jeannine."

"That is correct," Arcadius said.

"You *look* like pictures of the commander," their challenger conceded.

"Because I am him," Arcadius said.

One of the soldier guards lost control and snorted with amusement. The young man seemed not to consider this as supporting Arcadius's claim. He crossed strong but skinny arms. Arcadius's naturally thunderous brows lowered.

"We understand your time is valuable," Elyse said before the standoff could escalate. "We'd certainly pay for it while you spoke to us."

This wasn't enough to satisfy the man. "I don't answer nosy questions from people who aren't naked."

"In the name of God!" Arcadius burst out.

The volume he used was sufficient to cause his adversary to back up a step and drop his arms nervously. At this rate, they wouldn't get anything out of him.

"Arcadius," Elyse said in a conciliatory tone. "He just wants to do his job." She shifted her attention to the young man. "Your bathhouse job, right? Not special services."

"Right," the young man agreed, whether that was what he'd meant or not. "I'm very good at it."

Arcadius narrowed his eyes at him. "You're not proposing to bathe *her*."

"Of course not." The young man tossed his head proudly. His hair was the color of canary feathers, but it seemed natural. "Follow me. I have just the room for you."

"*Rooms*," Arcadius corrected. The bath boy didn't slow his roll down an adjoining hall. Arcadius jerked his head for two of the guards to move ahead of them and make sure the way was safe.

"Good cop, bad cop?" Arcadius muttered under his breath to her.

Elyse smiled. She guessed he'd seen some human television too.

~

Rooms weren't what Arcadius got, but he supposed the setup could have been worse. An open stonework screen provided partial privacy between the chamber's separate soaping benches and plunge tubs. The advantage was that Arcadius would be able to question two bathhouse employees for the price of one—with Elyse helping to smooth the proceedings, as she'd already proved she could.

The disadvantage was that, unless he was especially self-controlled, he'd see Elyse naked again.

"I'm Sindil," said the pretty bath girl who came in. "And that idiot is Kyros."

"I told them that," said the boy.

"You didn't," she disagreed. "You're always forgetting."

"I'm Kyros," he huffed to Elyse and Arcadius, "assistant manager to the Thirty-Fourth Street Bathhouse."

This was obviously a source of pride. Arcadius concealed his amusement with the process of disrobing. He took care not to watch Elyse doing the same on the privacy barrier's other side. Kyros didn't behave as if sneaking peeks tempted him. Arcadius supposed he'd seen too many undressed bodies to be curious anymore.

The room was warm enough to make Arcadius sweat but, fortunately, not too warm for Elyse. Her sigh of enjoyment as she stretched out on the cedar bench sounded as if it were an inch away.

"Face down, commander," Kyros instructed him.

The bench was planed to fit the general shape of a male body. Kyros worked a foot pedal to bring him to a convenient level. Wet slapping sounds announced that both bathhouse employees were whipping their soaping towels in the age-old manner for creating a thick lather. Arcadius waited until Kyros dropped the warm creamy cloth onto his shoulders. Though it felt good on his tense muscles, he wasn't here to relax.

"Tell me about Jeannine," he said.

"She was a bath girl," Kyros said unhelpfully. "She'd been here about a year before she disappeared."

Arcadius turned his head to the side on his folded arms. "Was she young?"

He felt the boy shrug as the nubbly towel rubbed his back up and down. "Twentyish. Around the same age as me. I got the impression she'd run away from her family."

"Did they come here to check on her?"

"Hardly."

"Did *you* report her missing to the authorities?"

"Why would I do that? She's just a bath girl. The police don't care if people like us wander off."

Considering the circumstances, Arcadius put off disputing that assumption. "If you didn't report her, how did word get out that she was gone?"

"You tell me," Kyros said. "You're the big guardian." He began soaping Arcadius's legs. His hands were strong as they pushed the towel up his calves and thighs. Arcadius sensed the boy was thinking, so he waited in silence. "We talked about it at the tavern, wondering if her ship had come in after all. Maybe someone overheard us there."

"Her ship?"

"That was a load of bull," Sindil put in from the other side of the screen. "Something Jeannine invented to make herself seem special compared to the rest of us."

"What did she say exactly?" Elyse asked.

"She hinted," Sindil said in a sneering tone. "Claimed she had a way out and she'd been 'chosen.' She was going somewhere she'd be at the top of the heap instead of at the bottom like she was here. She'd have riches and parties and she'd never say 'yes' to sleeping with anyone unless she wanted to."

"That's quite a prospect," Elyse said. "Did she drop clues as to where this wonderful life would be?"

"She couldn't," Sindil said. "Because it was nonsense. Probably she ran off to pretend it was true."

Kyros's hands hesitated behind Arcadius's knees.

"Is that what you think?" Arcadius asked. "That Jeannine made it up?"

"I don't know. She asked me once if I wanted to go with her. She said I was pretty enough to interest the recruiter."

Arcadius's ears pricked up. "The recruiter?"

"That's what she called him. She said he only chose djinn who were beautiful and smart, djinn who deserved to better their fortunes. I told her it sounded like a scam."

Sindil made a sarcastic noise. "I bet she hated that. She had a thing for you."

Arcadius suspected Sindil had a thing for Kyros too. The yellow-haired bath boy was out of the ordinary good-looking. "Did Jeannine ever point the recruiter out to you?"

"No. And I can't remember her exact words. A lot of what she said was chatter. Sometimes I tuned her out. She did seem convinced he'd want me. Like maybe she'd pointed *me* out to him." The bath boy's tone was uneasy. "Do you think I'm in danger of disappearing too?"

"I don't know," Arcadius said honestly. "Probably you and your friends should stick together. Avoid walking anywhere alone. I'll speak to the police in the area. Have them include this bathhouse in their patrols."

"Like that'll help," Sindil said, more resigned than angry.

Her reaction saddened him. "All right," he said, his next decision firmer than he expected. "I'll leave a personal scroll with Kyros. If anything alarming happens, as long as you and your friends are with him, you'll be able to reach me instantly."

"Even if we're just afraid?"

"Even if," Arcadius said, privately hoping he wouldn't regret the promise. "At the least, I'll read your message immediately."

He sensed Sindil and Kyros exchanging glances through the privacy screen.

"That's fair," Kyros said.

Arcadius smiled and put his head back down.

"Turn over," Sindil said briskly to Elyse. "I need to get your front."

"Um," Elyse hemmed. "I washed that side of me this morning."

"Really?" Sindil exclaimed. "You're going to be modest in a place like this?"

"Yes," Elyse said, adding politely: "If you wouldn't mind."

"Fine, then. You can plunge and rinse off."

She helped Elyse off the table, leading her to the step-in bath. Elyse's naked skin shone with wetness, suds dripping down her slender back to trickle over her perky ass and surprisingly strong legs. One lashing of suds flirted with the crack between her butt cheeks. Realizing he was staring, Arcadius turned his head the other way on his arms. The formerly comfortable molded bench wasn't providing comfort anymore. He fought against his urge to lift his hips and let one particular part of him adjust.

"Ah," Kyros observed softly. "Your companion is *not* your lover."

"Are you forgetting which of us is the interrogator?" Arcadius murmured back.

"I was simply going to suggest I hook you up with Sindil before you go. She's good with soap in more ways than one."

What sort of slang was *hook you up?* he wondered.

"Thank you, but no," Arcadius said, less coolly than he might have. It had occurred to him—though hopefully not to Kyros—that giving the bath boy his personal scroll could potentially turn him into a longer-term informant.

"She could get your rocks off quick," Kyros said. "Your companion need never know."

Arcadius believed he understood the meaning of getting his rocks off. For a moment, he was tempted. His cock throbbed between the wood and his groin, his balls aching like they'd shoot their load in no time.

"I can make my own arrangements," he said gruffly.

"As you like," Kyros said. "I assume you know an oil rub follows the plunge bath. There isn't a woman alive who won't moan like she's coming when Sindil massages her."

"Nonetheless," Arcadius declined, privately praying he'd survive it.

~

"Oh. My. God," Elyse moaned as they stepped back onto the sun-dappled street with their escort of guards. "That was the best massage ever." She rolled her shoulders, the muscles of her back warmer and more relaxed than she'd known they could be. "Did Sindil use magic on me? Because it felt like she used magic."

Arcadius grunted. Elyse checked his expression.

"Did something go wrong that I didn't notice? You're looking dourer than usual."

Arcadius stopped at the side of their parked carpet, where the fifth member of their escort, the pilot, patiently awaited. Arcadius rested his hand on the carpet's upfolded edge. His fingers combed the fringe idly.

"Elyse," he said. "Is 'hook you up' human slang?"

"It can be. People say they'll 'hook you up' with something you want, or to 'hook up' means to get together sexually. Why?"

"Kyros used that phrasing. And Sindil must have noticed you were human, but it didn't startle her."

Elyse saw he thought this was important. "Maybe they go to those view cafés. I know Kyros and Sindil didn't recognize the other names on Yasmin's list, but maybe different cafés are the link between the disappearances."

"Maybe." He pinched his lower lip. Cade did the same thing sometimes.

Elyse fought an inappropriate impulse to press her thighs together. Arcadius probably didn't realize the gesture was sexy. "I think it's interesting that Jeannine referred to her mystery man as a recruiter."

"These missing kids are being cherry picked."

"It seems so."

"You were kind to them," Elyse said, wondering if she could coax him to let down his guard with her. "Giving them that scroll so they could call you."

He'd told Kyros and Sindil to notify him if they or their friends noticed anything suspicious. Someone hanging around or approaching them with offers that sounded too good to be true.

What if they are true? Kyros had responded. *Come on, Kyros,* Arcadius had said. *What are the odds the disappearing djinn end up living out their dreams?*

"I wasn't being kind," Arcadius said. "I made them my eyes and ears. Also, I gave them your scroll."

"My scroll?"

"The one I was holding for you so you could contact the other me if anything went wrong."

"Oh." Elyse had forgotten all about that. She laughed. "That was sneaky."

"I'll have Joseph transfer the receiver spell to me. Cade won't have to answer their messages."

"He won't like that you gave away my panic button. You'll have to make sure nothing bad happens on the way home."

Elyse was teasing. The blue green gaze that locked onto hers was not. Arcadius's stare was so penetrating it was hot. Her toes curled inside the slippers he'd given her. Had he seen something while they were in the bathhouse, something he liked maybe? She'd checked a couple times, admittedly shy about undressing with him present. Every time she looked, he'd been turned away. In truth, she'd caught more of an eyeful than she'd intended.

Even through a screen, Arcadius's back view was just as spectacular as Cade's.

"I'll keep you safe," he promised.

His voice was rumbly. Elyse's vocal chords didn't feel up to telling him she hadn't doubted that for a second. She looked away and cleared her throat.

Apart from the rustle of leaves and the chirp of birds, the shady street was quiet. The traffic sounds all New Yorkers grew accustomed to didn't disturb this place. Magic was the power that ran things, for the most part. The hair on her arms stood up as she had the thought. A man had stepped out of the next building down the block and was walking away from them. He wasn't close enough to see distinctly, but he was tall and wore dark blue robes. Something about his silhouette made her skin prickle.

Arcadius asked if she was ready to get back on the rug.

She heard him with half an ear. "Wait," she said, touching his sleeve lightly.

She began walking after the unknown man. His stride was longer, and he had a head start. Even hurrying, she'd have trouble catching up.

"Excuse me," she called. "Sir, could I speak to you one moment?"

The man glanced briefly over his shoulder. She caught a flash of dark brows and eyes she didn't recognize. Her pulse sped up for no good reason.

"Wait!" she cried, and began running.

The man started running too.

"I just want to talk," she pleaded nonsensically. If the man didn't want to speak to her, this wouldn't convince him to. Realizing this, she nearly gave up the chase, but why was *he* running? She was just a woman, no danger to him at all. He *was* acting suspiciously.

Her illogical desire to apprehend him intensified. She hauled up her tunic's hem and pushed her trousered legs faster.

"Elyse!" Arcadius called, now sprinting after her.

Elyse kept going. The running man rounded the next corner. She saw . . . she wasn't sure what. A sparkle reflecting off a window? A brightening of the air?

"Stop!" she yelled. Her slippers didn't have much traction. She skidded to a wobbly halt at the intersection of the next shady street.

Her quarry had disappeared.

"Damn it," she swore, swiveling her head to look for him. She was out of breath. She needed more exercise. Caught up to her already, Arcadius seized her arm angrily.

"What are you doing?" he demanded.

She spotted a sweet shop with a few empty tables on its sidewalk. Hadn't she heard the jingle of an over-the-door chime?

"Come," she said, tugging him after her. "I think he ducked in there."

"Elyse—"

"Come," she insisted.

He gave in and jogged with her to the shop. What she saw through the large front window astonished her. The sweet shop's dozen or so customers were stone. White marble figures occupied the indoor tables' chairs, little cups of coffee frozen halfway to their mouths, little plates of Turkish delight still set in front of them. She supposed the djinn had wanted one last treat before Armageddon descended. She spied one last statue behind the display counter, standing beside an old fashioned cash register.

"No," she said, deeply disappointed at losing her quarry.

The statue behind the counter blinked.

"That's him!" she exclaimed excitedly. "He's disguising himself with magic!"

Arcadius didn't get a chance to respond. The front window with the swirly *Sweet Delights* lettering shattered without warning. The hundred knife-like shards didn't drop. They floated into the air instead, every pointy tip separating and turning until it was aimed at her.

"Shit," Elyse breathed, frozen like stone herself.

Arcadius had drawn his scimitar. She guessed it wasn't good for throwing, because he flung up his other hand, palm out. "In God's name, I command you to fall harmless."

Elyse had forgotten he could do magic. Cade could too, though not as much as Joseph. The air around them trembled as if intimidated by Arcadius's authority. At least half the shards fell to the sidewalk and broke.

The other half jerked like they were conscious and sped toward her.

What happened next happened lightning quick. The glass was only feet away. Arcadius grabbed her wrist, taking such control of her body that she had no say in her own movements. Her arm wrenched in its socket as he yanked her behind him and turned his front toward her. Then he tackled her and dropped them both. Her heels stayed on the pavement, her upper half smacking the street hard enough to knock the breath out of her. The shards of glass went *thunk-thunk-thunk* as they struck her protector's back and went in. Arcadius gasped but didn't let go of her.

Then everything was quiet.

Her heart pounded crazily. His did too, his whole body vibrating with the force of its contractions. He tried to get up and groaned.

"Don't move," she said, in case this caused the glass to do more damage. No one was attacking them right that second, so it seemed better not to run. She sucked in something near a whole breath.

"Guards," she called as loudly as she could. "We need help!"

They were there before she finished shouting, having jumped on the carpet and flown after them. Trapped beneath Arcadius's bulk, she heard four sets of boots leap out.

"You two," one guard barked. "Guard them. We'll check the area."

"Someone was in the sweet shop," Elyse said shakily. "Be careful of his magic."

"Are you all right, miss?" a soldier asked.

"Yes. Only Arcadius was hit."

Arcadius made pain noises as a guard checked him. The other two guards returned. "We didn't find the attacker, and I don't think we should search longer. We need to get the commander out of here for treatment."

"Get the glass . . . out," Arcadius rasped. "It isn't safe to move me until you do."

"Sir, are you sure?"

"Enchant it out," Arcadius ordered.

They didn't question him again. The senior guard led the others in a group prayer, which they repeated quite a number of times until all the glass was gone. Probably it didn't take more than two minutes. It simply felt to Elyse like it lasted forever.

Arcadius sighed when the final shard backed out of him. He couldn't stand. He could hardly even move. Amazingly, the hand that gripped his scimitar hadn't let go of it.

"Help me lift him and load him in," the lead guard said to the others.

The removal of his weight allowed Elyse to breathe normally again.

"Watch your step, miss," said the soldier who hopped back out to help her. "There's still glass underfoot."

It crackled under her slippers until he swung her off them.

"Oh, my God," she moaned when she got her first clear look at Arcadius.

Cade's double lay on his face on the rug, his back and legs a mass of wounds that overflowed with blood. He'd managed to protect his head with his hands, but they too were cut up. As the carpet rose smoothly and shot forward, two soldiers stripped off their shirts to staunch his worst bleeding.

Elyse knelt and stroked his hair, the only part of him that seemed safe to touch.

"He'll heal, miss," one of the men assured her. "Djinn aren't fragile like humans."

"Are we going to the hospital?"

"We're taking him to the palace. The magician can patch him up."

They meant Joseph. The thought of him immediately comforted her. He'd do anything to help either of his masters.

"Take me in *quietly*," Arcadius croaked. "I don't want our enemies catching wind of any more weaknesses."

The soldiers exchanged glances. Elyse assumed they were wondering which of those enemies was responsible.

CHAPTER FIVE

THE quickest way for Arcadius to heal would have been shifting into his smoke form. Some djinni couldn't change if they were in shock or pain, but Arcadius had relied on the trick many times on the battlefield. Like the troops who served him, he'd trained himself to do it under adverse conditions.

That knack was lost, he feared. He truly might be less powerful now that he'd split in two.

Their escort took him at his word about wanting to slip into the palace quietly. He wasn't sure how they convinced the royal flight controllers to wave their carpet past the main landing site, but they set down in the secluded courtyard outside the sultan's rooms.

Alarmingly, he didn't have sufficient strength in his limbs to rise.

"Don't struggle," Elyse advised, her fingers combing his hair gently—as she'd been doing all along. "Let the soldiers do the work of moving you until you feel better."

He wanted to ask her to stay with him. Fortunately for his pride, he had to bite his lip against the discomfort of the guards lifting him. Compounding the pain of his wounds, being carried made him dizzy.

He recognized the bed they laid him on as Iksander's. Though neatly made, the covers smelled of Elyse and the other him. Something primitive inside him couldn't help but find that comforting. When he closed his eyes, he almost fell asleep.

"I'll summon the magician," a male voice said.

Maybe he had drifted off. Only a second seemed to have passed before he heard Joseph and the other him speaking.

"Holy hell," breathed his double, leaving Arcadius in no doubt as to how bad he looked. "Who did this to him?"

"We were attacked," Elyse said from her perch beside him on the bed. "It was my fault. I ran after someone I thought looked suspicious. I should have waited for the guards. Arcadius had to shield me."

Arcadius didn't like her blaming herself. He was the one who knew magic. He should have spotted the danger. *Not your fault,* he tried to say but only got out a useless groan.

"Why were you—"

Joseph cut his double off. "Let me see if I can spell Arcadius to shift. Both of them can answer your questions then."

"Of course," Cade said, sounding stiff and chastened at the same time. "Let me know if I can help."

Arcadius nearly smiled. He'd forgotten that ability of Joseph's: to boss anyone he chose when he felt sure of his position. The sultan himself hadn't been immune to it.

He tried not to fight Joseph's magic. Resisting would make the shift harder. Despite knowing this, it wasn't natural for him to yield control to someone else. Finally, after a few minutes of chanting, Arcadius's particles flashed hot and spread out. He was a man-shaped cloud, larger than before, with the pleasant sensation of being feather light. The pain he'd been suffering ceased. That was a relief . . . until Joseph spelled him back to solidity. Then he had thirty tricky seconds while he struggled not to throw up. Being shifted by someone else's was stressful for djinn systems.

"I'll never get used to you guys doing that," Elyse murmured.

Being referred to as a *guy* was odd for Arcadius.

He was shaky but able to sit up. Blood dried unpleasantly on his clothes, gluing them to his back.

"Do you want to bathe?" Cade asked.

"That can wait until you question me," he said.

Perhaps he sounded prim. The corners of his double's mouth turned up. "Okay then. Why don't you start by telling me what happened?"

He and Elyse told the tale by turns, including their discoveries at the bathhouse. Cade listened quietly, letting them speak until they ran out.

"This man you saw," Cade said to Elyse. "What made you go after him?"

"I'm not sure," she said, still beside Arcadius. "Something about him seemed familiar, though when he turned to me for a second, I didn't recognize his face. I guess he struck me as suspicious."

"You don't chase everyone you see as suspicious."

Elyse pulled her mouth into a funny shape. "I can't explain it. Some gut instinct took hold of me. I know it was stupid, but I felt like I had to go after him."

"You weren't stupid," Arcadius chided. "Maybe running after him was but not your suspicions. They were more on the mark than mine."

Cade's eyebrows rose at the admission. "The man she chased didn't set off red flags for you?"

"No," Arcadius confessed. "Or for the guards. I should also tell you I found the spell our attacker cast on the glass hard to override."

"How hard?" Joseph asked sharply.

Arcadius shrugged, uncomfortable with the question. "That's difficult to say. Maybe it would have been easy for me before. My abilities seem . . . diminished."

"Mine too," Cade said absently. "Though I wouldn't say they were halved."

"I wouldn't say mine were either," Arcadius retorted.

His huffy response caused his opposite to smile creamily. "I can change on my own. In case you were wondering."

"Now who's being an ass's hat?" Arcadius snapped.

Elyse coughed out a little laugh. "Let's not argue about that. I'm sure you'll both admit we have more important things to focus on."

The other him rubbed his chin and returned to seriousness. "If the man you encountered was the mysterious recruiter, perhaps he returned to the bathhouse to scoop up the boy you talked to. We should set a guard on him."

"Can we spare the manpower, considering?"

"If the guard posed as the bath boy's friend, it wouldn't put the wind up your attacker. Posting a man there could improve our chances of catching him."

Arcadius weighed the pros and cons.

"All right," he agreed. "Let's do that."

Considering the matter settled, he scooted toward the edge of the massive bed and got out. This was a tactical error. Before his knees were properly under him, they buckled and he pitched forward. Elyse cried out in alarm. To his dismay, his arms failed to stop his fall. His teeth hit his lip so hard he tasted blood.

Joseph and Cade rushed to him. They sat him up and gripped his arms while he swayed like a pitiful drunkard. Arcadius couldn't look away from Cade's hands. Those were his knuckles, his veins. Cade wasn't him but he was.

It was like meeting a future self.

Elyse was the event he'd missed out on.

"This isn't good," Joseph said, his mind on its own track. "Having two commanders helps make up for Iksander's absence. If our enemies know one of you is weak, they'll pounce."

"I'm not weak," Arcadius objected. "Just temporarily . . . out of sorts."

Cade laughed dryly, still kneeling beside him. "You can't hold yourself upright. If it were me sitting there, would you call it 'out of sorts?'"

Arcadius glared, which he had plenty of strength for. "I'm strong enough to sit on my ass in our office. You can run around the city chasing unidentified sorcerers."

"That might work," Joseph said. "At least until it comes time for Arcadius to go home. I expect staff would notice he had to crawl."

"I'll stay here," Arcadius said rashly. "If I'm shaky, I'll use the servant's passage to come and go."

The other him's brows lowered. "I hope you're not proposing to stay here with Elyse. If I'm pretending to be you, I can't take her to your residence."

"We'll all stay in Iksander's rooms. People will assume we've reached an arrangement to share her. Nothing could be more natural than doubles being attracted to the same female."

"Um," Elyse said. "What about your not very secret opinion that I'm plain and inferior?"

"I'll pretend I got over it."

He realized the words were insulting only after he'd uttered them. Fortunately, his cheeks were already hot from having fallen flat on his face. He considered apologizing, but that seemed awkward too. And maybe Elyse wasn't plain, simply an acquired taste. Because his reaction at the bathhouse suggested he was acquiring it, the topic was probably best dropped.

"Arcadius might recover faster in your proximity," Joseph ruminated. "We don't really know how the doubling process affects us."

Cade pinched his lower lip. "Are you okay with this?" he asked Elyse.

She looked at Arcadius. He tried to maintain an impassive face. Interestingly, Elyse's expression was cautious. It hadn't occurred to him she might feel a similar erotic pull. The possibility that she did made his scalp tingle with awareness.

Other parts of him tingled too, but he was ignoring them.

"I suppose it would be all right," she said. "There certainly is room."

"All right," Cade decided. "But only until he recuperates."

Arcadius stubbornly refused to let himself change his mind.

~

Arcadius hadn't realized how exhausting a single afternoon and evening behind a desk could be. Somehow he got through dealing with the people he had to see. On the bright side, the meetings kept him busy. He didn't wonder more than once or twice what Cade and Elyse were doing.

The pair returned after sunset, which came late this time of year.

Arcadius was going over the happenings of the day with Philip's father Murat, who was Iksander's vizier. They'd moved their discussion to the small sitting area in the office, where they were drinking much needed tea. Cade and Elyse entered laughing, their arms slung loosely around each other's backs.

Their ease with one another inspired a pang he pushed away.

"You seem to have spent an agreeable afternoon," he observed dryly.

Elyse straightened, pushing her curls back as she sobered. He couldn't decide if he was sorry to have turned her serious. "Cade made sure Kyros got his guard, and we checked on the new food banks. We discovered the *valide sultana* had been there ahead of us."

"Per usual, Iksander's mother put the fear of God into everyone." Cade's eyes twinkled. "Everything is functioning efficiently."

"I imagine," Arcadius said.

Murat rose to greet Elyse and Cade. "Do the food banks have enough supplies?"

"More than," Cade said. "The sultana also put the fear of God into a few of the city's wealthier families. They've all made donations."

"You should leave that job to her," Elyse said. "We weren't needed at all."

"You mean *I* wasn't," Cade countered with an easy laugh. "Females were running the whole operation. I had to sit on my hands while Elyse talked to everyone."

That didn't sound right to Arcadius. Some male ought to oversee the business. Seeing that people were fed in this trying time was critical. He opened his mouth to say so. Elyse looked at him and smiled.

"You don't know what I'm thinking," he accused.

Her smile broadened. She walked to his chair, hesitated for a second, then bent to kiss his cheek. He stiffened in surprise. Her lips were soft and warm.

"I don't know," she agreed, "but I can guess."

Murat watched this exchange with raised eyebrows. Arcadius concluded Elyse was trying out their fiction that the three of them were involved. Seeming *almost* natural, she sat on the arm of his chair facing him. She laid her hand on his aching shoulder. Though he would rather have had the strength to rise, gazing into her soft green eyes was pleasant.

"The women will be fine," she said. "Iksander's mother gave the workers special golden badges, saying she'd picked them and they were under her protection. I don't think anyone, male or female, will dare put a foot wrong in their presence."

"I hope that's true," he said gravely.

She patted his shoulder. "We're going to call for dinner. Are you able to join us?"

Philip's father could be trusted to keep any vulnerability to himself. He'd already figured out which double Arcadius was. Arcadius could have suggested he eat with them as well. Nonetheless, he had a strong and sudden preference not to add even one extra person to their company.

"I believe that's my cue," Murat said. "If it suits you, commander, I'll meet with you again tomorrow."

Arcadius nodded and Cade clapped the vizier on his shoulder.

"Good night," Murat said as he bowed himself away.

~

Keeping up the front that everything was normal seemed to have drained Arcadius. He didn't argue when Elyse and Cade helped him up the back stairs to Iksander's rooms. How heavily he leaned on them worried her. Joseph had admitted they didn't know how the doubling process affected djinn. What if

Cade's original didn't have sufficient resources to recover from the stress to his system? Was there a way to divvy up the men's shared spirit more evenly? But maybe that would put both doubles in danger. Elyse dreaded the thought of Arcadius getting worse—or even not returning to the vital person he'd been when she first met him.

In the brief time they'd spent together, she'd grown attached to him.

The back stairway took them to a door concealed in the paneling outside the sultan's apartment. Cade held Arcadius upright while Elyse opened the double doors.

"I'm fine," Arcadius huffed when she looked anxiously back at him.

That made her smile. She liked his growly antediluvian personality.

That gave her food for thought while they ate their quiet dinner around the long table. Arcadius was too tired to snipe, merely nodding at Cade's report on how they'd spent their afternoon. His motions had slowed noticeably by the time the servants cleared the meat course.

"No dessert," Cade instructed as they withdrew. "We won't need you again tonight."

He'd noticed Arcadius fading too.

"Keep an eye on him," Cade said. "I'll make up an extra bed."

When Elyse glanced back at Arcadius, he was asleep in his chair. Slumped like that, with tracks of weariness on his face, he looked ten years older than his copy.

Cade came back in a few minutes, pausing in the doorway. Elyse couldn't identify the full range of his emotions as he gazed at his duplicate, but among them she certainly saw worry.

"I can feel you staring," Arcadius warned without opening his eyes.

Could he? He hadn't seemed to feel her.

"Help me up if you're going to," he said. "My knees are stiff from sitting."

Cade helped him, giving her a small headshake when she would have assisted. He was strong enough to handle Arcadius on his own and probably knew his preferences. Elyse debated leaving them to it but decided she'd rather know what happened. She followed the men into the vast bedroom.

Cade had pulled a large divan close to the sultan's bed. Sheets draped its well-stuffed cushion and a fresh white pillow lay at its head. There was room for all of them on the huge mattress, but she supposed Cade wasn't ready to share his territory to that extent.

Arcadius wasn't ready either. "You think I *want* to spy on you two snuggling up?" he exclaimed when he saw the cozy arrangement. "Just put my bed in the dressing room."

"You heard Joseph. Sticking close to me might help you recover."

"Time will take care of that."

Arcadius scowl would have intimidated a lesser man. Cade set his jaw stubbornly. "Time is going to pass no matter where you sleep. You may as well hedge your bets."

Cade settled the matter by letting go of Arcadius, thereby forcing him to drop onto the divan. Arcadius glared at him.

"Do you want help undressing?" Cade asked sweetly.

"If you want to help," Arcadius enunciated, "find me something to use as a walking stick. Unless you'd rather drag me across this stupid ballroom every time I have to pee."

Cade offered him a crisp but mocking salute, then turned on his heel and left.

"Bastard," Arcadius muttered under his breath. A moment later, he remembered she was there. "Pardon. I shouldn't use such language in front of you."

"I've heard worse. And said worse, for that matter."

Arcadius surprised her by smiling. As it turned out, her words weren't what amused him. "That man of yours is forgetting I know exactly which buttons to push to revenge myself on him."

Elyse smiled back. "I guess that man of mine better brace himself."

She pretended not to see how shaky the battle of wills had left Arcadius.

She was relieved when Cade returned. With all the things she wasn't saying, waiting with his original was awkward. Cade grinned like a triumphant hunter, a pair of bejeweled golden crutches held up in one hand.

"I found these among Iksander's father's things. I tried them out. They seem like they're tall enough."

Arcadius accepted them without rising from the divan. "I don't remember these."

"And you would, gaudy as they are. I think Iksander's father must have died before he got a chance to use them. His final decline was pretty swift."

"That I recall." Arcadius set the crutches on the floor where he could reach them. "Iksander losing his father and taking the throne that young seemed like the the biggest challenge he'd have to face."

"And then he fell in love with Najat."

"And then he lost her."

The two men looked at each other, their faces matching pictures of sadness.

"I believe he'd have married her even if he'd known where it would lead."

"Yes," Arcadius said. "Which may be the difference between Iksander and ourselves."

Elyse realized he meant marrying Najat had led to the sorceress cursing the city, not that marrying her had led to personal loss.

"Well," Arcadius said, shaking off the solemn moment. "Let's hope these crutches don't signal *my* last decline."

Elyse didn't think the joke was funny. It was even less amusing when Arcadius eased stiffly down on his side, closed his eyes, and went unconscious so swiftly it looked like he'd passed out.

"Is that normal?" she asked Cade. "Maybe we should call Joseph back."

"I suspect we've fussed as much as he can tolerate."

Cade would know, she supposed. She bit her thumbnail.

Cade hugged her from behind. "Why don't you and I wash up and get some rest ourselves?"

This was a reasonable plan. As they followed it, they didn't fool around the way they might have. That seemed insensitive with Arcadius there. Rather than sleep naked, Elyse threw on a loose silk tunic for modesty. Dressed and clean, she crawled onto the big bed and under the covers. Cade settled in behind her. She was nearest to Arcadius, but both of them faced him. Though he slept, his features remained strained. Proud too. Maybe that quality never went away.

"Is it okay to admit I like him?" she asked impulsively.

Cade's arm tightened around her. "Of course it is."

"I think—" She gathered her thoughts. "I think it's like if I met your mother and she showed me pictures of you as a kid. I'd have thought you were adorable even if your ears were big. Not that Arcadius is a kid."

Cade's soft laugh rumbled in her ear. "I understand what you mean, though I should disclose my mother wasn't the picture taking type."

Elyse squirmed onto her back so she could look at him. They'd talked about her childhood but not his. At the time, Cade had been trying to discover what she knew about the portal hidden in her basement. They'd had a strange courtship—an incomplete one, in her opinion. Maybe this was her chance to address that.

"What was your mother like?" she asked.

"Strict. She wanted me to be a soldier like my father. He died in battle when I was five."

"That must have been hard on both of you."

"I suppose." Cade's expression was distant. "I don't know if she truly loved him. Looking back, I think she was happy to be able to train me without his interference, according to her ideal of what a warrior should be."

"She *trained* you?"

"Not to fight. For that, she hired tutors. She trained me to be tough, to withstand deprivation and accept discipline. She'd make me live on half rations for a week and march around our village with loads of firewood strapped to my back. The other children teased me over that. 'Arcadius the Burro' was the nickname I recall. I hated it at the time, but she proved to me I could survive that and more. She wanted me to have confidence in myself. I can't deny she succeeded."

"Goodness," Elyse said, unsure how else to comment. Though he'd traveled a lot, her father had treated her like a cherished princess. Cade's description of his upbringing sounded horrible, but he didn't seem bitter. "Is your mother alive?"

Cade shook his head. "She lived to see Iksander appoint me his commander, which didn't please her as I expected."

"It didn't?"

His mouth slanted with memory. "No. She warned me not to let it make me soft. That was her idea of a sin." He turned his eyes to Arcadius's sleeping form. "I know why he is the way he is. He's what I would have been if I hadn't fallen in love with you."

His voice thickened with emotion. Did he really think she'd had that much effect on him? She didn't see how this was possible even if, as he said, he was in love with her.

"Arcadius isn't a bad man," she felt compelled to say. "Honestly, I think he's quite a good one. His perspective is just different from yours."

"So you would have loved me, big ears and all," he teased.

"I would," she said.

She'd answered easily, but once she had, the truth of the words shocked her. What exactly had she admitted to? She knew Cade's original attracted her. She'd been trying not to make too much of that. Probably, it was natural. Being with someone didn't mean you never thought another man was hot, especially when the man in question had many of the same characteristics that had drawn you. To say she could love Arcadius, however, was a more serious matter than attraction.

Cade didn't seem to notice what she'd implied. He'd moved to hang slightly over her, his thumb stroking her right brow's arch as he gazed into her eyes. "You have no idea what I'd give to make love to you right now."

Elyse's pulse accelerated. His thumb moved to brush her lower lip, causing her skin to tingle there—and between her legs as well. She reminded herself there couldn't be a worse way to make Arcadius feel like the odd man out.

"That wouldn't be considerate," she said breathily.

"No, it wouldn't."

Cade pressed his lips softly over hers. Her body knew what his had to offer. Though the touch was light, her pussy flooded as the tip of his tongue touched her. He backed off but slid his hand up the silk she wore. The way his fingers covered her breast felt incredible.

"Better turn around," he murmured. "Before I change my mind."

She couldn't right away. He was warm and big and, unlike her, he was naked. She dragged her hand down his chest, her touch pulled irresistibly over his ribs, around his navel, and onto one lean hipbone. His erection jerked, the bare head bumping lightly against her thigh.

She knew precisely how satiny that skin felt pushing inside her.

"Elyse," he said even softer than before. "If you don't turn away, I won't be able to."

She thought of his double, mere feet away on the divan. Arcadius seemed asleep but could conceivably be feigning out of politeness. It wouldn't be nice to make him watch them have sex, not when he couldn't get away, not when he might become aroused himself. Desire gripped her body at that idea, the sudden intensification of her lust causing her to shudder. Oh, that was wrong for sure.

She wriggled around so that her back faced Cade.

He spooned himself to her, groaning softly as he pushed his groin against her bottom. His erection was long and thick, and he rubbed it in little passes over the silk that draped her butt cheeks. She'd noticed how much he liked her ass before. Maybe she could suggest he take her from this position. Just ease her leg up and slide his throbbing cock into her. They could be really quiet. Arcadius would never have to know.

No, she thought, curling her hands into fists. Her pussy ached but she ignored it. They'd had plenty of sex since coming here. It wouldn't kill them to go without for one night.

She didn't think it would anyway. At the moment, her burning body was begging to differ.

~

Arcadius had gotten up once already to hobble the bloody mile from the bed to the bathing room. Completing the journey without waking Elyse and Cade had felt like the equivalent of two-day march. He'd collapsed on the divan afterwards and dropped back to sleep, fully expecting not to wake again until morning.

He should have been so lucky.

Apparently, the pair hadn't taken advantage of his comatose state to get their rocks off—as the bath boy put it. The other him was dreaming about Elyse, the intensity of his lust most definitely *not* recently satisfied.

The images Arcadius received seemed like memories. In them, his copy lay in a tent in the Great Desert. Elyse was above him, naked, riding his rigid prick with a fervor that caused her delectable breasts to bounce. Arcadius could feel her wetness on his own cock; could taste the sweat running down her skin. Most interestingly, Elyse seemed to have attached his wrist to a pole. Being bound was exciting him as much as the slick friction of her sheath. He'd never been taken captive in battle. To submit voluntarily, at the hands of a female he'd come to love, did strange things to his libido. He wanted to fight her control and revel in it at the same time.

My ***double*** *wanted to revel in it*, Arcadius corrected in his mind. His double's reaction was what had stiffened his cock to the point of pain. Arcadius preferred control to submission.

His double moaned in his sleep, shifting restlessly behind Elyse.

Damn it, Arcadius thought. He could feel Elyse's firm round butt against his groin. Even if he refrained from taking himself in hand, Cade's current dream seemed likely to drive him to explosion. Arcadius would rather not advertise this susceptibility to Elyse. He wasn't some pubescent youth. He ought to be able to last the night without shooting into his bed sheets.

He didn't have the luxury of cursing. As silently as he could, he retrieved his fancy golden crutches and levered his weight off the divan. The persistence of his erection added a layer of difficulty to crossing the endless room. He was tired and in pain. He shouldn't be capable of getting this damned hard.

His body was unaffected by his logic. He sensed Cade approaching orgasm in the dream. He hobbled faster, determined to reach the relative privacy of the dressing room. There was a small couch in there. Maybe a bit more distance between him and his double would break the link. He'd be able to sleep unmolested by Cade's salacious imaginings.

As if to mock him, his cock throbbed harder, bouncing with each swing of the crutches. Too late, he recalled his double's lusts had no trouble reaching him in his residence. As to that, they'd swapped consciousness across the same divide.

He'd reached the arch to Iksander's closet. Struck by a new idea, he stopped. Desire and exertion had deepened his breathing. Distracted from that by his thoughts, he leaned his shoulder against the door.

Their connection worked both ways. If Arcadius could reach Cade's sleeping awareness, he might be able to influence what happened within it.

He closed his eyes, willfully ignoring the jolt and hum of his aroused blood. *Turn away,* he thought to his double. *You need to help your city. You can finish taking Elyse another night.*

He felt Cade's resistance as if it were his own. He was so close to pouring that hot need inside of her.

Think of your people, Arcadius insisted ruthlessly. *They need you to be unselfish.*

His cock jerked once and then the sensation of imminent orgasm receded.

When the words "damn it" went through his head, he wasn't certain whether he or Cade had thought them.

~

Elyse woke to the sensation that something wasn't right. Cade had turned behind her to face the other way, but she didn't think that had disturbed her. He was near enough for his warmth to reach her, his breathing soothing and even. She took a moment to marvel at how quickly she'd grown accustomed to his presence, how soon he'd come to spell comfort and safety.

Then she realized Cade's was the only breathing she heard.

The divan where Arcadius had lain was empty. Her throat clenched, but then she saw the crutches were gone. Arcadius hadn't magically winked out of existence. Wherever he was, he'd gotten there on his own steam.

She rolled onto her back. She was sure he was fine. People got up at night.

Arcadius was a grown man. She'd insult him if she went to check.

Except . . . what if he hadn't simply gotten up? She remembered what he'd said earlier: *You think I want to spy on you two snuggling up?*

Something more than irascibility had colored the question.

Maybe the odd man out longed to feel the kind of closeness she and Cade were sharing. Maybe rather than have it shoved in his face, he'd decided to sleep in the dressing room. The choice would be natural—just not the best idea right then.

She sat up, suddenly certain that's where he was. So he'd be angry if she chivvied him to come back. That didn't matter as long his strength returned. She'd tell him she felt guilty because he'd gotten injured protecting her. Until he got better, she'd continue to feel bad. He was a chivalrous chauvinist. That would totally get him.

She slipped across the room as silently as she could, not wanting to wake her bed partner.

Because the large dressing room had no windows, it was too dark inside to see. She did, however, think she heard breathing. Unlike Cade's, it wasn't even.

"Arcadius?" she asked.

"Damn it," was his answer.

"Are you okay? I can't see a thing in here."

"I'd rather . . . you didn't see."

"You don't sound right. Did you injure yourself?"

He cursed again, then said a spell for light. The room was lined with fitted shelves and wardrobes, between which elegant sconces glowed. Arcadius's magic had turned them on.

She didn't find him on the couch. He knelt on his heels on a rug in front of the dressing mirror. One arm braced on a nearby tower of shelves for support. The decorated gold crutches leaned nearby. His back was to her. If it hadn't been for his reflection in the mirror, she wouldn't have seen his right hand clutching his massively hard boner. He'd shoved his trousers down to expose it. His shaft was thick, the flushed skin of the head stretched tight. The waistband of his pants lifted his swollen balls, putting them pornographically on offer.

"Jesus," she said without thinking.

Her voice betrayed how much the sight affected her. Arcadius's fingers tightened around the veiny rod. His thumb rubbed a patch along the side as if even with her looking he couldn't stop.

"It's ironic," he said on a breathy laugh. "I've never been this aroused in my life and I'm too tired to get off."

"But we didn't do anything!" Elyse burst out. "Cade and I didn't want to make you uncomfortable."

Arcadius's gaze met hers in the mirror. The extraordinary eyes he shared with his double looked like the sea burning. "Cade and I have been trading thoughts on and off. He was dreaming about you and woke me up. Something about you riding him in a tent with his wrist tied up. If the dream didn't actually happen, you might want to try light bondage. I believe the other me would react favorably."

His tone was wry. Elyse's cheeks blazed. She remembered the night in Sheik Zayd's encampment well.

"It . . . actually happened," she said haltingly. "I didn't know that. About you and he sharing thoughts. I'm sorry."

"Are you?" Arcadius's head tilted to the side. He hadn't released his erection. The thing throbbed hard as she looked at it. She forced her attention back to his face. His expression hid more than Cade's, but she noticed a ghost of a smile.

"Sorry," she said. "I . . . you . . . you're . . . constructed just like him. It's disconcerting."

"Disconcerting." His arm moved and her gaze fell inexorably. He stroked his prick upward once, gracefully, firmly, squeezing the swollen flare of the head before dragging down again. Elyse's nails dug into her palms. His fist made a shorter journey than hers would have. Her tongue curled out to wet her lip.

"Perhaps you could help me," he suggested.

"*What?*"

He laughed at her reaction. "So you *would* consider it cheating."

"Cade would. I don't want to hurt him."

"But he's me." Her attention or perhaps her attraction seemed to have endowed him with more vigor. He used the handhold of a shelf to pull himself to his feet.

The effort dragged a small grunt from him. He must have known he was anything but pathetic when he stood up to full height. His shoulders were squared, his solid legs braced wide on the plush carpet. He hadn't turned away from the mirror, and his right hand still gripped his cock. Somehow, him not facing her made it easier to ogle him. He had thin white knife scars on his fingers that Cade lacked—from magical blades, she guessed. The sight of the marks wrapped tight around his cock was disturbingly exciting. Elyse cursed her lack of panties. She just knew she was about to overflow.

When she pressed her trembling thighs together, Arcadius's faint smile deepened. "Do you think Cade would be too principled to seduce you if he were in my shoes?"

Elyse swallowed audibly "You only want me because he does. You think I'm plain and obnoxious."

"I could paint you from a single glimpse of you naked at the bathhouse. Your little ass dripping lather was truly a sight for joy."

Elyse gasped, one hot trickle squeezing between her labia. Alarmed, she took a step back from him. "It's a competition thing then. Like squabbling over who Joseph should answer to."

"Oh, I'd like you to answer to me," Arcadius purred.

He did turn then. He stepped toward her, swayed slightly, but kept his footing.

"You're not strong enough to be playing at this."

He outright grinned at her. "If I fall, will you catch me?"

He swayed again and—stupidly—she assumed the weakness was for real. She put her hands out to steady him and found herself wrapped in his arms instead.

"Elyse." He said her name differently than Cade. There was more arrogance in his voice, more sureness that she'd find him irresistible. She wished she could prove him wrong. Seeming to know she couldn't, he gazed down into her face with a combination of mischief and male triumph.

She pushed at his chest but to her amazement he wouldn't budge. "I'm not agreeing to this. You need to let me go."

"You're wet for me," he said smokily. "Or didn't the other me warn you about our people's sharp sense of smell?"

"That doesn't matter. If I say 'no,' you have to stop."

He considered her, his smile fading. "I suppose I do, but I think you ought to kiss me before you decide for sure."

She had decided. And she'd told him. Or she thought she had. Had she somehow failed to be clear?

She was trying to get her mouth to form lucid words when he molded his gently over it. Elyse jerked. Sensation seemed to spangle from her lips through her whole body. As she recalled, the same thing happened when Cade first kissed her.

"One kiss," he murmured, his lips pressing hers again. "I saved your life. Don't I deserve a taste of you?"

He was using the guilt she'd planned to use on him. Unfortunately, it worked. She couldn't deny he'd earned her gratitude, and—really—what could one kiss hurt?

She knew this reasoning was idiotic even as she succumbed to it. He slanted his head and assumed full control of her.

His mouth was Cade's but his manner was different. The components were similar: the way his tongue stroked and sucked, his taste, the exciting sound of his hastened breath. What differed were the amounts of assertiveness versus coaxing versus attentiveness to her reactions. Arcadius asked less and took more than Cade. His hands roved her as if he needed to explore every curve before she took it away from him. He liked her butt the same as Cade did, and her waist, and the oddly vulnerable plane between her shoulder blades. He stroked them all with fingertips and palms. Within moments he found the same shivery spot on her neck Cade so often exploited. When he nipped it, he put more teeth into it.

Everything Arcadius did was just a bit rougher.

She knew she shouldn't like that so much. She pushed his chest harder and managed to get away. "You don't think he's you," she half huffed and half panted. "You think you're better."

His thumb stroked the underside of her lower lip. Elyse fought another shiver. "You think he wouldn't stretch the truth to get what he wanted from a woman?"

"Actually, no."

"But I'm him, Elyse. How can I do what he wouldn't? Besides which, aren't I in a position to know his sins?"

"Maybe he left them behind with you when your shared spirit split."

Arcadius flinched. A second later, his face tightened. "If I'm that awful, why do you want me too?"

She'd spoken without thinking. Immediately remorseful, she stroked his chest. "I'm sorry. I didn't mean that. You're not awful."

"You said it."

"Because I didn't think. You're confusing me."

His stare was hard. It should have warned her. So should the contraction of his fingers around her upper arms. Before she could move, he yanked her up and kissed her twice as aggressively as before. She resisted for about two seconds, then melted and kissed him back.

He knew what her clinging meant. His soft groan reverberated from deep within his chest. His hips shoved closer to rub his cock against her. That was a shock—for one, because it felt amazing through the thin silk she wore and, for two, because she realized he hadn't done it already.

He *had* thought some things were off limits unless she encouraged them.

"God," he said. "*God.*" He caught her hand and dragged it down and around him. He forced it against his cock, thrusting up her palm even as her fingers curled irresistibly around him.

It must have felt good. He staggered slightly but didn't fall. She guessed the momentary weakening was worth it. The next time she pulled upward, he locked his knees, bent her thumb over the crown of his prick, and moaned.

His slit was leaking. She couldn't resist rubbing the silky wetness around the delicate skin. His quiver of response pleased her shamefully.

He dropped his mouth to her ear. "You see," he growled. "I'm wet for you too."

"I'm just doing this," she warned. "I won't take you inside me."

"Yes," he agreed, panting harder as she began to jerk him off in earnest. His pelvis undulated like he was making love to her hand. "Between your legs is his territory." He hissed with need and pleasure. "Just help me find release."

She wanted to but her conscience started fighting back. Cade would *not* be okay with this. Did she want to risk what she'd found with him? She didn't want to hurt Arcadius either. She'd already said she'd do this. Taking it back was rude. Not that being rude mattered compared to betraying someone you loved.

Unless she loved Arcadius too . . . She shook her head. That was silly. She'd only just met him. Not that she'd known Cade all that long.

"God," she said, taking her hand off him to squeeze her temples in confusion.

"*Don't*," said a voice behind her.

She spun. Cade had woken. Naked, he stood like an avenging angel in the arch to the dressing room. To her eyes, he looked furious.

"She was stopping," Arcadius said in defense of her. He'd put his hands on her shoulders. He was squeezing them in support.

"I know what she was doing," Cade said levelly. "And I can imagine why. You look like me. You feel like me. She can't help wanting you."

Arcadius's grip tightened. "I played on her sympathy."

"Perhaps you deserve it. No, I don't mean because you're injured. I mean because you can't help wanting her. We're linked," he said to Elyse. "When I want you, he feels it too."

"He told me," she said. Should she divulge what he'd said about seeing her in the bath? "He, um, he seems to think he's attracted to me on his own."

Cade's eyes widened slightly in surprise. He looked from her to Arcadius. Elyse felt him shrug. "She's . . . grown on me."

"She does that," Cade observed.

Well. That took Elyse aback. Had Cade thought her plain initially too?

His next words drove the question from her head. "Do what he wants."

"Excuse me?"

"Do what he wants. When he's unsatisfied, so am I. As you can see."

He spread his hands. Elyse blinked in a quick flurry. The fact that she hadn't noticed his erection proved how distressed she'd been at him walking in. His cock was huge, the rigid shaft standing nearly vertical. Probably it wasn't appropriate to compare, but he was a teensy bit longer than Arcadius.

How was that possible anyway?

"Um," she said, wondering how a woman was supposed to think under these conditions. "You're sure you're okay with me giving him a hand job?"

"That isn't what he really wants," Cade said in a low rough tone.

The flood of heat that washed through her temporarily blanked her mind. Arcadius's hands went very tight on her shoulders.

"You'd let me . . . have intercourse with your consort?" Arcadius's disbelief was apparent, as was his arousal. His voice was as husky as Cade's had been.

"She is my beloved," Cade said. "And, yes, I would allow that. I will remain here while you take her."

He announced this as autocratically as Arcadius would have.

"I don't think he can take you standing," he added. "He isn't steady enough for that."

Elyse couldn't help but gape at him.

"Fine," he said, crossing the room to her. "I see you need my help to get this started."

He took the neck of her tunic and ripped it to the hem.

"Cade," she gasped.

He kissed her as hard and deep as his double had. Elyse's nerves had just long enough to go crazy for new reasons.

"Do it," Cade broke the kiss to say tightly. "Feeling how much he needs this is making me crazy."

Arcadius got on board sooner than she did, though perhaps he was crazy too. Positioned behind her, he pulled the torn tunic down her arms.

"Kneel," he ordered. "Hands and knees on the rug."

Her will couldn't stand against both men's. She started to obey, but apparently not in the manner Cade's double wished. He shifted her to the side so that the tri-fold mirror reflected her. "Brace your arms on the shelves. And spread your legs wider."

Cade didn't object, so she did as he asked. Arcadius went to his knees behind her. He wasn't well enough to do it without lumbering but he got there. As he did, Cade's breathing got quicker.

Maybe, given how alike they looked, this was like watching yourself have sex in a home movie.

Arcadius probably wasn't concerned with that. He folded himself around her, hard hot muscle and male bulk. His cock rested on her butt as he played his right hand over her breasts and belly—as if claiming these parts of her for his own. Elyse couldn't stop quivering. Arcadius kissed the nape of her neck where her messy curls fell forward.

"Turn your head," he said, the instruction firm without being hard. "Watch me go into you."

She turned, her eyes automatically rising to catch Cade's in the mirror. He stared at them with his lips parted. When he saw her attention was on him, he fell to his knees as well. His hands curled on his thighs like he wanted to touch something—either himself or her. Arcadius's caresses traveled lower, burrowing between her labia to find the creamy wetness her clit and pussy were swimming in. Cade bit his lip hard enough to whiten it.

"Watch *me*," Arcadius said softly.

This time she complied. He pulled his hips back, his cock teasing around her ass as he shifted lower for entry. Her quivers became a shiver. He drove two fingers inside her so deeply they disappeared. Watching that was exciting —and never mind how good it felt.

A moan of pleasure wrenched from her.

"Good," he said, softer yet. His eyes closed. He was concentrating on her reactions as he simultaneously explored her pussy and thumbed her clit. His stroking was delicious but too gentle. She squirmed around his fingers, wanting to plead for more but feeling like she shouldn't with Cade watching.

Maybe Arcadius knew. Maybe he liked tormenting her.

Finally, Arcadius's lashes lifted again.

He removed his hand from her, his fingers shining with her juices. He used those fingers to aim his cock at her. Her stomach jerked with anticipation, her hips tilting higher instinctively. Her eyes were locked to his in the mirror. He touched her entrance with his smooth tip.

Cade would have said something at this point. His double simply held her gaze and pushed slo-owly into her.

The sound she made lasted as long as his entry. Only when he drew slowly back did she get to gulp for breath.

"Fuck." Cade's shaky curse held a kind of awe. "No," he said when she would have looked at him. "You two go on doing what you are."

Had Arcadius glanced over at Cade too? She couldn't see Cade in the mirror anymore. Arcadius's reflection was blocking his. Did Cade prefer to keep his reactions to himself? Maybe they were more intense than he wanted to let on. The possibility tightened her sheath in an aching clench. Arcadius grunted at the pressure around his flesh. Oh, this situation pushed her buttons to the max. In truth, she hadn't known she *had* buttons for these things.

Arcadius pushed into her again, not quite as slowly as before. His nonverbal style was provocative. She had to watch and listen closely to figure out what he was feeling. His heart beat harder as he came into her. His head fell forward, his mouth opening on her shoulder. His ragged breathing washed over her.

"Please," she whispered, driven past refraining. "Go faster than you are."

He filled his lungs with air and started pistoning into her.

It was instant heaven. She stretched one arm back to catch at his hip and encourage him. Arcadius might not have been saying words but he was making noise. Given the urgency of the sounds, she didn't expect him to last long. She came herself in two minutes, and still he went at her.

"Damn it," Arcadius panted, pumping his length into her from a new angle.

Elyse bent both arms on the shelving so she could push harder back at him. It didn't seem to help. "What's wrong?"

"I can't go over. Maybe I really am too tired."

"Maybe—" She sucked in air as she nearly went over again herself. "Maybe you should let me be on top."

He laughed breathlessly.

"It isn't a joke. I can do the work."

His cock pulsed and got harder. Whatever he might think, he didn't hate the idea.

"Sit her on your lap," Cade said. Their rhythm hitched as they looked at him. "Shift her around to face me. I think I know what the problem is."

"You think *you* know." Despite the raggedness of his breath, Arcadius's tone was snide.

Cade's eyes narrowed. "Do you want to come or not?"

Arcadius cursed but did as Cade advised. He banded one arm around her ribs to lift her against him. She felt the thudding of his heart on her spine.

"Move back," Cade said. "You can brace your weight on the other shelf."

Arcadius moved, making room for Cade to shift into the space before the mirror. The second man faced her on his knees. His diaphragm bellowed in and out, his erection standing up bold and flushed. Elyse's pulse went crazy.

Apart from where his kneecaps bumped hers, he hadn't touched her yet. Every muscle in his chest and arms was tight. Both men vibrated with passion.

She searched Cade's eyes.

"I'm okay," he said, registering her worry. "I'm going to raise you. He can come up with you."

Cade gripped her beneath the arms and lifted. Both men shifted and suddenly she was sandwiched between their hard bodies, suspended by their weight and strength. The vibration she'd sensed a moment ago heightened. The effect was more than their blood pulsing through their veins. It was their energy joining up and flaring. She felt like she'd been plunged into a pool of electric force, the sensation penetrating right through her bones.

She wasn't the only one affected. As they all made contact, the men's cocks jerked: Arcadius's inside her and Cade's pressed to her belly.

Arcadius inhaled sharply beside her ear.

"You see?" Cade said. "We're *too* linked. I don't think you can climax unless I do."

The idea performed a kind of magic on her desire. An ache swelled between her legs like nothing she'd ever felt. She wanted both of them to come and needed desperately to herself. It didn't matter that she just had. Nothing would satisfy her until they found release too.

She held her breath until Arcadius answered.

"Very well," he said after a weighted pause. His voice was raspier than before. "I'm in no condition to debate your theory."

Elyse rubbed his hip. She meant the gesture to be reassuring, but her hand shook.

"How do you want this?" Arcadius asked her, perhaps needing to establish that he wasn't simply going along with Cade's arrangement.

"Fast," she said as audibly as she could. "And—" She hesitated. "Kind of hard."

"*Kind of hard,*" Arcadius repeated, shaking his head at her vagueness. "No," he said when Cade would have tried to explain. "She can tell me if she needs more or less."

Cade ducked his head. She was pretty sure he was hiding amusement. If Arcadius saw, he ignored it. He set his hands on her waist and drew his cock back far enough that she sucked in a breath.

Then he went at her like she was his personal doorway to paradise and he needed to beat it down.

The hammering was harder than she expected. Maybe he couldn't be gentler than he was. It didn't matter. She was so aroused the force he used felt perfect—especially when Cade drove at her just as powerfully from the front. She wasn't squished, simply wonderfully buffeted between them. Her head went back with agonizing pleasure, and Arcadius's shoulder was there to support it. Her back arched, and Cade's hands slid up to engulf her breasts. Her nipples went hard as diamonds as his thumbs depressed them. When he circled the pressure around the points, she creamed down Arcadius.

Both men jerked at the wet sounds his thrusts made then.

Arcadius swore and picked up his pace, sliding his hands around her hipbones to her pubis. Evidently, he didn't intend to be shown up by his copy. He'd see to her pleasure too. His fingertips pressed her labia, squeezing them around her clitoris to massage the swelling from either side.

"God," she gasped a second before his teeth clamped around her nape.

He reminded her of an animal holding its mate in place.

His grunts were as primal as the bite. Cade, too, was caught up in the imperative to come, one hand gripping her ass so he could rub his cock up her front harder. He writhed so close his pubic hair rasped her. She clutched his shoulders, feeling their muscles bunch, wanting both the men against every inch of her. Cade's shaft was hard as steel on her belly, her sweat and his slicking its friction. Arcadius bucked into her vigorously enough that his pelvis spanked her bottom. Somehow the men's urgent motions didn't interfere with each other—or maybe that wasn't a surprise.

They were definitely of one mind, pleasuring her and themselves as if the fate of more than one world hung in the balance. She didn't have to do anything, only hold on for dear life and take what they were giving. Her cries grew wilder, her climax impossible to hold off with so much pleasure bombarding her.

"*Yes*," Arcadius said, jolting deep into her pussy as he felt her begin to go. His cock seemed impossibly big, the ideal hot thickness to contract on. This was ecstasy enough, but suddenly her clit was directly in his fingers, being rubbed hard and quick.

Then Cade pinched her nipples.

She didn't have breath to scream. The energy inside her spiked and then the men's combined electricity did as well. They cried out with matching hoarseness, two voices with one chorus. In unison, their cocks shot into and against her. Her orgasm streaked like lightning out all her nerve endings.

She didn't come down for quite a while.

When she did, all her limbs trembled.

"Elyse," Cade said, his hands stroking her down her sides.

"I'm good."

He clasped her face.

"I am," she insisted. Body humming with repletion, she let her breath sigh out. Arcadius sat down behind her and she did too. His cock was still erect enough to stay inside her. He wrapped his arms in a sort of hug around her waist. She became aware how copiously she was sweating. Being made love to by two men was a workout. "God, I'd kill for a shower."

The djinn didn't have them; they were bath-obsessed. Since Cade had spent time in her world, he knew what she was missing. He smiled indulgently. "Would you settle for me soaping you down?"

"I'll help," Arcadius said, raising her up so he could pull out of her.

She guessed their truce was over, because Cade bristled. "Your help isn't necessary."

"Yeesh," Elyse said. "If you're going to fight, I'll wash up by myself."

"We're *not* fighting," Arcadius said. "I helped you overheat. Therefore, I'll help you wash."

He had a knack for making her laugh, though he probably didn't intend to.

"All right," she said. "Both of you can help me."

~

Cade was reasonably skilled at hiding when he was knocked off balance. He'd instigated their threesome in the heat of the moment. Seized by the psychic link, he'd been focused on getting off before he went insane. He hadn't guessed he'd enjoy the experience so intensely. *Earthshaking* was a good word for his orgasm. He hadn't even been inside Elyse.

He'd given that honor—voluntarily—to his original.

Watching Arcadius fuck her had done incredible things to his excitement.

He kept his disconcertion to himself as he and Arcadius soaped their now mutual lover. Elyse lay face down on the special alabaster bench in the tiled bath nook. This was the women's niche, and the bench was sized for a female's form. Arcadius's manner was similarly evasive to Cade's, though Cade couldn't mistake the way his hands roamed Elyse for anything businesslike. He reveled in touching her with the soaping towel, in exploring her slender muscles and smooth warm skin. His motions were tender even if his face was a mask.

Did he want to repeat the experience? Was he, like Cade, feeling certain warning signs in his groin? The link between them had broken with the climax. Cade could have used it back, at least for a few seconds. He was damned if he wanted to *ask* what the other him was thinking.

"Mm," Elyse hummed, wriggling happily as Arcadius lifted her foot and rubbed its sole. "I could get used to this."

Arcadius jerked. That made one of them, Cade guessed.

~

Arcadius knew he shouldn't enjoy having his hands on his double's lover quite as much as he did. Elyse belonged to Cade. He was only borrowing her—who knew how temporarily? To wish to repeat the experience was reckless.

All the same, he couldn't deny making love to her had been earthshaking.

He also couldn't deny Cade's presence had driven his excitement higher.

When Elyse implied she could get used to having both of them, one corner of his psyche wondered if that also held true for him.

Too soon Cade was rinsing her down and drying her with a towel. She sat sleepily on the bench while he worked it vigorously over her wet curls.

"I'm going to look a fright tomorrow," she said, yawning.

Arcadius had been standing back, trying to mentally disengage himself from the intimate couple. Her comment ruined his intent. "I like your hair," he blurted.

She looked at him and smiled. "You look better. Not so shaky anymore."

He was better. He hadn't thought about the crutches since they'd finished having sex.

Cade considered him thoughtfully. "I wonder if you're up to changing into your smoke form now."

Was he trying to get rid of him? "I don't know," Arcadius said.

"Tomorrow should be soon enough to try," Cade said with breathtaking casualness, immediately shooting down his suspicion. "Probably we could all use a good night's sleep."

"And how." Elyse pushed onto her feet. "Come on, you," she said to him. "No more hiding out in the dressing room."

Though he felt like he should have argued, he trailed after her.

~

Elyse flopped onto her back. Arcadius was on the divan again, so deeply under he was snoring.

"Okay," she said. "Why is he the only one sleeping? We have to get up and work tomorrow too."

Cade rolled toward her on his side. His finger stroked around her temple and down her cheek. "Are you worried about what we did?"

"Aren't you?"

"Maybe not the same way you are."

His answer was cautious. She guessed she had to go first. "Why is he suddenly better? Not that I don't want him to be, but did he take some of your energy?"

"Take it?"

"When you two joined up spirits or whatever the heck that was."

"You felt that?"

"It was hard to miss."

Cade thought a moment. "I don't think he took anything from me. I don't feel any less than I was before. When we . . . when we all came together, it seemed to break the link."

"So you don't know what he's dreaming now."

"No."

She could tell he wasn't trying to listen in. She didn't push. If she'd been in his shoes, she might not have wanted to either. "Was that weird for you? You know, both of you having me."

"Yes."

She laughed softly. "Ask a silly question."

"You liked it," he said.

She rolled to face him and touched his chest. It seemed important to be honest. "It was exciting."

"For me too. Just awkward after." He rubbed her shoulder. "I'm not sure I want to explain to Joseph what happened, though I can't imagine who else we'd consult on what it means."

"I don't think he'll judge."

Cade's nod was vague. "This feels okay," he said. "Him sleeping in the same room with us."

"Like something was missing before and we didn't know what it was?"

"Yes," he agreed, not entirely happy to acknowledge it. "That's exactly what it's like."

CHAPTER SIX

ONCE again, Yasmin the concubine had been forgotten. She'd waited and waited for Elyse to return with an update on the search for her missing brother. She knew the commander's consort must have other priorities, but she could have sent a note. Didn't the human know how frustrating being stuck in a harem was?

"Phooey," she cursed, tossing aside the novel she couldn't convince herself she was reading.

Though she probably ought to give the habit a rest, she transformed into her cat.

A number of the harem's residents were awake. Iksander's mother was a night owl. Any concubine wishing to suck up could do so by keeping her company. Yasmin pattered silently on her paws to the main salon, pausing inside a concealing shadow by the entry. Seated on a tuffet above the others, the sultana was embroidering fancy patterns onto slippers. Her usual coterie surrounded her, their artificially graceful poses designed to impress a man who was even less likely to show up than previously. Hope sprang eternal, Yasmin guessed. With languid motions, they combed each other's hair and sipped tea, which a female servant was preparing over a small burner.

Yasmin had already heard about the sultana's venture into establishing soup kitchens. She hadn't been invited on the charitable expedition, but sometimes it was just as well not to be a favorite. Out of sight, out of mind had advantages.

"You say they're *all* staying in Iksander's rooms?" Iksander's mother was asking.

"Yes," replied the servant, the gossip she carried from the palace as welcome as the refreshments. "The kitchen staff served all three of them dinner. Apparently, both commanders are infatuated with the human."

"Extraordinary," mused the sultana. "I wonder if being doubled damaged their minds. Let us pray not. We need sound leaders until my son returns."

The other women murmured appropriately in agreement, though whether they disapproved or were simply jealous of the human's romantic fortunes Yasmin wouldn't have bet on. Yasmin herself was a bit annoyed. With two men to occupy her, no wonder Elyse was neglecting her.

What about my brother? Yasmin thought, wishing she could will the servant to mention that.

"I hear they went to a bathhouse," the servant continued. "The old one on Thirty-Fourth Street, where you can buy 'extras' with your massage."

The sultana's eyebrows rose. "They all went?"

"Just the female and one commander. The double who went to the human world, I believe. They're hard to tell apart. My friend on the guards said they interrogated a bath girl *and* a bath boy."

"Interrogated them? What on earth about?"

"Someone went missing is what I hear."

The sultana let the slippers she was embroidering fall into her lap. "From a third rate bathhouse? Why would my son's commander trouble himself with that?"

"I don't know, your highness. The guards go where they're told. Whichever commander went, some rogue sorcerer attacked him as they were leaving."

Now *that* was interesting. Eager to catch every word, Yasmin pricked her ears forward. As she did, her crooked tail began twitching.

The motion caught one of the harem women's attention.

"There's that cat again!" she exclaimed.

"Throw a pillow at it," urged another. "That ugly thing makes me sneeze."

Yasmin darted away before the suggestion could be followed. She wasn't afraid of being hit, but the sultana had a good nose for enchantments. The last thing Yasmin wanted was for her very handy disguise to be exposed.

Since she had an address—even a lead, one might say—she directed her running cat feet to the Thirty-Fourth Street bathhouse. One of the young people on her list had come to her attention while eavesdropping at a tavern around the corner. She hadn't known where the missing girl was employed, but it could have been the establishment the commander visited.

Finding the place was easy. With all her roaming, she'd developed a sense for where things were in the city.

A bathhouse like this was busier at night. She could slip in the front door with clientele but once there, she was likely to be noticed . . . and unlikely to be welcomed. No one wanted cat hairs mixed in with their massage oil. Reluctant to be cornered somewhere unfamiliar, she trotted to the long building's back. An open basement window would make a good entry point.

Leaping to the top of a thick brick wall provided her a vantage for studying the terrain. Employee apartments took up the rear of the bathhouse.

On the second floor in one of the lit windows, she spied a familiar face. It was the striking yellow-haired boy she'd overheard at the tavern wondering why his female colleague hadn't shown up for work. Another man was in the room with him, fully dressed and reading a newspaper. He didn't seem the right age to be a friend, but he wasn't acting like a client.

Guard? she wondered. If he were, it suggested the commander agreed with her assessment that young people weren't disappearing randomly. In one way, that was satisfying. In another, it was cause for concern. If there really were a pattern, Balu had been taken for a reason.

Security was tighter than she expected. She found no open windows to sneak into. She would have tried smoking in, but the spells against it had been refreshed.

All right, she thought. *Where should I nose off to instead?*

A howl of laughter split the night, spooking her. She took off on all four legs down the narrow portage road between Thirty-Fourth and Fifth. Rough weeds grew up between the cobbles, sharp pebbles threatening to cut her paws. The strange laugh rose and fell again, like it was following her. Was the rogue sorcerer who attacked the commander hanging around somewhere? Maybe it wasn't safe to be here in any shape. She thought a prayer for strength and sped faster.

Stop panicking, she ordered. The laugh had been farther behind her the second time, nothing to do with her. You'd think she was a real cat, as skittish as she was being.

As she slowed, a man stepped onto the throughway in front of her. She darted around him, trotting now but short of breath.

"Yasmin," he called after her. "Don't you recognize your brother?"

For a second, she thought . . . Hope tightened her throat as she turned back to face the djinni. It wasn't Balu standing tall and graceful in the road. It was her older brother, who'd murdered his friend in a jealous rage and become ifrit.

She hadn't seen Ramis in five years, not since her parents disowned him.

Her heart thudded so hard with shock she couldn't move.

Ramis came closer. His strides were calm, unhurried, his three-piece black suit an admittedly pleasing human style. His shoes were human too, their soles echoing slightly on the cobbles. Was that where he'd been all this time? Hiding out on the human plane? He came to a halt before her. She craned her feline head to see him.

"Won't you change?" he asked gently, his tone a blend of amusement and wistfulness. "We can't talk when you're in that form."

She took a moment to shift; she was practiced at it by now, enough that her harem robes weren't disarranged when she and they materialized. She glanced around to make sure no one was watching. It was late. A woman dressed as fancily as her wasn't a common sight in this neighborhood.

"You always were good at those kind of tricks," Ramis observed.

Now that she was her regular height, she examined him more closely. He looked like a normal djinn—like her, in fact. His hair was the same dark glossy brown as hers, his eyes the same luminous gray. His mouth had the same full shape that made people want to see him smile. Then he did smile, and he was breathtaking.

"Checking me for devil horns?" he teased.

"How did you know it was me?" she asked, not admitting it.

Ramis's eyes crinkled. "Do you think I wouldn't know my sister? What are you doing out here anyway? I thought you'd been selected for the royal harem."

It was rich for him to be questioning her. She wasn't a murdering ifrit. "What I do isn't your business."

He laughed softly. "Your mulishness hasn't changed. Come." He stroked the side of one of the arms she'd folded beneath her breasts. "Have coffee with me. There's a little place nearby where we can talk. No one will look twice at us."

He was her brother, and his manner had its old charm. He'd been wonderful when his moods were sunny: fun and loving and extraordinarily quick-witted. Their parents had been so proud of him. They'd denied the signs of what his less sunny side might do. In truth, he'd been all their favorite—Balu not excepted.

Ramis must be lonely without them to adore him.

"I'll share one pot," she relented. "I can't stay out all night with you."

The coffee shop was in the cellar of a nearby building, the entrance accessed from the alley they walked along. The moment they stepped in she understood why he'd said no one would look twice at them. It didn't matter that she hadn't veiled her face. The place was smoky and packed and everyone in it was strangely garbed.

Ramis pushed through the crowd to grab a small table with floor cushions. As she sat, Yasmin goggled at the colorful young people around them. "Why are they dressed up?"

"This is a cosplay club."

"A what?"

"Costume play. They use their magic to disguise themselves as different human characters. That's Beyoncé and Prince Harry and I believe that fellow over there in the sunglasses is a Hollywood director."

"And I thought view cafés were strange."

Ramis shrugged, the shoulders of his black suit going up and down. "Humans fascinate our kind. Always have and probably always will."

He spoke as if he were the same kind as her. Yasmin decided not to comment. "They don't seem worried about curfew."

She'd heard the commander had established one for djinn under twenty-one, at least until order was restored.

"They probably know the police are too busy to enforce it." He dug a golden coin from his pocket, waving it toward a coffee boy as a way of placing their order.

"You're supporting yourself," Yasmin said.

"Needs must," Ramis said dryly. "Since my silver spoon was forcibly removed from my privileged mouth. Tell me, do you ever wonder why human parents forgive their offspring countless sins, but ours cannot bend at all?"

"I'm not sure that's true," Yasmin said. "We don't know what all of them are like."

"Perhaps," Ramis said, but not as if her opinion had shifted his.

The coffee boy returned. He set a small shining samovar and a pair of cups and saucers on their table. Ramis handed him the coin before drawing her a serving.

Yasmin pulled the coffee closer but didn't sip. "Why are you back?"

"I missed my family. I know I can't stay in the Glorious City, but I wanted to make sure you were all right."

She had no idea if this were true. Ramis had never hesitated to lie when it suited him. "Balu has gone missing," she said and watched his expression.

His eyes widened. "Missing? Since when?"

"Soon after the sorceress's spell was broken." She pulled a face. "Or half broken."

"But . . . what happened?"

"No one knows. I'm here trying to find out."

"Here?"

"A girl disappeared from the bathhouse too, around the same time."

"Was she friends with Balu?"

"Not that I'm aware of."

Ramis leaned back straight-armed from the table. He seemed genuinely shocked. "But why are *you* looking for him? Why not Father or the police?"

"You said it yourself: the police have other concerns. I thought my cat form might hear something they couldn't."

"And has it?"

Was this question too eager? "It's too soon to tell."

Ramis dropped a sugar cube into his coffee cup. He stirred with his eyes on her. "Shouldn't you speak to the higher ups at the palace? Someone with authority could put their weight behind the investigation—not that I mean to tell you your duty."

"Perhaps I will speak to them," she said, "though there's no guarantee they'll listen. I'm not an important harem girl."

"Well." He stirred some more, his sugar surely dissolved by then. "You're important enough to be missed if you're not back in your room soon. I don't want to get you into trouble."

For someone who wanted to make sure she was all right, he suddenly seemed eager to have her go. She pushed her untouched coffee away and rose. "Should we try to meet again?"

Ramis's head had turned, his attention caught by a very large tattooed djinni just then coming in the door. The newcomer's size was noteworthy. He was at least six-six, thickly built, and no teenager. If that weren't enough to draw glances, the pattern of the ink he wore was unusual: thorny black swirls that appeared to cover all his skin—even underneath his clothes. Magic flickered at the marks' edges, causing Yasmin to wonder if this too were a "cosplay" disguise.

Though the gesture was subtle, she was almost certain the tattooed man and Ramis exchanged nods.

"What did you say?" Ramis asked, turning back to her.

Instinct kept her from inquiring if he knew the other man. "I asked if we should try to meet again."

"That would be wonderful. I'll see if I can send you a sign somehow. Let me walk you out and make sure you change safely."

His response was affectionate and smooth and she didn't trust it all. Was she like her parents, unable to see past his sin?

"Thank you," she said, her head lowered modestly to hide her thoughts. "That would be kind of you."

~

Yasmin had the journey back to the palace to decide what she ought to do. Ramis was her brother and perhaps was serving a hard sentence, cut off from all he knew. He'd always cared for Balu and had a vested interest in helping him. Joseph the Magician was simply a distant figure she had a tendre for. She had even less reason to trust the commander's human companion. By failing to keep her informed, Elyse had already let her down. To add to the confusion, Yasmin's own motivations were suspect.

Maybe she was more interested in seeking attention from the object of her crush than in finding her brother. She hoped that wasn't true. It certainly wouldn't reflect well on her.

She wasn't sure she'd decided even when she stopped outside Joseph's apartments. The magician was inside. Her cat nose could scent him.

All right, she thought, lifting her forepaw to give the door a bat. *Here goes nothing.*

~

Joseph's thoughts were on the portal in the palace's treasure room, which he'd just returned from checking on. The magicians he'd assigned to charging it were working around the clock in shifts. They'd made good progress, but as yet the nexus wasn't more than a quarter charged. If he put more men on it, other city services would suffer. If he didn't, it would take that much longer to start their search for Iksander and the sorceress in the human realm. He'd have said a prayer for patience if he'd thought it would work. He only hoped the bath he was preparing for would help him sleep a few hours tonight.

A rattling at the door brought his head up from disrobing. It wasn't a knock—more like something soft batting on the wood. Not alarmed but cautious, he retrieved his scimitar from the bed and went to see what had caused the disturbance.

He opened the door, saw nothing, then jumped as a small black streak zipped past his ankles into the room.

"Stop that," he said, recognizing the cat by its three white socks and its crooked tail. "You're not supposed to come in here."

He strode toward the creature, but the cat dodged the other way. Its furry shoulder hit the door, bumping it closed again. Joseph's skin tingled with awareness. That wasn't normal feline behavior. The cat sat and looked at him. To himself, he admitted he was impressed. Generally speaking, he could spot shifting magic a mile away.

"Okay," he said. "You're not a cat, you're a djinni in cat form. Perhaps you'd like to take your real shape so we can talk."

The cat blinked, lowered its head, and shimmered back to its actual self.

Joseph got his second shock. The cat was a young woman—and a beautiful one at that. Her luxurious garb was that of a harem girl.

He couldn't imagine what she was doing here.

"Forgive me," she said, lowering her head humbly. Her uncovered hair was long and shining. "I know my being here isn't proper, but I need to speak to you on a matter of importance."

He managed to shut his jaw before she glanced up at him. She looked down again at once. The color on her soft cheeks heightened. *Shit.* He stood before her in nothing but trousers. Probably he was lucky he wore that much. He grabbed a robe and tied it.

"Who are you?" he demanded, perhaps a bit rudely.

She'd clutched her hands together in front of her. "My name is Yasmin. The commander's human was gracious enough to see me the other day."

His memory clicked. "You're the girl whose brother went missing."

She seemed relieved that he remembered. "Yes. His name is Balu. I've been . . . scouting the city in search of him. That's how I heard about the other children who disappeared."

A harem girl had been running around the city as a cat? He didn't bother asking if she had permission. In a million years, Iksander's mother wouldn't have given it. A serious beating would be the least she'd face if her actions were discovered. She was Iksander's possession, sworn to obey his rule. Under more conservative administrations, what she'd done would constitute treason.

He rubbed the frown lines beside his mouth. "Perhaps this conversation calls for tea."

Deciding he wasn't in immediate danger, he set the scimitar on the table so he could brew the drink. Yasmin must have been impatient. She didn't wait for him to finish.

"I think my other brother is involved somehow," she blurted.

Joseph turned to face her again. "Your *other* brother?"

"His name is Ramis. Five years ago, when he was nineteen, his best friend of won an honor he'd been hoping to claim himself. Ramis accused him of cheating. When the friend refused to say he had, my brother stabbed him in the heart. It was clear he hadn't killed him by accident. He'd used an enchanted knife that blocked his friend from healing. The murder turned him ifrit and my parents disowned him."

"And you think he's involved because—?"

She wrung her hands. "Ramis showed up near the bathhouse. Perhaps I shouldn't have gone, but no one told me anything, and I had to see if I could find clues to what was going on."

"You *had* to," Joseph said.

"No one told me anything," the girl repeated. "I'm worried about Balu. Anyway, me running around in my cat form isn't what's important."

Under the circumstances, Joseph supposed that was true. Giving up on preparing tea, he poured some brandy into a snifter and handed it to her. "What did Ramis do that made you suspicious?"

She drank the liquor down and coughed. "He was there, for one thing, where the other girl disappeared. I saw the guard the commander put on the other bath boy. I think Ramis or whoever he's working with might have come back to try for him."

"But you didn't see him try for him."

"Well, the police guard was in his room—not blending very well, by the way. And then when Ramis recognized me in my cat shape, he told me to change out of it so we could talk and have coffee. I think he wanted to discover what I knew."

"Why would he think you knew anything?"

"Because he knows I was accepted into the harem, and we—" She gnawed her lip and stopped.

"You hear lots of good gossip there?"

"Yes." She seemed grateful he understood. "If these missing children have been the target of a criminal operation, whoever's running it would want to know if the official investigation is close to closing in. They'll be wondering if they dare take more djinn, or if they should settle for what they have and run. That's what I'd ask if it were me."

Her conclusions were a leap but not illogical. Joseph retrieved the empty glass her fingers were clamped on. He offered to pour more brandy in it, but she shook her head.

"You believe me, don't you?" she asked earnestly.

He wasn't ready to say that. "Why bring this story to me? I gather you were impatient, but why not seek out Elyse? Surely speaking to a woman would be easier."

Yasmin blushed even harder than she had at seeing him without a shirt. "I, um, it seemed as if she might be busy. I didn't wish to interrupt."

Joseph's own cheeks heated. He realized she meant interrupt Elyse with her two lovers. That juicy morsel of disinformation would have reached the harem too. Actually, he wasn't sure how much *dis* there was in the information. His original employer's fascination with Elyse hadn't escaped him.

"I see," he said and cleared his throat. "I'm afraid the commanders will want to hear your account. Do you suppose, since you've already spoken to me, that you'd be willing to address them directly? We'd be discreet about it, obviously."

Yasmin bowed her head. "I could do that. I want to be helpful."

Her pose was a picture of grace and modesty, exactly what a dutiful harem girl should be. Her tone, he couldn't help but notice, was the teensiest bit eager.

He glanced at the pendulum of a nearby table clock. Yasmin had already pushed her luck by sneaking from her rooms. Even if she were agreeable to staying, for her sake, he didn't dare keep her with him for the remainder of the night. The best thing would be to take her to the commanders immediately, thus giving her a chance to get back where she belonged before sunrise. The only drawback was popping in on the threesome unannounced.

"Are we going now?" Yasmin asked hopefully.

Joseph sighed to himself. "We're going now," he confirmed.

~

Cade was deeply asleep one moment and shockingly alert the next. A rustle of sheets informed him Arcadius had just sat up on the divan. Cade's hand moved protectively to Elyse's hip. Reaching out to her was instinctive—for his double as well, it seemed.

Noting what he'd done, Arcadius withdrew his hand.

"Your scroll," Arcadius said, nodding toward the bedside table where Cade had left it along with his harness of throwing knives. "It's flashing. Someone must be trying to contact you."

Wondering what the emergency was, Cade retrieved the parchment from the drawer and unrolled it. Familiar writing spilled across the surface. "It's Joseph. He's asking the three of us to meet him and the harem girl in Iksander's private library."

"Now?"

"Apparently."

Elyse made a grumbling noise. She'd curled up on her side, facing him. Cade gave her hip a pat. "Get up, sweetheart. We need more clothes than our skin for this."

They dressed without conversation, though the quiet wasn't uncomfortable. Curiosity drew Cade's gaze toward his double as he pulled on clothes with little evidence of lingering weakness. Cade wasn't over the strangeness of seeing his own body with—essentially—someone else in it. Those were his legs, his chest and arms, his dark hair falling down his brow. Had he and Arcadius really shared Elyse in this very closet? Arousal threatened to expand in him, but he pushed it down. He'd think about that later . . . maybe much. For his part, Arcadius cut more than one glance toward Elyse, smiling when she slid her feet into the sparkly jewel-studded slippers he'd given her. His gift was a success. Cade struggled not to mind.

Knowing Elyse, she hadn't realized the gems weren't rhinestones.

"Do I need a head scarf?" she asked.

"Only if you want one," Arcadius said. "We're in our own rooms, and this harem girl has broken protocol already."

Since Cade would have said the same, he tried not to resent the other him answering.

When they reached the small book-lined library, Joseph and the concubine hopped up from slightly distant separate armchairs. Though Joseph was a eunuch, Cade supposed the customary man-woman divide still applied. They definitely didn't seem easy with each other.

"You're better," Joseph said, seeing Arcadius walk in without support.

"Yes," Arcadius answered with a curtness that shut off discussion of that topic.

Joseph seemed to see the wisdom of dropping it. He introduced Yasmin, who was extraordinarily pretty but shy enough to blush. Cade assumed it was shyness anyway. As Joseph and she related her recent doings, his amazement expanded. While her motivation might be understandable, Yasmin might as well have torched the agreement her parents signed with Iksander. Putting herself recklessly in danger was a slap to Iksander's face. She was his concubine. She owed him more respect than running around the city like a literal wild thing.

Elyse, by contrast, listened to the young woman's account with admiration and interest. Cade suspected she'd enjoy the ability to turn into a cat. Too, a harem girl rebelling was probably more understandable to her than one who obeyed every rule. Interestingly, as he imagined how Yasmin's actions appeared to Elyse, his outrage subsided.

Was this what being part of a couple meant: that you automatically had access to another perspective? He'd have to think about that. Maybe it was just what being part of a couple meant for him.

"Your brother didn't appear different from when you knew him?" Elyse asked.

"No," Yasmin said. "I thought he would, but I haven't known ifrits before him."

She glanced at Joseph to consult him.

"Sometimes djinn who damn themselves look different, but not in every case. The sorceress looked the same before and after she killed Najat. The biggest change was that Luna had more power. Once she'd crossed that forbidden line, she didn't cavil at crossing more to boost her magic."

"Ramis always had a knack for spells. Our whole family does, though nothing compared to yourself, of course."

Elyse seemed to find Yasmin's high regard for Joseph amusing. Cade watched her humor fade as a new thought occurred to her. "If Ramis took your brother, that would explain why the emotion Joseph sensed when he touched his portrait was surprise. Balu wouldn't have been afraid of someone familiar."

"But why do it?" Yasmin asked. "I suppose Ramis misses Balu, but then why take the others?"

"Some ritual?" Arcadius suggested with analytical coolness. "Maybe he's using the djinn as sacrifices. The sorceress did as much to augment her curse."

"Ramis wouldn't kill his own brother!" Yasmin cried. "I spoke to him. He couldn't be that lost."

Cade suspected he could but preferred not to be as blunt as the other him. He switched to another tack. "The human connection is interesting. Balu was last seen at a view café. The bath girl Jeannine may have frequented the cosplay club, since it was near her work. Perhaps Ramis was her mysterious 'recruiter' and the first contact was made there." He turned to Arcadius. "Didn't the bath boy say she'd been bragging that she had a way out of the life she was living in our city? That she'd been chosen to go somewhere she'd be at the top of the heap and not the bottom?"

"Yes," Arcadius said.

"We didn't find a link like that for the kids who disappeared from the bottle house," Elyse pointed out.

"Not finding it doesn't mean it wasn't there. They were down on their luck. And romantics, by the priest's account. Like the others, they may have been vulnerable to promises of better lives on the human plane."

Cade thought his double's theory was possible. He pinched his lower lip. "The promise doesn't explain what Ramis gets out of it."

Yasmin piped up with that answer. "He had money. Maybe the tattooed man is paying him."

She didn't anticipate the reaction she got from Elyse and Cade. Her eyes went round as they turned to her, dumbstruck.

"What tattooed man?" Cade asked, trying not to alarm her with the intensity of his interest. They'd crossed paths with a tattooed man in Elyse's realm, an individual Cade had been hoping to put off dealing with for a while.

"He came into the club while Ramis and I were there," Yasmin said. "He didn't speak to my brother, but I got the impression they knew each other."

"Was he tall?" Elyse stretched her hand high to demonstrate. "Muscular build? Shaved head? Black swirly tattoos sort of liked thick barbed wire?"

"You know who he is?" Yasmin asked.

Elyse nodded. "Unfortunately. His name is Mario. He worked for my uncle as hired muscle until he joined forces with my cousin Cara and shot him dead." Yasmin looked confused so she elaborated. "My home in the human world had a portal nexus in its basement. My father figured out how to access your plane with it. He was an explorer, I guess you'd say. His idea of wealth was having new cultures to learn about. My uncle preferred cold hard cash. He resented my dad keeping a secret world of riches to himself and had him thrown into a volcano so he could claim the door for himself. The reasons are complicated, but we thought we'd prevented Mario from following us here."

"We left breadcrumbs," Joseph said resignedly. "A smart male like Mario would have followed them sooner or later."

"But—" Yasmin hesitated, her gaze shifting between them. "The man I saw in the cosplay club wasn't human. He was djinn."

"His *tattoos* were djinn," Cade corrected. "Animated by a trapped djinni's spirit. We're not sure where Mario got them, but we've seen evidence that his spirit and the djinni's are starting to intertwine."

"Hm," Arcadius said, not having heard this part of the story. "I wonder if he'll lose the advantage of his magic overruling ours as that happens."

None of them had sat since entering the library, and Cade's original was tiring. Without being obvious about it, Arcadius lowered his weight to the gilded arm of a long sapphire couch. He tapped one finger on his lips. "Actually, I wonder if this Mario was the rogue sorcerer who attacked myself and Elyse as we left the bathhouse. Perhaps, because she's human too, Elyse saw through his disguise. Her subconscious might have recognized him as the man she knew and urged her conscious self to go after him. The combination of djinni and human in his magic could be why I was able to counter his assault at all."

"That seems possible," Cade said. In truth, he wished he'd thought of the explanation. Seeming to know this, Arcadius smiled smugly.

His smirk faltered just a little when Elyse rubbed Cade's arm to draw his attention. "If Mario is here and he's behind the disappearances, how do we stop him?"

"I might be able to help you set a trap for my brother," Yasmin said.

"That is *not* a good idea," Joseph protested.

"You haven't heard what I'm going to say!"

"Let her speak," Cade said. "She's gone to some risk already. Perhaps we owe it to her to listen."

"The risks she's already taken are what I'm worried about." Joseph's mutter was uncharacteristically ill tempered.

"The girl has shown bravery," Arcadius put in—also unexpectedly. "I say we hear her out."

He and the others turned to her. Given the floor, Yasmin twisted her fingers nervously. "Before we parted, my brother said he'd try to send me a message so we could talk again. I don't think he realized I suspect him of anything. If I tell you where we're meeting, surely you could formulate some way to catch him. Maybe you can get him to rat on this Mario."

"If your brother sees the trick coming, you'll be in danger." This warning came from Elyse.

"Ramis wouldn't truly hurt me," Yasmin said.

"I'm sure the friend he stabbed in the heart would have said the same," Elyse pointed out gently. "You didn't know him then, and you don't really know him now."

Yasmin looked like she wanted to argue. "Fine," she said after a brief struggle. "But I'm still the most reliable way you have of locating my brother."

"We know his likely recruiting grounds," Arcadius said. "We could put a watch on the view cafés and the cosplay club. See if he or Mario shows up again."

"Respectfully," Yasmin said, "you can't. That guard you put on the bath boy stood out like a sore thumb. He's probably the reason Ramis risked exposing his presence here to me. He wanted to know what the scuttlebutt at the palace was. If you make him more nervous, he and Mario will run."

"We can't be sure he'll contact you," Joseph said.

"He probably will," Yasmin countered. "My brother always thought no one else was as smart as him. I'm willing to bet that didn't change when he turned dark."

~

Yasmin was proud of herself for getting through the interview with the commanders and Elyse. She'd been nervous but thought she expressed herself clearly. She'd even stood her ground against Joseph. In hindsight, maybe she wasn't *happy* she'd contradicted him, but it proved she had spine. Fortunately, no one guessed how long she'd been watching the handsome magician. Also fortunately, she slipped back into the harem unobserved.

All that remained for her to do was hope she'd judged her brother correctly. She was pretty sure she had, but wished she knew how Ramis would contact her. What if he had trouble getting a message through the palace's magical protections? Maybe she should ask Joseph to do something to make it easier.

Worries like these kept her awake for what was left of the night.

She wasn't at her best when she joined the other concubines for the morning meal. Their dining room held one long table with cushioned couches along the sides. Per usual, the sultana presided at the head. She liked the meal to be quiet, given the early hour. Yasmin slid into her customary place and was offered bread and cheese and fruit. Many of the table's seats were empty. Stupidly, she almost opened her mouth to ask where the rest of the women were. They were in the storeroom, their marble bodies wrapped in quilts to protect them from damage. Her life was currently so alive and interesting she'd forgotten them.

"Pardon, your highness," said one of the servers. "Some flowers have arrived for you. Shall I bring them in?"

"Flowers?" the sultana asked. "For me?"

"From one of the neighborhoods where you established an emergency food pantry. The residents wish to show their gratitude. The package checkers have vetted them. They're perfectly safe to bring in."

"Fine," she said. "Find a vase and put them in the middle of the table. We can all enjoy them."

The server grinned. When she returned a minute later they saw why. The bouquet was huge and absolutely gorgeous—a tumble of sunset orange roses, decorative palm leaf sprays, and fragrant sprigs of tiny white lime blossoms.

"Oh, my," the sultana breathed, actually lighting up with pleasure. It wasn't a look they often saw on her. It reminded Yasmin she was a person and not just a battleax. "They're beautiful."

"I misted them with spelled water," the server said. "They'll stay fresh for a while."

All the women got up to coo and sniff. Yasmin was no different except in one respect. When she leaned closer to the flowers, a single petal jumped from a rose and landed in her palm.

Startled, she looked at it. The orange petal glittered, only for a second, as if gold dust had been brushed over it. She didn't see words, but this had to be her brother's message. The spelled spritz water ought to have prevented blooms from falling off. Yasmin closed her fingers around the petal and forced herself to sit normally.

Her heart beat faster at the thought of taking this to Joseph.

~

Joseph was exiting the vizier's office when Yasmin's mostly black cat gamboled around the corner of the corridor.

"Cat!" exclaimed a passing cleaner, raising his broom to shoo her.

"Wait!" Joseph startled the man by rushing forward. "Don't hurt her. I'll carry her away."

The cleaner bowed when he saw who'd stopped him. Joseph tried to nod like this was all perfectly normal and picked up the waiting cat. She hung from his hand perfectly relaxed, though he felt slightly rude carrying her. Resisting an urge to stroke her between the ears, he ducked into the nearest empty room. As it happened, this was a storage space for extra cushions and de-spelled scrolls. He shut the door behind them and set Yasmin down.

She shimmered swiftly into her true form. The colorful stacked up cushions didn't leave much floor space. Yasmin tried to retreat and nearly fell into them.

"Sorry," she said with a breathless laugh. "Suddenly, I'm very big."

She was certainly very close, the curves of her figure abruptly making the air feel hot. Joseph took a step back himself. "You shouldn't be sneaking out from the harem in broad daylight."

He sounded an awful priss, but she simply shook her head guiltily. "I know. I should have waited. I got a message and couldn't control myself." She opened her hand to show him. "It's disguised as a rose petal. Ramis smuggled it in with a bouquet for the sultana. Right under the package checkers' noses."

Joseph lifted the petal carefully from her palm, simultaneously impressed and alarmed. "How does it work?"

"Say 'one for all and all for one' and then tap it twice with your fingertip. It's a code Ramis, Balu, and I made up when we were kids. For when we wanted to hide things from our parents."

Joseph did as she instructed. The spell had been miniaturized to avoid detection, its activation instantaneous and neat—as good as anything Joseph himself could work. A brief burst of golden sparklers preceded the petal turning into a three-inch square of orange notepaper. The sort of handwriting only taught at exclusive schools conveyed a short message.

Sultan's Circle in Victory Park. Midnight tomorrow. Come alone.

No sooner had he read it than the paper shifted back to a rose petal.

"That's clever," he admitted reluctantly.

"Ramis was a lot of fun when we were kids," Yasmin said.

She sounded sad. Joseph wanted to squeeze her shoulder, but touching her wouldn't have been proper. She shook off her melancholy without his help. "I should get back. You'll contact me when you've made a plan?"

"We'll send Elyse," he said, sounding like a priss again.

Yasmin didn't seem to notice. "Until then," she answered with polite elegance.

CHAPTER SEVEN

WHEN Joseph called her and Cade to the library, Elyse assumed the message from Ramis had arrived. Arcadius was there already, thumbing through the pages of a heavy volume that lay on a table heaped with books. Joseph sat on a long blue couch leaning forward, his attention on a small orange something in his hand. The room wasn't bright, but a sunbeam from one of the high windows spotlighted the item. For the space of a blink, Joseph's fingers looked like they were on fire.

"Is that it?" Cade asked as they approached him.

Joseph looked up. How handsome he was struck her, his face weary but masculine. She wondered what he made of Yasmin, if he found it hard not to be moved by her beauty. How did a man pretend to be a eunuch when he wasn't one anymore?

"This is it," he said. "Would you like to sit while I demonstrate how it works?"

They took chairs facing him across a lovely stretch of carpet. She guessed Arcadius had seen the show already. He remained standing where he was with his back to them. Only Elyse gasped when the flower petal changed to a piece of paper and back again.

Cade patted her forearm where it rested on her chair. She enjoyed his habit of reaching out to touch her, though she wasn't afraid. Even an enemy's magic had the power to delight her.

Cade's response was more strategic. "Midnight tomorrow isn't a lot of time to prepare a trap. Not when the person we're trying to catch is as adept as that spell suggests."

"No," Joseph agreed. "I thought the same myself."

"Was it really that good?" Elyse asked. "I mean, I don't know how you judge, but I've seen you pull off bigger things."

"He miniaturized the spell," Joseph said. "And snuck it past a team of screeners with years of experience. That's high level. My level, in point of fact."

"I regret to say this," Arcadius said, turning to them at last, "but whatever plan we come up with, I don't see a way around involving Elyse in it."

"Me?" She knew she sounded startled. Cade patted her arm again. She looked at him. He wasn't denying his double's words.

"Human magic overrules djinn magic," Joseph reminded.

"You've done spells before," Cade said.

"Only with your help!"

"You'll have our help this time. We simply need the advantage your nature can bring us."

"I'm afraid we do," Arcadius concurred. "Believe me, I wouldn't suggest it otherwise. I find putting women in danger abhorrent."

Elyse wriggled uncomfortably in her chair. It wasn't necessarily the danger that bothered her, but that the outcome depended on her not screwing up. "I won't have to be in charge? I'll just be pitching in?" Pitching in she enjoyed. Pitching in was her specialty.

The men exchanged glances with each other. She didn't like that they knew something she didn't—especially when the something might be that her worst fear was true. Cade took her hand and squeezed.

"We'll work with you," he said. "Anyone can develop sufficient confidence with practice."

Ulp, Elyse thought, praying her expression didn't betray how *un*confident she was. Arcadius moved from the book-heaped table to sit beside Joseph on the couch. He leaned forward across his knees very much like the magician was.

"Tell me," he said, "since I wasn't there to see. What sorts of spells have you done already?"

She thought back to their time in Sheikh Zayd's Bedouin camp. "I made a kettle boil by cursing at it. It ran on ifrit magic, and Joseph explained praying wouldn't work. I put Sheikh Zayd's men to sleep when we were escaping on the flying carpet. I guess that was impressive, but they were shooting at us and I was using panic strength—like those women who lift Volkswagens off their babies."

"Okay," Arcadius said, maybe a bit confused by that example. "That's good. Anything else?"

"Oh!" She hopped a little in her chair. "I freed Joseph from an Aladdin's lamp. That was the first magic I ever did. Mario cursed him into it, and since he was human, Cade said only another human could get him out. That was fun. For me, anyway. Maybe not for Joseph."

"It sounds as if you three had a few adventures. And also that you have enough natural talent to pull off what we'll ask of you."

"Ah," she said, realizing where his line of questioning had led. "You're trying to build me up. That was pretty slick."

When Arcadius smiled, she felt like a foot soldier a famous general had patted on the back.

Joseph was thinking ahead. "Sucking Ramis in a lamp might be feasible. Elyse has accomplished the reverse already. Better still, being turned to smoke won't kill him. We could question him about Mario and their operation at our leisure."

"She'll need to practice," Cade pointed out.

"Not on you," Joseph said. "And not on me, if you'd allow me to bow out. I've finally recovered from Mario forcing me into smoke form. I'd rather not risk losing my ability to change again."

The men turned their eyes to Arcadius. He sat straighter in alarm, his former smile wiped away. "You want me to be her guinea pig? What if my abilities get screwed up like Joseph's?"

"They probably won't," Joseph said.

"Probably!"

"Cade recovered from Mario's compulsion much sooner than I did. And you're made of the same stuff as him."

"It's for a good cause," Cade added.

"You do it then."

"I trust her too much. She needs resistance to work against. Plus, you've been having trouble changing on your own. You haven't got full-strength skills to lose. Really, you're the ideal test subject."

Arcadius heaved a sigh.

"Guys," Elyse said. "If he doesn't want to, I don't think we should force him."

"No, no," Arcadius said with his head wagging. "As your people say, I'll take one for the team."

~

The first thing Joseph did was help her memorize the chant. Some djinn magic seemed to be made up on the fly. This was a specific formula, done in the name of King Solomon from the Bible and requiring her to visualize a special seal at the same time that she said it.

"What if I forget a word?" she asked after twenty minutes hunched with Joseph over the leather bound spell book.

"You'll practice," Joseph said—not the most reassuring answer. "Here." He slid her a piece of paper and a quill pen. "Copy the spell a couple times. That will help you remember it."

Naturally, the pen required magic to function.

She thought she had it pretty good in an hour, which was when Joseph began fine-tuning her intonation. Trying not to complain, she knuckled the increasing ache between her brows.

"It's supposed to be hard," he said. "It wouldn't be fair if humans could enslave djinn any time they wanted to."

"It wouldn't occur to most humans that they could."

"Nonetheless," Joseph said. "There's meant to be a balance between our races. On top of which, that three wishes business really can create havoc."

Elyse had forgotten about that part. "If I'm practicing on Arcadius, will he owe me three new wishes each time I let him out?"

"No," Arcadius said very firmly from the nearby writing table where he'd occupied himself with paperwork. Cade had returned to their office, but her future test subject remained with them in the library.

"Yes, actually," Joseph contradicted quietly. "But it's considered rude to demand them and sometimes it's dangerous."

"You still owe me three," she teased.

"We're friends," he said. "I'm sure you don't want to put our bond on that footing."

"I like being your friend," Elyse admitted, a smile tugging at her lips. "I guess I'll let you off the hook."

Arcadius snorted. When she glanced at him, he was smiling faintly too.

"Let's go over this a few more times," Joseph said. "Then we'll test it out on him."

~

Iksander's bed would have been more comfortable, but Arcadius preferred not to let Elyse experiment on him in those surroundings. His attraction to her wasn't Joseph's business, though—given how sharp he was—the magician had probably noticed it. He wondered how the other him and Joseph had become so familiar in so short a time. Being friends with one's associates opened one to all sorts of awkwardness.

He felt ornery and slightly nervous as he stretched on his back on the long sapphire couch. The cushions were too overstuffed for his taste, the velvet reminding him of stroking Elyse's breasts. He shifted and willed himself not to get an erection. What had happened with Elyse and Cade in the closet had been a one-time thing.

Neither Elyse nor Joseph was paying him any attention.

"We'll use this in place of a lamp," Joseph said, handing her a fat bellied brass vessel. "I've drawn Solomon's seal on the side. Feel free to stare at it and get it set in your mind before you start your chant. Once all the commander's smoke is inside, slap this fitted iron stopper into the opening. It also has the seal on it and will prevent him from smoking right back out. I want you to cultivate the habit of securing your captive immediately."

"Right," Elyse said, not sounding sure at all. She looked at Arcadius and pulled an apologetic face.

It really was sort of sweet. *Resist her,* he thought. *She needs something to work against.*

"Just do it," he said grumpily.

Nothing happened the first ten times she said the chant.

"Keep repeating it," Joseph instructed. "And relax your shoulders. You're too tense."

Her tongue began to stumble on the words.

Arcadius lost patience. "Pull yourself together. This is important!"

"I'm not one of your recruits."

"More's the pity. I'd whip you into shape."

Her soft green eyes narrowed angrily, her arm tightening on the squat brass vase. She restarted the invocation, her will focused behind it now. His edges began to slip and by instinct, he fought against giving up control. He belonged to himself. No one forced him to change form but him. She chanted faster. Now his insides began to turn. It felt awful, far worse than when Joseph triggered him to shift. Joseph was a fellow djinni, and he'd been trying to be gentle. Elyse couldn't have been gentle even if she'd wanted to. Her raw human power was a hammer, his desire to command himself the nail it was smashing on. His cells were on fire, their molecules trying to fly apart. His vision blurred. He groaned with what was left of his vocal chords.

Elyse lost her nerve and let go.

His physical self snapped back from the half-smoke state. The sensation was like packing two hours of spinning into two seconds. He jumped up to escape the effect and his head whirled the other way. Before he could do a single thing to stop it, his vision went black. He had a sick sense of falling and then nothing.

He woke on the floor with Joseph's palms smacking his cheeks sharply.

"Oh, my God," Elyse cried. "Arcadius, I'm sorry!"

"Fuck," he gasped. His head hurt as he sat up.

"Careful," Joseph said. "You fainted. And broke a statuette on the way. I'll get something to spell the shards into."

He fainted? That was embarrassing. Groaning, he heaved himself back onto the couch. He touched his temple, which felt sticky. His fingers came away bloody, but the cut the blood had come from seemed to have healed.

He guessed he was glad that much of his power functioned.

"I'm sorry," Elyse repeated miserably. She'd laid her hand on his shaking shoulder. "I shouldn't have stopped, should I?"

At least she understood that much. He found the steadiness to cover her hand with his. "Next time, you'll do better."

"Err," she said. "Couldn't I practice on a houseplant instead?"

He collapsed against the couch's arm and considered her. Despite how terrible he felt, part of him longed to laugh. Humans weren't supposed to be as tenderhearted as this woman. They were the rival race, the Creator's preferred pet project. Elyse bit her lip when she saw how warmly he was gazing up at her.

"I'll make tea," she offered. "I know Joseph keeps some here."

He didn't want it to happen, but his heart softened: a bit of the tightness that was always there relaxing. "Tea would be good," he admitted.

~

Joseph was magically good at cleaning, but Elyse suggested they switch to a different corner of the room anyway. Fresh spot, fresh start, and all that. A big leather chair with an ottoman gave Arcadius a new place to sit.

Joseph took up his coaching position behind her. "Think about taking charge of him, like you take charge of your brownstone back home. You don't second-guess yourself about collecting rent or whether the walks need shoveling. You just do it."

"That's not magic," Elyse said.

"Magic is simply another form of control. When you believe you have the authority, you do."

Believe, she thought but wasn't convinced she did.

Oh, screw it, she countered. *Just give it your best shot.*

She closed her eyes, pictured the Solomon seal, and started the chant again. Two minutes later, the air grew hot and gave a palpable little pop. Her eyes flew open. The chair was empty. Arcadius's cinder gray smoke was streaming into the brass vase she held.

"I did it!" she exclaimed, her heart thundering madly with excitement.

"Stopper," Joseph reminded.

Elyse readied it. She waited for the last wisp to disappear and popped in the iron plug. Supported snugly in the crook of her arm, the metal vessel vibrated. *Whoa,* she thought. *I really put Arcadius in there.*

"Hm," Joseph said, one finger across his lips.

"Hm, what? Didn't I do that right?"

"As far as I can tell, you did, but I think he may have helped you along."

"Helped me!"

"Not on purpose. He saw how troubled you were over making him pass out. I suspect he didn't want you to experience hurting him again."

"I thought his ability to change was on the fritz."

"He's gotten better faster than I expected."

"Well, how am I supposed to practice if he's doing half the work?"

Joseph rubbed his upper lip and considered. "You could try getting him angry. Or at least be less likable."

Elyse rolled her eyes. "Too bad I didn't try to turn him to smoke when he first met me."

"Yes," Joseph said, not at all jokingly. "That probably would have worked better."

Him tacitly agreeing that Arcadius hadn't liked her wasn't worth getting upset about. "Shall I let him out?"

"Yes. Circle the seal three times clockwise and say the formula."

Luckily, she remembered it. She rubbed as she recited. "If you are one who honors the Holy Name, I free you from captivity."

The vessel shuddered. She removed the stopper and Arcadius's cloud billowed out. In a matter of seconds, he coalesced back into a solid man.

"You helped me," she accused immediately.

"I certainly did not!"

"You did. Joseph could tell. Are you really so . . ." She searched around for an insult. ". . . so biddable you'd *help* a measly human female order you around?"

Arcadius looked at her like she was crazy but not like he was irate.

"Okay, then you must be desperate for affection! You're jealous of Cade having someone in his life so you're trying to make me like you too."

She didn't relish saying that. She actually thought it was mean. The only rise she got from Arcadius was his head tilting to the side.

"Cade is bigger than you," she burst out.

Arcadius's eyebrows rose. "Bigger than me?"

"His cock," she said, fighting not to blush with Joseph listening in. "And, trust me, I can tell the difference!"

Arcadius's eyes slitted. "If Cade felt a need to increase his size, he's either childish or insecure."

"He was you when he did it! *You're* the one who's insecure."

"What *are* you on about?" Arcadius asked.

Elyse heaved a sigh. "This isn't working."

"What isn't working?"

"She's trying to make you mad," Joseph said.

"Well, it's irritating. She should stop."

Elyse broke into a laugh.

"Try the spell again," Joseph said. "Irritation might be the best result you get."

~

Joseph was a patient teacher, but even he needed a break by the time the dinner hour rolled around. Elyse succeeded in changing Arcadius a few more times, but Joseph kept claiming he was helping. Neither Elyse nor Arcadius knew how to stop this from happening, though Arcadius complained that repeatedly shifting back and forth was giving him a headache.

"I could have told you goading him wouldn't work," Cade said when he rejoined Elyse and Arcadius. "Arcadius's pride wouldn't let him admit your jibes hit home. If he'd resisted, he'd have proved they did."

"You're making my brain hurt now," Arcadius said from his slump on the side of the sultan's bed.

"Would you let *me* force you into your smoke form?" Cade asked.

"I'd like to see you try!"

Cade smiled sweetly. "I believe I rest my case."

"Guys," Elyse broke in. "I still need to learn to cast this spell. On an *unwilling* participant."

Cade pulled her against him into a hug. Although Elyse appreciated his support, they had a limited amount of time for her to get this right.

He stroked her curls, his hand coaxing her to look up at him. His smile was wonderfully affectionate. "Sweetheart, I don't think Arcadius is the participant we need to work on."

"No kidding," she responded, her frustration spiking past the boiling point. "I'm the one who's fucking up."

"Ah," Arcadius said as if he suddenly understood something she didn't.

"Don't *do* that," she demanded, dangerously close to tears. "I'm honestly trying."

"Elyse," Cade said, drawing her attention back to him. "Do you remember our first morning here, what you said when we made love in the bath?"

"I'm sure I said a lot of things."

Her tone was grouchy. Cade's vibrant eyes crinkled. "You said one day you were going to take me in the ass. I think you need to do that . . . but not to me."

"No-o," she denied at the same time Arcadius said, "I beg your pardon."

"You need to assert command," Cade explained, ignoring Arcadius. "Without hesitation or apologies."

"If you're so interested, have her do it to you!" his original huffed.

"I can't force him to do that against his will," Elyse said.

"You won't have to. He understands how important this is and he'll . . . like you commanding him. He just won't like that he likes it."

"Speak for yourself!" Arcadius snapped.

Elyse glanced at him. His face was flushed, his nostrils flaring with anger. His expression wasn't dissimilar to arousal. And Cade was in a position to guess at his secret kinks.

"I don't know," she said unsurely. "I wouldn't know how to take charge of him."

"You've done it to me."

"Only sort of."

"More than sort of. Don't you remember when you tied me up and rode me?"

She flashed back to the tent in the Bedouin camp, suddenly warm underneath her clothes. That had been fun, but Cade was talking about really pushing Arcadius's limits, and that made her uneasy. "Will you help?"

Cade shook his head. "If I tell you what to do, it undermines the point."

"Don't I get a say?" Arcadius broke in.

His arms were crossed, his upper lip twisted into a handsome sneer. Awareness clicked inside Elyse's mind. If she was going to do this, now was the time to start, before Arcadius realized she'd never push past his limits, only right up to them.

"No," she said. "At the moment, your say isn't important."

Arcadius's eyes widened. She didn't give him a chance to speak.

"I think you *will* have to help," she added to Cade, deciding she might as well push him too. "Not to give me ideas. I have plenty. It's just some of the things I want to do to him require muscle."

Cade's jaw fell.

"You ought to say 'yes, mistress,'" she pointed out. "If he has to answer to me, you should as well."

Arcadius snorted out a laugh.

"This isn't a game," she said, firm and calm. "I expect both of you to obey me."

Arcadius blinked.

"Answer me appropriately," she insisted.

"Yes, mistress," he responded.

"Yes, mistress," Cade echoed a beat later.

They didn't mean it yet. Nonetheless, a little thrill went through her, unexpected and intoxicating. These men were more powerful than she was—in every way, she would have said. They had more mass, more muscle, certainly more experience with magic. They'd commanded armies and devised winning strategies. Both possessed the sort of beauty that turned heads. Elyse was petite and had only a female's strength. Aside from that, she was a passably attractive, passably smart, small-time human landlady. Just this once, though, maybe she had an opportunity to outthink them.

Fake it till you make it, she told herself. Chances were, her two commanders had never heard of that.

Channeling her inner dominatrix—and hoping she had one—she put her fists on her waist. "Does Iksander have a toy drawer?"

"A toy drawer?" Arcadius was confused.

"Sex toys," Cade explained to the less traveled him.

"I can call down to the harem if he doesn't," Elyse said. "I expect they have all sorts."

"He might have one in the closet," Arcadius answered, his tone bemused. "Perhaps in the large wardrobe?"

"I'll check," she said. "You two have your clothes off before I return."

"Both of us?" Cade was startled.

"Both of you," she confirmed. "If I'm taking charge, I'm not doing it halfway."

She smiled to herself as she crossed the large bedroom. Cade and Arcadius's expressions were priceless.

The absent sultan didn't have a toy drawer. He had what looked like a pirate's treasure chest with straps. She found the thing at the rear of the large wardrobe Arcadius had suggested looking in. She had no idea what some of the contents did. The symbols carved and painted on them suggested they might be magical. A box within the box held a selection of dildos whose function was obvious enough, despite being unusually decorative. The unguent jars also seemed self-explanatory. Deciding it was best not to leave anything behind, she carried the entire chest back into the bedroom.

The men were naked. Cade sat on the side of the mattress, hands braced on his knees, trying to look casual. Arcadius stood by the heavily gilded footboard, his mood stubborn and angry. Neither had an erection but something about the way their cocks were hanging—the slightly greater thickness of the shafts—made her think they'd be easy to arouse. It amused her that she had no trouble telling them apart. They were as alike as twins but each man inhabited his body differently.

"Good," she said, slightly breathless from lugging the heavy box. She dropped it on the bed and tipped up the lid.

Both men leaned in to see. Presumably they knew what the unidentifiable items did.

"That's a lot of toys," Cade observed.

"Iksander does have his quirks," Arcadius agreed.

"What's this?" she asked, pulling out a tangle of dog collar-ish leather straps.

"An outfit," Cade said. "You recite the spell and it fits itself to you."

She looked to Arcadius for confirmation.

"He isn't lying. That's what it does."

"Is it for a woman or a man?"

"Either," Arcadius said. He was braced and trying to hide it. She sensed he didn't want her to order him to put it on himself.

Pick your battles, she thought. She stroked a length of the leather harness. It was dark brown, sturdy, and broken in. Arcadius's gaze followed the movements of her fingers like he was hypnotized.

"How do you think I'd look in it?" she asked softly.

Her answer came in the sudden flush that washed up his cheeks. The color deepened when he saw her notice it.

"Well," she said on a low chuckle. "You'd better tell me that spell, hadn't you?"

He pointed to the place where the incantation was stamped onto a strap.

"I expect I take my clothes off first?"

"Yes," he said throatily.

The men watched as she disrobed, neither trying to hide his fascination with her body. Their genitals filled and jerked, at least half-mast by the time she finished. That was good for her confidence. When all her garments were pooled around her feet, she lifted the harness and read the words.

Garb me, the enchantment said, *if it pleases the Source of all pleasure.*

The magic must have been coded into the straps. She only had to recite the incantation once and the leather slapped securely but not hurtfully around her.

The harness fit as if it were designed for her. One strap covered her contracting nipples, while others tilted her small breasts upward. Bands circled different portions of her body: her waist, her arms, her thighs and knees and ankles. Apart from the leather strips, she was bare.

Their constriction was weirdly empowering. She felt like a perverted gladiator—and probably looked like one. A *V* of leather drew attention to the triangle at her groin. The straps passed between her thighs and around her butt, tightening beneath her cheeks so that they were lifted up. She was sharply aware of her various erogenous zones. The men's awareness of them seemed sharper too. They were more erect than before. The spots where Cade's fingers gripped his knees had paled.

Seeing that, Elyse's pussy went soft and wet.

"Well," Arcadius said, rubbing his chin in bemusement. "That outfit certainly suits you."

"It suits you, *mistress*," she corrected.

"Mistress," he conceded, inclining his head. He remained a bit sardonic. Elyse would have to address that.

"Get on the bed," she ordered. "Stretched out on your front."

"Me?" Arcadius pointed to himself.

"Yes, you. You're my subject. He's just my assistant."

She'd said she needed Cade's muscle, but Arcadius moved into position without being urged further. Perhaps he wanted to avoid wrestling with himself.

She noticed he had to lift his hips to settle his hard-on beneath him.

"Arms up and out. You may look at me but don't speak."

He almost did speak, but pressed his lips together at the last moment. His reaction seemed irritated, which she told herself was an improvement. He was beginning to take this seriously. She dug two chains out of the treasure box. Their rattle caused him to jerk reflexively. The sultan's carved and gilded bedframe seemed too fancy to risk damaging it. She used the spells she found on the chains to anchor them to the floor instead. The opposite ends of the links held rings. She tossed one of these to Cade. He caught it without fumbling but looked surprised.

"Spell that onto his left wrist."

Cade obeyed. Elyse took Arcadius's right arm, sliding the bracelet gently over his clenched fist. His head craned around to watch her, his gaze cautious. She stroked his knuckles, silently coaxing him to relax. Seeming reluctant, Arcadius straightened his long fingers.

"You have beautiful hands," she said as she continued to caress them.

"I have scars."

She'd noticed them before—and that Cade had none. "The correct response is: thank you, mistress."

"Thank you, mistress," he said.

Elyse smiled. "When I spell this ring to clasp your wrist, you won't be able to smoke out of it, will you?"

"No, mistress."

"Does the one Cade attached to you hurt?"

"No, mistress. The chains aren't designed for pain."

Satisfied, she repeated the same spell as Cade. The second ring closed snugly around Arcadius's wrist.

He felt the imprisonment—at least psychologically. His body rolled, his wide, muscled shoulders coming off the bed. His hips followed. His cock was hard and red. He couldn't resist rubbing it on the mattress when he came down again.

"That won't do," she said, though she went hot all over watching him. "I didn't tell you to give yourself pleasure."

"Perhaps you should punish him," his double suggested.

She cocked her head at Cade.

"Mistress," he amended.

What was going through her lover's head? He'd locked down his expression the way Arcadius liked to. He was aroused, regardless, his fully-fledged erection pulsing straight up in front of him. The organ was powerful, its veins engorged and dark. She suspected Arcadius's cock was in a similar state.

Cade flushed when he saw her look at his.

"Will you imagine yourself in his place if I punish him?"

His diaphragm jerked with a quick breath. "Yes, mistress," he grated out.

For the first time, the title sounded natural in his mouth. Hearing that made the little swelling between her legs ache harder. Maybe there was more than she knew to this dominatrix thing.

"Is there a good toy for discipline in this box?"

"There's a whip," he said, his voice even rougher than before. "It's the same as we use on soldiers for serious infractions. It won't break skin. It simply feels as if it does."

He'd thought about this before . . . which meant Arcadius had as well.

She found the bullwhip among the jumble of other things. The tail was long braided leather, the stiffer handle portion thick. Cade wet his lips as she curled her fingers around the grip, the shape reminding her—ironically enough—of an erect penis. She shifted her attention to Arcadius. Sweat glistened on his gorgeous face. He rolled his lips together like he was tempted to lick them too. His hips shifted restlessly, almost but not quite buffing his cock on the bed again.

"I have a feeling," she said, "that you're too proud to admit if I hurt you more than I should."

His gaze sharpened. "Why would you worry about that?"

"Because I'd rather make you desperate for pleasure than for a surcease from pain. I think Cade had better tell me when you've had enough."

"You think he will?"

"I know he will. He understands you better than you do him, and he knows what I want from you."

"What do you want from me . . . mistress?"

Elyse dragged the tail of the whip down Arcadius's spine to the first rise of his buttocks. The strong muscles clenched as she flirted the leather into his crack. "I want what any mistress would: your complete surrender."

"You're fooling yourself if you think I'll give you that." He wasn't bragging, just stating what he thought was fact.

She drew the braided tail up the other way, causing him to grimace at the tickling sensation. The answer she needed came so easily she wasn't aware she'd searched for it. "I don't think that's true. I think you want someone to tell you what to do. I think that's why you let your mother order you to carry those loads of firewood around your village when you were young. You believed doing what she said would turn you into a good soldier. 'Arcadius the Burro' wanted her approval."

Arcadius's face tightened. He didn't appreciate Cade having told her this private story, though it had been Cade's childhood too. Elyse ignored his displeasure and leaned closer to his ear.

"I'll tell you another secret." She laid the hand that held the whip across his tailbone. His skin was hot, his pulse beating strongly everywhere. She dropped the truth bomb on him in a whisper. "It doesn't matter that I'm a human. You want my approval too."

"Shh," she said when he opened his mouth to argue. "If you fight me, I'll assume you want more punishment."

He closed his mouth and glared.

"You're beautiful when you're angry," she teased.

With the aid of the footboard, she climbed onto the bed. She nudged Arcadius's calf with her toes. "Spread your legs. I want to stand between them."

He spread them and she stepped over. He couldn't watch her now because she was directly behind him. Cade's attention would have to satisfy her need for an audience. She stroked the length of the whip thoughtfully. "I suppose I should test this out before I use it. I imagine it's something like fly-fishing."

Either it was or the whip was spelled to allow any user to wield it successfully. Her first attempt produced a beautiful cracking in the air. Arcadius tensed but didn't jerk.

Please God, don't let me really hurt him, she prayed.

She brought the lash down across his shoulders. Arcadius hissed as a stripe of pink appeared and then almost instantly vanished from his skin. She glanced over at Cade. He nodded, letting her know that hadn't been too much. She brought the whip down the other way, crisscrossing the stripe that had disappeared.

Arcadius sucked in air again. "Is that all you've got?" he goaded.

"I have what I decide to have," she countered. "I control what happens here."

She felt in control of herself. Neither angry nor afraid, she stepped back on the soft mattress so she could reach more of him. She made the whip whistle onto his back six times more. As a soldier, he was used to refusing to let pain weaken him. This wasn't simply pride: it was him proving he was man. If she wavered, she wouldn't win the prize she was aiming for. Trusting Cade to warn her if she went too far, she licked the leather more determinedly across his buttocks. Arcadius took six lashes, his jerks of response increasing, though he made no more sounds.

"That's the idea," Cade said softly.

She didn't look at him. She brought the whip down a seventh time. The most vibrant welt yet appeared and faded. An idea came to her of how to make the experience more powerful for him.

"You're mine, recruit," she barked.

She didn't know if it was the final whip stroke or her choice of words, but Arcadius clenched his ass and groaned.

The sound went through her like a caress—deep and low and unmistakably aroused. The same instinct as before gripped her mind and her arm muscles. This was what he needed. This was what she had to do.

Once more, she thought, raising her arm and slashing it sharply down.

Her victim writhed with abandon on the covers.

"Be still," she ordered in her harshest voice.

Arcadius ceased moving and just panted.

"Better," she said grudgingly. "Though I suspect you need more discipline."

She put her foot on his cheeks, her weight pushing his hips deeper into the mattress. If he were as excited as she suspected, this would feel both bad and good. Arcadius groaned again.

"That's right," she said. "This ass is mine, soldier."

"Don't." His voice was so soft Elyse barely heard the plea.

"*Don't?*" she repeated in disbelief, fully immersed in her role of sexual drill sergeant. She dropped to her palms and knees. Her fingers still clenched the bullwhip. She threw it aside and drove her hand under his pelvis. He gasped when she found him. His cock was so hard it shuddered. She gripped it tightly and pulled one long stroke up the pounding shaft. "This is saying *do,* soldier. This is saying *pretty please.*"

She let him go abruptly.

"Fuck," he breathed, his whole body shaken by sensual tremors.

"Now that request I can fulfill." She turned to Cade, who was watching her openmouthed. Shock wasn't his only reaction. His penis was shuddering too. "Dig out the box of dildos."

"Don't," Arcadius repeated.

Elyse reared up and spanked his ass with her open palm. She didn't hold back. She was certain this didn't hurt like the whip. It was, however, more personal. "There's only one man here who I trust to tell me *no,* and—forgive me—but you aren't him."

Arcadius twisted his head around. Sweat rolled down his near temple. "You put him ahead of me?"

"Don't kid yourself. I'm doing you a favor, and both of you know it. He'd pay to be where you are right now."

"Then he's an idiot."

"He's you, Arcadius. He knows all your dark secrets—all the things you've ever wanted but never dared to say. The difference is he's not afraid to embrace them."

"I'm not afraid of anything."

She almost spanked him again but stopped. The angry glint in his eyes was too close to an *I dare you.*

"That's interesting," she observed. "You'd rather I hit you than pleasure you anally."

Taking this as his cue, Cade handed her a dildo carved of cobalt semi-translucent stone—possibly an actual sapphire. Djinn did like real gemstones. "The size of this one seems good."

Arcadius looked at it, then clamped his mouth tightly shut. He wasn't denying his double had chosen well. Tellingly, he didn't look away when she tapped the smooth object against her lips. He might dread what was happening, but he didn't really want to escape.

"This dildo has a nice shape, doesn't it?" she asked. "The way it curves. The rounded flare beneath the head. I bet it feels like a real penis going in. Like you're really submitting to being fucked."

"I am not a lover of men."

His protest was surly but shaken. She dragged the tip of the dildo down the perspiring channel of his spine. "Who says you have to be? It's a symbol of submission. Submission to me, in this case."

"Maybe I should lubricate him," Cade volunteered.

That was an interesting suggestion, considering Arcadius's recent objection.

"We're . . . linked up again," he explained, blushing. "I can tell exactly what he likes best."

This revelation sent a long hard tingle up her most erotic nerves. "That's a convenient development." She studied him, waiting patiently for her decision. Cade was going along with this game more voluntarily than his double, but she sensed he wasn't quite his normal self. Part of this wasn't pretend for him.

"No," she said. "I prefer to prepare this recruit myself. I'll enjoy it twice as much knowing I'm affecting both of you. You can ensure he doesn't hide anything from me."

Cade didn't have to say *yes, mistress*. She read that in the respectful manner with which he bowed his head.

~

Arcadius couldn't grit his teeth hard enough to stop his body from reacting. He didn't want what he knew was coming but also couldn't bear to wait. The link with Cade made it worse. He craved everything for two.

Get it over with, he thought, desiring and dreading Elyse's next touch on him.

She was right. Taking the whipping had been easier for him.

That was over, though the jolts of pain seemed to have wakened every nerve he had. Hot chills chased in waves down his trembling spine and limbs. His groin was pounding, silky wetness seeping steadily from his slit. The sound of Elyse unscrewing the lid of an unguent jar inspired a further shiver of excitement. He hid his face in the covers under him. Though that was cowardly, he couldn't stop himself.

Two of her fingers spread warm slick lubricant down his crack. When they rubbed his asshole, hot chills became hot tingles.

"Stop clenching," she said. "You're a soldier. You can take anything."

He was so tense he didn't think he could relax. One slender finger pushed into him anyway. He groaned at the sensation. The slow penetration was intensely pleasurable, more than he expected. He'd never had this done to him. No woman had ever tried. Did Elyse want to because human females had no proper sense of place?

Was that what made it—and her—so exciting?

He gasped as she continued rubbing, his head arching off the bed with enjoyment. She leaned closer, her harness-covered breasts touching his back lightly.

"You see," she said. "You like giving in to me."

"No." he said. He didn't mean it, but something about denying her claim was thrilling—as if striving against her was part of the excitement.

"Yes," she contradicted, her teeth closing on his nape in a quick light nip. He'd done that to her in the closet. Now it seemed she was claiming him. The way that made him feel, the bone-deep longing for it to be true, threatened to strip him to his soul. He couldn't let that happen, not when this was simply an exercise.

"Get on with it," he growled.

"Get on with what?" she responded mockingly.

"Get on with fucking me, *mistress*." The shudder that rolled through him as he addressed her by the title put the lie to his belligerence. He cursed silently.

He might as well have begged her.

She laughed the same as if he had. "I'll get on with fucking you, recruit. I just hope you're man enough to take it."

She moved back, wet slapping noises informing him she was slathering the dildo.

"You need a cushion for your hips," she announced. "Cade, put one under him."

Cade got a name. Arcadius was only *soldier* or *recruit.*

Chains rattled as Cade lifted him at the waist. The bolster he shoved under him tilted his ass upward. The position was hardly one of authority. Arcadius should have fought it. God forbid any of his men saw him offered up like this. Instead he hitched his legs wider and panted.

"Did I tell you to do that?" She struck his cheeks openhanded, putting enough strength behind the action that it didn't seem like play. Each smack resounded through him, driving the heat that wasn't pain deep inside.

"Sorry, mistress," he said.

She quickened the rain of blows. "You're not sorry. You want this."

He grunted when she stopped, every sexual part of him seeming to expand and contract in its own rhythm. To his amazement, she pressed her lips gently to his ass.

Was it an insult, or did she mean the kiss to be tender?

"Now you're ready for me," she said.

She pressed the dildo's head against his hole. The stone was warm, perhaps from her holding it. It was slick as well, easing the flared tip past his constriction. She pushed, and the hard smooth bulb glided farther in. A sound broke in his throat that wasn't a complaint. The toy filled him more completely than her finger. Cade let out a muted version of his moan. Obviously, the echoes of his sensations were reaching the double.

When the toy crossed his prostate, Arcadius gave up caring what anyone but him experienced.

"You're mine," Elyse whispered—those words his hidden heart wanted to believe. "You and your ass belong to me."

She drew the dildo back within his tingling passage, fucking him slowly, deeply with the warm stone penis. He moaned louder, his hips beginning to rock back to get more from her motions. On every level, he was at her mercy.

"Tell me you're mine," she ordered.

"I'm not," he lied.

"Shall I stop?" She suited action to word.

Arcadius clenched his jaw.

"Perhaps I should remind you what you're missing." She stroked the dildo in and out a single time. Stimulated all too briefly, his prostate cried for more. His testicles clenched with readiness.

Someone besides himself knew this.

"Tug his balls," his traitor double suggested.

Their mistress reached under him. The oiled hand that caught and massaged his sac was as bold as the rest of her. Though she was a small woman, no one could mistake her fingers for those of a female who was pampered. He believed then that she took care of a residence—that she hammered and shoveled and repaired things. That seemed a good thing to his secret self. She had strength and didn't hesitate to use it. He sucked in a breath as she hurt him just a bit. Maybe he shouldn't have reacted. The next time her fingers surrounded his scrotal sac and pulled, the pressure was perfect.

The slow tug made him want to come that second, to have her fuck him with the dildo until it happened. He couldn't reach backward to urge her on. The chains didn't allow his arms to move far enough. Wound up by that too, he squirmed helplessly.

The word "please" burst unwillingly from him.

"There is no *please*. There's only *I'm yours, mistress*."

Her voice was hard. He struggled two more delicious seconds and then gave in. "I'm yours, mistress."

"Very well," she said. "I'll give you what you need."

The warm stone penis went into him again. She positioned herself behind it as if the appendage belonged to her. When her hand pushed it inward, her hips followed. Her thighs were smooth where they hit the backs of his. She used her left arm to prop herself above him. His ribcage was right beside it and nothing about her arm's shape said anything but *female*. All these things underscored the fact that a woman was fucking him.

The effect that had on his mind and body drew a long moan from him.

"You're close," she murmured beside his ear. "That's the sound *he* makes."

He growled, his hands clenching on the chains. He didn't want the reminder of his rival, though in truth it heightened his feelings of imminence. He was so close to coming he was about to scream.

"Finish me," he demanded. "Fucking finish me, mistress."

She laughed and picked up the pace. His head flung back, his ass writhing on the hardness that went in and out of him. The outermost inches of his passage tingled and itched at the quick friction. The good sensations shot much further than what she touched, as if the vigor of her strokes propelled them deep into his body. His cock jerked with pleasure, though she wasn't touching that. He didn't want her to. He wanted her to bring him off through tormenting a different ache: the ache that proved she'd driven him to submit.

"There," he snarled as she ran over his inner sweet spot just so. "*There*."

She knew what he meant. She shimmied the dildo's head over and over the hidden swelling, as if she meant to wear it smooth. He gasped, needing to regain the air the uptick in his pleasure stole. What she did felt insanely nice. The sharpness of the almost-climax was too much, and yet the last thing he wanted was for her to stop doing exactly what she was. He tried to say *yes* and could only groan.

"My God, you're sexy," she praised.

He loved that she approved. His body gathered and clenched and then he went like the fuse on a bomb catching fire. Seed shot from him onto the sultan's bed, the violence of the ejaculation both delicious and shocking. Goosebumps rolled along his skin at the force of it, and the hair on his arms stood up. He collapsed as the climax ended, his strained muscles giving out. He was sweating like a pig and utterly relaxed. The only thing that could have improved his afterglow was if Elyse had sagged down on top of him.

She sat back on her feet instead, gently pulling out the dildo. "He came without you this time," she said.

Arcadius couldn't remember why that was worth noting.

~

Elyse had rocked Cade to his foundations. He hadn't known she had this in her. She'd gotten him—the other him—to submit to her. Cade knew genuine surrender when he heard it. Now he knew how it sounded groaned out from his own throat.

I'm yours, mistress.

Arcadius had truly meant the words.

Just as astonishing was the effect her victory had on him. Cade was a man of action. Voyeurism wasn't his fantasy of choice. Nonetheless, more than the link with his double gripped him. Yes, he'd caught the fallout of Arcadius's sensations, but he'd experienced plenty of his own. Standing there stark naked, watching the woman he loved subdue his mirror image, caused sweat to break out on his body. His cock was harder than he'd known it could get. When Arcadius came, he was unable to look away. A normal man would have ground his dick on the hip bolster. The other him hadn't. Instead, he'd let Elyse and her dildo push him over the precipice. Seeing him come made Cade desire things he couldn't put in words. Certainly, what he'd wanted was more complicated than a release.

Maybe Cade had fantasies he hadn't guessed at yet.

Elyse sat back, her adorable butt resting on her heels. The strappy leather outfit suited her lean body. She was a human sex assassin, designed to devastate helpless males. Cade's hands fisted at his sides. Did he want her to devastate him too?

"He came without you this time," she said.

"Yes." He locked his eyes onto hers. "I guess he healed from his injuries."

"You still felt what he did."

"Yes," he said. "Much of it."

Elyse's gaze slid to his rigid erection and back up to his face. She licked the soft pink lips that had gotten his lust going since the day they met. "Do you want to come?"

His desire crystalized in a series of erotic images, his cock jolting with each one.

"I want to make you come," he said hoarsely. "I want to lay you across him and make you moan with pleasure."

Her eyes widened. "Across him . . ."

She touched Arcadius's hip. His double lay like a toppled tree. Now his head twisted on the pillow to look at Cade. Someone who didn't see that face in a mirror every morning might have mistaken the sharpening of his gaze for anger. Cade knew better. Cade could read how very interested his doppelganger was.

"We should take Elyse together," Cade said, absolutely convinced of it. "We should intensify her pleasure the same way she did for us."

"I'm done in," Arcadius cautioned, though Cade noticed his butt cheeks tensed.

"That won't matter. She'll enjoy feeling you under her. You can be the bed I fuck her on."

Arcadius's eyes probed his a second longer. "Do it. Fuck her nice and hard for me."

Elyse let out a startled *oh*. Because it didn't seem to indicate reluctance, Cade gripped her beneath the arms. He lifted her negligible weight, laying her across the dip of Arcadius's back.

"Oh," she said again as he stretched over both of them.

He'd taken her by surprise. Her legs weren't splayed wide enough to fit his hips between. He pulled them apart firmly. Sliding his fingers up her silky inner thighs was irresistible. He played the pads of his thumbs along the valleys between her legs and her labia. As he'd expected, mastering Arcadius had excited her. Her wetness overflowed her folds. He pushed the plump flesh into her pubic bone, rubbing it up and down, tugging at her clitoris without actually touching it.

Elyse inhaled sharply and grew wetter.

"He wants me to do this hard," he warned.

"I, um, wouldn't mind that," she admitted.

Her body lifted. Arcadius had shifted under her, like he might not be as *done in* as he'd thought. Cade swung one knee onto the covers, his other foot planted firmly on the carpet. Elyse's hands skated up and down his ribs. Taking her when she was this eager was going to be good.

"You're mine," he said, echoing her.

She crooked her legs behind him as he fit himself to her entrance. Her gaze held his as he pushed in. Penetrating her felt incredible. She was soft and hot and wet enough that her inner tightness was no barrier to his highly excited state. Cade tried not to lose his breath, but the streaks of bliss sparking in his cock made it difficult. Reaching her end caused her eyes to close and her sheath to flicker. He gripped her bottom to steady her for what he intended next.

Her heels dug in behind him.

Don't warn her, he thought. *She's already given you permission. Take her like you and Arcadius want to.*

Seeing his resolve, she bit her lip. Cade dragged back within her slowly, teasingly, then let his stored-up desires loose. He pumped his hips like he'd go right through her, like it wasn't enough to fuck her pussy—he had to reach her heart. To overwhelm her was the prize he craved, to claim her as his in truth. Confusing matters was the fact that he wanted this for Arcadius too. Cade needed to possess her for both of them. He didn't care if this was the influence of the link. He drove into her with absolute single-mindedness.

The unsteadiness of their platform didn't hamper him at all.

She began to cry out with pleasure. Cade answered her with groans. Her fingers dug into his shoulders, then shifted to his butt, urging his efforts on. He wanted her to have everything she desired and more. He changed the tilt of his pelvis, each crazed stroke catching her higher, where her passage was sensitive. She came, and he simply went faster. Licks of sharp white heat ran up his dick and balls. He was going to go. He couldn't hold on longer. He sucked a breath and tried to anyway. Arcadius groaned and heaved beneath both of them.

The chains that held him clashed as his need to move caused him to yank them straight.

Elyse squirmed on his double's back. Cade wondered how that felt for both of them. Arousing, probably. Arcadius jerked in telltale motions against the bed. Obviously, he was too excited not to try to get off with them.

Cade was sure Elyse noticed.

"*Cade*," she groaned, her whole body arching with orgasm.

That was it for him. He jammed inside her, the licks of heat that had been lashing him blazing out. He came lengthily.

"Cade," she sighed more softly.

One of her hands fell from him. He pushed up to check that she was all right. She seemed to be. Her face had flushed with pleasure, dark curls clinging at her hairline, lovely green eyes as lustrous as a djinni's. The hand she'd pulled away from him rubbed Arcadius's outstretched and still chained arm. The leather straps that wrapped hers created the impression that she was bound as well.

"We should get those chains off him," Cade said.

"'m fine," Arcadius mumbled with a lassitude that suggested he'd climaxed too.

"Go ahead," Elyse said to Cade, ignoring the other man's refusal.

Cade kissed her cheek and pulled gently out of her.

Arcadius groaned a small complaint when Elyse sat up.

She laughed at that. "We must have squished you."

"Didn't care," was all he allowed himself to admit.

She climbed over him to release the chain she'd spelled on. Cade noted she reversed the magic like an old hand at it. Thinking it might be better not to make her self-conscious, he didn't point this out.

Arcadius rolled over once he was free, then sat up and rubbed his wrists. Elyse remained kneeling beside him.

"Did that hurt?" she asked.

He shook his head. "The marks are already fading."

She took his hand and looked. As she touched him, Arcadius was suddenly the one who looked self-conscious. Elyse peered into his eyes. "Are you okay?"

They all knew she wasn't talking about his wrists.

"Yes." He hesitated. "I enjoyed that."

"Thank you for trusting me," Elyse said shyly.

Arcadius furrowed his brow, seeming confused by her changed demeanor. She wasn't a dominatrix now. "You did a good job. I promise you, I wasn't helping you along."

She smiled and rubbed her forehead. "Well, um, good. I enjoyed it too."

"Good." Arcadius scooted toward the mattress edge. "I'll get out of your way."

Elyse shot Cade a concerned look. Cade was pretty sure he understood its meaning.

"You're not in our way," he said.

"I'm healed now. I can return to my rooms."

Cade should have welcomed his departure. Maybe if the pleasure they'd shared hadn't dulled his sense of rivalry, he would have. "You don't have to spend tonight alone."

Arcadius snorted. "Since when have I dreaded that?"

"Never," Cade said. "Except when a little corner of you has."

The other him pretended to ignore that. He found his trousers and pulled them on.

"What if we need you?" Elyse said. "For planning or suppose there's an attack? Wouldn't it be better if you were close by?"

Arcadius shook wrinkles from his tunic. "I'd sense if Cade were alarmed. I could smoke here in an instant."

"Could you?"

"Yes." He met her gaze with a crooked smile. "Being your guinea pig all day seems to have fixed that problem."

Elyse frowned, probably not realizing how adorable the scowl was on her. More or less dressed, Arcadius cupped the side of her face. Seeing the connection between them made Cade feel . . . not displeasure but off balance. Elyse felt things for Arcadius that were separate and different from what she felt for him.

This also seemed true for Arcadius. His emotions for Elyse weren't the same as Cade's. His expression was that of a fond uncle—as if he were more comfortable regarding her as a young person who wasn't his equal. Cade knew better. He'd experienced firsthand how brave and capable Elyse was.

"I'm fine," Arcadius said. "You and Cade need your privacy."

Her mouth twisted out of shape. Cade suspected she wanted to argue. In the end, she let Arcadius have his way. "You'll come back first thing tomorrow?"

"First thing," he promised.

~

Arcadius paused outside the doors to Iksander's chambers and looked back. Now that he was alone, he allowed himself second thoughts. He could change his mind about spending the night with them. Elyse had invited him, and Cade hadn't protested.

He wondered at that. *Was* the other him a better person? More generous and less territorial? As to that, maybe Arcadius was changing. He'd never put himself in a woman's power the way he'd put himself in Elyse's. He wasn't sure, but he thought his double's presence had made it easier.

Cade hadn't seemed like a rival in those moments. Arcadius had trusted his double to have his back.

Was it strange or simply horribly narcissistic to consider a version of yourself a potential friend?

He wagged his head and forced himself to walk off. He was a soldier, not a philosopher. He'd think about these questions when there weren't more pressing issues to consider.

CHAPTER EIGHT

THE following morning, Elyse, Joseph, and the two commanders met up with Vizier Murat in his office in the main palace. As might be expected for a space that entertained dignitaries, the decor exhibited the djinn's love for excessive furnishings.

Elyse couldn't help goggling at an odd globe on the corner of Murat's desk. Its shape wasn't a ball but a wide circular ribbon. The usual brown bumps stood for mountain ranges with green swaths for fertile plains. What really caught her eye was that the various landmasses were animated, seeming to float on an ocean of realistically swirling clouds.

Cade had warned her the lands of djinn didn't have the sort of geographical locations she was used to.

Understandably, the vizier's attention was on the commanders. The dignified white-haired man leaned back in his tall desk chair. "I assume we're meeting because you've decided you kept me in the dark long enough."

"We didn't mean to insult you," Cade said. "You had plenty on your plate already."

Murat waved the words away. "Never mind that. Just tell me what you've been dealing with."

They told him about the missing young people and the plan to catch Yasmin's brother in Victory Park.

"Myself, Cade, and Joseph are taking part," Arcadius said. "If worse comes to worse and something happens to all of us, you need to be prepared to take the reins."

The calmness with which Arcadius mentioned this potential catastrophe caused Murat's brows to shoot up. "You're too kind," he returned. "If the three of you do die, I'm sure having the hours between now and midnight to 'prepare' will make all the difference."

"We need to handle this ourselves," Arcadius said. "The threat Ramis and the human sorcerer pose to our city might seem slight, but it's significant. We cannot allow our people, however humble their origins, to be nabbed for unknown nefarious purposes. This plot needs to be stopped before it grows larger."

"And no one can be trusted to stop it but the city's three most irreplaceable personnel?"

"Not really," Cade said.

"Not really," Arcadius agreed.

The vizier laughed wearily. "Very well. If you want to get to the park unnoticed, you should use the underground waterways."

The two commanders stiffened. "What underground waterways?" they demanded in unison.

Murat smiled. "They're part of an old cistern system we don't use anymore. The sultan who ruled prior to Iksander's father magically shielded them from discovery. The waterways are how Iksander eluded the tails you put on him when he wanted to temporarily escape his responsibilities."

"They're navigable?" Arcadius asked. "And you have a map?"

"Yes and yes," Murat said. "Iksander was sensible enough to want someone to be able to find him if his adventuring went awry."

Both commanders appeared annoyed by this reminder.

"If you wish," Murat said, smoothly ignoring this, "I can arrange for Yasmin to be called away from the harem on a family emergency. The sultana might check her story but probably not right away. You'll have time to work out the details of your strategy."

"That would be useful," Arcadius admitted.

"Thank you for thinking of it," Cade added.

Joseph cut off a coughing noise that could have been laughter.

"Are *you* ready for this, young lady?" Murat suddenly asked her. "An important part of this plan seems to depend on you."

Elyse had grown used to being invisible. Was she ready? Her recent experiences with Cade and Arcadius had given her more confidence, but would it be enough?

"She's ready," Arcadius answered before she could. "In truth, if she weren't on our side, we'd have to put her on a watch list right after Mario."

Elyse gaped at him. Was he trying to buck her up or did he actually think she was dangerous?

"Very well," Murat said, taking him at his word. "I'll do my bit to move this scheme forward."

~

Because so few djinn knew the old waterways existed, it made sense to set their final meet-up in the palace's main cistern. The antique glow lights were dusty but still functioned. Their blue-tinged illumination revealed an underground chamber that reminded Cade of a pagan temple, with long lines of marble columns, a tall cathedral ceiling, and three feet of surprisingly clear water covering the tiled basin. The former reservoir was grimier than most places in the Glorious City, and the squeaks that occasionally echoed through the shadowy space suggested rats had taken up residence. As in a temple, more than the absence of noise created an atmosphere of quiet.

They probably didn't need to, but they spoke in hushed voices.

The harem girl, Yasmin, was allowing Joseph to fit her with a listening device disguised as a pearl earring. Because Joseph was being careful not to touch her familiarly, securing the thing was taking a while. Like the rest of their compact group, Yasmin wore muted color robes. In the daytime, this would have made her stand out. At night, it was camouflage.

Cade found himself wondering what was going through her head. In their eagerness to set this trap, they hadn't asked themselves how reliable she'd be. She seemed nervous but was controlling it. Part of this must be due to being in the company of males who were neither her family nor her consort. She also might be worrying if she could trick her brother. Cade hoped she didn't have second thoughts while they were underway. Loyalty among siblings wasn't necessarily logical.

Joseph finished securing the pearls in Yasmin's ears and stepped back from her. One of her hands went anxiously to the enchanted one.

"You're sure Ramis won't sense the eavesdropping spell?" she asked. "I know you shrank it, but my brother has a sharp nose for magic."

"Elyse is going to help with that," Joseph said. Elyse jumped and then took the piece of parchment Joseph was holding out to her. "This is a concealment spell. Nothing tricky. Just read the words. I've already created a little channel for them to run into." He turned back to Yasmin. "No matter how adept your brother is, her human power will keep him from spotting what we've done."

Elyse read the words. Cade didn't sense anything happening, but Joseph nodded as if what *he* sensed had satisfied.

"Perfect," he said, taking the paper back. He addressed the harem girl. "All you have to do is keep your brother talking long enough for Elyse to suck him into her brass vessel. We won't be able to speak to you, but we'll hear everything. Tell Ramis whatever feels natural, whatever you think he wants to hear. We're not looking for a confession, just sufficient time for Elyse to perform the spell. We'll have guards posted in hidden places around the park. If you seem to be in danger, they'll move in."

"But don't try to find the guards," Cade said, aware that this was difficult for civilians to resist.

Yasmin's anxious hand shifted to her throat. "Just act natural."

"Don't worry too much about that either," Cade advised. "Your brother hasn't seen you in a long time. You two don't have a natural mode anymore.

He won't think it's strange if you're nervous. You'll be out alone at night—and not just in your cat form."

"So don't be nervous if I'm nervous."

"Exactly," Cade confirmed.

Ever vigilant, Arcadius had been watching their surroundings and not Yasmin. As a result, he heard the muted footsteps first. "The guards are coming," he announced.

They'd recruited three to serve as additional backup. They emerged from the base of the secret staircase, robed in black and well armed with throwing knives. Yasmin veiled her face hastily. Cade glanced around. Everyone appeared to be ready.

"All right," he said. "Time to saddle up."

His double gave him a funny look. "We don't have saddles."

Cade had soaked up more human idiom than he realized. "I mean mount our carpets."

"We're not wading?" Elyse asked.

"No," he said. "That wouldn't be efficient. And as you can see, one of the guards brought a roll of rugs."

"Good." She sounded relieved. "I saw fish in that water."

"They're minnows."

"I don't want them sneaking up on me and nibbling my toes."

Cade broke into a laugh. Of all the things to make her afraid . . . "You can ride with me if you wish. I'll protect you."

She grinned, her face lighting up like a ray of sun. "You're my hero."

Affection welled potently inside him. He loved that she could joke at a time like this, loved everything about her actually. The silly reasons seemed as important as the serious. *I'm lucky,* he thought. No matter what they risked, he was glad in that moment that she was there. These shared experiences bound them together, helping each understand what made the other tick. His lingering unease about Arcadius fell away. Elyse was his, no fooling.

Despite the witnesses all around, he couldn't resist bending down to lightly kiss her cheek. Elyse gave *his* cheek an answering pat. She was still smiling when he pulled back.

Love you, her lips shaped secretly to him.

Or maybe not so secretly. As he straightened, he caught Yasmin staring at them. Though her face was covered, the expression in her eyes was wistful.

"If you're done billing and cooing," Arcadius said dryly, "I'd like to set up in the park *before* our target arrives."

~

Cade didn't expect to encounter trouble, and happily this proved true. Their squadron of flying carpets glided through the tunnels without getting lost, ambushed, or eaten by minnows.

The trip was short. Victory Park was in the palace sector, conveniently close to one of the forgotten waterway's exits. The three guards left first, smoking up a hidden set of steps a block away from the city's premiere green space. The guards would take up positions on different ministry building roofs, from which they'd survey the meeting place. Arcadius smoked out behind them, returning minutes later to report on conditions.

"Your brother isn't here yet," he told Yasmin. "Or not that I can tell. The last of the enchanted statues have been removed, but the landscaping and the monuments might offer hiding spots. Chances are, he'll watch you approach to ensure you've come alone."

Yasmin nodded, her nervousness apparent even in her concealing clothes.

"You'll be fine," Arcadius said, surprising Cade a bit with his warmth. "Go ahead and change into your cat form."

Yasmin did and immediately bounded up the crumbly steps. Arcadius turned to Cade and Elyse. "You two are ready?"

Cade didn't waste breath pointing out that his double wasn't in charge of them.

"We're ready," he confirmed. "Joseph will unlock the spells he set on the Arch of Triumph, and Elyse and I will climb to the portal room."

The Arch of Triumph straddled the Avenue of Palms and overlooked the park. The portal room itself had no windows, but a small gallery behind it would provide him and Elyse a view.

"And you?" Arcadius asked Joseph.

"I circle the park in vapor form and watch for Mario." His tone was as patient as Cade's had been. "If the human sorcerer shows up, I notify you or Cade."

"Good," Arcadius said. "I'll be on the roof of the Ministry of Transport." He thrust one finger toward Cade for emphasis. "Use our link if you need to. I can be with you in an instant."

"I will," Cade promised and meant it. When it came to watching out for Elyse, he wouldn't hesitate to call his original for backup.

~

"Brr," Elyse said as she and Cade went into the portal room. "This place is creepy."

The hollow was built into the top of the giant arch. Despite being high in the air, the worn stone floor and cracked tiling reminded her of a derelict subway stop—one where psychotic villains dragged their exsanguinated victims to mummify. She could *almost* see the guttering energy of the portal, the suspended flicker there and then gone at the corner of her eye.

"This space wasn't meant to be used," Cade explained absently. His palm cupped a tiny glow he'd created with magic, and he was checking the room's corners. "The previous sultan decided to establish a door to your dimension here because the structure is easy to secure."

Secure wasn't what Elyse felt. The skin along her shoulders crawled, and tiny goosebumps washed up her arms.

"Sheesh," she said, catching sight of a ghost-shaped hump draped in a white sheet. "Is that Joseph's statue?"

"Yes. Arcadius must have covered it when he woke."

Joseph's statue held a kneeling position. Elyse experienced a weird compulsion to lift the cloth and peek at the stone version of her friend. That would be rude, right? She should probably leave his copy alone.

She jumped when Cade's warm hand squeezed the ball of her shoulder.

"He's perfectly fine there. Certainly not aware that anything's going on." He rubbed her arm. "I know this place seems strange, but don't let your imagination give you the jitters."

She hugged the brass vase she was carrying a bit tighter. "Right. I'm just going to concentrate on what I need to do."

"You're ready," he said, sounding sure of it. He jerked his head to the side. "The observation gallery is this way."

There was a door with a metal knob. Cade yanked it open, displacing a puff of dust. He let the little light he carried wink out before he went through.

The narrow gallery the door led to was enclosed, but a series of decorative piercings in the stone created a screen where the arch loomed above the park. The view of the avenue and the green space was unobstructed, and they could see without being seen. Because this seemed so handy, Elyse conjectured the gallery had been used as a spy post before. Better still, the rays of a near-half moon allowed her to move along the passage without tripping. She was glad she'd memorized the pattern of the Solomon seal on her brass container. That design was no longer distinct to her human eyes.

She noticed Cade propped the door to the portal room open behind them. "Sightlines," he said. "Best not to let someone approach from the rear unseen. Not that they could. Joseph refreshed the locks after he let us in."

"But better safe than sorry?" Elyse suggested.

He smiled, pleased she'd understood. He dug in the pocket of his military style trousers. When his hand came out, he held two marble-sized creamy pearls.

"Take one," he said. "Joseph linked them to Yasmin's earrings. If you hold it close to your ear, you'll hear what she and her brother say. Sorry I only have one pair of binoculars. We could take turns, but I think I should probably keep them."

"You're the professional," she said, not at all offended. "Just warn me when Ramis arrives."

Cade positioned himself in front of an opening and put the lenses to his eyes. Fortunately, some of the holes in the screen were low enough for her.

He was right to urge her not to worry. They seemed far from danger here. The palm-dotted park spread out quite a ways below and in front of them. She spied a pretty swirl of paths and flowerbeds that was probably the Sultan's Circle Yasmin's brother mentioned in his instructions. At the moment, it was empty of everything but shadows.

"I've been meaning to ask," Cade said from beside her. "That name, Ramis, does it seem strange to you?"

"Well, I'm more used to names like Sam or Dave, but, no, I can't say it does."

"I feel like I should know it." He focused the binoculars. "I wonder if we crossed paths before he turned ifrit."

She didn't get a chance to come up with a response. His shoulders straightened abruptly. "There's Yasmin's cat. She's nosing around the meeting place."

Elyse's heart rate picked up, a tingle of nervousness streaking across her palms.

Please God, she thought. *Help me to do this well.*

~

Yasmin found a patch of shadow beneath a palm where she changed into her normal form. She remained in the concealing darkness when she was done. The moonlight made the Sultan's Circle seem too bright to wait in.

Hanging back makes sense, she assured herself. *I wouldn't stand in the open for anyone to see no matter what I'd come here to accomplish.*

A twig snapped and she spun in the direction of the sound. She saw nothing. Maybe it was a rabbit that had frozen. *Don't look at the roofs,* she ordered. *Scan the park around you, like a normal person would.*

She scanned, her shoulders as tight as if they were made of iron. She felt as if crowds of people were watching her. She started to touch the earring Joseph had fastened in her earlobe, the one with the listening spell. Before her fingers reached it, she jerked her hand back down. Joseph was watching out for her and so were his friends. She could rely on that. She didn't need to add another prayer to the dozens she's already said.

God, she hoped Elyse the human could close the trap. Did the men recognize the irony of their strategy depending on two women?

"You came," said her brother's voice.

She turned the other way and saw him. Ramis was dressed in djinn robes tonight: rich silk layers in shades of black and gray. The moon caught his eyes, the glow it kindled in his irises pure silver. He seemed lovelier than the last time they'd met, lovelier than he'd been even as a boy. It occurred to her—belatedly—that the image she was seeing might be an illusion. He possessed a great deal of magic. Maybe he was using it to disguise a more monstrous appearance. What did people like her really know about ifrits?

"Of course I came," she said, trying to ignore the alarming possibilities pushing at her mind. "We haven't seen each other in a long time."

Smiling gently, he waved toward a bench shaded by the furled purple flowers of a jacaranda tree. "Shall we sit while we talk?"

Aware that the bench was in view of her watchers, Yasmin followed his suggestion. As she pressed her knees together and smoothed her robes, her joints were tight with tension. If Ramis noticed, he didn't remark on it.

"I have a gift for you," he said. "I hope you don't mind."

She didn't mind but she was surprised.

"It won't bite," he said, dangling a pretty printed wax paper bag. "It's Turkish Delight. From the shop in the spice market you used to like as a girl. I believe I remembered your favorite flavor."

She peeked inside the white tissue paper. "Honey lime with rose sugar! I haven't eaten these in ages. Ramis . . . " In spite of everything she knew he'd done, her throat closed with sentiment. The love she'd once felt for him was rising. She missed those days when the three of them were children. Simpler times, she supposed. "Thank you. You were thoughtful to remember."

"My memories of my family are all that sustain me now," he said.

She looked away from him and at her hands instead. Her fingers were pinching the small bag shut. Ramis seemed to realize he'd struck a discordant note.

"Well," he said, his palms rubbing at his knees. "I take it you managed to sneak back into the palace without getting caught last time?"

"Yes. I'm not important enough to watch closely."

"I'm sure that's not true." He shifted slightly on the bench. "And the investigation into our brother's disappearance? Have you taken your suspicions to the authorities?"

"It seems they were already looking into it," she answered, having decided this would account for the bodyguard that had been placed in the bath boy's room—which Ramis probably had noticed. She shook her head dolefully. "They didn't act as if my findings added anything to theirs."

She expected Ramis to press her for more details. He rubbed his knees again instead, staring into space as if she'd given him more to think about than she realized.

The silence made her nerves tighten. How long would Elyse's spell take to work? Yasmin didn't sense any magic yet. She could, however, feel a fat drop of sweat rolling down her spine.

After pausing a few more heartbeats, her brother spoke. "Are you happy, Yasmin?"

She didn't have to feign her jerk of shock. "What do you mean?"

"With your life." Ramis's gray eyes looked sympathetic as well as beautiful. "I don't mean to be insulting, but Mother and Father sold you into the harem to be a sultan's toy. Your acceptance there enhanced their status, but what did you get except—at most—a moment or two beneath a virtual stranger who wouldn't recall your name afterwards? What has the great Iksander done for you besides use you for his pleasure? Now that he's gone, you won't even have that much. Why do you owe them loyalty?"

"*Them*?" she asked faintly.

"Your masters," he said, waving one hand impatiently. "Everyone's masters here. No matter how soft your bed or how rich your clothes, you're their prisoner. Why not throw off their shackles? Why not build a free new life, one you can shape to suit your own desires?"

His questions were unexpectedly compelling. She'd barely been Iksander's lover, and she'd come to hate being a concubine. In her heart of hearts, she knew she deserved better.

This is how he seduced them, she thought. *How he got those children to willingly go with him.* But she couldn't give away that she knew.

"I don't . . . understand," she said haltingly.

Ramis's silver gaze gleamed with intensity. "What if I told you Balu was alive and I know where he is?"

"What?" Her hand pressed her chest, her heart thudding beneath her palm.

He took her other hand and squeezed it. "Come with me. The three of us can be a family in a wonderful new world. I know that's what Balu wants."

Hearing him admit he had their brother was different from suspecting it. Yasmin felt as if he'd yanked a rug out from under her. "You know what Balu wants? Ramis, where is he? Is he all right?"

"He's better than all right. He's—"

Ramis stopped speaking. His head cocked slightly to one side, as if he were listening to faint music. Yasmin hadn't been paying attention to anything but him, but now she noticed a subtle thickening in the air, a tingling where it brushed it her skin. Elyse's spell must be starting to take effect. She gripped Ramis's hands to pull his focus back to her.

"Where is he?" she asked. "Where is Balu?"

"I—" Ramis swayed on the park bench. His eyes flared bright yellow, as blinding as little suns. When the glare receded, his irises didn't return to their normal gray. They stayed the alien color, like flickering candle flames. His pupils were different too. Blacker. Smaller. And not quite round anymore.

These are his real eyes, Yasmin thought. *This is what he looks like now.*

Ramis's expression changed as he took in her reaction.

"What did you do?" he demanded. He held out his right hand and stared at it. The tips of his fingers smoked. Notably, the blurring wasn't restricted to his hands. Over all his edges wisps pulled off—as if a distant vacuum were dragging bits off him. He looked at her, horrified. "You betrayed me to them?"

"Ramis," she begged, knowing she might only have seconds. Who knew if he'd speak once he was imprisoned? "Please tell me where Balu is."

He threw off her pleading hold, leaping to his feet. "Damn you to hell for this!"

She was lucky he could only curse her with words. Caught up in resisting the human's spell, he couldn't spare power to do magic. More and more of his body turned to smoke. He was also shrinking rapidly, until he was no taller than a four-year-old. Yasmin gasped as new appendages suddenly sprouted on his back. He was all smoke then: a monkey-sized, roiling smoke demon with bat wings.

Was this what murder turned good djinn into?

"God help us," she murmured unthinkingly.

The Ramis monkey let out a scream of rage. His smoke form—his true form?—was sucked up into the air . . . unwillingly, from what she could tell. Willing or not, the struggling ball of smoke sped toward the top of the Arch of Triumph, where Elyse and one of the commanders were posted. Yasmin wanted to fly after it. How else would she get answers about what had happened to Balu?

She was about to transform when Joseph materialized beside her. He put his hand on her arm, the unexpected familiarity startling her.

"Wait," he said, not seeming to realize he'd done something he shouldn't. "This situation isn't settled. Your brother has a confederate, possibly more than one. We need to stay alert down here, not up there confusing things."

"He actually took our brother," she said, her voice trembling on the edge of tears. "He knows where Balu is!"

Joseph rubbed her arm through her sleeve. "I heard," he said. "Just trust Cade to get the truth out of him."

~

Cade was peering through the binoculars as Elyse succeeded in turning Ramis into smoke. Cade's body jerked, his mind unprepared to accept the being his eyes had identified.

"Shit," he said softly. "Ramis is Samir."

He couldn't be mistaken. The ifrit Samir had snuck into Elyse's brownstone through the portal in her basement. He'd popped up again when they journeyed to the desert and met Sheikh Zayd's Bedouins. When Cade, Elyse, and Joseph escaped the sheikh's plot to do them harm, Samir had helped navigate their flying carpet here.

Cade hadn't thought Samir might be *from* the Glorious City. In truth, he hadn't imagined Samir started life as a light djinni. His smoke shape was distinctive, his mannerisms those of a low-level born demon: alternately unctuous and sly. He'd seemed childish in his emotions, though canny in intelligence. Samir was easy to be annoyed by and even easier to underestimate. The ifrit had never once assumed solid form in front of them.

Cade hadn't thought he could.

Cade and Joseph's ignorance must have amused him.

"What?" Elyse asked, noting the change in his demeanor.

"Nothing," he said, not wanting to distract her. "You're doing perfectly. Keep chanting."

She didn't lose her stride as she resumed. The thrashing ball of vapor streaked toward their perch, yanked helplessly toward the brass vessel Elyse held.

"Ready the stopper," Cade advised.

The thing was iron, and would have singed his fingers. Elyse readied it without a bobble in her spell. She truly had grown in confidence. An ifrit's shriek was a frightening noise, and Samir was wailing one out nonstop. Cade was prepared to assist, but Elyse braced her feet. This was a wise precaution. Samir's smoke practically exploded through the gallery piercings on its way into the brass vessel.

"Now," Cade said as the last smoky trail whisked in.

Elyse slammed the stopper into the opening. "Gotcha," she said and grinned.

The vessel clanged and vibrated as Samir ricocheted inside, trying to find an opening to get out. Elyse wrapped her arm more tightly around the vase, but Samir's escape attempts were violent. Holding the vessel took physical and not magic strength.

"Shall I?" Cade offered.

"Please," she said and handed the prize to him.

Samir took a minute to realize his struggle was futile. His shrieks cut off as he finally settled. Cade resisted the impulse to rub his ringing ears. He patted the vase instead.

"Hello, Samir," he said.

Samir? Elyse mouthed, her eyes gone wide. She hadn't seen the ifrit through the binoculars. Cade nodded in acknowledgment.

"You've confused me with someone else," the ifrit huffed, his angry upper-class voice distorted by the vase. "My name is Ramis, and I'm a free djinni citizen. I demand that you release me."

Did he really think he could fool them? Cade considered the now still vessel. He supposed was possible Samir thought they were idiots.

"*I* can't release you," he answered reasonably. "As you might have noticed, a human trapped you. Only another human can let you out. To be honest, I'm not certain anyone but my friend could do it. Her skill with that particular incantation is impressive."

Cade wanted their captive to abandon hope that his accomplice could free him. The claim might be true, actually. Mario's djinni-infused tattoos had adulterated his human power. Given how few humans could work spells at this level, Elyse could well be Samir's sole option.

"Fine," the ifrit said after a brief silence. "Have your friend let me out."

"She'll want three wishes in return," he warned. "You know how humans like to insist on that." Cade winked at Elyse, whose eyebrows shot up quizzically. "Are you prepared to tell her everything you know about the plot to abduct our city's djinn? Because I assure you, that would be her first request."

Another silence stretched. "I don't know what you're talking about," Samir said.

"Well, if you don't know what I'm talking about, that wish would cost you nothing to fulfill. If you do, however, you'd be compelled to spill your guts. Plus, she'd still have two wishes left. She could order you to become a worm. Doom you to being digested by birds for eternity. I know ifrits are tough, but I doubt you'd enjoy that."

This time, Samir had no response at all.

"We could come to a more comfortable agreement," Cade suggested. "You answer our questions voluntarily, and Elyse releases you into the custody of our court system. You'd face justice for your actions but not endless suffering."

Once again, Cade waited for an answer that didn't come.

"Oh, give the vase back to me," Elyse snapped. "I don't care if that pipsqueak suffers. I want answers."

He gaped at her in surprise. She certainly seemed to mean the threat. She put out her arms and gestured for him to hand Samir to her. With Samir listening to everything they said, Cade was obliged to comply. He hoped Elyse understood how tricky wording wishes could be.

"Very well," he said and passed the vase over.

She began the ritual rubbing motion around the Solomon seal.

"Wait!" Samir cried from inside. "Maybe I know something."

Samir's wheedling anxiety sounded more like the ifrit they'd known before. Elyse surprised Cade again by smiling. She *had* been bluffing.

"We want good answers," she said sternly. "And we're going to confirm them before I set you free."

"Yes," Samir agreed. "I'll give you good answers."

Cade gave Elyse the go-ahead to begin. She thought for a moment. "Okay, you work with a tattooed human. We want to know his name."

Cade thought this a clever means of confirming if the ifrit would tell the truth.

"His name is Mario," Samir said. "I met him in your cellar ten weeks ago. He'd just killed someone, and the extra death energy allowed me to squeeze through a hole in your locked portal."

The *someone* Mario killed was Elyse's husband. Elyse knew this, though the reminder couldn't be pleasant.

She tightened her jaw. "What was the nature of your agreement?"

"He'd never been to our world. He needed a partner who knew his way around."

"And what did *you* need?" Cade asked.

"The same. Someone who understood the lay of the human land. You could call it a cross border alliance."

"To traffick abducted djinn from your world to mine."

"Among other things," Samir said. "And they weren't abducted. Every one of those young people came willingly."

Cade could see Elyse wanted to argue that they'd been tricked into coming with false promises. Cade touched her arm to stop her. Disputing semantics with Samir wouldn't make him more forthcoming.

"Where are the young people now?" Cade asked.

"Safe," Samir said.

"Safe *where*?" Elyse pressed. Samir was silent. Elyse moved her hand to the jar's Solomon seal. "Do I need to force you to give me a straight answer?"

"You're welcome to try," Samir said pleasantly.

His sudden self assurance took Cade aback. What did Samir know that they didn't? Alarms went off in his head. Cade reached for his scimitar.

He didn't have time to stop the threat Samir sensed was near. A man shaped of empty air and snarled thorny branches materialized in the door between the portal room and the gallery. The thing was a nightmare from a tale. Two red eyes glowed within its tangled head.

Mario, Cade thought. Or rather Mario's demon-infused tattoo. He had a nanosecond to wonder where it had come from, along with why Joseph's magical barriers hadn't kept it from intruding. Joseph had given Cade the necessary *open sesame* to enter. The enchanted shields hadn't been broken. Plus, Cade had reactivated them afterward.

Samir was considerably happier than Cade to greet the new arrival.

"Over here!" he cried. "Free me from this container!"

Cade swung his sword at the creature, but the thorn man was as quick as if he were smoke. One branch arm snapped out to twice its original length, snatching the brass container from Elyse's arms with surprising dexterity. Elyse cursed as the creature's other arm uncoiled and lashed at him. Cade ignored the tears it made in his chest to take another swing. This time, he managed to lop off its thorny hand. Hoping to disable the whole thing, he swung again and missed.

The thorn being had flashed back to the portal room.

"*Stay,*" Cade ordered Elyse, peripherally aware that the tattoo demon had scratched her arm and face bloody. "You're safer here."

He shouldn't have been surprised that she bolted right after him. They reached the other room together, in time to see the thorn demon smash full speed into its master. Mario staggered, then spread his bulging arms in welcome as the black ink raced over his skin again. His right hand, whose thorn counterpart Cade had severed, was the only part that stayed bare. When the admittedly fascinating process finished, the strapping sorcerer held Samir's vase. He immediately began trying to tug out the stopper.

He wasn't successful. More than Elyse's hand had affixed it there. Her magic had soldered a bond between the iron plug and the vessel's neck. Interestingly, Mario hissed as if the iron stung his fingers. Joseph's theory was correct. Mario was becoming part ifrit.

If that was true, Cade had nothing to lose by attacking him.

"Halt!" Mario ordered before he could.

The former fake handyman was showing his true colors. The one-word enchantment stopped Cade as handily as an elaborate spell. His feet stuck in place like they'd been cemented to the smooth stone floor. The rest of his body kept going. He had to shoot his hands in front of him to keep from face planting.

Elyse let out a startled cry as he fell. Her alarm was natural but counterproductive.

"You can outspell him," Cade told her, wishing he had a way to convey this knowledge to her with just his voice. "You have more power than him."

"Shut up!" Mario commanded, effectively clamping his mouth shut.

Elyse gaped helplessly at Cade, the white of fear showing around her widened eyes.

You can, Cade willed her to understand. *You're more human than he is now.*

Elyse jerked—almost as if she'd heard. Then to his amazement and everlasting pride, she began chanting the spell she'd just used successfully on Samir. She was attempting to put Mario in the very jar he was holding. It was a bold idea. Mario was only partly djinni, but it seemed like it might work. At the least, fighting her influence split his attention. He growled with annoyance as his hand slipped on the stopper he was still struggling with. He couldn't do everything at once. Cade felt his feet start to unstick from the floor.

A moment later, he noticed something else. The edges of Mario's tattoos were fogging, as if Elyse's chant were turning them to smoke.

"Enough," Mario snapped. He went still and closed his eyes.

Cade knew letting the sorcerer concentrate wasn't a good idea.

"No," he roared even as a streak of motion whipped through the air toward Elyse.

She screamed and scrabbled at her throat. The thorn hand from Mario's tattoo was strangling her. Cade hadn't rendered it inactive when he cut it off.

"I co-c—" *command,* she tried to say. The demon hand wouldn't let her. Rivulets of blood trickled down her neck where its thorns pierced her.

Cade struggled harder but only succeeded in making his hip joints feel like they were going to dislocate. No quitter, Elyse was fighting the thorn hand with everything she had. She fell onto her hip on a crumpled sheet that lay on the floor near her. Possibly she'd done it on purpose. She immediately grabbed a wad of cloth, using it to drag at the thorns without cutting up her hands. She seemed to be holding off the thing somewhat, though she wasn't able to try a spell.

Wait, Cade thought. *That sheet she's using was covering Joseph's statue. Where the hell is his double?*

It wasn't jumping out to save them—but maybe someone could.

Arcadius, Cade thought, reaching along the link between him and his spirit twin. *By all that's holy, get here now.*

~

The moment he heard the call, Arcadius flashed into his smoke form. He changed so quickly he made himself dizzy. Ignoring his discomfort, he zoomed to the commemorative arch and through the openings in the gallery overlook. Joseph's *open sesame* got him through the barrier. He followed the noise of fighting to the portal room.

He gauged the situation in one swift glance: Cade stuck to the floor, the rogue magician radiating spell-power like an almost visible lightning bolt. The mortal danger Elyse confronted caused his heart to contract with uncustomary terror. He didn't let the emotion paralyze him. He smoked straight to her and materialized, immediately straddling her body and adding his strength to prying the animated bramble-hand from her throat. For one inappropriate second, the position felt sexual. What would it be like to take her for himself, not to further any cause but because he wanted to?

He didn't have time for inane questions. The ifrit spirit that infused the tattoo might not be particularly smart, but it was vicious. Stubborn too. Even with both himself and Elyse tugging it away, blood trickled from the spots it clutched. Arcadius grunted at the force required to keep the thorns from puncturing her deeper.

His double would have to wait for help. Arcadius wasn't free to turn and check on him. It didn't matter. The other him would endorse his priorities. Elyse's magical advantage was the only trick they had up their sleeve, on top of which Cade was in love with her.

Arcadius bit out a curse, but not because of that. The thorns had gnawed through the cloth Elyse was using to muffle them. They were slicing up his fingers—hers too, he imagined. He refused to be distracted by the fear in her eyes. With one last determined wrench, he gained her sufficient breathing room to speak. He didn't waste the opening.

"Repeat after me," he said in his sternest you-can-and-will-do-what-I-say voice. "By the power of the Light, I banish this Dark to hell."

She had to gasp to do it. "*By the power . . . of the Light, I . . . banish this Dark to hell.*"

The spell was old and simple, its efficacy springing from the countless times djinn had used it successfully. Luckily, Arcadius's authority steadied

Elyse enough for the charm to work. The bramble-hand disappeared in a black puff of smoke.

Freed, Elyse struggled to sit up with her bleeding hand pressed over her bleeding throat. She swayed with weakness and shock.

Arcadius took an instant to ascertain that none of her wounds were fatal. Then he whipped around to attack the sorcerer who'd inflicted them.

"*Stop right there*," the man commanded.

Suddenly, Arcadius strove against an opposing force as strong as a hurricane. A wall would have given more, though he called on every ounce of his considerable djinn muscle. A trickle of fear ran through him. He wanted to deny it, but superior skill might not be enough to defeat this man's raw power. With the sole exception of the enchantress who'd cursed their city, Mario was stronger than any magician Arcadius had come up against.

He glanced sideways at Cade. Sweat drenched his spirit twin, who struggled just as ineffectually. Unsure what else to do, Arcadius turned his gaze to the magician, getting his first clear look at the mostly human male. He'd caught a glimpse of him when Elyse chased him around the corner from the bathhouse. Mario had been slighter then, the magical disguise he'd assumed nowhere near as imposing as his brawny six-and-a-half foot frame. Tattoos and shaved head aside, Arcadius supposed he wasn't bad looking. He looked rough and ready, like a promising soldier candidate. Clearly, he was also intelligent.

Stupid people couldn't pull of these kinds of enchantments—not even one at a time.

The human had gone pale, at least; tense from the energy he was exerting. He stood near the center of the tile-lined room, perhaps two feet from the drained portal. The vessel in which Elyse had trapped Yasmin's brother was securely cradled in his left arm. His right hung less assuredly at his side. He clenched and unclenched the hand that had lost its tattoo, as if the appendage bothered him. Arcadius rather doubted it bothered him enough.

Despite all the magical plates he juggled, Mario wasn't out of breath.

"You can't control us both forever," Arcadius said conversationally, not wanting to remind him Elyse could do anything.

Light gleamed in the sorcerer's dark eyes. "Who says I need forever?"

"Let me out!" his cohort urged hollowly from inside the vase. "I'll help you defeat them."

Mario's feral grin wouldn't have heartened the ifrit. "Sorry, Samir," he said. "I have a better use for you."

What better use? Arcadius wondered.

He got his answer soon enough.

Samir sputtered objections as Mario began a new incantation. The words rolled so quickly from his tongue they weren't intelligible. Arcadius tensed, but the spell wasn't directed at him or Cade. It wasn't directed at Elyse either.

"What are you doing?" Samir demanded, fear cranking his voice higher. "Stop that! I told you I'd help you!"

"He's killing him," Cade said, figuring it out quicker than Arcadius could. "He's going to use him for death magic."

The portal, Arcadius thought, his mind racing to catch up. Joseph's team had ignored this door in favor of restoring the one Iksander had left through. Mario super-infusing this nexus with Samir's spirit would circumvent the need for the lengthy charging process that *didn't* break light djinn law.

If the sorcerer was so keen to get away that he'd sacrifice his partner, maybe he felt more threatened than they realized.

Arcadius looked at Elyse. Her dismayed expression conveyed the unfortunate truth. She had no experience improvising spells.

"I don't know what to chant," she confessed.

He didn't know what to tell her. His class of djinn didn't practice death magic. Joseph studied broadly. He might have been aware of a counter spell. Like Elyse, however, Arcadius couldn't swim beyond his depth.

Fuck, he thought. Cade's grimace said the same thing.

Inside the brass vessel, Samir screeched like a banshee as his life force was wrenched from him. Arcadius didn't have time to pity him. The iron stopper, which Elyse had remembered to secure, suddenly popped spinning from the jar. The ifrit's departing spirit had forced it out, his essence spuming like a solar flare from its prison. The sun the flare fell into was the portal's power source. The nexus flashed white with a tall blue slit, blinding rainbow sparks and rays shooting out of both. The air was abruptly so dense with magic Arcadius's ears felt stuffed with cotton.

Despite this, he heard his double call to Elyse.

"Take my hand," Cade said hoarsely.

Mario's magic didn't affect her like it did them. She wasn't immobilized. She ran through the glare even as Mario tossed the vase aside and bounded into his escape route.

Elyse's bloodied palm slapped around Arcadius's double's. The pair reminded him of children swearing a "friends forever" oath. Cade must be hoping to use her human magic to strengthen his. He'd better hurry. The portal's slit had already swallowed the sorcerer. If Mario escaped, they'd have little chance of catching him . . . or finding the lost young people.

His spirit twin bowed his head. "If it please my Creator, whither this man now goes, so go my love and I." It wasn't a spell, merely a humble prayer. "Say *Amen*," he added to Elyse.

No, Arcadius thought, realizing what Cade had asked. He shouldn't be taking Elyse with him into danger. Yes, he needed her power, but what if he got her killed?

"Amen," Elyse agreed.

The air buzzed as she said the word. A second later, Arcadius's feet unstuck from the floor. Mario must have gotten completely through the door. Without him to sustain it, the spell he'd put on Cade and Arcadius fell away. Still holding hands, Cade and Elyse stepped into the whirling radiance.

"No!" Arcadius protested.

Elyse glanced back at him. Her green eyes were brighter than he'd ever seen them, lustrous light green jewels blazing within dark lashes. Her curls floated crazily, her smile for him as warm as sunshine. What did that smile mean? Did she care about him too? His blood roared in his ears from the intense magic. Her lips moved.

"We'll be back," he thought she assured him.

Arcadius had perhaps three heartbeats to decide. The portal's surge of energy couldn't last. His breastbone felt as if a hot poker were stabbing it. One of them should stay. The city needed a commander. Elyse's head turned back in the direction of wherever she and Cade were going. Cade could protect her.

Probably.

"Damn it," Arcadius muttered as he jumped after them.

~

Though it frustrated him to wait, Joseph couldn't leave Yasmin. From what he'd overheard of her conversation with her unexpectedly familiar brother, the ifrit wanted her for his scheme. Samir/Ramis had already collected enough victims. Until they knew the risk was over, he wouldn't give him the chance to claim another.

Not that Yasmin was defenseless. He glanced at the fine gray eyes that showed above her veil. He knew she'd been nervous, but she'd proved her mettle.

At the moment, her attention wasn't on him.

"Something is going on up there," she observed, nodding toward the Arch of Triumph.

Joseph turned. Soft gold light radiated through the normally invisible openings in the gallery overlook. He stiffened as the glow suddenly turned sun-bright.

"Crap," he said. "Someone's charging the portal."

Did Samir have enough power to do it? Little hairs on his arms stood up.

The ifrit would if he didn't bother following light rules.

"That's death magic," Yasmin said, shivering as she identified the vibration.

The glaring light winked out, causing his nerves to jolt. If Samir had killed someone to fuel the portal, chances were Joseph was friends with them.

"Stay," he ordered his companion. "I'll call a guard to protect you."

"You aren't going without me. And we don't have time to argue."

They didn't. He changed and she did too. They streaked side by side through the gallery's decorative piercings, materializing silently behind them. Yasmin took a moment to shake her robes straighter. The door to the portal room was open, the space inside almost completely dark. Joseph's nostrils flared. He smelled blood but not enough to signify a death.

The magic he'd sensed from the park was now no more than a vapor trail.

Yasmin began to speak and he held up a hand to silence her. Though the entire structure seemed empty, he had a sick feeling in the pit of his stomach, as if there were something inside that room he didn't want to see.

He went in first. No one attacked. Elyse and Cade weren't there. The portal was even dimmer than the last time he'd checked—more a cinder with a single spark than a guttering candle flame. The recent influx of power must have been exhausted by whoever had gone through it. Joseph couldn't read the location it had been keyed to connect to.

"I think the tattooed man was here," Yasmin said softly from behind him. "I caught a whiff of him at the cosplay club."

Joseph turned. "You read scents that well?"

She hugged herself and shrugged. "I've been in my cat form a lot lately."

Joseph rubbed his upper lip. Mario could have charged the portal if he'd been here. Possibly, he could have slipped around Joseph's barriers as well. Joseph had come up against the human sorcerer back in Elyse's world and hadn't emerged victorious. Mario's skills were formidable. On his own, Joseph wasn't sure he could counter them.

It also seemed using the arch as a vantage point wasn't an original concept. Though he'd known Samir might ask Mario to observe his meeting with his sister, in case it was a trap, he'd hadn't guessed *this* would be his lookout.

He tapped his teeth in frustration. Cade had chided him now and then for taking too much weight on his own shoulders. Tonight Joseph deserved a different sort of rebuke. He'd screwed up royally.

"Can I spell a light?" Yasmin asked. "It's really dark in here."

"Sure," he said absently.

She called up a handheld glow. The soft illumination pushed back the thick shadows. As it turned out, the space wasn't as empty as he'd thought. One very lifeless body stretched face down on the floor.

Yasmin gasped sharply. "Is that—?"

The corpse was child-sized. Its skin was gray and sunken, its limbs too skinny and vaguely simian. One foot remained within the brass vase that lay nearby, but Joseph didn't need the clue to identify who it was. This was the physical counterpart to Samir's smoke form—or rather the husk of it. Every scrap of soul energy had been sucked from it. Though the sight was terrible, Joseph was relieved.

At least he knew whose life force had recharged the portal.

"Yes," he said to Yasmin. "I'm afraid that's your brother. The form he showed you must have been a disguise."

She leaned rather than stepped closer. One slim hand pressed her face veil against her mouth in shock. "Ramis must have hated looking like that after he turned ifrit. He was so proud." She choked out a breathy laugh. "Pride was what led him to murder in the first place."

Joseph didn't know how to comfort her. He had no siblings and couldn't comprehend the shadings of what must be a complicated wound.

"I'm all right," she said, waving his concern away. "Should we . . . do something with his body?"

He couldn't answer. He was too distracted. Rather than feeling better that his friends weren't dead, his unease worsened. Something was still wrong. His stomach was in knots. Dreading what he'd find, he scanned the room again.

What he *didn't* find finally set off his alarms.

His statue double was gone. The sheet Arcadius had draped over him lay twisted on the floor a few feet from where the stone form had knelt. The blood he'd smelled before stained it. With his skin gone icy, he bent to examine it.

As he lifted the cloth, a few chips of stone fell off.

"Shit," he hissed.

"What's wrong?" Yasmin asked.

"My statue's gone." He looked around wildly. There, against the base of wall, where the tiles met the floor, a long trail of shattered marble stretched.

"You left your copy here?"

"It seemed safe enough." His voice sounded far away. "I spelled the locks on the place myself."

He moved to the line of rubble like he was sleepwalking. He didn't want to, but he stooped to gather up a handful of stone debris. The statue had been destroyed so violently some of the stone was dust. His double's spirit was gone—along with the remaining portion of Joseph's power.

"Did someone break it?" Yasmin asked.

"Mario, I expect." Yasmin sounded more horrified than he did. He simply sounded numb. He rose. He almost smacked his palm clean against his thigh before he stopped himself. He ought to show respect for the loss. He'd never be the magician he was before.

He also didn't have to be a eunuch.

A joy so fierce it shamed him spread through his chest. In seconds, he flashed hot from the crown of his head to the soles of his feet.

Stupid, he thought. And selfish. If he'd had his full power, he might not have failed everyone tonight.

"Why do you suppose he broke it?" Yasmin asked.

Who cares? the selfish part of him chortled.

"I don't know," he said aloud. His second hand clenched the sheet he was still holding. "Maybe he heard Cade and Elyse coming up the stairs. Maybe he shattered my statue so he could hide under this."

"They would have sensed him," Yasmin objected.

"Maybe not. Human magic works differently on us. And Elyse isn't experienced. If she did sense his presence, she might not have known what the feeling meant."

"At least they're not dead," Yasmin said.

She'd stepped closer, as if she were tempted to comfort him with a touch. Tingles swept his skin as he registered her nearness. His selfish side pointed out he had nothing to lose by taking a woman now. He couldn't screw up his chances of reuniting with his double. That ship hadn't simply left the harbor. It had sunk.

His cock began to harden, the heat and heaviness of his arousal incredibly seductive.

Stop, he ordered. He might be able to take "a" woman, but not this one. This one was Iksander's.

He forced his mind back to her last comment.

"I hope they're alive," he said. "I can't be sure without knowing where they went or what menace Mario might have waiting on the other side."

"Did he re key the portal from the last time it was used?"

"I don't know. With so low a charge remaining, I can't tell." He rubbed the ache between his eyebrows. "I suppose I could pull some of palace's magicians off other jobs, but everything they're doing is important."

"Do you have to use *palace* magicians?" she asked.

He looked at her. To his surprise, she'd pulled her veil down to speak. He supposed she thought it didn't matter. She didn't know he was capable.

He struggled not to react to her extraordinary beauty. Looks like hers explained why the practice of veiling had begun. "Recharging nexuses is a special skill, not to mention taking a lot of power."

"But I was thinking," she said, her cheeks gone pink from her own boldness. "The kids who start up the view cafés have a lot of power. They're self-taught, but maybe you could train them well enough for this. You know, if it isn't a breach of security or something."

"That *is* an idea," he said, immediately seeing the possibilities.

"We could maybe start at the café my brother Balu frequented. I hear people liked him there. If they knew it was for him, they'd be happy to help you. Better still, those magic geeks all know each other. They could point you to more candidates."

"Well," Joseph said. "You certainly are more than a pretty face."

At this, Yasmin blushed so hotly she could have powered a nexus with that alone.

CHAPTER NINE

THE trip through the nexus was as dizzying as Elyse remembered. Her brain felt like a clock whose hands spun in both directions. She couldn't tell if she were big or small, awake or dreaming. Light beamed all around her or maybe she was the light. Her ears rang with music that played a thousand tunes. Then, like a guillotine chopping the illusory from the real, she was in an actual place again.

Fortunately, Cade's hold on her hand saved her from stumbling.

Weirdly, her palm wasn't bleeding anymore. Her face and neck weren't either. Maybe going through a door was like shifting?

"Whew," she said, unable to hold back a breathless laugh. "Those portal thingies are quite the ride."

Cade grinned and both of them looked around. It was nighttime, and they were on the roof of a broad building, easily a block long but just a few stories tall. Elyse didn't see or hear Mario. She did, however, recognize the skyline.

"That's the Empire State Building!" she exclaimed delightedly. "We're back in New York. Mario mustn't have had a chance to re-key the door."

"You're right. This is the same post office Joseph and I originally landed on."

A thud and a curse behind them caused them to snap around.

"It's me," Arcadius said, pushing up from his hands and knees. "Don't attack."

Cade had drawn his scimitar. He slid it away slowly. When he spoke, he seemed amazed. "You followed us."

"I . . . obeyed an impulse," his double said. "The portal was closing. I had to make up my mind quickly."

Elyse thought his usual unemotional tone held a hint of embarrassment. Maybe her heart shouldn't have sped up, but it did. Had his *impulse* involved her? She couldn't deny the possibility was appealing. She'd experienced a definite wrench at leaving him behind, and he'd looked forlorn to see them go. Now that he was with them, she felt as if someone she liked quite a bit had brightened up a party.

His arrival made it perfect.

She glanced at Cade to check his reaction. He wasn't angry or displeased. Surprised, she thought, and maybe a bit doubtful.

"We did warn Murat he might have to stand in for us," Arcadius reminded. "And he has Joseph to help him." He scanned their surroundings with the same professional composure Cade had displayed. "I take it the sorcerer got here too far ahead of you to catch. Do you know where this is?"

"This is Manhattan," Cade said. "Elyse's home."

"Well." Arcadius's expression was better guarded than his double's. What a poker player Cade must have been once upon a time! "Is it always this cold?"

She laughed. Cade had put his arm around her shoulders. She wasn't chilled at all. "The temperature has got to be in the forties. The real icebox weather was back when Cade arrived."

"I'll take your word for it." Arcadius drew half a breath and spoke. "Perhaps, since this is your city, you'd like to suggest how we proceed?"

His formality reminded her of Cade when she first met him—that wonderful old world politeness. Happiness she simply could not control welled up inside her. She was very glad both of them were here. If she got the chance, she'd show Arcadius everything.

"I suggest I take you home," she said. "Wherever Mario slithered off to, we won't find him now. Once we warm up and catch our breath, some means of tracking him will occur to us."

"You're certain you want me in your residence?" Arcadius asked.

"Actually, we need you there," Cade broke in, chafing her arm as if she and not his twin needed reassurance. "Mario knows where Elyse lives. He might have people watching her building."

This was true. Nonetheless, she knew Cade was saying it to spare Arcadius awkwardness. He was being kind to the other man—and not because he had to. Elyse couldn't recall him doing this before. She was startled and touched and secretly amused.

How often did a man get a chance to befriend himself?

More to the point, how many people would want to if they met who they used to be?

Since they had no carpet, Arcadius added to her amusement by proposing he and Cade fly her home in their smoke forms. While this would have been exciting in a slightly scary way for Elyse, Cade warned his double it would attract unwanted attention. He suggested they take a taxi, but Elyse had to put the kibosh on that. Between them, they didn't have one normal U.S. cent.

"I'm afraid we're stuck with foot power. Luckily, we're only a mile or so from my home. Walking will give Arcadius a chance to take in his surroundings."

The two djinn spelled the roof door open and then they were on their way. Cade was even more entertained than Elyse by the way his original gawked. While she was sure Arcadius had studied up on the human plane, a man like him didn't spend his days hanging out at view cafés. The information he'd have about her world couldn't replace experience. The rush of traffic on the avenue caused him to jerk and touch his weapon, though he watched the vehicles with interest. The skyscrapers left him slack-jawed—and some of the people too.

"This place is . . . lively," he said as two Goths with matching foot-high blue Mohawks strode by them on the sidewalk. The pair was chattering animatedly about where to eat in Little Korea.

"This is the city that never sleeps," Cade informed him.

Arcadius nodded, his gaze on the surrounding scene. Like his double, he was naturally coordinated. Even as he craned around to watch a passing stretch Hummer, he sidestepped a manhole from which a cloud of subway steam issued. "No one is dressed quite like us."

"We'll fix that," Cade said. "The jewels on our slippers are worth quite a bit of cash, as Joseph and I discovered."

"I'm surprised we aren't drawing more attention."

"New Yorkers pride themselves on not being startled by eccentricity."

"But you shouldn't do spells in public," Elyse put in—in case Cade's answer misled his twin.

Arcadius grinned at her. "I understood that much."

His smile was as wonderful as Cade's—a ray of sunlight breaking through somber clouds. She rubbed her cheek to hide the fact that it had heated.

Arcadius jolted to a halt in front of a lit-up boutique window.

"What's a golem doing there?" he demanded, pointing at the mannequin. "Suppose someone puts a spirit inside it!"

"It's only plastic," Cade said. "Those forms are for displaying goods, to entice people to buy them."

Arcadius frowned. "Those garments aren't high quality."

"Don't worry," Cade reassured. "Other establishments sell better."

Elyse couldn't restrain a laugh. This wasn't a Dollar Store. Those were expensive designer duds! "You djinn men sure don't like roughing it."

Arcadius pulled himself haughtily straighter. "I shall wear whatever I need to without complaint."

Elyse patted his beautiful embroidered tunic sleeve. He wore black and navy for stealth but had still dressed richly by her standards. "I'm sure you will. I'm only teasing you."

"You deserve nice clothes as well," he said stiffly. "Not those flimsy . . . *blah* garments."

He pulled the word from the air, the way Cade used to.

"Thank you," she said, striving to be polite in spite of her amusement. "I appreciate the sentiment."

Given how many sights distracted Arcadius and how much Cade enjoyed playing tour guide, they took longer than they might have to reach her house. Elyse had worried while she was away, but the place looked fine. The front stoop was clean, the façade showing no more wear and tear than before she'd left. The vestibule light was on, and the bike rack for tenants was orderly.

It was as if the brownstone hadn't missed her at all.

"This is your home?" Arcadius asked, pausing on the sidewalk to regard its six stories.

"Yes," she said, hoping the building made a better impression than the mannequin and its clothes. She remembered how dubious Cade had seemed when he first viewed it. "I live in an apartment on the top floor. I rent out the other eleven units. Twelve actually, counting the basement Cade and Joseph shared."

"The *basement*," Arcadius said, his dark brows arching.

"The nexus is in the cellar behind it. Your double did what he had to without complaining too."

Arcadius double-checked that she was pulling his leg. He returned his attention to the house. "I don't sense anyone watching us."

"Nor do I," Cade said. He'd been surveying the nearby street.

"We should proceed with caution," Arcadius advised.

"Crap," Elyse said, causing both men to look at her. "I don't have my keys. You'll have to spell our way in here."

They went up the steps together. Cade took hold of the knob and muttered a quick chant. "Hm," he said when it wouldn't give to his twist. "That should have worked."

Arcadius leaned closer and peered at it. "There's a spell on this lock. To prevent it from being charmed open."

"I wonder if Mario put it there," Cade mused. "Or Cara—assuming your cousin and the sorcerer are still together."

This didn't strike her as logical. "If it was them, who are they trying to keep out? They'd expect me—and by association *you*—to get in with a regular key."

Cade rubbed his chin. "I could smoke around the house. See if I spot them inside."

"But what if someone spots *you*? Screw it." Elyse made up her mind. "I'll buzz a tenant. The lights on the second floor are on. One of them will recognize me and let us up."

Her strategy worked. Susan Gunnarson from 2B came down with her terrier Ivan whuffling happily in her arms. Perhaps to make up for his annoyance over her initiative, Arcadius insisted he and Cade guard her fore and aft as they went up the stairs. Susan watched their procession go by wide-eyed. It wasn't every day her landlady arrived looking like an Arabian Nights princess with two equally opulent matching men.

"That must have been some vacation," she observed, "to lose your luggage *and* come back with souvenirs like those."

Elyse was happy the woman bought her explanation for appearing the way she did. The hint of envy in her tone she understood perfectly. Odd dress aside, the handsome djinn invited coveting.

"This is it," she said as they reached the sixth floor landing. She noticed neither man was winded from climbing all the steps.

Arcadius surveyed the quiet hall. He rubbed the back of neck, perhaps confused by how plain the brownstone was compared to domiciles in his dimension. "It's warm," was the nicest thing he thought to say.

Cade laughed beneath his breath. "You'll like the inside," he predicted.

Both men pulled their swords as footsteps approached from behind the door to 6B.

Shoot, Elyse thought. She'd forgotten her crotchety neighbor, Mrs. Goldberg, who'd spied on Elyse for Cara and nearly got her killed.

"Don't attack," Cade whispered to Arcadius. "That resident keeps dangerous company, but she's an old lady."

Except . . . the person who exited the opposite apartment wasn't an old lady. It was a male with a rangy build on which faded jeans hung loosely. His salt and pepper hair waved so much it almost curled.

The shape of the body beneath the black turtleneck was stunningly familiar.

Elyse felt like her heart would explode. This couldn't be who she thought it was. The man that profile belonged to was dead. This had to be a cruel joke. Or a magic trick. Or maybe this person just resembled the one she knew.

The man locked the deadbolt and turned. They'd been so silent he hadn't noticed they were there.

"Oh," he said, dropping his keys in shock.

His face *was* his face: his nose strong, his mouth made for laughing, his eyes sharp with humor and intelligence. The only change was that he was leaner and a few years older.

Two years, she thought, her head gone light from too much or too little blood. Gray mist crept across her vision.

"Dad," she gasped, and crumpled to the floor.

~

Her dad's gentle hand stroked her forehead. "Hey, sweetie. Time to wake up."

Eyes still closed, she smiled at the love in the simple touch. "'s not a school day."

"She must be dreaming," her dad chuckled to someone.

A different set of hands touched Elyse's arm. They were gentle too.

Elyse's eyes snapped open. She was back home in her living room, on her back on the long leather couch. Her dad's face moved into view.

"Oh, my God," she said.

"It's okay," her dad soothed. "I can explain everything."

"You're alive."

"Yes," he agreed.

She looked at Cade. He was hunkered beside the couch. His were the hands on her arm. Arcadius hovered a few feet behind him, as if he weren't sure he was a part of this scene but didn't want to withdraw farther. Her father saw the direction her gaze had gone.

"Those men of yours are protective," he observed. "They nearly killed me when they thought I'd cast a spell to knock you out."

Elyse struggled onto her elbows, her brain scrambling to respond. The way he said *those men of yours* implied he knew their arrangement wasn't platonic. Plus, they'd accused her father of doing spells, which they wouldn't have done if they'd been hiding what they were. Of course, Leo *did* do spells—or so she'd discovered. Chances were, her father knew right off that Cade and Arcadius were djinn.

Her dad patted her shoulder. "Don't worry, honey. While you were unconscious, your friends caught me up on what you've been up to."

"It's okay." Cade's normally low voice was deepened by concern. "We're satisfied we can trust him."

That made the corners of her mouth tug up. He meant *we* as him and his spirit twin.

"Dad," she said, her brain finally settling on the topic she most wanted to address. She took his hand and squeezed it. "Where the hell have you been?"

"Can't I get a hug from my daughter first?"

She released everything but that, flinging her arms around him and letting him hug her back. He smelled just as she remembered, giving her the little growl of welcome he always did. She buried her face in his familiar shoulder. It had been two years since she'd embraced him. She'd honestly thought she never would again.

"You lost weight," she said when she pulled back at last.

His dad wiped his eyes and laughed. "I fell into a volcano. The fat melted."

That was her dad—always ready with a joke.

"Did you really fall into Mt. Etna?"

Her dad sobered. "I did."

"Do you know about Uncle Vince?"

"That my brother is dead and that he arranged my 'accident'? Yes and yes, I'm afraid."

Elyse bit her lip. "I'm sorry. That must have been hard to learn."

Her dad stroked her curls from her face. "Harder for you to learn, I imagine, since—at the time—he and your cousin were trying to force the secret to the brownstone's portal out of you."

"You were unconscious for a while," Cade said when she shifted her gaze to him. "I explained that bit."

His face was serious, the worry in his eyes not hidden by humor. Love for Cade expanded inside of her. She realized she'd never felt this way for anyone before—not her father, not her husband or closest friend. She was in love with him, and there was no going back. The realization was a little frightening. She found herself hoping she wouldn't let him down.

"What?" Cade asked, noting the change in her expression.

She smiled and shook her head. Now wasn't the time for sappy romantic declarations. "Thank you for explaining. You're better at telling stories than I am." She turned back to her dad. "You have one to tell us, I assume."

"You want to know how I survived." She nodded, and he glanced at the men. "You want them to hear everything?"

"I trust them with my life," she said. "And I'd trust them with yours too."

Her father accepted that. As at-home as if he'd never been away, he settled into an armchair and began. "It was a case of Solomon luck, though I didn't feel that fortunate when the guide I'd hired to sightsee the crater shoved me in. You probably know Etna is an active volcano, the tallest in Europe. It was relatively quiet then. You can't get close when it's full-on erupting.

"Anyway, I thought I was done for. The caldera was hot and fumy as I fell, and my mind went to a protective prayer I'd read in one of your grandfather's arcane books. I guess the volcano had a power spot, because as soon as I recited it everything flashed bright. The next thing I knew, I'd tumbled onto a forgotten island in the djinn world. The ifrits who live there call it Shadow Wood."

Her father looked at Cade to see if he recognized the name.

Cade shook his head. "Our dimension has more corners than any of us knows."

"Certainly more than *I* know," her father agreed. "Wherever it was precisely, Shadow Wood wasn't big. A few square miles and beyond that, nothing but dangerous 'in-between' banks of mist. Seeing I'd be stuck there for a while, I made friends with the natives as best I could. Possibly I did too good a job. The ifrits were bored and decided to make a pet of me. Every mention I made of leaving riled them up. I took a year to find their nexus in the wood and another year to charge it, bit by bit, behind their backs. They didn't use the door themselves. They were hiding out from an upper level demon who was after them for I don't know what reason. I escaped by the skin of my teeth, leaving them squawking with outrage as I went. I'd keyed the nexus to spit me out in Sicily—thankfully not in the volcano. From there, I made my way back here."

He said this as if the adventure were ordinary. Perhaps for him it had been.

"I'm sorry you worried," he added with comic offhandedness.

If her father had a flaw, it was that his sunny disposition didn't comprehend darker emotions. Grief he might catch a whiff of but not despair. The homicidal envy Uncle Vince had experienced in the face of his brother's charm was a mystery to him.

"Do other people know you're alive?" she asked.

"The tenants do, of course. Your Aunt June was managing the place. I don't think she knew what her husband did. She barely batted an eye when I turned up. You know how oblivious she can be."

Aunt June's grasp of what went on around her could be vague—a trait she'd probably developed in self defense married to a man who was, at best, a puffed up blowhard and, at worst, a murderer.

"How is she handling Uncle Vince's death?"

"Well, she *says* she can't get used to him being gone, but to be honest she seems cheerful. She doesn't know Mario shot her husband, or that her daughter played a part. Mario's underlings staged the scene so that his death looked like a robbery gone wrong."

The mention of Cara reminded Elyse of a whole 'nother can of worms. "What about Cara? She can't have been happy you're not dead."

"Not even a little." Her father cracked a grin. "She hid it, mind you. Gave me a big hug and exclaimed how 'amazed' and 'over the moon' she was. For my part, I pretended I hadn't figured out my accident wasn't one. She and Mario are engaged, by the way. Not by Cara's choosing, I don't think. She put that love whammy on him, and now she's stuck with the results. She must not have realized him falling in love with her wouldn't guarantee she could control him."

Elyse could vouch for the whammy's effectiveness. Her now-deceased husband had bound her to him with the same enchanted book of poems. He'd gotten the volume from Cara originally. Cara enlisted David to marry Elyse so that she and Uncle Vince could steal the secret to controlling her dad's portal. Mario started out as Vince's hired muscle, but developed ambitions of his own. Failing to notice that had cost Uncle Vince his life. Though Cara hadn't meant for her dad to die, she'd unwittingly caused it by bespelling Mario. He'd thought her dad's continued existence wasn't in his beloved's best interest.

Apparently, Cara had decided to stick with him anyway.

"You spelled the door to keep Cara out," Elyse realized. She rubbed her brow in the hope that it would help her brain wake up. "She must have stayed behind in New York when Mario crossed dimensions."

"Yes," her dad affirmed. "I changed the locks after I took back control from your Aunt June. I wasn't sure what your cousin and Mario planned to do in the other world, but I figured I'd make it harder by blocking the nexus here." He shrugged philosophically. "I should have guessed he'd find a portal there that he could get back with."

"And you evicted Mrs. Goldberg?"

"She evicted herself. Since her unit was empty, I moved in. You shouldn't have to give up this apartment just because I'm alive again."

Elyse sat back with a little jolt. That was something else to get used to. She supposed she wasn't a landlady anymore.

Her father had no trouble reading her expression. "The brownstone is yours as long as you want it. I'm happy to hand back the reins." His gaze cut to the two listening djinn. "Unless, of course, you've made other plans for your future?"

Sorting out her future was a nut she couldn't crack right then. "I don't know what I'm planning. We need to find those djinn kids who went missing."

"We should watch your cousin," Arcadius said. "If she cast a love spell on the sorcerer, he'll go to her sooner or later. In truth, he may be with her now."

"We should catch a few hours sleep," his double contradicted. "Elyse is exhausted."

"*I* can go," Arcadius said. "All I need are directions to where she is."

"You don't look much better than Elyse."

Arcadius glowered. Now that she checked, he did look dead on his feet.

"He's right," Elyse said. "We had an eventful night *before* we got here. We all need rest, food, and human clothes. And maybe a nice hot shower. We can start fresh tomorrow."

Arcadius frowned harder.

"It's the *strategic* choice," Cade said. "You shouldn't flail blindly around this dimension just because you're impatient."

"I concede your point for now," his double relented grudgingly.

Elyse's father laughed and bent to kiss her cheek. "Perhaps I should leave you to it. I can see your hands are full. I'll be across the way. Call me if you need anything."

She needed him. She wasn't done reassuring herself that he was back.

"You'll be fine," he said. "These men of yours will take good care of you."

Arcadius opened his mouth, probably to deny that he was hers. He must have decided not to explain. He looked extremely stubborn when he clamped his jaw shut again.

~

Arcadius was alone in Elyse's living room. Elyse was showering and singing—not very well, if he were honest. Cade had descended to the basement to retrieve his old human clothes. Had Cade and Joseph truly not minded staying in a dank cellar? Roughing it on campaign was one thing. Taking up residence underground was another.

Djinn weren't meant to live like mushrooms.

Arcadius stood drawn slightly back from the window, gazing out at the lamplit street while remaining unseen himself. He was half on the watch for danger, half simply surveying the area. The narrow connected houses had a sense of age like the ones he knew but not as much of one. Though Elyse's neighborhood seemed cared for, there was more dirt here than in his city—more *grit*, he guessed he'd say. Their environs weren't wholly unpleasant. The parked cars squeezed up against the curb were intriguing.

Would he be here long enough to drive one?

He turned at a sound. The door to the apartment opened. "It's me," Cade said, coming in. "I have clothes for both of us. Plus Joseph's survival supply briefcase. He left it lying under a chair. I guess Mario and his boys didn't notice it."

Though Arcadius wasn't sure what briefcase he referred to, he nodded. Cade draped a pile of garments over the spine of the leather couch.

Curious, Arcadius went to look at them.

"Underwear," Cade identified. "Business shirt. Trousers. I grabbed a couple T-shirts and jeans in case we need to look casual. We never bought pajamas, but the underwear is fine for sleeping in."

The pair Arcadius picked up was soft and formfitting. It certainly wouldn't hide much if he had any . . . reactions to Elyse.

"They're clean," Cade said. "Not that my germs are anything you haven't met before."

Arcadius guessed he'd looked dubious. A fear of germs wasn't the reason. He decided it was time to stop beating around the bush. "How are we going to handle this?"

Cade sat on the sofa arm. "You're not talking about what to wear, are you?"

"How do we handle being together with Elyse? How do we handle both of us wanting her?"

Cade met Arcadius's eyes. "You don't just want her."

"I don't just want her," he admitted.

"Do you love her?"

He started to deny it. "I'm not certain," he said instead.

Cade scratched the knee of his djinn trousers. "I didn't realize I was in love with her until Fate shoved it in my face."

That was vaguely alarming. "I'm not you—or not entirely."

Cade looked away toward a wall of nice bookcases. Arcadius knew the other man was gathering his thoughts. Because it was what he would have wanted, he didn't interrupt. Finally, Cade was ready to speak again.

"I think we should focus on what we agree on. We both want her safe and we both want her happy. We won't be able to stop her from helping us find those kids, so it's important we work together to protect her."

Arcadius saw no cause for argument in this. There were, however, more matters to discuss. Following Cade and Elyse through the portal had taught him a few new things about his sentiments.

"What about Elyse's bed? Would you be agreeable to both of us pleasuring her?"

Cade's lips twisted into a less comfortable expression. "You've healed from your injuries. We don't have to do that again."

"Are you implying you didn't enjoy sharing her?"

"I . . . enjoyed it," Cade admitted.

"As did I. As did Elyse, I believe. She might have stronger emotional ties to you, but she finds me attractive."

Cade's chest sank with a sigh. "I can't speak for her."

Arcadius wanted a straighter answer. "If she wishes to repeat the experience, would you object?"

"I don't know," Cade said.

"Would you be unhappy?"

"I don't know," he repeated a little angrily. He stood and strode to the bookcase. Once there, he pulled out a book and shoved it in again. "What we did was exciting, but it complicates matters. And I feel strange about how much it appealed to me."

Arcadius felt strange about it too. He sensed this wasn't the moment to mention his interest in sleeping with Elyse solo. "Perhaps we need more time to consider this."

Cade nodded and sighed again. He was facing Arcadius, his shoulders against the shelves. "She's happy to be back," he said as if he wanted someone to confide in but wasn't sure Arcadius ought to be that person.

"This is her home," Arcadius said. "I'm sure that's natural."

"I was happy too when I realized where we'd landed. This place grows on a person."

If Cade was suggesting this was a problem, Arcadius thought they had bigger ones. "I'm sure it's possible to love more than one city."

The question for him was: was it possible for a woman to love more than one djinni?

Cade wasn't thinking along those lines. He rubbed his mouth and contemplated the apartment door. "Now that she's discovered her father is alive, she'll be even more attached to New York."

Ah, Arcadius thought. *That's the ill wind he's conjured up.*

"Don't borrow trouble," he advised, surprised he could see the issue clearly when the other him could not. "For one thing, her father isn't averse to exotic travel. For another, should it become necessary, I have no doubt Elyse will choose to stay with you."

"You can't know that," Cade said.

"Can't I?" Arcadius asked. "Perhaps in this instance I have a cooler head. Emotion clouds reason."

Cade grimaced, but didn't get a chance to retort. The distant waterfall of Elyse's seemingly endless shower cut off. As if it were on a swivel, Cade's head yanked around in the direction of where she was.

Arcadius's snort of amusement was soft but audible. "Go on," he said as Cade glanced at him. "Go to her. I've conceded we can't settle our . . . complications this minute."

The other him utterly failed to hide his eagerness. He pushed off and went to her, leaving Arcadius forgotten.

God help me if ***I*** *ever look that lovesick,* Arcadius thought wryly.

~

Elyse was back in her own bedroom, squeaky clean from her long hot shower. Her head rested on Cade's bare chest. He was relaxed but not asleep, just lying there silently holding her. His heart beat a soothing rhythm beneath her ear. Elyse drew a circle on his ribs with one finger.

"I should be conked out," she said.

"You have a lot in your head."

"Don't you?"

His chest rocked with a quiet laugh. "Of course."

He didn't volunteer what it was. "I like being in my home with you," she said.

His muscular arms tightened slightly around her. "Me too. I mean I like being in your home with you."

She smiled, wriggling comfortably against him. She wondered if she should ask what she wanted to. "Is he awake?"

He was bunked on the couch in the living room, which he'd chosen as a better vantage point than David's office for listening to street noises. The living room was also the furthest spot in the house from them.

Cade seemed likely to be aware of this. His hand glided down her spine. "I don't know. Do you want me to check our link?"

"No. Unless you can't help it, maybe that's a breach of his privacy." She listened but couldn't hear if Arcadius moved around.

"You want to check on him," Cade guessed.

"Would you mind?" Elyse pushed up on her forearms to gaze in his face.

"I think we've established you make your own decisions, especially in your world."

"But will me worrying about Arcadius bother you?"

He touched her face, his fingertips skating lightly around its shape. His expression didn't give much away, but she could tell he was mulling over the question. "I think you should be your authentic self."

She smiled. Where he'd picked up that term she didn't know. Her *authentic self* thought she needed to ask permission. Sleeping together had changed their dynamic, opening them to possibilities that she, at least, wasn't ready to look straight at. Thankful she didn't have to, she dropped a kiss onto Cade's mouth and rolled out of bed.

"I love you," she said, remembering she'd wanted to say it.

"And I you," he responded.

~

Elyse's gut hadn't misled her. Arcadius was awake. When she padded into the living room in her oversized Mets T-shirt, he was sitting up on the couch. Then again, why would he be asleep? He was in a stranger's home, a stranger's world—and no doubt feeling third-wheely.

"What's wrong?" he asked even as his gaze dropped to her bare knees and calves.

Maybe the Mets shirt wasn't as modest as she'd thought.

"Nothing," she said. "The sun's coming up. It'll be bright in here. I didn't show you how to pull the shades." She pulled them down the two front windows, the nape of her neck prickling with the awareness that he watched her. "There. Maybe you can sleep now."

"I feel like someone should stand sentry."

"That defeats the purpose of coming here to rest."

"Still," he said.

Elyse shook her head, admiring his dedication if not his approach to taking care of himself. "I'm not an expert like you and Cade, but didn't Mario kill Samir because we made him feel cornered? He ran *from* us. I don't think he's going to come here."

"His courage might recover. Cade mentioned he had allies in your dimension."

"Okay, but won't your commander instincts kick in if someone tries to sneak in?"

Arcadius's mouth curved the slightest bit. "Maybe."

"Probably," she countered. "You and Cade have ears like bats. I suspect something else is keeping you awake."

The curve of his lips deepened. "What if I said it was you?"

She sensed he was testing her reaction—testing his own, perhaps. She tried not to make a big deal of it. "I'd say I was flattered."

He crossed his arms, his slight smile gone skeptical. Either that or he was fishing for her to prove it.

"Oh, whatever," she huffed. She strode to him and fluffed the pillow he should have been sleeping on. "Lie back." Her tone held a hint of the dominatrix she'd pretended to be before. She guessed the approach worked. Arcadius reclined and looked up at her, waiting for what came next. She pulled a footstool up beside him, sitting on it and reaching over to stroke her thumb across his forehead.

Arcadius must have expected something else. His expression was puzzled.

"My father used to do this when I was little," she explained. "I never could sleep the night before he went on trips."

"He didn't take you with him?"

"Not if I had school or if he was going somewhere politically tricky."

"Tricky?"

"He wouldn't admit it to my face, but my dad is a bit of a risk junkie."

Arcadius shifted onto his side. "Humans have interesting ways of phrasing things."

"So you *do* like something about us."

She was teasing, but he answered seriously. "You're different, but I was wrong to think you were less."

She grinned. "I bet you don't say *that* often."

"If I start choking, you can . . . give me CPR."

His unexpected joke surprised her into laughing.

"I said that right?" he asked.

"Yes, you did." She considered him as she continued to pet his brow. "You have a good smile."

"I have the same smile as him."

Oh, that was fishing for sure. "It's not exactly the same."

He smirked. "Is mine prettier?"

She shoved his chest. "Now you're being silly."

He caught the hand she'd pushed him with, turning it gently but firmly to kiss the underside of her wrist. As his lips brushed her there, Elyse's nerves tingled all the way up her arm. His eyes locked onto hers knowingly.

"Thank you, Elyse," he said, his voice mock-grave. "I believe I will sleep now."

Elyse pulled her hand back and rose, more unsettled than she was prepared for. "I'll leave you then," she said.

"Sleep well," was his sly answer.

CHAPTER TEN

AMAZINGLY, none of them woke until eleven the next day. Elyse was peering into her refrigerator, futilely trying to wish food onto its empty shelves, when her father knocked on the door. Cade went to let him in. She'd noticed he was at ease in her home—and with her father, for that matter.

"Leo," he said, like a long-time boyfriend—respectful but friendly too.

Her dad clapped Cade on his big shoulder. "I've got bagels and news." He looked around. "Where's the other one?"

"In the shower," Cade said. "He's discovered the second thing he likes about your world."

"What's the first?"

"Cars. He asked if we could buy one."

"God help him if he tries driving in Manhattan. Better he should memorize subway lines." As he spoke, Leo unpacked the breakfast bag on the island. Elyse started making coffee, interrupting herself to open a drawer and pass him the bagel knife before he asked for it.

Falling back into their old rhythm was surreal. They'd done this divvying up of morning duties too many times to count. She was gladder than she could say that they were doing it now. She would have hugged him again, but he was being casual.

"What's the news?" she asked.

"Well, you don't have to stake out your cousin Cara. Your Aunt June invited you and me to dinner. An official celebration of both our homecomings."

"Where does she think I was?"

Her dad pried open the cream cheese tub. "On vacation in Turkey. I mentioned you brought friends back. She said the more the merrier."

Elyse had her doubts about it being merry. "Did she say Cara would be there?"

"She practically guaranteed it. June says she's been seeing a lot of her since Vince died."

That surprised her. Cara was more of a daddy's girl. But maybe guilt explained it. Perhaps, given everything she'd done, Cara craved her remaining parent's love.

"Is Aunt June making dinner?" she had to ask.

Aunt June's cooking was famously erratic. You never knew if you'd survive eating it.

"I convinced her you missed Moscato's pasta something awful while you were in Istanbul. She's having them cater."

Moscato's was a nice restaurant in Scarsdale. Elyse's *phew* was heartfelt.

Her dad handed her a cream cheese bagel topped with a transparent slice of lox, everything arranged exactly as she liked. Elyse bit into the treat and sighed. She'd enjoyed the food in the Glorious City, but this was nirvana.

"You like toasted or plain, kid?" Leo asked her lover.

"Toasted," Cade said, watching him prepare it with interest. Elyse smiled. He was like a kid waiting for his own sundae.

"Hey," Elyse said, realizing the implication of something else her dad said. "If Cara and Mario are engaged, won't he be at dinner too?"

Leo grinned like he was ten years old. "That's what I'm thinking."

"Oh, boy," Elyse said.

"Oh, boy," Cade agreed.

This should be interesting.

~

Having to do laundry underscored the fact that Elyse was in the real world again. Having a handsome djinni appear in her bedroom door while she folded pointed up that her life wasn't quite normal. Arcadius observed her at the chore for a few heartbeats.

"You do that yourself?" he asked curiously.

"If I don't, it won't get done." She laid a folded T-shirt on top of a pile of them.

"Fewer people have servants here."

He didn't sound judgmental. "Probably," she answered.

"In the Glorious City, if people are rich, their servants use magic to clean their clothes."

"I'm just glad I don't have to go to the Laundromat."

Arcadius nodded, no doubt plucking the word's meaning from the ethers. "Where's Cade?"

"Across the hall. He's grilling Dad about the layout of my aunt's house. Cade is hoping we'll get the chance to corner Mario on his own."

She'd already explained about the invitation to her Aunt June's. Arcadius shifted his weight against the doorframe. "You don't want to upset your aunt by apprehending the sorcerer in her presence?"

"My aunt has servants. And neighbors. It might be best if we don't have a magical shootout in front of witnesses."

"I see," Arcadius said.

Elyse tried not to color up as she extracted one of her nicer bras from the plastic basket of clean clothes. Arcadius was noticeably silent as she shook out and folded it. Losing her nerve, she ignored the underwear she saw next and pulled out a towel instead.

Arcadius cleared his throat. "I want to ask, what are your intentions toward the other me?"

"My intentions?" she responded, unprepared for this tack.

Arcadius looked sober. "Do you intend to marry him? To be with him forever?"

"I . . . well, he hasn't asked me, and forever isn't something I can predict but, yes, I'd be happy to spend the rest of my life with him."

"You love him."

Elyse gave up on folding and faced him. "Yes," she said, wanting no mistake about it.

Arcadius had crossed his arms but didn't appear upset. "You care about me too."

"You *are* direct," she said, reluctant to get into this.

"Directness can be useful." He dropped his arms and moved from the threshold into the room. His eyes had the same glow Cade's sometimes got, as if his single-minded concentration narrowed them to lasers. To her dismay, her heart rate went rabbity. Maybe Arcadius noticed. His gaze dropped for a second to the pulse in her neck. Elyse willed herself not to retreat.

Retreat equaled weakness for men like him.

"I won't compete with him for you," Arcadius announced.

"That's fortunate," she retorted a bit sharply. "As it happens, I'm not up for grabs. What we did . . ." She trailed off. Could she say for certain it wouldn't happen again? She couldn't deny they'd all enjoyed it.

Her hesitation gave Arcadius an opening to exploit. "Yes," he said in a low purring tone. "I haven't forgotten *what we did*. In the closet. In the bed. With your whip burning up my ass."

Suddenly, his big tall body was right in front of her. He'd backed her against the mattress without even touching her. She couldn't go any farther without toppling onto it. That didn't seem like a good idea. Warmth radiated from the wall of muscle that was his chest. The image of him bound to the sultan's bed—naked, writhing—rose too vividly in her mind.

It was followed by the memory of Cade fucking her on top of Arcadius. The small of her back could almost feel his skin.

"I won't cheat on Cade," she said with unfortunate breathiness.

A hot flush suffused his face, not embarrassment but arousal. "I won't make you," he promised in a counterproductively sexy growl.

She didn't have long to be relieved. He seized her face between his hands and covered her mouth with his.

Her hormones didn't mind his roughness. They went wild, her pussy instantly going wet. His lips were strong and agile, his tongue sleek and hungry. Raw sounds broke in his throat as he plundered and pulled at her. She loved those signs of his need for her: the too bold, too plain human. Aware that thinking like this was dangerous, she shoved at him.

Not hard enough, she guessed. Then again, maybe he was paying more attention to the reactions that weren't saying *no* to him. She'd done the same when she had him at her mercy. Rather than stop, he groaned and wrapped his arms around her. He didn't hurt her. His hands caressed as much as they controlled, but his greater strength—which was more than a human's—squeezed her tight to him.

She couldn't miss that his cock was erect, the big ridge grinding against her belly in stripper-style body rolls. God, that felt good. When his hand clamped around her bottom, her clit twitched with excitement.

She ached for his hardness to slide over that swollen button and into her.

"Stop," she said, shoving more forcefully at his chest. "*Please.*"

This time he listened. He pulled his head back and released her. His fingers curled toward his palms as if he itched to grab her again.

"I want you to myself," he said defensively. "I want to make love to you, without him."

"How is that not competing?" she demanded.

The flush in his cheeks took on a hint of embarrassment. "I didn't say I wouldn't give you back after I was done."

Elyse snorted. "I hope you realize that's not very flattering."

"Do you want to be flattered?" he challenged.

She had to think about that. David's hold on her hadn't been completely due to the magical poetry book. Her double-dealing husband had stroked her ego too, showering her with compliments she'd been hungry to believe. Some of the praise he'd meant. The rest he'd used to scam what he—and Cara—wanted out of her.

"I want to be told the truth," she said. "A*nd* I want to be loved. By someone I can count on."

Arcadius stared at her. She got the impression he'd taken in every word and stored it for later use. She expected him to speak, but he nodded curtly and turned away. Then at the door, he paused.

"I understand better now," he said over his shoulder.

When he went for good, he left her totally off balance.

Her hands were shaking. Should she interpret Arcadius's withdrawal as surrender? He didn't seem the sort to surrender a single inch unless it suited him. But maybe he'd decided he couldn't be the person she'd described and was leaving the field to his spirit twin. Cade *was* the man she'd spoken of. More than, actually, because his good qualities didn't end at her minimum. She admired as well as loved him. He'd earned her trust and her laughs and—God knows—her desire. He wasn't one gift; he was a hundred birthdays' worth. No woman could deserve a man like him. She could only feel lucky.

Secretly wishing she could have everything she wanted was worse than ungrateful.

~

Arcadius had a lot to consider as he dressed for dinner in Elyse's small home office. Though he'd kissed his double's woman impulsively, the results were informative. Fortunately, his brain felt steadier now that he'd decided—or perhaps admitted—that he wanted Elyse as a more than a fleeting presence in his life. He couldn't predict if he'd achieve his goal. What he had ruled out was waiting passively for Cade to determine what would happen between the three of them.

It would have to be the three of them. Elyse was too attached to Cade—and too principled a person in general—to expect her to cast him off. Arcadius didn't think less of her for that. A woman who would cheat on one man would assuredly cheat on another. In truth, Arcadius's natural competitiveness was getting more difficult to muster in regards to Cade. Arcadius was a logical man. It made *sense* to work with and not against the other him. Though it had nothing to do with logic, it also *felt* pleasant.

Pleasant didn't begin to describe working with his twin to satisfy Elyse.

Heat flooded his body, causing his fingers to falter on the smooth white shirt's buttons. The garment fit perfectly, of course. It was well made, as promised, and he and his double were the same size. Well, the same size excepting the aspect Elyse had mentioned when she'd been trying to anger him. She'd succeeded more than he'd let on but not so much that he'd dwell on it. In any case, smaller men were easier to "go down" on.

His mouth curved as the slang popped into his mind. He hadn't lied when he said he wanted to take Elyse without Cade. Since gratifying the wish might be difficult, making Cade watch her do him that favor would be a fine substitute. Getting his twin wound up offered multiple rewards—not the least being that Elyse enjoyed it.

Probably he shouldn't be thinking along those lines. When he shoved the dress shirt's tails into the tailored trousers, his hand met more obstruction than was ideal.

If he didn't get his libido under control, this would be a long evening.

He recognized his double's tap on the door. Since he was dressed, he opened it. He tried not to take offense as Cade examined him up and down.

"Good," Cade said. "You're ready. I assume you're armed?"

"Ankle sheath," Arcadius answered. "I figured our hostess wouldn't notice one small dagger."

"Breast pocket." Cade patted his jacket to indicate where his weapon was. He frowned at Arcadius's feet. "You can't wear slippers."

"These match." Black like the trousers, jet beads and dark blue sapphires decorated his footwear. "Those human shoes pinched my feet."

His pulse jumped when Elyse appeared in the door. He hadn't seen her since he'd left her in her bedroom. She'd finished her chores and then she'd been with Cade. For just an instant as her gaze met his, her eyes were self-conscious.

She hasn't told him about the kiss, he realized. He and Elyse shared a secret. But maybe she'd tell Cade later. Maybe she was working up to it. Was Arcadius upset that she hadn't told him? Should he have told Cade himself? Ridiculously, he found himself wishing he could ask Cade's opinion. The moral in and outs of this situation were difficult to sort out. All he knew for sure was that Elyse wasn't taking their talk lightly.

Neither are you, he thought as her attention dropped to the article of dress he and Cade were debating.

"Those are all right," she said. "Some men wear slippers in New York, and at least they're not bright colors."

Her stepping closer gave him a better view of her. She was wearing a garment he was too stupefied to find a name for. It was snug and black and showed off far too many inches of her fine legs. Her shoes were black and extremely shiny. They had heels that hoisted them off the ground, plus eye-catching scarlet soles. The display they made of her excellent calves and ankles literally stole his breath.

The words "Good Lord" burst from him unplanned.

His loss of control seemed worth it when she grinned delightedly. Then he noticed that her pillowy lips—her best feature after her eyes and rear—were painted a soft red. Her lashes had some sort of paint on them too, making her eyes greener. Djinn women sometimes wore cosmetics, but he'd never seen Elyse in them. How stunning she was didn't strike him as fair. He'd resigned himself to hankering after a somewhat ordinary looking woman. He wasn't prepared for the effect she had fully kitted out. His cock jerked inside his trousers, the warning he'd given it earlier forgotten.

"This is my little black dress," she said, turning in an obliging circle so his mouth could water from all angles. "I take it you approve."

"I'm not sure *approve* is the right word." Though he admired her appearance, he experienced a measure of alarm at the thought of her wearing those instruments of seduction in public. Wouldn't every man want to leap on her?

"The weather's cold," Cade reminded him, his slightly grim expression saying he understood. "She'll have a coat over it."

His comment took Elyse by surprise. "Come on, guys. This outfit isn't that revealing. And it shows zero cleavage."

Cade wagged his head and Arcadius did too. "You're lucky you have us to guard you," was all Arcadius said.

~

The village of Scarsdale, where Uncle Vince had established his family seat, was a ritzy suburb thirty minutes outside Manhattan on the Metro-North express. Vince had chosen it to suit his pretensions as a master of commerce and all-around important man. Elyse was familiar with the area and the journey. When she was young, she'd ridden this train many times, staying with Cara and Aunt June if her father was out of the country for more than a day or two. She'd attended Cara's fancy high school nearly as often as her own.

That she hadn't fit in there was an understatement of epic proportions.

She shook the memories off. This visit would be different. Tonight she had her father with her. And Cade and Arcadius. The dangers she faced had nothing to do with social awkwardness.

It said something that she'd rather confront a murderous magician than a clique of teenage girls.

They'd been lucky enough to find four seats facing each other on the train. Cade and Leo had their heads together and were going over possible scenarios by which they might get the jump on Mario and Cara. Arcadius's attention stayed on the remaining passengers—scanning them for threats, she presumed. He spared Leo and Cade half an ear, occasionally pulling a dubious face over their discussions.

"Would you stop that?" Cade complained quietly. "It can't hurt to consider the angles."

"It might not hurt," Arcadius said in the same low tone. "But it's likely a waste of time. The sorcerer will have his own plans, and if Elyse's cousin is anything like her, she's neither stupid nor cowardly. We need to resign ourselves to playing it by ear."

Elyse's eyes widened. Had Arcadius complimented her?

"Moreover," Arcadius went on before she could savor his approval, "what if the aunt is in on it? This dinner invitation could be a trap."

Elyse and Leo burst out laughing at the same time.

Arcadius's eyebrows lowered. "It could," he insisted.

"Sorry," her father said. "You're right. It could be a trap, but June won't be in on it. She's . . . well, you'll see when you meet her."

"She could be more devious than you realize."

Their arrival at the Scarsdale stop saved her father from answering. Aunt June had sent the car to meet them at the faux English half-timbered train station. The limo was the same classic silver Daimler she remembered. She couldn't deny it was a lovely car. Uncle Vince had demonstrated good taste about some things.

Mr. Pickering, the family's ancient driver, was holding the door for them. "Welcome back," he said to her and her father. "I'm very pleased you're not dead."

"Douglas," her dad replied, with his usual unfeigned pleasure. "How's that daughter of yours? Didn't I hear she shot under par at the Women's Open?"

"Yes, Mr. Solomon. We're all very proud of her."

Golf, Cade mouthed to Arcadius.

They slid into the Daimler's spacious rear section, which was a masterwork of hand-stitched leather, burled wood details, and silk wool carpeting. Arcadius gazed around like he thought it was pretty swell. "Does this automobile go fast?" he asked hopefully.

Her father smiled. "If that's your priority, you'd do better with a sports car."

Arcadius appeared to consider this seriously, which amused Leo more. Elyse guessed both the commanders were growing on her dad. She wished Arcadius's future vehicular adventures were all she was dwelling on. As they rode along Scarsdale's oak-lined streets, her uptightness increased.

You're not a kid anymore, she told herself. This place and Cara had no hold over her. Even if they did, it was moot tonight. She and her companions had more important fish to fry.

Uncle Vince's estate was on exclusive Heathcote Road. Mr. Pickering buzzed the iron gate open with his remote. The curving drive to the house was cobbled, the handsome, two-story wide brick front shown off by spotlights. The five acres of grass and trees on which the historic home was set were lusher than a golf course. Uncle Vince had paid four mill for property and liked to brag it was now worth eight.

She guessed he'd have to brag from the afterlife.

When Mr. Pickering opened the Daimler's door, Arcadius and Cade had a little scuffle over who would help her out.

It was good to be amused by that . . . and to see Aunt June. She appeared on the portico as bubbly and eager as if she'd been listening for the car. June was tall like her daughter—curvy too, though not as fashionably. Regular visits to the salon maintained her beautiful gold blonde hair. She liked big jewelry, bright colors, and—so she always said—pleasing her smart husband. She'd never had a job apart from that. Her tendency toward literalness had sometimes led Vince to tease her unkindly. Cara had never seemed to respect her, though perhaps that had changed.

"How wonderful!" June exclaimed. "Cara will be so happy to know you're here."

Leo hugged her gently and handed her a wine bottle.

"My favorite!" she said. "How good you are to remember. Come in, all of you. Georgia will take your coats."

Georgia was the housekeeper. There was a cook who came in sometimes, plus a pair of men who did odd jobs and took care of the landscaping. Once upon a time there had been string of nannies. Cara had gone through a lot of them.

"You look marvelous," June said to Elyse. "You must be happy to have your father back. Imagine him not being dead but wandering around Europe with amnesia! It's like a soap opera, don't you think? Oh, I do love your hair that way!"

Elyse touched it, unavoidably embarrassed about her mop of curls. Now that she was home, maybe she should have used her flatiron. She forced herself to pull her hand down. "Where is Cara? Dad told me she's engaged."

"Cara's . . . somewhere," her aunt said, waving her arm vaguely. "I'm afraid her young man won't be joining us tonight. He had business he couldn't get out of. I swear he's as busy a fellow as my Vince used to be."

She looked sort of sad for about two seconds. Elyse couldn't quite choke out that she was sorry for her loss.

She saw the djinn exchange looks at this development.

"That's too bad," Leo said, smoothly patting Aunt June's shoulder. "Shall I introduce you to Elyse's friends from Turkey?"

"Oh, *do*," she said, recovering quick as a wink. "It's so nice to meet new people!"

~

The aunt reminded Arcadius of a friendly but nervous bird that perpetually chittered and fluffed its wings. She led them—if such fits and starts could be called *leading*—to a small formal dining room. The table was beautifully appointed with fine china and lit candles. Sadly, the papered walls spoiled the space. The whole room was pasted over with faded caricatures of Chinamen in green robes. Mountains cragged in the background, their colors muddy and unpleasant. Mindful he was a guest, Arcadius tried to hide his distaste.

"You're admiring our wallpaper," the aunt burbled, noting his glance if not his expression. "Vince was so proud of that. It's real Victorian."

"Very nice," he said solemnly.

Cade coughed into his napkin. He was across the table next to Leo, with a view of the dining room's broad entry. Arcadius had snagged the seat beside Elyse, his vantage the two "French" doors to the softly lit garden. Elyse seemed tense. He wondered if it would help to rub her hand. Cade did that frequently. Before he could decide, the aunt turned to him. She'd taken the position of authority at the table's head, where—despite her dithery manner—she appeared comfortable.

"How long have you been twins?" she asked interestedly.

Arcadius had to pick up his jaw. What did she mean: how long had they been twins? Leo had presented him and Cade as siblings. Could this human have recognized them as not the ordinary sort?

"All our lives, ma'am," Cade answered for him with careful gravity.

The aunt broke into a laugh, her hand covering her mouth. "Of course. Forgive me. Vince always said I should think before I speak. I simply can't get over how much alike you look."

"I'm the handsome one," Cade said straight-faced.

The aunt gaped a moment and then laughed at that as well. "Call me, June, won't you?"

"June," Cade agreed, bowing his head to her.

Arcadius saw his shoulders had relaxed. His double seemed to have dismissed June as a threat. He'd have to watch her on his own, he guessed.

Cade's body language changed again as someone new came to the doorway.

"Hello, Cara," he said coolly. "Nice to see you again."

"Arcadius," a smooth feminine voice replied.

Her spicy perfume had arrived ahead of her. Arcadius turned to find a younger, more confident version of the aunt in the broad archway. Now this was a striking woman. Tall and curvaceous, Cara's voluptuous figure stretched all the right sections of her burgundy velvet dress. Modesty seemed not to concern her. A handsome garnet necklace drew attention to the valley of her cleavage. Her hair was honey blonde like her mother's but shiny and shoulder length. She flicked it behind her and pursed her painted mouth.

She made him think of a harem girl who couldn't conceive of the sultan choosing anyone but her as the favorite.

"That one's Cade, I think," June corrected. "Do you two know each other?"

Cade answered before her daughter could. "We met when I visited Elyse in New York by myself earlier." He held Cara's gaze steadily. "I'm sorry your fiancé won't be joining us tonight. I looked forward to seeing him again."

Cara narrowed her cool green eyes. Although expertly made up, they weren't as tender and lovely as Elyse's. "I wouldn't worry about that. I'm sure you'll meet up with him soon enough." She turned to Arcadius and cocked her head. "So. There really are two of you. Elyse gets herself into the oddest spots sometimes."

"Elyse is woman enough to handle any . . . oddity," he returned.

She didn't like the suggestiveness he injected into that. She frowned, and he smiled, and then she jerked her gaze from him with a small head toss.

Elyse had twisted around in her chair to watch this exchange. Cara greeted her by name and bent toward her, instantly causing both men to tense. Neither would bet Elyse's safety that this woman wouldn't harm her in front of her mother. Arcadius ground his teeth as Cara touched Elyse's shoulders, leaning in as if to kiss her cheek. He supposed Cara didn't have as much experience with djinn as her fiancé. She must not have known they heard every word she said.

"You blab to my mom, you die," she said in an undertone.

Elyse's head jerked back, her eyes locking onto her cousin's. "I guess that answers my question about whether you regret your choices."

"Girls," their hostess scolded, reading their demeanor if not their words. "This is a celebration. Don't start up your old squabbling."

Her daughter smiled as if she didn't know what a squabble was. "I was just admiring what Elyse has done, or rather *not* done with her hair."

"It is nice, isn't it?" June said. Arcadius noticed Elyse had blushed.

"As a bird's nest," Cara sniped creamily. She sauntered behind Elyse to the remaining place setting, which was located at the foot of the white-draped table. On the way, her manicured nail tapped Elyse's silver spoon. It was a playful gesture, idle to most people's perception.

Cade and Arcadius weren't most people. Their brows shot up as the shimmer of a pre-made spell leaped from her fingertip to the utensil.

"Goodness," Arcadius exclaimed, immediately leaning across Elyse to wrap the thing in a white napkin. "I think there's a spot on this. Perhaps it should be returned to the kitchen."

June made dismayed noises he didn't pay attention to. He checked the spell carefully. It wasn't poison but a compulsion that Elyse wouldn't "blab"—should Cara's whispered threat not prove effective. He sent Cade a look to say as much and sat back again.

"What was that about?" Elyse asked softly.

"I'll tell you later," he said. "Everything's fine for now."

When he smiled at her, somehow he couldn't restrict his response to that. A spot of warmth was expanding inside of him, as penetrating as sunshine. The perhaps misleading sense that she was his to protect was pleasurable. He squeezed her hand as he'd wanted to before.

Though Elyse's expression was perplexed, she didn't pull away.

"Okay," she said. "I guess I'll wait till then."

~

Cade had decided to be the less paranoid member of his and Arcadius's alliance. Nonetheless, he didn't like the vibe Elyse's cousin was giving off. Cara picked at her food, was borderline rude to her own mother, and sent hooded hostile looks toward Elyse. No doubt about it: she was up to something.

All through dinner she'd been periodically touching a small clutch purse, which she'd laid within reach beside her plate. The contents buzzed as her mother's housekeeper set dishes of sorbet in front of them for dessert.

Cara pushed back her chair and rose. "Excuse me. I need to take this call."

"We're still eating," her mother said. "Can't it wait?"

"Sorry," Cara said and slipped away hurriedly.

Her spiky shoes clacked into the hallway and kept going. At the rate she was moving, she'd soon be out of eavesdropping range.

"Forgive me," Cade said to June. "Could you tell me where to find the facilities?"

She gave him more convoluted directions than were convenient, considering he didn't actually need them. He strove to hide his impatience until she trailed off.

"Got it," he said and went after her daughter. A quick glance up and down the hall assured him it was clear of servants. He changed swiftly into his least visible smoke form. The corridors weren't well lit. Even if she was on alert, Cara was unlikely to notice his vaporous shimmer.

He found her in a study whose masculine furniture must have been her father's. Her profile faced him, her attention on her cell phone.

"Can't you handle it yourself?" she was asking into it.

The voice that came back was buzzy, but he thought it was Mario's. "I need the extra juice," he said. "Tonight's pair is resisting me."

"This isn't what we planned."

"Just get here," the male voice snapped.

Cara's caller hung up. She shoved the cell phone back in her bag as if it had annoyed her. She tapped her lips thoughtfully. A moment later, she dug out a set of keys—car keys, he concluded from the beeper gadget they were attached to.

This presented him with a dilemma. He could follow her in his smoke form, but that would split up their team. Given Mario's experience with magic, he might well spot Cade in vapor form. Depending on the nature of the "pair" he'd mentioned, Cade would be up against a superior force. He'd also be leaving Elyse with only Arcadius and Leo to protect her. From what he knew of Cara, she was a good actress. This business with the call might be a ruse to divide and conquer.

Cara appeared to have made up her mind. The study had its own window doors to the outside. She exited through them without bothering to grab a coat—or to say goodbye to her mother's guests. Cade watched her stride across the lawn until she disappeared into a large separate garage. Half a minute later, a car revved. Doors rolled up and a sleek green Jaguar zipped down the drive.

Damn it, he thought, still not following her.

He sincerely hoped he'd made the right decision.

When he rejoined the others, they were drinking coffee from delicate cups in a large white-on-white parlor.

"There you are," their hostess burbled. "We thought you'd fallen in."

Cade blinked at that idea. His gaze traveled automatically to Elyse. She sat on a spindly sofa next to her father, her cup and saucer perched on her stockinged knees. She was so different from her cousin—endearingly awkward, certainly less dramatic—and yet to him she was infinitely more beautiful.

The heart creates beauty, he thought, surprising himself a bit. *Both in the lover and in the loved.*

"Aunt June was telling us Cara has been staying in her old rooms," Elyse informed him. Her manner said she thought this significant.

"I was surprised she wanted to," June confessed. "She has her own apartment in the city and, well, to be truthful, Cara always was closer to Vince than she is to me. Peas in a pod, those two. Not that Cara and I don't love each other."

"She's just worried because you're on your own," Leo said soothingly.

"I suppose so," June said. "Or she misses Vince and feels like his spirit's here. Anyway, it's touching." She shook her head and *tched* sympathetically.

"Could I speak to you a moment?" Cade took the opportunity to ask Arcadius.

"Perhaps that could wait," Leo said.

Elyse's father stood. The way his suit hung on him gave it a sort of dash. His hand went into his trouser pocket, coming out with a small wrapped object. "I have one more guest gift for you, June."

"For me?" Her hand pressed her soft bosom.

"Because I missed your birthday while I had amnesia. I found it in Italy. It's really quite special."

June opened the crinkling tissue. Something colorful was inside. "Oh!" she gasped. "A majolica nightingale! You remembered I collect—"

Her chin dropped to her chest mid-sentence and she began to snore.

"Dad!" Elyse exclaimed. "What did you do to her?"

"It's just a harmless djinn artifact. People use them in your boyfriends' world instead of sleeping pills."

June began to list forward in her chair. Leo pushed her back gently. Cade understood then how Elyse's seemingly nonviolent father had maintained control of the nexus for all those years. Friendly though he was, when it came to accomplishing what he thought was important, Leo was pragmatic.

"There we go," he said, satisfied their hostess wouldn't topple onto the floor. "Now we can search the house without upsetting her. Cara left to meet Mario, I take it?"

"How did you know?" Cade asked.

"Lucky guess," he said, waving it away. "I believe both Elyse and myself have been wondering why Cara is sticking close to her childhood home . . . unless she wants to keep an eye on something here."

"Exactly," Elyse said. "She doesn't show any signs of enjoying her mother's company, or of being worried about her."

"You think the missing djinn might be here," Cade deduced.

"They might," Leo said. "The property is big enough."

"What are we waiting for?" Arcadius asked, rubbing his hands together.

"Let's search this pile of bricks."

They moved together into the hall. Only Elyse glanced back at her slumbering aunt. Cade guessed June seemed okay, because Elyse shrugged her worry off. Leo shut the door quietly behind them.

"We should toss Cara's rooms first," he said.

Elyse rubbed her cheek unsurely. "Wouldn't the servants have noticed if she were keeping people there?"

"Not if the djinn are sealed in containers. Cara and Mario might only be letting them out when they have a use for them. They wouldn't even require feeding."

Cade and Arcadius winced. Being imprisoned for long periods was disagreeable. Unless you stayed in your smoke form, you got hungry or ran out of oxygen. The longer you were prevented from turning physical, the greater the risk of mental confusion—which could become permanent.

"All right," Elyse said. "Cara's old rooms are on the second floor."

They succeeded in avoiding servants along the way. Elyse's nervousness increased as they climbed the stairs. Cade wasn't the only one who noticed.

"Are you okay?" Arcadius asked her.

"Fine," she said. "Just . . . remembering past visits. Sleepovers with Cara weren't exactly the highlight of my childhood."

"You never told me that," Leo said. "I thought you idolized your cousin."

"I did. But that made it harder when she was mean. Even when she wasn't, constantly remembering to let her be the star was stressful."

Spread out for safety, they progressed down a carpeted hall. Elyse was in the cautious lead. No lamps were on in this corridor, but a window at the end let in the subdued landscape lighting. Elyse stopped at the final door.

"This should be it," she said.

She didn't seem inclined to open it.

Arcadius reached past her and turned the knob. "Wait here. I'll take a look around." He returned a minute later. "It seems fine. I don't sense any magical booby-traps."

Leo entered and flipped on the light switch.

Cade restrained a whistle. A daughter from a good djinn family wouldn't have minded sleeping here. The walls were pink, of course, the furnishings frilly. They were good quality, though, and the space was large. Windows deep enough to enclose reading seats offered a view of the house's grounds. Other doors led to a bathroom, a large partitioned closet, and what appeared to be a sitting room with a nice antique desk.

Elyse didn't gaze around like the others. She'd come to a halt in one corner in front of a large dollhouse. Two stories tall plus an attic, the elaborate structure was fully furnished inside and out—and nearly as tall as her. The "grounds" for the house included trees and a swing set. The creation was so detailed that, had it not been a human toy, Cade would have concluded it was magically shrunken. Within the house were little rugs and light fixtures and dolls dressed up in old-fashioned human clothes. The dining room table had plates of food on it.

"Good Lord," Arcadius exclaimed.

Elyse shivered and turned away from it. "I'll search Cara's desk. See if she's bought or rented new property. That thing gives me the creeps. Whenever we played, I had to be the ugly doll."

Leo shot her a surprised look, so Cade guessed he hadn't known that either. Leo had already started on the bedroom bookshelves, removing vases and treasure boxes to scan for animate contents. Since he seemed competent to do so, Arcadius checked around the bed.

Left to watch their backs, Cade probed the area for magic. Every sign he sensed was extremely faint. Cara seemed not to practice on the same level as her boyfriend. By this point, Elyse might have the edge in experience.

Cade was willing to bet Mario had supplied Cara with the "don't blab" spell.

"If anyone notices a small book of love poems, they should grab it," he said. "Carefully."

"Haven't seen one," Leo answered. "I assume it's an artifact."

"Cara used it to make Mario fall in love with her. We might gain an advantage if we can break the spell."

Arcadius rummaged through a bureau drawer full of colorful silk and lace. "I haven't seen anything like that."

"Cara wouldn't leave that book where we could find it," Elyse added from the sitting room. "David wasn't as paranoid as her, and even he hid it well."

"David?" Arcadius asked Cade.

"Her former husband. Now dead. By Mario's hand."

"Her husband spelled her to love him? That's unconscionable."

"It wasn't quite that simple, but yes."

"I'm not finding anything," Elyse called from her search area. "Dad, how long does that sleep spell last?"

"Forty minutes or thereabouts. I've struck out here. I'm starting on the closet."

Arcadius had finished searching around the bed. He moved as if he intended to join Leo, then paused to look at Cade.

"*Is* she all right?" he asked in an undertone. "It's not like Elyse to let her imagination run away with her."

He jerked his head to indicate the dollhouse, which she'd mentioned gave her the creeps. Suddenly, a memory prodded Cade. Elyse had claimed the nexus room above the Arch of Triumph was creepy too. He hadn't thought it through at the time, but Mario must have been there already, impersonating Joseph's statue. What if she were more sensitive to magic than they realized? What if she'd known, subconsciously, that the sorcerer was there?

"Elyse," he called. "Come back here for a moment."

She came to the doorway.

"Check the dollhouse," he said. "I'm not sensing magic in it, but you might."

"There's nothing there," she protested.

"It could be small. A shrunken spell like Samir put in the bouquet of roses to contact his sister."

"Or a shrunken *thing*," Arcadius added, seeing what Cade was getting at. "The missing djinn could be trapped in miniature containers. Look for anything brass, Elyse. Especially if it's sealed."

Still Elyse hesitated. Arcadius held out his hand to encourage her to come. "I'll be right with you. You might be uneasy due to a magical repulsion."

She went to him and took his hand. Cade was oddly touched to see how gentle his double was with her. Together, they bent closer to the dollhouse: one broad-shouldered back and one slender. Cade pointed out possible containers, but Elyse repeatedly shook her head.

"They're nothing. I don't think –" She stopped speaking and wrinkled her forehead.

"What is it?" Arcadius asked her.

"The root cellar," she said. "I remember it opens."

Arcadius unlatched the tiny doors for her. She'd drawn back, so he looked inside first. Cade sensed his excitement even before he spoke.

"They're here," he announced.

CHAPTER ELEVEN

IT had been a while since she'd seen it, but the same black painted compartment Elyse recalled was under the miniature doors. Cara had used it to hide contraband—forbidden lipstick when she was little, inappropriate gifts from boyfriends as she got older.

Tonight Arcadius pulled out four teensy Aladdin lamps, none bigger than her thumb from the nail to its first knuckle. Though the patterns on the containers' sides were small, she recognized the King Solomon seal.

Arcadius cradled his discovery carefully in one palm. The caution was necessary. One good sneeze could have tumbled them away.

"Holy smokes," Elyse said, too shocked to avoid the pun. "Are they alive in there?"

"We'll see when you let them out," he said gravely.

"Should I? I mean, won't they be disoriented? What if they think we're working with Mario and panic?"

"We have to risk it," Arcadius said. "Keeping them in smoke form any longer could lead to damage they can't recover from. On the other hand, maybe Cade should shift first. Prevent them from fleeing or attacking before we have a chance to explain."

Cade nodded, dissolving into a fog that spread across the window seats. He did this so easily it was breathtaking.

"Release them one at a time," Leo suggested, positioning himself in front of the hallway door.

If this worked, it was going to be interesting explaining four news guests to Aunt June.

"Okay," she said. "Hand me the first brass lamp."

The thing didn't weigh much more than a stick of gum. Troublingly, she didn't feel the smallest tingle of magic. She breathed slowly in and out and told herself to focus. She drew the ritual circle with the tip of her pinkie. "If you are one who honors the Holy Name, I free you from captivity."

Nothing happened.

"You forgot to remove the lid," her father said. "I'll fetch a tweezers from the bathroom."

She prized out the bit of metal and tried again.

A trickle of smoke wisped from the small opening.

Please God, she thought. *Let this kid be all right.*

"We're here to help," Leo said soothingly. "It's safe for you to come out."

Her dad was the djinn whisperer, she guessed. The wisp grew stronger, and bigger, and then the air in front of her shook with a muffled *whump.* A very pale, very thin teenage boy materialized in front of her—full size, to her relief. He swayed on his feet, and she shot her hands out to catch his wrists. The skin she clasped was clammy.

"Balu," she said, unable to mistake his beautiful gray eyes. "Yasmin will be overjoyed you're alive."

He tried to pull away but staggered again. She could tell he was afraid to accept her help. "Who are you?" he demanded. "How do you know my sister?"

"Explanations later," Arcadius said in his steady commander way. "We'd like to free your companions too."

Elyse repeated the process she'd used to get Balu out. Two girls appeared and then another boy. Balu turned out to be in the best shape. The others were white as paper and too shaky to stand, much less run. Arcadius helped each to Cara's flowery princess bed, where they sat in a huddle together.

Elyse felt like she was meeting characters who'd escaped a storybook. The kids were dressed like normal teenagers in Wal-Mart type jeans and flannel shirts, but something about their eyes—or maybe *behind* their eyes—declared them to be not human.

Yasmin's brother seemed to be the group's spokesperson.

"Excuse me, ma'am," he said politely. "Could we have some water?"

"I'll fetch it," Leo said, striding to the bathroom. He returned with a single glass, probably all he found. The way the kids shared the drink with each other was touching. Elyse was glad to see their color returning.

Recovering or not, they continued to throw their rescuers nervous looks, as if freedom were a state they'd given up on believing in. Elyse thought maybe she could ease their minds.

"You must be Patrizio and Celia," she said to the pair who appeared the most romantic. The girl's wavy cloud of golden hair hadn't once left Patrizio's skinny but broad shoulder. "Arcadius and I saw your pictures at the bottle house. I'm very glad you got through this together." She turned to the remaining girl, who looked less soft and more defensive. Her sharp looks were very pretty, her auburn hair chopped in a punk human style. "Are you Jeannine?"

Her eyes went wide as she nodded. "How do you know who we are?"

"Balu's sister Yasmin pieced together that you'd all gone missing."

"How could she do that?" Balu burst out in confusion. "She's stuck in the harem."

Arcadius put his hand on the boy's shoulder. "Your sister is resourceful. And very concerned for you."

Balu's expression revealed the struggle inside of him. "What about . . . did she realize our brother Ramis helped the human sorcerer kidnap us?"

His lips shook with shame and anger, his lustrous eyes on the verge of tears.

"She knows it now," Arcadius said. "I don't know if this will upset you, but your brother is dead."

"Good," Balu said. "I hope he rots in hell."

Arcadius gave his arm a pat.

"What about the sorcerer?" Patrizio asked.

"Mario is still alive, as is his woman. Don't be alarmed. They're not here now, and we'll protect you."

Cade must have realized his double's claim would be more convincing if he took physical form. He materialized where they could see him, right next to Arcadius. Standing side by side that way, they formed an impressive wall.

"Whoa," Jeannine exclaimed with humorously human inflection.

"Hey," Balu said. "Aren't you two the sultan's commander?"

"We are." Cade's boyish grin pointed up the difference between him and his spirit twin. "Your sister wasn't messing around when she got help for you." He touched Elyse's shoulder. "This is Elyse and her father Leo. They're friendly humans who are experienced in magic."

"Especially my father," Elyse said, not wanting her skills exaggerated beyond what they really were.

"Can you tell us what's been happening to you?" Arcadius asked.

"You don't know?" Balu sounded surprised.

"Our information is sketchy," Cade responded.

"Okay," Balu said. "I guess I'll fill you in . . ."

Balu's Tale

So . . . we're all lost kids, in one way or another. My situation wasn't too bad—though I thought it was at the time. My brother turned ifrit, which you know. My sister left home to join the harem, sticking me with parents who didn't understand me blah blah blah. I hung out at the view café because I like human stuff, but a privileged kid like me didn't really fit in there either.

Jeannine's parents were actually worth running from. They beat her and . . . other stuff, and working at the bathhouse—while not the best—was an improvement.

Patrizio and Celia were on the streets due to having no folks at all. When they got tired of being poor and hungry, they asked the bottle house to store them. They were hoping a good foster situation or job would come in that would let them stay together. They're in love, you see, and can't bear to be split up.

Ramis selected them from the pictures in the bottle house's record book. Mario hired my brother to find good-looking young djinn who weren't likely to be missed. Jeannine he discovered at the cosplay club. Me, well, I didn't take much convincing. I wanted to believe Ramis was the same big brother I'd loved before. He promised us new lives in the human world. Said we could be supermodels or princes of industry—anything we wanted, because our magic would give us a leg up.

Ramis convinced me Yasmin would join us here someday, and we could be a family again. I could tell he wanted that. I just didn't realize that was the only thing he told the truth about. He'd never been the djinni I thought he was. Yasmin and I wouldn't have been free in the human world. We'd have been his and Mario's slave labor.

Anyway, none of us guessed what we were in for.

Mario said he had to make us small to send us through a portal without it needing a big charge. Crossing dimensions like we planned to do was illegal. If someone official noticed the door was used, the operation would be shut down. Worse, the sultan might send men after us. Because we knew this was true, we let Mario spell us into those lamps voluntarily. Probably we should have refused when we saw they had seals. We wouldn't be able to smoke out on our own. Mario talked his way around us, claiming the seals were there to protect us from damage on the journey.

He promised another human would pick us up on the other side.

He also promised she'd let us out.

We don't know where we landed except that it was cold. The oil lamps got really chilly once we arrived. Someone collected us—Mario's girlfriend, we guess—but no one let us out for days. After a while, we discovered we could hear each other if we yelled loud enough. Jeannine was the one who badgered us into turning physical periodically. We weren't going to otherwise. We didn't have food or drink, and we were afraid we'd use up the air. She was right, though. We got thin and shaky but not crazy. When Mario finally let us out, usually one at a time, we had our wits about us.

He had a bunch of things he wanted us to do for him. We smoked through walls to steal stuff and spy on his rivals—drug dealers, we think they were. He used the girls a couple times to seduce people he wanted favors from. None of us wanted Celia and Jeannine to have to do that, but we didn't know how to prevent it. Each time we went out on Mario's assignments, he used his wishing rights to compel us. We couldn't resist obeying, no matter how hard we tried.

He also wanted us to be assassins. He didn't care if we turned ifrit and went to hell once we died. It wouldn't be him burning. Luckily, I convinced him none of us were as good at illusion as my brother. Ramis could pass as human, but I warned Mario we'd look too frightening.

He bought it, I think, because he gave up the idea for the time being.

Then again, that might have been because he had another brainstorm to keep him occupied. He thinks the way portals work is too inconvenient. You can only go one way between dimensions, and then you have to find *another* door to bring you back where you came from. Mario didn't like that. We overheard him and Cara talking about a pair of linked portals here in the human world. Twin nexuses, they called them. He said wouldn't it be good if they could use them to make round trips? You know, go to our world and then turn around and come back through the same door. He said if the nexuses had the right energy source, he wouldn't need to recharge them. They'd be a magical perpetual motion thingummy.

I didn't think that was possible, but Patrizio says if Mario infuses the nexuses with djinn spirits, the same as was done to his tattoo, they might stay powered as long as the life force he puts in them survives.

Also . . . I'm not sure you're aware of this, but when Cara heard Mario's plan, she said they should "use the twins." She claimed they would keep the portals in synch with each other. That confused us until we saw you two. For everybody's sake, you need to be sure they don't get their hands on you.

~

"Would they dare?" Elyse asked as Balu finished speaking. The idea that Mario wanted to use her men this way was alarming.

"They might," Cade said. "The potential reward would be worth a risk."

"Where in the world did they find *twin* nexuses?" Leo asked. "Elyse's grandfather and I had a hard enough time getting the single one in the cellar to function."

Elyse knew the answer to that question.

"Cade's friend Joseph made a mirror space," she explained. "It wasn't very big, but it replicated the portal too."

"And the copy worked?" Leo said in amazement.

"We used it to escape Mario and Cara the first time they attacked us."

"So Cara was meeting Mario at the brownstone tonight." Leo furrowed his brow in thought. "I wonder how he got past my wards. I admit I'm not a genius at magic, but I'm more experienced than him."

"Maybe that's why he needed Cara," Elyse theorized. "To add her power to his. Especially if he's losing his human advantage."

"Six names," Arcadius suddenly interjected. Everyone looked at him. "Yasmin's list had six names on it: six djinn teenagers who disappeared in the same span of time. There are only four of you."

"We don't know of any more," Balu said. "Unless Cara stored them separately."

"Could the others simply be missing and not abducted?" Elyse wondered.

Arcadius started to respond, but Cade broke in.

"No, they couldn't," he said, anger kindling in his eyes. "When I eavesdropped on Cara's call, Mario said—and I quote—'Tonight's pair is resisting me.' We never did track down the last two names. What do you want to bet he meant a pair of twins? He intends to sacrifice them, not by killing them but by imprisoning their souls alive in the nexuses. Mario and Cara didn't want to divide and conquer us. They engineered tonight's invitation from your aunt to get us out of the brownstone."

"Shit," Arcadius breathed. "We've been incredibly stupid."

"We have to stop them," Leo said. "A man like Mario can't be allowed unrestricted access to your dimension. He's already proven that."

"We can help," Balu said.

"Yes," Patrizio agreed. "We're feeling a lot better."

Matching expressions of doubt entered Arcadius and Cade's faces. Elyse knew they were thinking these were just kids, but they didn't get a chance to voice their objections.

"You have to let us fight," Jeannine put in. She'd taken Celia's hand and was squeezing it fiercely. Truth be told, the angelic blonde looked pretty fierce herself. "We're not letting a single other djinni suffer like we did."

"Well," Leo said, a hint of humor playing around his mouth. "It looks like you commanders have some new foot soldiers."

~

Aunt June simplified matters by sleeping through their mass exodus. It was hard to know if it was the right choice, but they took the train back to Manhattan. If they'd flown, Leo and Elyse would have needed carrying. That would have drained the commanders' strength—in addition to which, the kids could use all the recuperation time they could get.

As they waited on the platform for the next express to arrive, Elyse had a strong suspicion Cade and Arcadius wished they could ditch everyone and tackle this themselves.

"Thank you," she said, taking Cade's fingers and squeezing them.

He looked startled. "For what?"

"For not playing reckless hero. For doing this the smart way."

"We hope it's the smart way," Arcadius said, injecting his personal dose of gloom and doom. He stood on her other side, a few feet farther off than Cade. "Look at those idiots."

He jerked his head toward the teenage djinn. They'd discovered the vending machines and were magicking all the candy bars out of them. Elyse appreciated the fact that they were giggling. Her dad was keeping a casual eye on them.

"They're strong," Cade said. "And just this once they can probably use a sugar rush."

"Hmph," Arcadius said.

His gemlike eyes told a different story. He was worried about the kids. Elyse gave in to impulse and clasped his hand as well. He rubbed his thumb across her knuckles without looking around at her. He drew up his shoulders. When he dropped them back to level, he seemed to have willed away his unease.

"Very well," he said. "We'll do the best we can with the tools we have."

The kids were all eyes and ears on the train, whispering comments to each other at the new things they saw. Her dad appointed himself to ride herd on them. Like most people who met Leo, they were soon won over. When they started whispering their questions to him, Elyse couldn't help smiling.

Cade shook his head in bemusement. "I'm beginning to understand how your father survived two years on an island of ifrit. He could charm a tree stump if he put his mind to it."

"He has a young spirit," Arcadius said. "They recognize him as one of them."

Elyse couldn't tell if he approved or not. Perhaps he hadn't decided yet.

The mood turned serious for the final leg of their journey, which they covered on the subway. Arcadius and Cade assumed command, cooperating without a hitch for once.

Climbing the exit steps to the street gave her an odd feeling. Scarsdale was a different world, but the four teenagers who bumped with them along the pavement proved even stranger worlds existed. She noticed they all had neon high-top sneakers. Whoever had shopped for them must have found a sale. Celia and Patrizio had drawn *C hearts P* on theirs. Elyse wagged her head. Though they were magical beings, they were still young and vulnerable.

Were Arcadius and Cade crazy for letting them join the fight?

They stopped short of the intersection near her brownstone, in a dim stretch between streetlights. Using the group to shield him from view, Cade changed and smoked around the corner to check on conditions. Though he wasn't gone long, Elyse's nerves tightened.

"Okay," he said when he returned. "Mario has two watchers on the street: one sitting on a stoop and one in a darkened car. Neither seems particularly alert. They might not know the nature of what he's doing, but we can't count on it. You three—" He indicated Patrizio, Celia, and Jeannine. "If you're up for shifting form this soon, I want you to take up positions on the roofs around the brownstone. Be sure you can see each other and the approaches to the house. If you think anyone has spotted you, just keep flying. I don't want some human Mario has clued in about our race trying a spell on you."

"We want to fight," Patrizio complained. "Not sit on our thumbs watching."

Cade leveled a look at him that his double wouldn't have been ashamed of. "You've seen the people Mario does business with. Do you think we ought to let them sneak up on our rear?"

"No," Patrizio admitted. "But—"

"No buts. You follow orders or I'll have Elyse put you back in the lamps. I brought them with me, in case you're wondering."

Patrizio looked horrified at this. Elyse did her best to appear hardhearted enough to return them to their prisons.

"How will we stay in touch?" Balu asked. "None of us have scrolls."

"Elyse will give Patrizio her cell phone."

"Ooh," Patrizio said, like this was exciting.

Elyse dug it from her coat and handed it over.

"I have one too," her dad said. "With an earpiece. If Patrizio speaks softly, only the person wearing it will hear."

Cade and Arcadius exchanged looks.

"Cade will take it," Arcadius said. "I expect he has experience with these devices."

"*I'm* coming with you," Balu said, trying to make it sound like this wasn't a question. "We have a stake in this. You can't keep all of us out of the line of fire."

"I'm allowing you to come provisionally," Arcadius said. "I know you're motivated. Now I'm counting on your nerves being as steady as your sister's."

Elyse thought reminding Balu his family had at least one admirable member was a good strategy. The young man squared his shoulders.

"I won't let you down, sir," he promised.

Balu nodded for the others to do as Cade instructed. They must have been feeling better, or maybe it was the sugar rush. They poofed away with no trouble.

"What's our best point of entry?" Arcadius asked.

"Back courtyard," Leo said. "The door there leads to the basement unit, which gives us access to the nexus. The scouts Mario posted shouldn't notice us entering, especially if you two airlift myself and Elyse in."

"We could do that," Cade said. He looked at Elyse.

"I'm up for it," she said.

They checked the small one-way street for approaching cars or other witnesses. Finding none, Cade swept her up in his arms and shifted into a man-shaped cloud in nearly the same second. She gasped but didn't have time to lose her nerve. She zoomed into the air like she was levitating. Cade's smoke form felt like an extra thick, extra tingly wind. The sense of speed was exhilarating. Up the nearest building's brick side they went, then over a line of roofs. Arcadius was carrying her father in similar fashion a few body lengths away. Because it was dark and Arcadius's smoke was sooty, only the most alert observer would have seen anything.

She looked back to see if Balu was following. His vaporous shape was barely visible.

It must be amazing to be able to do that, she thought. It was pretty amazing to be flown around by someone who could.

They landed in the small enclosed courtyard in less than fifteen seconds. The djinn changed back into solid form. Elyse's dad didn't try to hide his grin, so she knew he'd enjoyed the ride. Naturally, he wasn't fazed. He dug out his keys as quietly as he could and opened the rear entry.

Cade gestured to the rest of them that he would go first. He'd been here before and knew the territory. Arcadius could follow up the rear. Once again, Arcadius didn't argue. Like Cade, he drew a dagger he'd hidden in his clothes. The two commanders were on the same page now.

The basement apartment didn't take up the whole cellar. The passage that led to it from the courtyard was draughty. As they slipped silently along it, the coldness of the air came as no surprise. Also familiar, though for different reasons, was the creeping sensation that rippled across her skin. Elyse identified it as the effect of dark magic: the same not-right vibe that had repelled her from the dollhouse. The further they went, the stronger the impression got—until she felt as if she were swallowing something noxious every time she breathed in.

Cara must have nerves of steel to tolerate Mario's practices.

They entered Cade and Joseph's former apartment without turning on the lights. A muted glow stretched through the bars of the street door window to where they stood.

Good old New York, Elyse thought. *Never completely dark.*

Djinn eyes needed less light than hers. Her companions glanced toward the living room/kitchen combo in the front. A hallway led from that space to the bath, followed by the door to the courtyard passage, the single bedroom, and the now unsecured entrance to the mechanical room. This door gave access to the unfinished portion of the basement. Prior to his "demise" in the volcano, Elyse's father put a magic lock on the brownstone's portal. He'd hidden the key in a screw for this very door. The hiding place was subtle and handy and very much in tune with her dad's humor.

Of course a key would be in a door. Where else would anyone put it?

With Cade's help, Elyse had discovered her dad's secret. The fact that the door was now off its hinges said Mario had too. Cade noted its dismantled state but only grimaced in response.

He signaled the others that he was going to inspect the room across from them. This was the single bedroom, where Joseph had put the entrance to the mirror space. The mirror space duplicated parts of the cellar . . . with djinn-style improvements. Everything in it was cleaner and more beautiful and just a bit sparkly. Because most humans wouldn't suspect the bolthole was there, Joseph had intended it for emergencies. Mario had learned of its existence during their last escape. Cade went in, presumably to check the status of the twin nexus.

He couldn't have explored very far. He was gone for less than a minute. When he returned, he spoke very quietly. His voice sounded tight, as if he didn't like nastiness in the atmosphere any more than Elyse did.

"No one is in the copied part of the cellar. Mario must be performing whatever ritual he's doing on this side."

"That is bad, bad mojo he's working," her father said—unnecessarily.

Cade nodded. "I think we need to stick together to approach them. If we try to attack singly, Mario will pick us off."

"Cara is his weakness," Arcadius said. "He needs her humanity to shore up his magic. And he's in love with her. She should be our first target."

"I'll take my niece," Leo volunteered. "I'm human too. Her magic won't disable me."

"All right," Cade said. "Balu, you stick with him."

"What about me?" Elyse asked. Her voice was a little rough but at least it didn't shake. Cade touched her cheek gently.

"Arcadius and I would like you to do a protective spell, to lessen Mario's influence over us. We'll make it a really simple one, much easier than sucking djinn into lamps."

"Lock of hair charm," her dad suggested. "I've done that for djinn friends before. You only need twine and a pair of shears."

"Kitchen," Elyse said and darted off to it.

She'd rented this apartment furnished, stocking it herself with basics. Joseph and Cade hadn't moved things around. She found the items she needed in the drawer she expected. A roll of duct tape was in there too. She grabbed it. Given a choice, her dad would probably prefer muzzling Cara to killing her.

She'd retrieved the implements so quickly she came back breathless. She handed Leo the tape, which he accepted without comment, and then she waited for instructions.

"Okay," her dad said. "Snip off a lock of each of your fella's hair and tie it to one of yours with the twine."

The tall djinn leaned down so she could reach. Both their hair was silky against her fingers, both their compliance suggesting trust of her. The only difference between them was that Arcadius was a little stiff.

"I'm not familiar with this spell," he said.

"It's no-fail," her dad assured. "You say the chant and you're good to go. All it needs is genuine affection to charge it."

Elyse thought she could she could handle that. She clipped a curl from her own head, bundling all three together and tying them.

"What are the words?" she asked.

She never got an answer. The most terrible sound she'd ever heard split the air. It was a moan and a wail and a tortured person begging *please, please, no* . . . with every note and syllable doubled. Elyse broke out in goosebumps at the hopelessness of the cry. She didn't know who made it, only that her heart ached for them.

"They're killing them," Balu gasped.

"Follow me," Cade said, low and sharp. "Watch your head on the pipes."

He sprang off through the boiler room. The other men followed—including her father.

"Sorry, Elyse," Leo threw over his shoulder. "Just wing it the best you can."

Elyse didn't *wing* things. Whenever possible, she practiced them to death. She didn't have a choice right then. She had to scramble after her *fellas*. If she didn't, Mario and Cara would have magical free reign over them.

She knew the cellar but couldn't see as well as the males in front of her. To make matters worse, she was wearing heels. She tried not to stumble over the contents of the various storage areas: the cardboard boxes and castoff furniture, the jumble of Christmas stuff, the mazelike pathways through all of it. She tripped on a crack in the cement floor, only just swallowing her curse as she skinned her palms when she caught herself. She got up frantically patting her coat pocket. Thankfully, the twine-tied bundle remained in it.

She'd reached the janitor's bathroom and paintbrush washing sink. For once, its filthy condition seemed friendly. It had a window, and some light from outside came in. She caught her breath and peered around the next corner. The cinderblock walls her dad had installed to surround and shield the nexus were up ahead. She gritted her teeth. More waves of Mario's black magic rolled out from it, along with the flickering glow she recognized as portal energy. She didn't see the men. They must be inside the enclosure. No sounds of fighting came to her. Was that a good sign or a bad one?

Crap, she thought, edging forward cautiously. Her heart thudded in her chest. She was sweating so much she was tempted to pull off her coat. She wished she'd reminded Cade to leave the tiny Aladdin's lamps behind. Elyse couldn't use them. She had no experience shrinking things. If Mario somehow discerned they were nearby and shot the djinn into them, she'd never forgive herself.

Her father's voice was the first she heard as she neared the opening.

"Let's none of us do anything crazy," he advised. "We've each got control of something the other is interested in."

Cara let out a muffled angry noise. Elyse guessed her father had put the duct tape to its intended use.

"You wouldn't kill your own niece," Mario asserted.

His voice sounded odd. Its belligerence was what she'd expect, but its timbre had more smokiness than she remembered—as if he were a djinni speaking in nonphysical form. As far as she knew, humans couldn't change state that way. Maybe the ifrit spirit in his tattoo was adding its two cents to his vocal chords.

"I wouldn't *want* to kill her," her dad admitted. "Then again, you and she almost killed Elyse. Maybe I'd get over my reluctance. Or I could just let my friend here do it. I don't think he's fond of either of you."

"We could work a trade," Cade suggested. "Arcadius and I for the two youngsters."

Sheesh, Elyse thought. But at least Cade's offer meant the last missing djinn were alive.

"Like I'd fall for that," Mario sneered. "I've been in your 'Glorious' city. I heard what happened to its commander. You aren't twins. You're two halves of the same person—and inferior halves at that. I need whole spirits like these kids' to power my twinned nexuses. Plus, I've almost finished separating their spirits from their bodies. Even if you two were good enough, why should I start again at the beginning?"

"You know," Arcadius said in his coolest tone. "If you're not willing to negotiate, there's no reason we *shouldn't* kill your woman. I have a feeling you can't finish your ritual without her."

Elyse couldn't stand it. She had to know what was going on. She went to her elbows and knees on the floor, where her enemies would be less likely to spot her. She edged her head around the opening in time to see Balu punch his smoke fist wrist-deep into Cara's midsection.

The blow made a sound like a mallet driven through sawdust.

It must have hurt. Cara cried out hoarsely behind her gag. Leo hadn't simply plastered the silver adhesive across her mouth. He'd also taped it around her head. His thoroughness was smart. His flinch at Cara's cry of pain: not so much. No wonder Mario didn't believe he'd kill her.

Not that Mario enjoyed seeing his lover hurt. The tattooed goliath growled in reaction to Balu's blow. The sound snapped Elyse's eyes across the room to him. What she saw behind him completely distracted her.

The last two kids he'd abducted looked terrible.

The djinn twins were female—coltish girls aged about sixteen with long red hair and blue eyes. Probably they were pretty, normally. Most djinn she'd met were attractive. At the moment, they resembled the famous Edvard Munch painting of the screaming man. They were on their knees in front of the nexus's floating glow, gasping and trembling and barely able to hold themselves upright. Though their eyes were panicked, they also seemed to have trouble keeping them open. Their sweat-slicked skin was sucked close against their skulls and their discount clothes hung on them—as if not just their life force but also their flesh were being drawn from them.

Elyse had read descriptions of metaphysical silver cords: the umbilicus-like connector between a person's astral and physical bodies. She thought that might be what she was seeing extending back from the girls' solar plexuses.

One girl's cord stretched from her center to the surface of the nexus behind her. The other's had a vanishing point deep within the semi-transparent orb. Elyse assumed her cord had been feeding energy to the nexus's mirror space copy. As far as she could tell, Mario wasn't actively draining either girl.

Presumably, her friends' arrival had interrupted him.

"Please," one girl rasped. "Just kill us."

Mario spun to her in a rage. He pointed his finger at each sister. The hand he used was his right, the same from which Cade had severed the tattoo. Was it more effective because the ifrit's spirit no longer tainted it?

"You may *not* die," he ordered the girls. "Your spirits need to live for as long as I have a use for them. That's my wish and you must obey it!"

If the twins owed Mario wishes, he must have stored them in lamps too. Their bodies jerked like puppets whose strings had been yanked taut. They knelt more upright then, but their eyes rolled back in their heads. Elyse wondered if it were a mercy that they were unconscious.

"Bastard," Balu cried. "Release them or my next punch rips through her heart!"

He cocked his smoke fist in front of Cara's chest. She struggled in Leo's hold but Elyse's dad had a good grip on her upper arms. Good grip notwithstanding, he didn't look happy about the prospect of Balu killing her.

"Wait," her dad advised the djinni in a low voice. "We haven't run out of chess moves yet."

Mario must have decided he couldn't bet on the boy obeying. He threw back his head and roared a word she didn't understand . . . or maybe it was a name. His slab-like chest strained the seams of his black T-shirt, his legs planted as thick as trees in his leather pants. Suddenly his thorn tattoo separated from his skin, blurring across the room to attack Balu. His regular body, which was formidable enough, went for Cade. The force of his rush knocked Cade to the ground, stunning him. Before he could recover, Mario grabbed his throat and began squeezing. Arcadius moved to help.

To her dismay, she noticed neither commander held his dagger. Had Mario spelled them away somehow?

"In the name of God, you serve me," Mario barked.

Elyse thought he was trying to freeze Arcadius like before. A second later, she realized this would have been preferable. Arcadius's feet weren't stuck to the ground. Instead, a seven-inch silver railroad spike slipped itself from Mario's pants pocket. The weapon flashed up into the air, its deadly point swerving around to target the startled commander.

Elyse didn't think she imagined the spike's wriggle of eagerness.

"Pierce his heart and he's yours to drink," Mario promised the artifact.

Crap, Elyse thought. Was the spike possessed like Mario's tattoo—and by a vampire djinni? When he said *drink*, did he mean literally?

Arcadius acted as if he did. He ducked and weaved while the spike darted at him quick as a wasp.

Elyse didn't understand how Mario was pulling off attacking three djinn at once. He was holding his own as he straddled and strangled Cade, and Cade was no pushover. She assumed Mario's tattoo and the spike had some autonomy, but Mario supplied the energy and will behind them. To make the sorcerer's multi-tasking more impressive, Elyse's dad was helping Balu fight his thorny attacker. Though Leo wasn't releasing Cara, he whispered spells to assist the boy.

What the hell had happened to Mario's power being on the wane?

It didn't matter. Elyse had to figure out a protective spell and get it working fast. Because watching was too upsetting, she ducked back out of the portal room's opening. She pressed her spine to the wall of cinderblock, the twine-tied bundle of locks clutched tight against her breast.

Think, she ordered. Arcadius and Cade couldn't hold her hand for this. She had to find her own way. Djinn always asked for things *in the name of God*, and *if it please the Creator*. Those weren't empty words to them. They wanted a higher power to take charge because they believed unquestioningly in one. As a human, Elyse was more comfortable with questions than she was in unswerving faith. All the same, she knew she must have faith inside her. If she hadn't, she couldn't have pulled off spells before.

How did Mario do this so easily anyway? Did he just not think about the deity he was praying to? Maybe belief in his own arrogant self was all he required.

God, she was overthinking this. She needed to concentrate.

"In the name of God," she mouthed as firmly as she could with only her lips moving. She didn't want to alert the sorcerer that she was trying to help. "Father in Heaven, please protect Cade and Arcadius. Let there be no favorites between djinn and human when You watch over Your children."

Nothing happened that she could tell. The grunts and growls of the men continued as alarmingly before. Arcadius cried out, forcing her to wonder if the bloodthirsty spike had succeeded in reaching him. She would have cursed, but the first rule of successful spelling came back to her.

If at first you don't succeed, repeat and repeat again.

She reprised her impromptu prayer, whispering the words this time. Leo said the spell needed affection to charge it, so she tried drawing her feelings for Cade and Arcadius up into her heart. They were good men, who'd dedicated their lives to caring for their people. Surely whatever power ran the Universe couldn't consider them less than Mario or her just because they were djinn. They deserved whatever protection He had to give. Elyse had to believe that. To her mind, any deity worth the name loved all its children equally.

For that matter, the Almighty ought to love Mario and Cara too.

Something clicked inside her, some fragmentary understanding of what universal love must be. Her spirit seemed to expand in sunlit ripples from her center.

Help them, she thought. *If it's Your will, help the men I love.*

She couldn't pray beyond that. She'd asked in accordance with her belief. If it weren't good enough, she'd have to accept failure.

Okay, that possibility wasn't so appealing. Elyse looked around her desperately. She hadn't noticed it before, but she spotted a rusty shovel lying on the floor a few feet away. She leaped up and grabbed it. So what if her spellwork sucked? Her arms worked fine, thank you very much. She ran with the shovel into the nexus room. The back of Mario's shaven head was within bashing range.

The old garden implement was heavier than she expected, made of wood and iron rather than aluminum or plastic. Before Elyse could swing it up and connect, Cara yelled a warning through the duct tape. Mario rolled out of reach, taking Cade with him. Cade's face was red from Mario's efforts to throttle him.

"Shove—" he choked out unhelpfully.

Arcadius seemed to understand the shorthand.

"Get the tattoo demon!" he cried. He gripped the spike that was attacking him in both hands. How long he could hold it off Elyse didn't want to guess. "That shovel head is iron!"

So it was. Probably ifrits didn't like iron any better than light djinn.

The tattoo demon was wrestling with Balu. Elyse ran over and jabbed the shovel's sharp end at it. To her great satisfaction, the thorny swirls shattered like bone china and clattered to the floor.

"*Yes,*" Balu crowed. Freed, he bounded off to help Cade . . . and was stopped short by an invisible wall of force.

Then the broken bits of tattoo demon began to slither back together.

No, Elyse thought. Mario couldn't be doing this by himself. They'd put him on the run in the Arch of Triumph portal room. He wasn't that powerful. She looked toward Cara, who her father was still restraining by the arms.

Elyse's cousin was doing something funny with her hands, tapping her fingertips in odd rhythms against her thighs. Elyse realized she was *typing* spells, because her mouth was gagged. Cara was the reason Mario's magic seemed unstoppable. She was lending her human juice to his experience and skill.

Elyse took a heartbeat to wish it were as easy to be brutal to her cousin as it was to attack a tattoo monster.

Don't lose your nerve, she ordered even as she hefted the shovel. Two running steps took her close enough to Cara, where she swung with all her might. She'd played baseball maybe ten times in her life. Luckily, her muscles understood what to do.

The duct tape couldn't silence Cara's scream as Elyse broke half the bones in her right hand.

Again, Elyse commanded herself.

She knocked her father *and* Cara over as she shattered the left one.

Chaos erupted as Cara's ability to bolster her boyfriend's magic was nullified. Though she was hurt, Cara flung herself away from Leo. Elyse's dad struggled to get up from where he'd dropped. Elyse couldn't tell if Cade threw Mario off, or if Mario let go of him so he could help his girlfriend. Whichever it was, Arcadius took advantage of Mario's lessened power. He roared like a Viking as he wrested control of the silver spike, driving it so far into the cinderblock that it stuck.

Tattoo demon, Elyse remembered, grabbing the chance to smash it into smaller fragments with her shovel. This time, the smithereens stayed down.

"The girls!" Balu cried.

Elyse spun back around. Both redheads had collapsed face down on the floor. Mario gripped their silver cords in one fist. The cords still glowed, so she guessed the twins weren't dead. Cara clung to Mario's side as well as a person could with two broken hands. The tape still muzzled her. Presumably her fingers hurt too much to pull it off. Elyse noticed her cousin's eyes blazed with rage. If Cara had ever had second thoughts about siding with Mario, she was over them.

Directly behind her and her boyfriend, the slowly spinning nexus pulsed.

"Stay back," Mario warned as the two commanders advanced on him. "I can kill these girls with one good tug."

"Let them go," Arcadius growled, his voice as deep as it got when he was in smoke form.

"Why should I?" Mario demanded. He looked different without his tattoo: more ordinary, like a big but basically normal bald football coach.

"If you let them go, we'll let you escape," Cade said.

No, we won't, Elyse protested in her head.

"We'll escape anyway," Mario blustered.

"Before he closes the portal?" Cade inquired politely.

He jerked his head toward her father. Leo was on his knees rapidly whispering a spell. Could her dad close it? If he could, he'd better hurry up.

Mario's naked face darkened. He took a securer grip on Cara's waist. Elyse held her breath, unsure which way he'd jump. He must have decided he couldn't fight anymore. He flung away the sisters' cords, digging the hand that had held them into his pants pocket. He withdrew a long spiral screw, the same her father had enchanted to let people pass through this portal to a particular location in the djinn world.

The screw had taken Elyse and Cade to the Great Desert. She didn't know where it was keyed to now. The Glorious City, maybe, or some other place Mario could start up his tricks again.

"Really, Cara?" Elyse said, appealing to her cousin one last time. "Your father's death was for this? Giving up your life, your family, people you used to feel affection for? You want to throw that over to support this crazy-ass power-hungry gangster who wouldn't actually love you if you hadn't spelled him to?"

Even with a broken hand, Cara giving her the finger was unmistakable. Seeing it, Mario grinned. Elyse concluded he hadn't registered everything she said.

"*Hasta la vista*," he signed off, turning to swipe the tip of the key down the flickering energy.

A brighter opening parted in the nexus, beautiful rainbow-sparking rays spiking out. Mario stepped into the slit with Cara hugged tight to him.

Damn it, Elyse thought as the light began to swallow them.

But it wasn't over. Her father leaped to his feet and flung something through the air. Though the object spun like a dagger, it didn't glint. It also didn't stop the couple from escaping. It disappeared right along with them as the seam in the portal closed. One last burst of radiance squeaked through.

Then everything went dark.

Elyse heard a lot of tired men panting. She guessed the djinn couldn't see through pitch black either. Cade pulled out the phone he'd borrowed and made its screen light up.

"Did they get through?" she asked. "Dad, what did you throw at them?"

Her dad surprised her by laughing. "I hope they got through. I threw a splinter from Shadow Wood after them. I charmed it to override the old key."

Arcadius and Cade were kneeling beside the fallen twins, checking their vital signs. Despite the seriousness of their conditions, Arcadius flashed a grin. "You sent them to the island of ifrits?"

"I did." Her dad looked pleased with himself. "Call me arrogant, but Mario and Cara aren't as charming as I am. I don't think they'll endear themselves to their hosts. I also don't think they'll get away. I triple-locked the door I escaped through behind me. I didn't want those ifrits pursuing. Even with Cara to shore him up, I doubt Mario will crack my system."

Cade pursed his lips. "He'll have plenty of time to work out Elyse's revelation that Cara spelled him to love her. That will make for some comfy chats. It certainly was smart of you to save a piece of wood."

"Benefit of experience," her dad dismissed. "If there's one thing I've learned about magic, it's that you never know what will turn out to be useful." He propped his hands on his hips and looked around the room. "This cellar needs a good cleansing. Why don't I take care of that while you get those girls somewhere comfortable to recuperate?"

"Don't forget that," Elyse said, waving at the spike now embedded in the wall.

"Yes." Her dad considered it thoughtfully. "That thing is dangerous."

CHAPTER TWELVE

CADE had never been so grateful a fight was over. The threat Mario posed to his people and Elyse had struck too close to home. Banishing the sorcerer and her cousin felt like real progress. Important hurdles remained, but the breaths he drew in the aftermath were his first easy ones in a while.

Since Leo was handling cleanup, Elyse led everyone back through the cellar's maze. Flipping on the lights made it a different place, though the illumination didn't rouse the injured girls. Cade and Arcadius each carried one. The twins seemed to be sleeping and not unconscious—a definite improvement. To his relief, their spirits had detached from the nexuses on their own, their life force returning naturally to their bodies. Once the last of Mario's spells wore off, he expected them to recover completely.

Also improved was the basement's atmosphere. Cade hoped Elyse didn't realize the spike her father had taken charge of was the same artifact Mario used to kill her husband. Though she didn't seem traumatized by battling supernatural dangers, he'd prefer she not have to revisit David's death—especially since the man had been sliced to pieces exactly where they'd fought.

Arcadius lifted a single brow, seeming to sense his thoughts weren't idle.

Cade pulled a face to warn him the topic was better avoided. "Let's get these girls to Elyse's place."

"Could we use the cellar apartment?" Balu piped up hopefully. "The others need somewhere to crash too."

Elyse regarded him with surprise. "There's only one bedroom. And now there's six of you."

"There's the mirror space. If Joseph the Magician created it, it's probably wicked rad."

Shaking her head in amusement, Elyse sidestepped a tower of boxes. "Joseph is a rock star to you kids, isn't he?"

"Yes," Balu said earnestly. "We'd love to study what he did. Probably the girls would recover faster if they were in that energy."

"Probably you think you'd have less oversight if you were down here alone." This dry observation came from Arcadius.

"That never occurred to me," Balu said with unconvincing innocence. "If you want, one of you commanders could stay with us."

Balu was no fool. Chances were, he'd calculated the likelihood of that happening. Cade had no intention of sleeping anywhere but next to Elyse. Given her obvious increasing pull on Arcadius, his double would—at the least—want to stay near as well. But Balu was right about one thing. The girls would benefit from being around djinn energy. Cade didn't doubt they'd feel more comfortable waking among other young people from their own race.

"Do you promise not to wander outside the brownstone?" he asked sternly.

Balu nodded too quickly.

"I mean it," Cade said. "Arcadius and I will hold you personally responsible for everyone's compliance."

The nervous glance Balu shot Arcadius revealed which of them intimidated him more. "Could we wander if Leo were taking us?"

"If Leo clears it with one of us beforehand."

"Cross my heart," Balu swore. "And we'll take really good care of the twins. We won't go anywhere or do anything we shouldn't until they feel better."

Arcadius and Cade sighed at the same time. "You won't do anything you shouldn't, period."

"Right," Balu said. "So, is it okay?"

This time the boy looked to Elyse for permission. They'd stopped outside the mechanical room. Elyse was stroking the forehead of the sleeping girl Arcadius carried. Cade noticed the girl's brow wasn't sweating anymore. He suspected her improvement swayed Elyse's response.

"You'd have to be extra responsible," she said. "More responsible than maybe you want to be. I know you think my world is cool, but it isn't safe if you don't know your way around. Sometimes it isn't safe even if you do. Imagine how you'd feel if you rescued your friends from danger only to have them fall into it again. You kids deserve the chance to have a bright future."

Balu gnawed his lip. "Is that a *yes*?"

Elyse sighed a lot like Arcadius and Cade had. "It's a *yes* for now. You'll have to prove you're trustworthy."

Balu victory-punched the air. Cade sincerely hoped they wouldn't regret this.

~

Arcadius couldn't quell his unease as the three of them returned to Elyse's residence. They'd been outside already. Mario's associates were no longer on "stake out." Either they'd grown tired of waiting for their boss to emerge or they had other criminal fish to fry. Since they posed no present danger, Cade informed Patrizio, Celia and Jeannine that the sorcerer was defeated and that they had permission to stay in the cellar apartment. Arcadius was surprised by how enthusiastically they received the news. For one thing, it was a *cellar.* For another, they'd hardly had good experiences in the human world. Teenagers must be more resilient than he remembered being himself. The first thing Patrizio had asked was if he could use Elyse's phone to order "real" New York pizza.

"Should we have agreed to that?" he asked.

"God knows," Elyse shrugged off her coat and tossed it wearily to the couch. "Patrizio did promise to order salad too. Those kids need actual nutrition."

"I mean about leaving them on their own."

She turned to him with a surprised expression. "You seemed like you trusted them."

"That was Cade."

"But you didn't argue. Anyway, I know which of you is which."

Cade seemed to find this funny. Arcadius wished he did. Vanquishing their enemies ought to have left him ebullient. Instead, he felt like part of him still fought. He wanted to dismiss Mario's shot at them but couldn't.

You aren't twins. You're two halves of the same person—and inferior halves at that.

If anyone were the inferior half, it was Arcadius. Supposedly, he had ten percent of their spirit. The other him had ninety. Arcadius might not feel like less of a person, but he couldn't know for sure.

Would the blood-drinking spike have slain him if Elyse hadn't intervened? Would he even have noticed she carried an implement capable of shattering Mario's tattoo if Cade hadn't seen it first? He didn't enjoy questioning himself this way, but his sense of duty demanded it.

Maybe he'd been wrong to think he deserved an equal share of her.

If Elyse noticed he was troubled, she didn't guess the cause. She leaned on the wall for balance, bending—rather fetchingly, he thought—to pull off her seductive high-heeled shoes. The casualness of the action, the intimacy she didn't even realize it implied, left his throat aching.

"Tell you what," she said, wriggling her toes in relief. "We'll call Balu in half an hour. Make sure they haven't gone AWOL and check if the twins have woken up."

Cade took her shoulders and kissed her mouth lightly. "Sounds like a plan. You hungry?"

"Sweaty," she said, grimacing as she plucked at front of her sexy dress. "Probably the effect of being scared spitless." She tiptoed up to return Cade's kiss and grinned. "I'm glad we're not dead. I'm going to take a shower."

She walked toward the bathroom, dragging down her dress's zipper with one hand on the way. She only bared a thin strip of skin, but Arcadius's eyes felt glued to the show. Elyse really was growing accustomed to his presence.

Cade was still smiling fondly when he turned back to Arcadius. Would Arcadius have looked that relaxed and happy if Elyse were his woman too?

"You okay?" Cade said. "You seem off."

"It really doesn't bother you," Arcadius said.

"What doesn't bother me?"

"That a woman—your woman—had to save our butts in a fight."

"That's what Elyse does, not the saving part, necessarily, but she always wants to contribute. I don't like her being in danger, but it's not like I can stop her."

"But you *could*," Arcadius said. "You could lock her in a closet or tie her to a chair."

"I guess it's lucky I didn't think of that tonight. She was pretty awesome with that shovel."

"It's wrong," Arcadius insisted.

Cade laughed. "I really have changed since I was you."

"You say that like you're the new, improved version, and I'm defective!"

Cade's humor receded. "I didn't mean to imply that."

"I'm not less than you." Considering he'd been worried that he was within the last five minutes, the claim was ironic. He ignored his lack of logic and continued. "I'd also like to point out, you never were the me I am. I've changed since that moment Joseph split us in two. I've had my own experiences and perspective."

"I suppose you have." Cade was serious for a couple heartbeats, an effect he spoiled by snickering. "When you first woke up from being a statue, you were convinced *I* was defective."

Arcadius missed the clarity of those days quite intensely for a moment. He let that go with a sigh. He was talking around the point, which he hoped wasn't characteristic of either of their current selves. He pulled himself back on track.

"About sharing her," he said. "You said you weren't sure that would make you happy, but I can't let go of the idea. I want to keep her in my life too."

Cade didn't look surprised. He propped the sole of one dress shoe against the wall, bracing his weight on it. "I suspected you were working around to that."

"I understand it's her decision to make—"

"At least you've figured out that much." When Arcadius narrowed his eyes, Cade raised a hand in apology. "Sorry. You were saying?"

"It's your decision too. I want to know if you plan to oppose me."

"When you say *share* . . . "

"I mean I'd commit myself to her as you have. I'd give her my affections and hope to receive hers. We wouldn't always need to share her favors in bed.

I'm interested in having her to myself sometimes. I assume you'd feel the same."

Cade rubbed his thumb across the center of one eyebrow.

"We could try taking her together again," Arcadius offered when Cade didn't speak. "See if you still enjoy it."

His double's laugh was dry. "I suspect you know I would."

This was true but Arcadius didn't apologize. Playing fair shouldn't rule out good strategy. If anyone knew that, it was the other him.

"Hell," Cade said, pushing off the wall. "Let me talk to her."

"Now?" Arcadius asked, disconcerted by this unexpected capitulation.

Cade shrugged. "We might as well find out what she's thinking. Mind you, don't interrupt. For now, this is between me and her."

"Understood." Sudden nerves made Arcadius's palms go damp. He fought an urge to tell Cade he needn't rush. Maybe the possibility of Elyse agreeing would be greater another day.

Cade snorted, having read every thought that crossed his face.

"Buck up," he said, giving Arcadius's shoulder a light punch. "If she says *no*, you'll be spared learning to let her be her own woman."

Somehow, Arcadius didn't think he'd take solace in that outcome.

~

Elyse's bathroom was one of her favorite places in the house. She'd renovated it herself in turn of the century repro style. The tiles were white with black accents, the fittings silvery brushed nickel. The steam shower was the exception to the historic theme. It was a futuristic glass cylinder with multiple jets and programmable temperature settings. She let it pound on her for five full minutes and didn't feel guilty.

Sometimes that's what it took for a shovel-wielding human to feel steady on her legs again.

When Cade stepped into the shower enclosure, she didn't scold him for stealing half the spray. He was breathtakingly big and naked as he smiled down at her. He put his hands on her hips, his thumbs fanning the wet skin there.

"Hey," he said.

"Hey," she answered. Her palms rested on his chest where his heart beat an even rhythm behind his ribs. The realization that she could have lost him washed over her. "Tonight was scary. I think I need a kiss."

He understood how much she meant it. He pulled her to him, wrapped her in his arms, and gave her a nice deep one. He didn't add his fears to hers; his kiss wasn't frantic but just solid. She held him tight, soaking up how comforting he was. His big bare feet bracketed either side of her smaller ones, the juxtaposition oddly protective. Though his cock thickened against her, he didn't turn the embrace sexual—or not any more sexual than kissing him always was. Elyse allowed herself to relax, enjoying the buzz he raised in her body without pushing it to be more.

This was part of being a couple too: just being there for each other.

"Better?" he asked, his eyes creasing with affection when he drew back.

"Yes." She knew her face was flushed as his hands smoothed up and down her spine. "I wanted to do that before, but it seemed mean to in front of Arcadius."

"Ah." He took one hand from her to scratch his cheek. His expression was interesting. "About that. Arcadius is who I came in to talk about."

"What about him?" She had one bad second during which she wondered if his double had told him about their kiss.

I really need to come clean about that, she thought.

Cade seemed to be having his own mental argument. Elyse waited for him to finish it. He drew breath before he spoke.

"Arcadius would like us to share you. Officially. I told him I'd bring it up with you."

Her heart did a funny flip. "He asked you to bring it up?"

"Well, we both realize you have a say . . ." Cade trailed off to take a sharper look at her. "You're less surprised by this than I expected."

Okay, there's your opening, she thought.

"Arcadius kissed me," she confessed, plunging in. "Yesterday, when you were across the hall with Dad. I stopped him before it went any farther. I told him I want to be loved by someone I can count on. He implied he'd give me back once he was done with me."

Simply repeating that made her temper rise.

"That annoyed you," Cade concluded.

She couldn't deny it. "You know I like him. I can't help it. It's insulting to be told someone you care about would toss you over after he's had you a couple times."

"You might have misunderstood how serious his interest is. In fact, I suspect he's only now realizing the extent of it himself. He told me he'd commit himself to you as I have."

"He said that?"

Cade stroked her wet curls back from her face. "He said exactly that, and that he hoped you'd return his affection. I think we both know you already do."

Elyse bit her lip. She saw he wasn't upset, but she couldn't tell what he was feeling exactly. "What about you?"

He smiled. "I definitely return your affection."

She rolled her eyes. "You know that's not what I'm asking. I need a serious answer. What's your position on all this?"

His expression grew less teasing but not less fond. His steady sea blue gaze cut through the steam billowing in the shower. He didn't speak right away. Was he going to insist she state her preference first? She didn't think she could without knowing how he felt—maybe not even to herself.

She wouldn't hurt Cade to please Arcadius.

"I think," he said slowly, as if the answer were even then coming clear, "that he's the only person in any dimension I could share you with. I think I want him to be happy, and I know I want you to. In a way, sharing you with him feels like giving you more of me. He's not me precisely, but I trust him to appreciate you. I want you to have that. An amazing woman like you deserves to be loved twice over."

Tears spilled over Elyse's lower lashes, running down her cheeks along with the shower spray. The things she felt for Cade were too big to contain. "God, I'm lucky to be in love with you."

The way his brows shot up took her by surprise. "You're *in* love with me, are you?"

"Of course I am. You knew that."

He shook his head. "You've admitted to loving me, but not to being in love. You made a point of it when we were in Sheikh Zayd's camp. You said you didn't know the difference between 'love' and 'in love' but you thought you could come to feel that way about me."

The memory nudged at her. She had said that, hadn't she? "I'd forgotten all about that. Sheesh, how insufferable of me!"

"I didn't like hearing it, but I understood what you meant. You said love that lasts takes time." His grin flashed out, his big hands chafing her shoulders. "I suppose this means you've had enough time to be certain."

"I suppose it does."

"Naturally you should take as long to fall in love with Cade as you did with me."

"Oh, please," she said. "It isn't a competition."

His face settled into peaceful lines that her own echoed. Evidently, saying she was in love did nice things for both of them.

"Are we doing this then?" he asked.

Were they? "It might not work out."

"Do you want to try?"

She searched her heart. She felt . . . excited by the idea. Not just physically, but in her emotions. She wanted to love both men. The thought that Arcadius might love her too touched and humbled her. How many people had an opportunity like the one Cade was offering her? Was it impulsive to say *yes* or the only logical answer?

Could three people be happy together?

"Let's try," she said, her pulse fluttering wildly. "Let's just be as careful as we can of each other."

~

Arcadius paced Elyse's living room back and forth. How long were Cade and Elyse going to discuss their decision? Admittedly, he didn't want them to choose lightly. To try the arrangement and then have it blow up in their faces would be uncomfortable. He forked his hands into his hair and pulled. Maybe he'd been crazy to suggest this in the first place. Maybe he should tell them he'd changed his mind.

The shower finally shut off, jolting his heart up into his throat.

You'd have thought *he* was a teenager, the way he was reacting.

He forced himself to stand calmly where he was, in the center of the room. Half a minute later, he wished he were still pacing. What the hell were they doing now? Didn't they realize he was waiting for an answer?

They'd been drying off, apparently. They returned to the living room in robes. Elyse's was a bulky white thing and Cade's djinn-style silk. Despite how unrevealing her garment was, Elyse looked adorable in it. Her feet were bare and her hair hung in wet ringlets. He couldn't fail to note that she was blushing furiously. She halted at the edge of the rug he stood on.

"Arcadius," she said, which he found exasperatingly uninformative.

"Have you decided?" he asked. "Are you agreeable to letting Cade share you?"

He didn't mean to sound so brusque. He guessed this was what Elyse expected of him, because she smiled. "I'm agreeable, but I think we should —"

He couldn't let her finish. His emotions and his urges were too pent-up, and maybe had been for longer than he realized. She said *agreeable*, and he crossed the carpet in two long strides, lifting her off her feet and into his arms. Her startled hands clutched his shoulders. He crashed his mouth down on hers.

He couldn't just kiss her once. He slanted their faces this way and that, sucking her tongue against his, probing her, conquering her, clutching her terry-wrapped naked body tight to his. After the first few shy—or perhaps shocked—moments she kissed him back. *That* was pleasurable, to put it mildly. His moan of response was hoarse, her repeated little cries astoundingly erotic. He hardened to the point of pain and didn't care.

He was never going to stop kissing her.

That thought startled him. He remembered Cade was watching. Though his awareness of his double's presence sent an undeniable rush through him, it occurred to him that perhaps his eagerness was insensitive. He set Elyse back onto her feet. Flatteringly, her arms took a moment to release him. She pressed three fingertips to her lips. Possibly her mouth was buzzing as heatedly as his.

"Sorry," he said. His human trousers were tight, his cock pounding like a drum inside their constriction. He cleared his throat. "I interrupted you."

"What?" was Elyse's dazed response.

His double chuckled in amusement. "You were going to remind Arcadius we need to be careful of each other's feelings."

"Right," she said. "And, um, we should try not to lose the bonds we've already formed. Learning to like and admire each other has been really enjoyable. Risking that is—well, we need to be sure it's worth it."

"You like us being allies," Arcadius said, wanting to be sure he understood.

Elyse nodded emphatically. "Yes. Allies and friends. Being lovers is good too, but being a team matters."

Cade looked at her with his head cocked, as if he hadn't known she was going to say this and was pleasantly surprised.

"I concur," Arcadius said. "Being a team matters."

Though he didn't intend his words to be erotic, they caused Elyse to blush. That was interesting. And arousing. His confidence surged back to more normal levels as tingles spread through his groin. "I assume we're activating our new team tonight."

"Oh, yes," Cade answered before Elyse found her voice. "No time like the present."

Arcadius had one more important question for their lover. "Are you amenable to me being in charge?"

Elyse rolled her lips together and smiled at the same time. "I believe you've earned you turn at that."

"Good," he said, not really caring whether he'd earned it. He swung her up in his arms, breezing past Cade to carry her down the hall to her bedroom. Elyse's jaw dropped, her hold on him automatic and not frightened. He didn't study her face. He'd worry about what she felt when he was sliding into her.

"Come if you intend to," he called to Cade over his shoulder.

Cade laughed but of course he followed. Arcadius didn't expect him to abandon Elyse to him. Having her in his arms was enough for now, knowing he was going to take her the way he'd wanted for what seemed like forever.

He set her gently on her bed and immediately started unbuttoning his dress shirt. He sensed Cade's arrival in the doorway behind him. He didn't turn. He liked the way Elyse was watching him disrobe. She had an up close view. He was only a foot away from her.

"Do you want help with that?" she asked.

"No," he said, already finished unbuttoning. Elyse laughed softly at his refusal. "I take it I amuse you."

"Only in a good way. It's kind of sexy that you know what you want."

He hoped it was. He couldn't be any other way. He removed his jacket and worked his arms free of the shirtsleeves. He threw both onto a chair and toed off his slippers. His chest was bare. He guessed Elyse liked the look of it. She rolled onto her knees, sitting on her heels as her gaze took him in. He breathed faster. Her admiration was an aphrodisiac. When she wet her lips, the sight of her little tongue set his blood on fire. Suddenly, he didn't have the patience to strip completely. Unzipping and shoving down would have to be good enough.

Possibly because he was so eager, the belt buckle thwarted him.

"Would you allow me?" she asked politely.

He was glaring, but she didn't seem to mind. He dropped his arms, and she scooted to the end of the bed to sit. Her calves and feet dangled to either side of his, both bare beneath her thick white robe. Her motions were assured as she undid the buckle and pulled the leather free of his trouser loops. The same part of him that had enjoyed being whipped got a secret charge from that. This wasn't his only thrill. His erection throbbed crazily at the proximity of her hands, at the idea that she might touch him there. Before he could attack the trousers' other fastenings, she pressed her lips to his navel.

He'd wondered if she'd want to be sweet to him like she was with Cade. Here was his answer. Coils unwound in his shoulders. He cupped the back of her head and exhaled.

Her hands were on his thighs, kneading the lust-tensed muscles beneath his pants. She kissed his belly again, brushing her mouth across hair and skin. Arcadius's spine just about melted.

"Could I suck your cock?" she asked. "Or would you rather just take me?"

Her voice was husky with arousal. He hadn't realized his eyes had drifted shut until he opened them and looked down at her. Her cheeks were pink, her every feature exquisite. Her lips were perfect, her nose the best nose in the world. Her eyes were the sort poets wrote dreamy words about. He didn't understand how he could have thought her plain.

Her hands moved again, sliding together over the hump of his aching prick—exactly where he wanted them. Without releasing his erection, her thumbs stretched over his balls and rubbed.

The combined sensations were so delicious chills rolled up his tailbone.

"Let me unzip," he said harshly.

She backed her hands off him. He undid the tabs and dragged the zipper down. The state of his cock caused the stretchy underwear he wore to swell into the opening. Elyse let out a little gasp. Liking that, Arcadius shoved both hands down into the garment and pulled his heavy erection out. Elyse's eyes followed every motion. Her attention put him in less of a hurry. He trailed his fingers over the places he most wanted her attention on. His raphe. The spot underneath the head. The silky circle of the crown where his pre-cum welled. She watched the map his fingers drew, then gratified him by licking her lips again.

"In a minute," he rumbled, "you're going to be grateful I'm not as big as him."

She laughed, breathless and delighted. "I always do the best I can with whatever challenge is set in front of me."

Cade laughed too, having come closer without Arcadius noticing.

"Don't let me interrupt," he said as Arcadius glanced at him. "I'm agreeable to observing this next bit."

Arcadius was too aroused—and too fixated on Elyse—to be offended by Cade's confidence. In any case, Cade feeling threatened wouldn't have benefited anything except Arcadius's ego. Throwing off that unproductive thought, Arcadius stroked a baby soft dark ringlet behind Elyse's ear. Her curls were damp but drying.

She waited for instructions.

"Do as you wish in this," he said.

She pushed her hands slowly upward so that his were displaced from his erection. Her thumbs rubbed his underside, her fingers crooked between his upright length and his abdomen. Very gently she kissed the neck of his cock. The soft press of her lips was as much an expression of affection as a sexual act.

"You don't have to be so nice," he said, wondering if she thought his feelings needed it.

She smiled and kissed him the same way again.

He couldn't deny he enjoyed it. Probably his little shiver was as good as admitting it.

The sight of her tongue coming out made him suck in a breath.

She dragged its flat up his underridge, moving her thumbs to the side so that nothing obstructed the slow, long lick. His hands tangled in her hair without him consciously deciding to. When her mouth and tongue approached his tip, he urged her head gently over it.

She didn't resist. She took his crown in her mouth, her lips and tongue sliding wetly down as her hands began massaging his lower shaft. His hips rolled toward her, the bliss of what she was doing pouring through him in sugared waves. She sucked and his fingers tightened in her hair.

"Careful," Cade said, but Arcadius knew he was neither hurting nor forcing her.

Her bobbing motions were too relaxed, the pull of her tongue and cheeks too passionate. She liked doing this. Her tongue was fluttering and rubbing, teasing him, slicking him, while her hands braced his shaft for her work. Her mouth was magic, but her fingers weren't far behind. They drove delight into the inches her tongue couldn't reach. They increased the pressure of everything she did.

"God," he moaned, unable to hold the outcry in.

He didn't startle her. She drew the ring of her lips upward, then pushed them down snugly. Suddenly everything felt too good. He swelled even more, his scrotum drawing higher, tighter, his nails pricking her scalp involuntarily.

She released him and looked up his body. "Enough?"

"Enough of *that*," he answered. His voice was gruff, more or less the opposite of his emotions. Rather than tell her this, he took her hands and tugged her weight upward.

"On your feet," he ordered.

She obeyed with a tiny shiver. He undid the tie of her figure-swallowing robe and flung the halves open. The shadows her body cast on itself were pretty: her little breasts with their budded nipples, her navel, the puff of dark curls between her legs. She was delicate and delectable, every inch of her calling out for kisses. Cade must have thought so too. Arcadius heard him breathing faster behind him.

Arcadius's own feelings were so strong he couldn't tell if Cade's were affecting him.

"Take that off," he said, gesturing to Elyse's robe.

She shrugged it off slowly. He liked her body just as well unveiled as hidden. An appropriate human phrase slipped into his mind. Elyse's hesitation revved his motor. She wasn't afraid. She simply seemed aware that he was a male of power.

She woke his desire to conquer *and* coddle.

"On the bed," was his next thick command.

She crawled back onto it, slightly awkward, her eyes big and bright as she locked her gaze to his. Her breathing had sped up like Cade's, her breasts trembling from the force of her heart racing behind them.

"You're very beautiful," Arcadius said, wanting her to know that. "Please lie back on your elbows and spread your legs. I want to look at you."

Self-consciousness tinged her compliance. She propped herself on her elbows but didn't sprawl her thighs. He remembered her story about Cara forcing her to be the ugly doll. Considering Arcadius hadn't been showered with praise as a child, this angered him more than he would have guessed.

He realized those early insults were still affecting her.

That was wrong. Perhaps some men would find another style of beauty more attractive, but Elyse was completely lovely in her own right. Even more important, she was lovely on the inside. Her strength, her courage, even her stubbornness had become a delight to him.

"Tell her," he said to Cade, suspecting he'd be better at making the point than him. "Tell her what you see when you look at her."

Cade understood. "I see a woman with so much beauty it makes me ache. I see a woman I'll never stop loving."

"Well," Elyse said, her cheeks gone pink. "Thank you."

"He speaks the truth," Arcadius said firmly. "No reasonable man could dislike any part of you."

This made her laugh softly. "No *reasonable* man."

He saw he'd misstepped. "*I'm* reasonable," he pointed out.

Her eyes were warm, her laughter dancing silently in them. "I'm grateful for that. As it happens, I believe no reasonable woman could dislike any part of you."

She was still amused. How did she mollify him and put his back up in the same breath? He fought his urge to cross his arms.

"Please," she said soothingly. "Give me your next command."

"I don't have any more right now. I just want to make love to you."

His answer was surly. Her brows twitched up and wagged suggestively. When she also let one knee fall to the side, he got the message she was sending. The sheen of moisture between her folds constricted his vocal cords.

"I see," he said. "You mean no one is stopping me."

"Please," she repeated, holding out her arms this time. "I want you to do as you wish."

His inconsequential irritation let go of him. Abruptly lighter—not to mention energized—he swung onto the mattress and over her. He planted his palms outside her shoulders, holding himself above her. That felt good, like he really was in charge now. One of his knees ended up within the angle of her bent leg. She shifted that leg to touch him and met his eyes, not teasing or laughing anymore.

His cock was heavy enough to dangle and stiff enough to hurt.

The discomfort reached him from a distance. Holding her gaze seemed strange, like he was about to fall or jump or be yanked into danger. People said the eyes were the windows to the soul.

Would his betray him as less than a whole man?

She touched his cheek, petting it before he could look away. He reminded himself he'd been inside her before. He knew he could pleasure her, with or without Cade's help.

Despite this knowledge, his next question burst from him.

"Do you want to make love to me?" he asked.

Her expression changed, her expanding pupils making her eyes darker. Her hands slid down his chest to lightly rub the groove inside his hipbones. Her touch was enchanted. His erection stretched another millimeter, actually stinging with fullness.

"Yes," she said. "Very much."

"Should I finish removing my trousers?"

She laughed. "What a beautiful idiot you are! Can't you tell when a woman wants you this second?"

He was no idiot. Given this clear green light, he began to move. As he did, Cade sat on the side of the bed, halting him where he was. Arcadius was startled but—to his surprise—not annoyed. Cade had removed his jacket and tie but was otherwise fully dressed. The crotch of his trousers humped as dramatically as Arcadius's had. Seeming prepared to ignore this for the time being, Cade held out a small packet with "Trojan" printed on its surface.

Arcadius's mind sorted out that it was a condom.

"Put this on first," Cade said. "It's a human prophylactic. It's easier than trying to use magic for prevention when you're . . . in the thick of things."

Arcadius assumed he knew this from experience.

"Give it here," Elyse said. "Arcadius won't know what to do with it."

Arcadius could have pulled the information from the ethers but chose not to. Letting her perform the task offered its own rewards, though he had to clench his jaw as she rolled it on. Unfamiliarity with the aid aside, he knew he wasn't supposed to explode at this stage of the proceedings.

"There," she said, smoothing the translucent covering down him with an air of accomplishment.

She'd certainly accomplished winding him to a fever pitch. Though she'd stopped sucking him, moisture continued to well from his slit, causing the condom to cling there. The jerking of his cock was somewhat alarming.

"This will hold?" he asked. "This sheath seems very thin. I felt your fingers perfectly through it."

"It will hold." She grinned. "And good. Imagine what else you'll feel perfectly."

He couldn't help imagining that. He jerked his chin, directing her to lie back again. As he descended over her, she slid her hands down his sides—probably intending to help him enter her. However enjoyable that would be, he realized he wanted something else.

Two commanders were in this room. Not taking advantage of Cade's presence would be wasteful. Arcadius caught his double's eye.

"Please control her arm," he instructed. "Just the left will be enough."

Elyse's lips parted in surprise. Cade didn't let that stop him from clasping her left hand against his chest. He trailed the fingertips of his other hand along the inside of her forearm. Elyse squirmed and broke into goosebumps at the same time. Maybe Arcadius should have been jealous, but he liked watching her respond to the other him.

"Good?" Cade asked Arcadius.

"Perfect. I want her to feel a bit constrained."

"You're ganging up on me," Elyse said.

Her accusation was breathless. Arcadius smiled. "That is one benefit of this arrangement."

He stroked her breast, then bent to kiss its contracted tip. Her skin was so buttery smooth he had to stay there and suck.

Elyse definitely responded to stimulation there. She twitched within Cade's control. "Arcadius," she gasped.

"Arcadius is my name," he agreed pleasantly. He sucked her second nipple harder than he had the first.

Elyse's twitch became a heave of impatience. "I want you now."

"Soon," he said. "When I'm done admiring you."

He might never be done with that. He backed up to caress her torso from collarbones to hips. His palms smoothed the shape of her, molding the strokes down her subtle curves until she thrashed. Her thighs were already open, but he nudged them wider with his knees. His thumbs rubbed the grooves to either side of her pubic triangle.

"Perhaps you'd like me to hold her labia apart for you," Cade offered politely.

"Yes," Arcadius agreed. "I would."

Elyse gasped as the other man's fingers pressed down and spread her there. The feel of both men touching her increased her excitement. Her clitoris stood out sharply, its swollen pinkness thrilling Arcadius.

She was so aroused he saw moisture well from her.

"That's good," he growled. "I like going in easily."

This time when he lowered himself to her he didn't intend to stop. Actually, he wasn't sure his cock would stand more delay. He gripped its base to steer it, adding a quick tight squeeze to calm its urgency. This only helped a bit. He grimaced at the electric zing that jumped from her to him when they made first contact. Her heat was astounding, her wetness gushing against him.

"God," she groaned, her back arching off the bed.

Waiting wasn't possible after that. He pushed and groaned louder than she had. Forging into her was heaven. He drew out the penetration as long as he could bear. At last his cock was buried in her softness. Their pulses beat together, a tormenting tickling sensation. Elyse wasn't able to stay still. She ground her pelvis against his in wonderful hard circles. In spite of how good this felt, he held one hip down to restrain her.

Elyse growled a small protest.

"Hush," he said. "Trust me . . . trust *us* to take care of you."

Her free hand formed a fist on his back. "I'm going crazy. You feel too good inside me."

He couldn't help but love hearing that. With her hip secure in his hold, he drew his cock back and pushed slowly in again.

"More," she said, her fist actually thumping him.

Though she wasn't the boss of this, he gave her a stronger thrust.

"Ah," she sighed, pushing up to meet him.

He couldn't resist this persuasion. His hold on himself unraveled before he finished pushing back. He needed a real rhythm too, needed stroke after stroke, harder, deeper, until they found release together. With each meeting of their bodies, his hunger built. The bed made protesting noises, their combined weight jerking the mattress against its frame. Arcadius fought for control, ready to explode but wanting this act of taking her to last forever.

Then Elyse locked her feet together behind his thighs.

His head flung back, his torso rearing up. She was adding her strength to his, intensifying the concussion of his flesh and hers. The sensations of his pleasure were too sharp for sanity. The pumping of his hips turned compulsive. He'd die if he had to stop, die if he couldn't come.

But he didn't want this position. Elyse was too far away. He wanted more of her, all of her against him. He came down onto his elbows and cupped her jiggling breasts, each thumb and index finger pinching a furled nipple. As he'd expected, the tiny bite of pain suited her. She cried out, her movements going completely wild, her pussy tightening desperately on his thrusts.

Arcadius knew what she needed but refused to release the points through which he was pleasuring her.

"Finger her," he rasped to his double.

Cade's grip had remained on her mons. He pinched all his fingers around her clit, rolling and rubbing the sensitive engorged bud. Experience must have told him what pressure she liked most. Elyse gasped for air, then came with a genuine scream.

Her pussy clutched Arcadius. God, that felt good: so good the pressure beneath his penis surged uncontrollably.

Just hold on, he thought, grunting in reaction. *Just long enough to make her go again.*

He shifted angles, his pelvis tilting to push the strongest friction into the upper wall of her sheath. This was a sensitive spot for her. He went at it good and fast. She whimpered, clutching Cade's hand hard enough that their knuckles were going white. Arcadius hadn't realized he was watching until the excitement the sight inspired sizzled through him like lightning.

The step-up of arousal triggered him, the wave impossible to hold back. Liquid ecstasy shot from more than his cock. His nerves fired along a hundred paths simultaneously: down his shaft, around his nipples, zooming through all his limbs and out his fingertips.

Such blinding bliss accompanied his climax that he almost missed Elyse's next orgasm. Fortunately, she groaned loudly enough to catch his attention.

She sagged beneath him after that: sweaty, sated, and gorgeously flushed. Her heart pounded so hard it shook her whole body.

"Wow," she sighed. Her eyes were closed, her lashes dark fans against her cheeks. Arcadius enjoyed the opportunity to gaze his fill of her.

"Need my hand back," she pointed out breathily.

Arcadius didn't have it. Cade released the extremity in question—along with her pubis. Both he and Elyse needed to flex their fingers to restart the circulation inside of them. The echo of a thrill rolled through Arcadius. He stroked Elyse's curls from her damp forehead. She smiled at the caress, then turned her head on the pillow toward where Cade was sitting.

Her lashes lifted so she could gaze at him.

"Hey," Arcadius's double said softly.

Her smile deepened. She touched Cade's upper thigh with her now free hand, her pinky brushing his big hard-on. "That left you all charged up."

"It was exciting."

The hoarseness of Cade's voice sent a visible shudder through Elyse. Cade's mouth curved as her eyes connected to and held his. Despite the fact that Arcadius remained inside her, the intimacy that passed between them excluded him.

~

Elyse seemed to have broken her own rule that they be careful of each other's feelings.

Everything had seemed fine. Arcadius was being his take-charge self, but she hadn't sensed this causing awkwardness between him and Cade. She certainly didn't mind Arcadius's assertive style. It did nice things for her libido, as did the pair of them joining forces to pleasure her. Her scream was proof of that, for goodness sake. They'd felt like a team—a well-oiled one.

Then Arcadius stiffened and backed off from her.

She withdrew her hand from Cade's leg. "Where are you going?"

Arcadius was already on his feet at the foot of the bed. His trousers hung open but didn't fall down his hips. He removed the spent condom, frowned, then looked up and smiled at her.

The smile *seemed* genuine, but she knew his poker face was good.

"You don't have to leave," Cade said.

Arcadius shrugged. "I could use a wash. And you two need time together."

Should Elyse tell him not to leave? Showing too much concern didn't seem like a good idea. Arcadius was a proud person. Then again, maybe he wanted her to push him to stay. Unless that would bother Cade. *Crap*. Trying to be a threesome was not simple.

"Come back after," she said, not sure that was right choice either. "If you want to, of course."

Seeming to sense she was off balance, Cade squeezed her shoulder. Arcadius fastened his pants and zipped. He glanced at Cade and back to her. "I'll keep your invitation in mind."

He turned and left, closing the bedroom door quietly behind him.

"He'll keep my invitation *in mind*?" Elyse repeated disbelievingly.

Cade snorted out a laugh. "You couldn't have expected this to work perfectly right away."

"What did I do wrong?"

Cade stroked the side of her face. "Nothing. If you tiptoe around him too hard, he won't like that either."

"I guess you'd know."

His eyes crinkled tenderly. "I guess I would."

"Are *you* okay?" she asked.

"I am, though I confess my condition could be improved."

His leer was adorable. Elyse's mood lightened. She smoothed her hands up and down his shirt. The muscles beneath it were hard and warm.

"Tell me what you'd like," she said, "and I'll see what I can do . . ."

~

Though he'd washed up, Arcadius couldn't bring himself to return to the bedroom. It was too quiet in there. Elyse and Cade were probably caught up in pleasuring each other.

He sighed and scrubbed at his hair. He shouldn't turn this into a competition. She and Cade had been together longer. It stood to reason their connection was closer. Arcadius needed to be patient. Hoping his bond with Elyse would one day be as strong wasn't unrealistic.

His hope notwithstanding, he turned left and not right, wandering back to the foyer where he stared at the bolted door. He could go check on the teenagers. Under the circumstances, Elyse seemed unlikely to remember her promise to call them in half an hour.

Good Lord, he thought, recognizing how sulky he sounded.

That wasn't who he was, not now and not ever. If it turned out Elyse couldn't love him the way she loved Cade, he'd accept it like a man.

With that resolved, he grabbed one of the T-shirts Cade had left in the living room and dragged it down his bare chest. He opened the hallway door.

He met Elyse's father coming up the building stairs.

"Hello," Leo said, smiling easily at him. "Is it Arcadius?"

Arcadius nodded. Then, because he didn't know else what to say, he gave in to curiosity. "How did you know?"

"You hold yourself differently—more like a general. Cade's military edges have worn off a bit."

This didn't seem like something Arcadius should correct. "Have you been visiting the young people?"

"Have I ever!" Leo laughed. "I forgot what a handful teenagers are. But they're all present and accounted for. The twins woke up, ate a slice of pizza, and went right back to bed. Probably that means they're okay." He cocked his head at Arcadius. "You look like you could use a beer. Or a cup of tea. I've got both across the hall."

Leo unlocked his apartment door, seeming to assume Arcadius would follow. Arcadius couldn't recall sharing drinks with a lover's father. Actually, he couldn't recall meeting one.

Leo's apartment smelled mainly of fresh paint. It was similar in style to Elyse's but had less furniture. He noticed he had no rugs on the bare floorboards.

"Sit anywhere you like," Leo said as he disappeared into another room. "I'm afraid this place isn't as cozy as my daughter's. I'm still making it my own."

Arcadius chose a large leather armchair next to the fireplace. The chair was old and comfortable. Leo returned with two cold beers in bottles.

"Here you go," he said, handing one to him. He took the chair opposite. Arcadius watched him twist off the cap and mimicked the gesture. Vapor wisped from the bottle's neck like an escaping djinn.

"I've had beer in your world," Leo said. "I don't think you'll hate this."

Arcadius drank cautiously. "It is good," he said, sounding a bit surprised.

Leo laughed, the chuckle reminiscent of his daughter's, though of course it was male. "The other you is smoother," he observed.

"Cade claims knowing Elyse has made him a different man."

"Elyse has her own version of the Solomon charm."

Arcadius considered this statement. For all his social ease, Leo didn't strike him as a person who shared every thought that went through his head. He was sharper than he let on . . . and possibly harder too. Arcadius sensed Leo was taking his measure. He reminded himself two could play that game. Though he had no wish to make an enemy of Elyse's sire, he wouldn't kowtow to him either.

"You didn't protect her very well when she was a child," he said.

Leo's dark brows went up. "I was a single father, with a demanding job. I did the best I could."

"You traveled to suit yourself. You abandoned her to the care of a family whose head you knew wasn't trustworthy, and at the mercy of a girl who wasn't a fit friend."

"Okay, a) June was around to look out for Elyse, and b) Cara wasn't that bad when they were girls. She and my daughter were fond of each other."

"Cara encouraged Elyse to hold a low opinion of herself."

Leo leaned back in his chair. "So that's how it is. Both of you are serious about her."

Arcadius's temper boiled over. "I'm not saying this because I love your daughter. I'm saying it because her cousin was a bully. I sincerely hope you don't intend to treat her safety and happiness that cavalierly now."

Anger gripped Leo's face for about five seconds. He earned Arcadius's respect by pushing it off again. "Fair enough," he said. "I wasn't a perfect dad. As for Elyse's safety and happiness, I suspect that's not going to be up to me so much. Maybe the men who love her have more say in that these days."

His response forced Arcadius to acknowledge that he'd said he loved Elyse. His gut tightened. He hadn't even thought about it. The words had simply come out his mouth.

I love her, he thought. It had crept up on him just as his double warned.

"She loves you," he said aloud.

Leo's face softened. "That I know, and believe me I'm grateful. If it weren't for her, my life would be nothing but my obsession with you folks."

"Obsessions can be dangerous."

"Yes, they can," Leo agreed wholeheartedly.

CHAPTER THIRTEEN

LIKE it or not, Elyse's circadian rhythm had switched back to landlady mode. She woke before the sun with the awareness that she ought to order some trundle beds and sheet sets for the kid downstairs. She sat up and scrubbed at her face.

"Do I need to get up?" Cade asked. His voice sounded awake but his eyes were closed.

He was her sole bed companion. Arcadius must have slept in the living room again. Should she worry about that? But maybe that was just how it would be: the three of them together for sex and then going their own way.

She tried not to let that idea sadden her.

"Go back to sleep," she said, patting Cade's leg gently. "I've got a couple landlady chores."

"Mmph," he said, and rolled over.

When she washed up, dressed, and made it to the kitchen, she spied Arcadius conked out the couch. His presence reassured her, though she wondered at neither man rousing. Last night's magical fight must have taken it out of them. Well, excepting the energy they'd spent on her.

She smiled—perhaps a bit smugly—and opened her laptop. With a couple clicks, she ordered what she needed from an online store that delivered. Despite the issues that remained unsettled, she hummed as she made coffee. Still, neither djinni woke. She found some bacon in her freezer and took it out to thaw in the microwave. No man from any dimension would sleep through her frying that.

She stiffened as a key turned without warning in her front door.

"It's just me," her dad whispered, sticking his head around. "I need the sheep figurine from the miniature farm I sent you from Mexico. Please tell me you didn't throw it out when I died."

Getting used to this sort of conversation would take time.

"I think it's on the bookcase in front of the *Poor Richard's Almanac*. Be quiet when you get it. Arcadius is sleeping."

Her dad tiptoed hurriedly into the living room. "Bless you," he said, coming back with it.

"What do you need it for?" she asked curiously.

"It's an artifact, from the djinn space associated with Chichen Itza. If you recite a spell while you hold it, it makes people suggestible."

"O-kay," she said, still not getting why he needed it.

"Mario's men came back. They're asking where he is."

"They're asking where he is?" She pressed her hand to her heart, alarmed by this development.

"They buzzed." Her dad gave her arm a pat. "Don't worry. While you were gone, I switched the manager's calls to go to my intercom."

Who got the manager calls hardly worried her. "Dad—"

"It's fine," he said, pausing at her door. "I'm going to convince them he and Cara took a long vacation in Canada."

Elyse's pulse palpitated in her throat. Should she wake Cade and Arcadius? Her dad seemed confident he could handle it. *Hell*, she thought and grabbed a frying pan. He shouldn't face this without backup.

He'd been quicker than she expected. Mario's men were leaving by the time she clattered all the way down the stairs. Her father shut the door.

"There," he said. "All sorted out. It was like I figured. Mario didn't prep his goons to resist magic because *he* wanted to spell them. You can have this back if you want."

He held out the innocent looking wooden sheep. Elyse accepted it dazedly. Her knees were shaking. She sat on the nicked old bench in the small lobby space, which was currently empty of tenants.

Companionable as ever, her father dropped to the cushion beside her. "What's the frying pan for?"

"In case you got into trouble," she said weakly.

"Huh. You're pluckier than I realized. Maybe I shouldn't have kept you in the dark about the djinn."

"Oh, that's okay." She rubbed her nose and laughed. "I may be plucky, but I think I have more of a fear gene than you."

"That just makes you braver," he said.

She set down the pan and rubbed her jeans' faded knees. "You're really back," she said, the truth hitting her. "God, my life is crazy."

"Too crazy?" he asked seriously.

His tone took her by surprise. "What do you mean?"

"Well, your fellas." He turned to face her. "I realized last night that they're both in love with you. Not that I'm judging. Maybe that's the way you want it. You just, um, seem more serious about Cade."

"I care about each of them. They're—" How did she explain it? That they were two sides of the same person? She wasn't sure the truth was that simple. "They're both important to me."

"You know the chance is high that someone will get hurt."

"I know," she said. "We're trying to be careful."

"And they're djinn. I'm not one to throw stones, but interdimensional love affairs aren't for everyone."

Him trying to act all mainstream paternal made her smile. "That doesn't bother me anymore. I'm not sure how Cade and I will arrange our lives, but I know we're committed to each other. Maybe that will mean I move to his world, or maybe we'll split our time here and there. I'll be happy—and home —as long as I'm with him."

She'd said the words easily, but she knew they were big—maybe bigger than acknowledging that she was in love. Bright spangles of excitement burst through her veins. She was glad about how she felt. It didn't make her afraid at all.

"You do hear how you're talking," her father said. "You said 'Cade and I,' not 'the three of us.'"

He startled her out of her sparkly glow. "Arcadius and I are newer."

"Maybe," he said, "but it's something to think about."

Elyse shifted uneasily on the bench. She didn't want to think about it. She liked the idea of keeping Arcadius, especially now that she knew Cade wasn't against it. Cade didn't want his double hurt any more than she did.

We'll find a way, she thought. *Somehow.*

That her brain was operating more on stubbornness than belief she didn't want to dwell on.

"Well," she said, getting to her feet. "Is your fridge better stocked than mine? I was going to make breakfast."

"It's not stocked well enough for six teenagers."

"Shoot," she said, momentarily having forgotten them.

"I *could* take them out to shop," he suggested unsurely. "They won't agree to stay indoors forever, and it *might* be good if they familiarize themselves with how life works here."

The sound of approaching male footsteps drew Elyse's gaze away. Cade appeared on the foyer's open stretch of stairs. Even as he trotted down them, he thrust his arms into a T-shirt and pulled it down his muscular chest. He must have been dressing on the fly.

He also must have heard what her father proposed. "You want chaperoning help?"

"Absolutely," Leo said.

Cade hugged her shoulders and kissed her cheek. "Everything okay? Sorry I didn't get here right away. I couldn't decide if I should smoke down or dress."

"Everything's fine." Elyse hugged him back, feeling pleasantly fussed over.

"Dad can fill you in on what happened."

"All right," Cade said. "Let's grab coats and round up those teenagers."

~

Arcadius had been half awake ever since Elyse started puttering in the kitchen. He'd enjoyed her unknowing company, soothed by the simple idea that she was there. Leo's arrival had woken him all the way, though he hadn't known how to say so politely. Elyse's frantic departure with the frying pan had pushed aside his concern for niceties. He'd snapped into his smoke form and streaked down the stairs after her father. He'd been prepared to intervene, but Leo tricked Mario's associates with a minimum of effort. When Elyse caught up, Arcadius was still there, hovering invisibly. For the second time that morning, he was undecided how to announce himself.

Because he couldn't make up his mind, he heard everything she and her father said. None of their conversation was surprising, but somehow all of it hurt.

She said she'd be happy as long as she was with Cade.

His envy made him angry—and the awareness that he was being cowardly by hiding. He rematerialized on the upper landing in front of the cozy group.

They all jolted to a halt. Arcadius forced his face to stay impassive.

"Oh," Elyse said, her palm pressed against her breasts. "How long have you been awake?"

"I accompanied your father on his errand to befuddle Mario's men. In case they turned violent and he needed assistance."

"Oh." She blinked rapidly, no doubt calculating what this meant. The faintest blush rose into her cheeks. "That was considerate."

"You must be good at taking vapor form," Leo said admiringly. "I never felt you there."

Arcadius returned his compliment with a bow. "You handled the criminals well."

"We're taking the kids food shopping," Cade broke in. "Maybe you'd like to come."

"Someone should guard the residence," he said.

He sounded stiff even to himself.

"Sure," Cade said. "Playing it safe isn't a bad idea."

"I'll stay too," Elyse volunteered. "If we're all eating together, I need to steal some chairs and dishes from dad's place."

Cade seemed to intuit this wasn't the whole story—and that Elyse didn't wish to elaborate right then. He kissed her lightly before he and her father left. Arcadius noticed Cade acted as much like a member of Elyse's family as Leo Solomon.

The apartment was very quiet once they were gone.

Arcadius didn't flinch when Elyse faced him. She put her hands on the hips of her snug blue jeans. The pants were distractingly formfitting, but he held onto his wits. "You heard what my father said. About me seeming more serious about Cade."

"The truth shouldn't be avoided. Especially in a situation such as the three of us are in."

"Other things I said are true too. You're important to me."

He nodded, accepting that. "I apologize for not announcing my presence. I shouldn't have eavesdropped."

She rubbed her brow and laughed softly. "I don't expect the people I love to be perfect."

Conceivably he expected this of himself. "I will keep that in mind," he said.

She surprised him by giving him a hug. His arms felt awkward as they circled her, unused to casual embraces. He did like holding her. Her smallness and her affection were pleasant. After a bit, she tipped her head up to smile at him. His heart wouldn't go along with his resolve to remain stoic. It beat unevenly.

She rubbed his back as if she thought he needed warming up.

Maybe he did. He didn't want to let go of her.

"Come on," she said, her hand sliding down his arm to clasp his fingers. "Let's go raid my dad's apartment."

~

By the time her dad and Cade returned with the excited teenagers and a cab load of groceries, the hour was more appropriate for lunch than breakfast. Elyse wished she'd accomplished as much in the time she'd spent with Arcadius. Though they'd done everything they needed, even setting up the kids' new beds, she couldn't shake the impression that she was dropping the ball with him. Arcadius was pleasant and polite—too polite, really. She ought to be able to figure out what to do or say to make things right for him. Somewhere the perfect words or gesture existed.

Unless they didn't, in which case they were screwed.

During the meal, Arcadius was the quietest person at the table. Even the twins, who'd so recently been released from their ordeal, spoke up more than him.

The glances Cade sent his double's way said he noticed how subdued he was. Her dad did too—though Leo was in his element, playing host to the exotic young people. They all exclaimed with disappointment when he announced he needed to excuse himself.

"You won't even miss me," he said, "because you're going to clear up and figure out how to use my daughter's dishwasher."

"You show us, Mr. Solomon," Celia pleaded. "We're not as good at plucking information from the ethers as old folks."

"All the more reason to practice. I know you want to be allowed to stay. You'll need to convince more than one 'old folk' that you can handle it."

This statement was moderately alarming. Elyse had assumed the kids would go home as soon as the cellar portal could be recharged and reprogrammed. Naturally, they'd need to return to better circumstances than they left, but she was certain the two commanders would arrange that.

Her dad spotted her look of doubt. "I didn't promise anything," he said, his hands up in denial. "Anyway, while the kids are busy, maybe the three of you would take a trip with me."

"The three of us," Arcadius repeated.

"The three of you," he confirmed. "I can't swear to it, but I might have a solution to your problem."

He wouldn't say where he was taking them, but her dad liked to be mysterious—more than she'd realized, actually. Evidently, their destination was close enough to walk. He led them north on her street and then a short ways east on 25th.

He stopped at a narrow storefront, in front of which a section of Manhattan's ubiquitous construction scaffolding stood. The business it overhung was a bookstore, its old-fashioned door a short ramp down from street level. Dusty yellowed volumes leaned in hodgepodge stacks behind the plate glass window, blocking much of the view to the interior. Peeling gold letters announced the establishment to be G. J. Wright's Antiquarian Book Trader. It was the sort of place elderly men and lost tourists went into. Elyse must have walked by it a thousand times without giving it a glance.

"Why are we here?"

"I wondered if you'd remember," her father said. "The last time I brought you here you were two. We realized around then it might be best to let my brother forget this place existed."

"This was your father Saul's bookstore," Cade said in a tone of discovery. "Elyse's grandfather."

"You researched our family."

"And the history of your brownstone. Joseph and I wanted to know how the nexus had gotten there."

"Who is G. J. Wright?" Arcadius asked.

"The man Saul Solomon pretended to sell the store to," her dad answered. "I pay his salary now."

A *Closed* sign hung in the door. Elyse supposed they wouldn't meet Mr. Wright today.

Her dad didn't need a key. He cupped his hand above the knob and murmured a little spell. The knob and bolt turned without him touching them. He pulled the door outward and gestured for the others to enter.

They picked their way in as best they could. Many tall overloaded shelves cramped the space. More volumes piled at their bases narrowed the paths between. Mr. Wright seemed not to have been hired for his housekeeping or his work ethic. The overwhelming smell of mildew and aging books caused Elyse to cover her nose and sneeze.

"Bless you," Cade said, rubbing her back as he looked around.

A bell jingled as her dad shut and locked the street door again.

"There's nothing we need to see in this front bit," he announced. "Keep going down the aisle until you spot the sign for military books."

The military books were in the back and around a corner.

Her father followed behind the three of them. "You see that *Training Horses for War* by Dunkirk? Knock on its spine and say, 'Please let me in, if you'd be so kind.'"

Elyse did as he instructed. The charm must have been easy to activate. A gritty grinding noise was her immediate reward. The tall shelf slid back and then swung around to the side. The area behind it was as dark as a cave.

"There's a light switch on the right," her father said helpfully.

Cade reached in and flipped it.

"Ooh," Elyse exclaimed.

They'd accessed a secret library. Perhaps ten feet in diameter, the space was octagonal and lined all around with mahogany shelves. The books that stood in ranks within them were less dusty than those out front and mostly leather bound. A dark flowered Persian carpet cushioned the wooden floor. Toward the back wall, opposite the door, two comfy armchairs, a reading table, and a double-headed banker's lamp supplied the furniture.

"Your grandfather and I would come here to read and practice spells in private. It took decades, but eventually we hit on how to make the nexus work. Well, I did. Dad didn't live long enough to travel through the door."

Saul Solomon had died when Elyse was nine or ten. She remembered him as an intense personality with a thin face and shaggy brows. He'd been very smart, very particular, and occasionally quite funny. She'd liked him but warily. It was no accident Saul's sons had ended up at odds. He hadn't been as easygoing as her dad, and his temper was sometimes sharp. Seeing this place, imagining him and Leo poring over books and conducting magic experiments, made him realer but also more peculiar.

"This is your heritage," her dad said. "Doing magic is officially in your blood."

That sounded odd to her. She walked deeper into the handsome room, trailing her fingers along the chest-height shelf. Would she read these books some day? Many weren't in English. They were Latin and Spanish and . . . djinn, she realized, as the titles blurred and rearranged themselves for her eyes. Her gift for translating the other dimension's language, which had magically rubbed off on her from Cade, was still functioning.

Arcadius's voice turned her back toward the door. "You mentioned you had a solution to our problem?"

His tone was circumspect, as it had been all day. His guardedness troubled her—and the way he deliberately kept his gaze on her father and avoided her. What exactly didn't he want her to see?

"I *may* have an answer," her father said. "Not to flatter myself, but I have a better than average memory. When Cade first told me how you two came to be, my brain started nudging me to remember something I'd read in here years ago. I know your friend Joseph is a skilled magician, and I'm sure he's done everything he can to help you recombine. The fact is, however, that he's a djinni. When it comes to magic, human power is top dog. Because djinn magic split you into a pair, possibly a human with the right spell could put you back together."

"And you think that spell is inside these books?"

"That one specifically." Her dad pointed toward the shelf Cade was near. "The smallish royal blue journal. I believe it's called *Mending With Magic: Broken Items Restored As Good As New.* I found it at a flea market in New Jersey. The title was obscured with a chocolate stain. No one noticed it but me."

Cade pulled the book from the shelf and opened it. "It's handwritten, in English. Dated August 12, 1967." He turned a page and his eyes widened. "The description says it's 'a manual for servants away from home.'"

Her father came to stand at Cade's shoulder. Inches shorter and lanky, he was downright skinny next to the brawny djinn.

"Yes," he said to Cade. "That's the book I recall. You didn't think you were the first of your kind to pop up on this continent, did you?"

"I suppose not. Samir found his way here, after all." Cade flipped a few pages. "Here's a spell for 'Returning Two to One: when copies become clutter.' The sorcerer who wrote this couldn't have meant people, but I imagine it could work."

"May I see it?" Arcadius held out his hand. "Not that I consider myself *clutter.*"

Cade smiled and handed the book to him. Arcadius read it without twitching one face muscle. "Yes," he said. "This seems do-able."

Elyse's stomach clenched. This was moving too fast for her. She had to swallow before she spoke. "We can think about this before we try it, right?"

The men turned to her as a group. Arcadius's expression was impossible to read, but Cade looked slightly surprised. Thank goodness her father seemed to understand what she felt.

"Of course you can," he said, his eyes soft with compassion. "You need to decide what's best for your heart . . . for all your hearts. I showed you this so you would have a choice. Just don't put it off too long. Cade and Arcadius have been doubled for quite a while. The more separate experiences they have, the more difficult it will be for even you to put them back together."

She went hot from a sudden rush of adrenaline. "You expect *me* to do the spell?"

"There's no one better," he asserted. "Emotion adds power to enchantments. This one is likely to take everything you've got."

In more ways than one, was her instant thought.

Her father must have seen her dismay. He clapped one hand on her shoulder. "I'll leave you three to discuss this among yourselves. I don't mean to rush you, but—if you can—you might want to decide here and now."

He went back into the store, working the mechanism to swing the secret bookshelf door shut again.

Cade looked at her, a hint of her same helplessness in his eyes.

The third member of their party had a different perspective.

"We should do it," Arcadius said firmly. "If this works, it would solve everything, for us and for our city. Now of all times, our people need their commander to be at full strength. In addition to this—though I don't think personal considerations should come first—neither of us would have to face losing you. We could truly share you, because we'd be one person."

"Neither of you have to face losing me now!"

"Don't we?" Arcadius asked, his naturally serious face pulled into even more solemn lines. "In truth, haven't you chosen which of us you care for more?"

Had she? Elyse wasn't sure of that.

"He has a point," Cade broke in even as he rubbed his upper lip doubtfully. "Since we're both in love with you, a combined commander would be unlikely to fall out of it. Maybe we'd love you even more."

"I like the way you love me now!" Okay, maybe that wasn't the best way to put it. She lost her fight with the blush that stung her cheeks. Cade noticed and cracked a grin. "I don't just mean I like having sex with both of you."

"One is less awkward," Arcadius pointed out. "You don't have to worry about making either of us jealous."

"You *do* worry about that," Cade said. "We can tell."

Hell, she thought. Was she resisting for selfish reasons, because making love to two men appealed to her kinky side? She didn't think that was the reason. Her heart was uneasy, not her sex organs.

"What if I screw this up like I did the protection spell?"

The men exchanged confused glances. "How did you screw that up?" Cade asked.

"I couldn't come up with an effective chant. I said words but they didn't work. If I hadn't noticed that shovel lying there, Mario might have beaten you."

"But you did notice the shovel," Arcadius said. "And you turned the tide of the battle by wielding it. That's the way magic works sometimes—not as you will but as the Almighty does. That's why light djinn petition Him."

"That's not magic. That's coincidence."

Arcadius smiled tolerantly. "You performed the right action at the right time. I call that inspiration."

"Arcadius thinks *he* screwed up," Cade teased. "Because a girl had to save our butts."

"I didn't call her a girl," Arcadius corrected. "I definitely said 'woman.'"

If Elyse turned the men back into one person, she'd never hear them bicker this way again. She frowned. She couldn't rationally explain why that felt like a bad thing.

"I want to do this," Arcadius said.

"Are you sure you're in the right frame of mind to decide?" she asked.

"Yes," he insisted.

She gnawed her lip, then extended her arm for the book. "Let me take a look at the instructions."

Arcadius handed her the journal with the page left open. Elyse had hoped for something complicated . . . a bunch of 'eye of newt'-type ingredients they'd have to scour the city for. Instead, the spell seemed simple. The doubled items needed to be placed close together while the spell worker chanted the incantation and pictured them as one.

"It's simple," Arcadius said, seeming to read her mind. "After what you've pulled off, you should be able to accomplish this with no problem."

No problem apart from a person she'd grown attached to ceasing to exist.

She reminded herself Arcadius's personality would be included in the mix, but how much of it would there be? He'd been allocated the smaller portion of their shared spirit. Would she even know he was there?

"Are *you* sure you want to try this?" she asked Cade. "We can't be certain how it will affect you."

"It's now or never," he answered soberly. "One more hour spent apart might make it impossible." He bent a little to look into her eyes. "I think we need to do this, sweetheart. I think we'll be making this situation right for all us."

So . . . he wanted to do it too. She couldn't squirm out of it that way. The palms of her hands turned clammy.

"Okay," she said reluctantly. "You two stand together in the center of the carpet."

The men stood together, muscular arms bumping each other. She looked at them: so tall, so handsome, their serious expressions almost a perfect match. Cade was dressed casually in a white T-shirt and gray sweats. Arcadius wore his trousers from the night before and a blue polo shirt. Both their shoulders were broad, both their chests beautifully developed. Other than their clothes, there appeared to be no difference between them.

They're the same, she tried to tell herself. *You won't be losing anything.*

She took few stiff steps backward and held the book before her.

"Relax," Cade said. "We have faith you can do this."

For once Elyse didn't doubt she could do a spell. Unfortunately, faith was her enemy now, the source of her growing dread. *It's their choice*, she told herself, *their city that needs them.*

She began to read the spell haltingly.

When she'd gone through it twice, Cade let out a quiet gasp. He seemed to be in pain. His face had drained of color and one fist pressed his breastbone. He and Arcadius had locked their free hands together.

"Just keep going," Cade instructed through gritted teeth.

"Please," Arcadius seconded in the same clenched tone.

She didn't want to, but she resumed. The air started thickening, the faintest glow beginning to glimmer around the djinn. Shit, should this feel so wrong? Like her heart was being twisted to face the wrong way around? She remembered she was supposed to visualize the men as one. The instant she had the thought, the glow brightened. The light formed an envelope around them, their divided spirits beginning to rejoin.

Suddenly, a slide show flicked through her mind. She saw herself sitting with Arcadius in the hot sunny garden outside the harem walls. His sly little grin after he'd tricked Cade into spending all day behind their desk. The sparkly slippers he bought for her from the bazaar. The kiss he'd stolen in her apartment. *I want you to myself,* he'd said. *I want to make love to you, without him.* Like it was occurring that very second, she glanced back over her shoulder as she and Cade stepped through the Arch of Triumph portal, seeing the yearning and the worry in Arcadius's face at being left behind.

That was the moment she first suspected he was in love with her.

Her chest hitched, the ache that gripped it making it hard to speak. She couldn't read anyway. The words of the spell had blurred. She was crying for Arcadius.

"I *can't*," she burst out, flinging the magic journal away from her. "I'm sorry. I love him too!"

She dropped to her knees and sobbed, too wracked to get up or even lift her head. She never let herself fall apart, but she couldn't help it then.

Please, she prayed. *Don't let the spell have worked yet.*

Warm male hands gripped her shoulders.

"Shh," Cade said, pulling her against him. "Hush, honey, it's all right."

He rubbed her back, but she couldn't stop crying.

"Is she ill?" asked Arcadius.

Her head jerked up. It was him. Conflicting reactions warred in his face: alarm, pleasure, and a weensy bit of disapproval that she'd so utterly lost control. She laughed at that through her tears. "You're still here."

"I am." Sighing, he came down on his knees like Cade. "You really love me?"

She turned and flung her arms around him, burying her face in his warm strong neck. He held her back with almost no hesitation. She didn't care if he did hesitate. She loved that about him too.

"I love you," she said, squeezing him even harder. "Exactly the way you are."

"Well," he said, like she'd astounded him.

She'd astounded herself. Until she fell for Cade, she hadn't thought she'd give her heart again. Her deceitful departed husband had broken it too well. Now here she was, risking it twice over.

Cade stroked her hair. "It's all right," he said, leaning to kiss her temple. "We'll make it work this way."

Elyse pushed back. "I'm sorry I couldn't do the spell. I know it was important."

Her cheeks were wet. Cade dried one at nearly the same time that Arcadius brushed the other. She really was a mess if they both had to coddle her.

"I didn't mean to be such a baby," she apologized.

"We'll make it work." Arcadius's voice was sterner than Cade's had been, his manner determined.

"Good." She finished wiping her face herself. "Can we go back to the brownstone now? I don't want to stay in this place."

~

Arcadius walked to Elyse's home in an unprecedented daze. An army of ifrits could have lurked on the roofs, and he wouldn't have noticed.

Cade was obliged to explain to Leo why they weren't doing the spell. Elyse was too shaken up.

Elyse loved Arcadius.

Not just a little, apparently. She loved him enough to have sobbed like her world was ending, enough—in truth—to look as if she were having a teensy fit. She loved him exactly the way he was; loved him as much as she loved his double . . . so far as he could tell.

That was an extraordinary development.

In all his life, Arcadius had never been that important to someone's happiness. He'd had friends and people who counted on him, but nothing as deep as this. The realization made him giddy. He wanted to slay a dragon, or maybe hug everyone he met. Well, perhaps that went a bit too far. He could have hugged Cade, though, and Leo too. Had he known he had this much affection inside of him? The sense that he and Cade were rivals had blown away.

They were meant to love Elyse together.

Leo shooed the kids out of Elyse's apartment and then disappeared himself.

"I guess they figured it out," Elyse said. "The dishwasher is running."

She was in the open kitchen, regarding the machine. Her face was still streaked with tears, her hair the sort of mess that helped him understand why she sometimes behaved as if she were at war with it. Her hands were propped on her hips. Her butt shaped her faded jeans so well they were indecent. Arcadius couldn't bring himself to disapprove. This was the butt of the woman who loved him.

Remembering what it looked like naked caused his cock to swell.

"Elyse," he said huskily.

She looked at him and blushed.

Cade cleared his throat. "Okay," he said. "You two go to the bedroom and have at it. I'll be out here if you need me."

"Cade," Elyse said, concern in her voice and eyes.

Cade shook his head. "I have to trust you alone together. I have to trust you'll love me even if you love him."

"I do." Her face glowed with it.

"I know," he said, "and, in time, Arcadius will too. You need chances to forge a separate bond with him. That's how we'll make this work: not just the three of us but also two and two."

She walked to Cade like he was the center of her universe, a sun that shone for her alone. When their gazes held, their expressions seemed beautiful to Arcadius. The pang their love stirred was less. And maybe the pang wasn't totally for him. Maybe he understood this was a challenge for Cade as well.

Elyse put her hands on his chest. Cade covered them gently. "Are you going to marry me someday?" she asked shyly.

He smiled. "Whenever you want in whichever dimension. For now, though, I'll just stand by your front window, watching the street for threats."

He deliberately made this sound pitiful. Elyse looked startled, but Arcadius rolled his eyes. "He's . . . pulling your leg. He'll be fine out here."

"Really?" Elyse asked. "Because he could—"

Arcadius steered her away by both shoulders. "Not this time."

Her gaze came up to his, and he saw a spark that was just for him.

"Treat her right," Cade called, halfway to his watching post.

"As if I wouldn't," Arcadius said mildly. He took Elyse's hand, weaving their fingers together. "Come with me, beautiful. Let's make a memory."

~

Was that going to be his pet name for her? Not *sweetheart*, not *honey*, but *beautiful*?

Elyse didn't ask. It would have felt like fishing for compliments. She let him draw her down the hall instead. The hand that held hers was the same shape and size as Cade's but it felt different.

"You have calluses," she blurted.

They were at her bedroom door. Arcadius paused to face her. "Calluses?"

"On your hands. Cade must have forgotten to project them into your copy."

Arcadius's gaze searched hers.

"I don't mind," she added. "You must have gotten them from sword practice."

"Yes," he said. "Normally djinn wouldn't, but I . . . *we* train a lot with our men. The magic that allows us to change form treats calluses as assets and not injuries. I imagine Cade will develop them again." He hesitated before stroking her curls back. "I can't be exactly like him."

"I don't want you to." She gnawed her lip unsurely.

"What troubles you?" he asked.

"Just that, when I'm with you, I can't be exactly like I am with him."

"But you love me."

"Oh, yes," she assured him.

He must have liked the way she said it. His normally stern mouth curved. "I'd like to kiss you now, Elyse."

"Yes, please," she said and stretched up to reach him.

His arms slid around her as his mouth covered hers, completely confident in this. Their tongues met, and he let out a sound. Wanting more of that, she drove her hands up his back and clung. He gripped her bottom, hitching her up his body and then turning to push her hard into the doorframe. With her secured by his weight, he ground his erection between her legs—as if their genitals could burn through their clothes. He gentled a moment later, but hot excitement had already streaked to her sex. He dropped his lips to her neck and nipped. Elyse gasped with quick pleasure.

"Elyse," he groaned. "I want you so much."

She reclaimed his mouth even as she started wrestling her T-shirt up her torso.

This didn't work, of course. She didn't have elbowroom. Arcadius's chuckle was low and male, his fingers squeezing her ass even as he turned to carry her into the bedroom. He laid her on the covers but she sat up. She couldn't let go of him. She kissed him and kissed him until he pushed firmly enough to break free.

Joy and lust danced together behind his eyes. He caught her wrists and pulled them away from clutching him. Then, with a quickness that stole her breath, he whipped her T-shirt over her head. Her bra followed just as swiftly, leaving her breasts swaying. His gaze dipped to her tightening nipples before returning to her face.

"I'm undressing you," he warned, "Every stitch, until you're stark naked."

"I'll help," she offered eagerly. Wet and aching with readiness, she moved her hands to the metal button at the waist of her jeans.

"No," he said, stopping her with the single commanding word. Seeing he had her compliance, he pulled his belt free of his trousers. In contrast to the night before, he had no trouble removing it. Her attention snagged on the leather accessory.

Fires gleamed hotter in his eyes.

"You want me to restrain you," he concluded. She shivered involuntarily. Naturally, he noticed that as well. "Cross your wrists in front of you."

She had no impulse to disobey. She crossed them, and he wrapped the leather strap around. She couldn't help squirming on the bed as her pussy grew wetter. Cade liked to control her too. The difference lay in Arcadius's edge, his slightly less careful willfulness. She remembered whipping him and how much he'd enjoyed that. Maybe Arcadius had more of both extremes in him.

When her wrists were securely trussed, he buckled the belt ends together.

"Stay where you are," he said. "You're not lying down for this."

He knelt to pull off her sneakers and socks. He rubbed the soles of her feet, his fingertips digging in to find interesting nerve bundles. Her breath sucked in as he found a spot that caused her clit to twitch uncontrollably.

"Like that?" he said, his smile saturnine.

"You djinn know sneaky things," she panted.

He bent forward to nip her thigh just above the knee, making her muscles jump. With his gaze on hers, he slid both hands slowly up her legs, from her ankles on upward.

She felt like his palms were staking ownership of her.

"I like these blue jeans," he growled. "More than you can imagine."

When his caresses reached her hips, he scooted her to the mattress edge. Her thighs widened automatically around his torso. Her breathing quickened. Their positions were suggestive.

She waited for his next instruction.

"Put your hands behind my head," he said.

She dropped the loop his belt made behind his neck, her forearms resting on his broad shoulders. He was kneeling. She had to look down to meet his eyes. Despite being above him, he felt very much in charge of her.

Possibly he wasn't in charge of himself. His heart pounded all through his body, his heat beating out in waves.

"You smell good," he said.

He lowered his face and rubbed it across her crotch.

"God," she said, her neck and back arching. Her fingers clenched in his hair, her hands forced to stay together.

He mouthed her then, widening his jaw to bite down lightly on her pubis. If he'd smelled her before, he certainly did then. She creamed like crazy at the pressure of his teeth.

He drew back from her, breathing heavier than before. Finally, he was ready to undo the fastenings of her jeans. He freed them quickly, tugging the pants down her legs the moment she lifted her hips enough. He ducked from beneath her hands and rose to his feet.

Then he made short work of removing his own garments.

Oh, his naked body was drool worthy—his skin, his muscles, the cloud of hair that made his chest look so male before it dove to his pubic thatch. His substantial shape was exactly what she liked. His cock stood hard and flushed from his groin, pulsing with excitement.

Too impatient to ask permission, she reached for it with her bound hands.

He let her catch it, groaning out little pleasured noises as she dropped kisses along his shaft. Over his veins she wandered, up to the swollen tip.

"Don't," he rasped when she sucked the hot head into her mouth.

She didn't obey. He was too delicious, too satiny and aroused. She flicked her tongue back and forth and pulled firmly with her cheeks. He couldn't resist pushing once. As he did, his cock pulsed strongly inside her oral clasp.

Maybe it felt too nice. He dragged her back from him with both hands. His chest went in and out, his diaphragm hollowing. Happy to tease him, Elyse licked her lower lip.

"You taste good," she said.

He considered her gravely. "I love you, Elyse."

She bit her grin before her humor could show too much. He was so wonderfully serious. "I love you back."

He nodded, so apparently this answer was acceptable.

"Do you like that chair?" He tilted his head toward the one nearest to the bed. It was a big armchair, well-stuffed and broken in, with a pattern of small blue flowers on its upholstery.

"I like it fine. You aren't planning on breaking it, are you?"

He cracked the slightest smile. "I thought I'd sit in it, and then perhaps you could sit on me."

"Oh." Her pussy clenched with anticipation. "Yes, I believe I would enjoy that."

He strode to it before she could move, lowering his body onto the cushion. His knees sprawled to take up more space, his hands curled around the ends of the arms as if he owned everything in sight. Her hormones reacted in spite of her amusement. No wonder he'd had no qualms about filling in for their lost sultan. He was a ruler in his own right.

"Come to me," he said sternly.

She came, step by step, with her wrapped wrists in front of her. She began to incline her head, thinking he'd enjoy the docile pose.

"No," he said, tipping her jaw back up with a gentle hand. "I don't want you to play that much at submissiveness."

"No?"

He shook his head. "I like your strength. I like looking into your eyes and knowing you won't break." He paused and drew breath. "I expect Cade finds it attractive too."

Emotion roughened his voice for the admission.

"I hope he does." Elyse broke into a laugh. "I like knowing you guys won't break either. Sometimes a girl likes a good hard ride."

His beautiful eyes kindled. "Allow me to help you . . . get into the saddle."

He steadied her by the hips. She swung her first knee into the chair and then the other. His big hands rubbed her from butt to waist. She put her bound hands behind his neck again. Arcadius studied her up and down.

"Very pretty," he murmured. "Especially here, where you've gone soft and wet for me."

His thumbs stroked into her folds, parting and sensitizing them.

"Lower yourself," he said. "I'll guide you where you need to be."

He took her hips again to do it, his attention on the place their bodies were about to meet. She felt his crown, and delight snapped through her.

His finger pads dug into on her skin.

"Come down," he said, nearly whispering. "Feel me going into you."

She felt him, inch by inch, pulsing, stretching, filling her until his cock seemed to reach her womb. Needing to express the incredible tension inside of her, she gripped the back of the chair and groaned.

"Yes," he said, enraptured by her writhing. "Ride me like that."

He held her hips so tight she could only rock. The lap dance was deliciously slow and intimate. His gaze traveled down her, to the spot where the thickness at his base rolled in and out of her. He'd shifted his hips a bit forward, giving her legs room within the chair. Suddenly, he leaned back to see their joining better. He couldn't hide his reaction to the improved view. His teeth caught his lower lip and his cheeks darkened. The ache in her pussy went nuclear.

"You like watching us," she said.

He looked up, his pupils as big as dimes. "I like watching you. You move like a harem girl. Will you keep doing that?"

"You mean without your hands guiding me?"

"Yes."

"I will," she promised. "It feels really good to me."

He hesitated for two heartbeats, then slid his hold up her sides and inward over her ribs. The gliding stopped when he cupped her bosom. She was small and his hands were large. They swallowed her breasts as his fingers contracted and massaged. Her nipples pebbled harder beneath his palms. Arcadius's breathing turned jerkier.

"That feels really good to me," he said.

She wasn't sure she could speak. He was so thick inside her. Working her hungry walls against him was driving her to the brink. She'd reached the point where she truly needed an orgasm.

"Could I move faster now?" she asked.

Arcadius groaned. Like her, he must have been impatient. "Harder, too, if you would."

His thumbs and fingers rolled her nipples just enough to stir a twinge of pleasure-pain. When Elyse undulated harder, his hips drove up to meet hers. He was tightening his glutes to lift him off the seat, thrusting his thick hard rod into her. His head flung back and then lowered.

His gaze locked on hers.

Their eyes told each other how close they were, the tensing of their facial muscles, the sweat glittering on their skin. Arcadius didn't hide from her, and she couldn't hide from him. This was just the two of them, their private moment together. Elyse couldn't hold back from chasing her orgasm. Arcadius grunted, lengthening his strokes so that she rose and fell more inches along him. The friction killed her, the way it pushed sweet sensations ever deeper into her.

Her hands were on his back again, where the solid muscles of his shoulders met those behind his neck. The leather that wrapped her wrists gave her something satisfying to strain against. Maybe too satisfying.

Her nails dug into him hard enough to leave marks.

He knew what that meant. He released her left breast. She was moving wildly, desperate to go over. His thumb and fingers found her clit anyway. He frigged the soft sheath fast and snug over the little rod. Bolts of pure ecstasy streaked up its nerves and out her fingertips.

Her body felt like it wasn't hers. The things he'd done to her and asked of her had remade it. She came with a banshee cry, her pussy contracting helplessly and hard. Her violent clenching around his shaft set off a response in him. He tightened all over, his muscles as hard as stone. He whispered something and his cock pumped into her crazy-strong. A handful of thrusts later, he roared and slammed all the way into her.

He held there like he didn't ever want to come out. Heat flooded her but not wetness. He'd remembered to turn his seed to smoke.

Cade wasn't the only responsible commander, apparently.

"Ah," Arcadius sighed, relaxing under her into the chair. His thighs no longer felt like they were made of obsidian.

Reminded to relax herself, Elyse unclamped her fingernails from his shoulders.

"I broke your skin," she exclaimed, *tsking* over the half-moon marks.

He smiled as she craned to check both sides. His hands settled on her hips. "I will heal. And how could I mind such flattering battle wounds?"

Because the battle was over, she lifted her wrists over his head and back in front of him. "Would you undo this?"

He unfastened the buckle, unwrapped the leather, and kissed the redness her straining had left inside her forearms—*her* battle wounds, she guessed. His lips were soft, his eyes closing for each kiss. When she first met him, she wouldn't have thought him capable of such tenderness. Then again, she wouldn't have thought herself capable of feeling so much for him.

Her hands finally back in her own control, she petted his face between her palms. "I love you, Arcadius."

"I do not mind hearing that," he acknowledged.

She laughed and laid her head on his broad shoulder. His arms came around her to rub her back. He was so warm, so protective and comforting that every scrap of tension in her body released at once.

"You may fall asleep if you wish," he said. "I will wake you after you've had a nap."

"You're ridiculously nice," she murmured—and took him up on his offer.

~

Cade had grown used to the rhythms of Elyse's neighborhood. Sensing nothing amiss, he retrieved a beer from her fridge, popped the metal cap with a flare of magic, and relaxed at her round table. As he took a swallow, his feet found a resting place on one of the chairs they'd squeezed in to seat the kids.

Though they needed to return to the Glorious City, he realized he was equally at home in Manhattan. He could be happy here, as long as he was with his beloved.

His contemplations were interrupted by a long female moan trailing up the hall from the main bedroom. Muted but interesting feelings rolled through his groin as his double orgasmed.

That would take adjusting to, but he still thought he'd made the right decision to leave Elyse and Arcadius to themselves. Looked at in a certain way, Arcadius's appeal for Elyse was reassuring. She loved who Cade used to be. To her, he'd always been a good man. It was even possible that meeting the missing part of Cade's spirit had completed a puzzle for her heart. Maybe she hadn't been able to fall in love until she knew all of him.

It was a theory anyway.

His beer was half gone by the time Arcadius entered the living area, looking considerably more relaxed. He wore baggy black cargo shorts that Cade didn't recognize.

"Elyse is asleep," Arcadius said as he sat across from him. "I believe these pants were her husband's. I found them in a box in his old office."

Cade nodded and slid the beer to him. "She has history besides us."

"We will treat her better than him," Arcadius declared.

His solemnity amused Cade. "That's the plan."

"We must come to an agreement, you and I." Cade's eyebrows rose, but Arcadius continued. "We shouldn't force Elyse to play peacemaker. It's too uncomfortable for her to be put in the middle. If we have differences, we should settle them ourselves."

"I'd get on board with that—though we need to be careful we don't keep too much from her. That undermines the idea of us being a team."

Arcadius narrowed his eyes. He didn't like being contradicted. "We *will* protect her."

"Not from everything," Cade countered. "That isn't going to work."

"She is proud," Arcadius acknowledged.

"Luckily for us, she's not as proud as you."

Arcadius surprised him by laughing. He lifted Cade's beer and drank. "You're proud too," he pointed out slyly.

Cade quirked his lips and shrugged. "I'm a work in progress. Kind of like our arrangement."

"All right," his double conceded. "I'm satisfied we understand each other well enough for now."

When he leaned across the table to shake on it, Cade returned his grip unreservedly.

CHAPTER FOURTEEN

THE muted thump of club music drew Elyse from her nap. As she pulled on fresh clothes, she noticed the floor was vibrating. The noise wasn't coming from her apartment or the outdoors. The best she could tell was that the music issued from the unit across the hall.

Good grief, she thought. What was her dad up to?

Whatever he was up to, he'd drawn Cade and Arcadius into it. They weren't in the kitchen or the front room. She scraped her hands through her sleep-mussed curls. Should she be worried? Had a gang of ifrits snuck in to assault their eardrums?

She closed her eyes and tried to concentrate like the djinn but didn't sense danger.

What the hell, she decided and opened her front door.

The noise immediately went up a lot of decibels. A party was in full swing in the hall outside her apartment. Multiple festoons of Christmas lights, probably liberated from storage boxes in the cellar, flashed in time with the dance music. All six djinn kids gyrated on the landing, looking far cooler doing it than Elyse could have. She supposed this was the result of their view café education. Evidently, they had way hipper taste in music. She had no idea who was playing.

She spotted her dad leaning in the open door to his place. He smiled as he watched the teenagers, his head bobbing with the beat. Elyse dodged between dancers, then touched his arm to get his attention.

"Dad! Turn this down. The other tenants will complain."

He grinned and shook his head. "It's fine. You see that line of lights shaped like cowboy boots? The twins cast a spell on it to keep the noise inside."

"I heard past it," she said.

"What?" He held his hand to his ear.

She laughed. "*I heard past it.*"

"Oh," he said. "I think that's Balu's fault. He poked a hole in the barrier by your door. He didn't want you to miss the party."

Yasmin's brother spotted her through the bouncing crowd. He waved her toward him, but she shook her head. She wasn't going to make a fool of herself.

The boy wasn't put off by her refusal. His smile flashed out as he said something she couldn't hear to his companions. Suddenly all the djinn were gyrating in her direction. The redheaded twins in particular looked amazing, their long hair whipping while their slender bodies writhed. Maybe their wildness was therapy? Whatever the case, Elyse's distraction with their talent allowed Balu to catch her hands.

"Dance with us, Elyse," he urged. "We're celebrating our freedom."

"Yes, Leo's daughter," the bathhouse girl Jeannine seconded. "This party isn't complete without our heroine."

Well, that was flattering. She hadn't thought of herself that way. And it *was* nice to feel in demand, even if their affection was partially spillover from their fondness for her dad.

"Dance," Celia urged, her manner as sweet as her angelic face. "We want to thank you for rescuing us."

"*I* didn't rescue you," she denied.

"You did!" chorused the twins. "The commanders admitted it."

Had they? "Where are Arcadius and Cade?"

"Foo on them," scoffed Patrizio. "We want you to dance with us!"

She couldn't resist them all. She let them tug her onto the floor, ordering herself not to care that she could only dance like it was ten years ago. The djinn didn't mind. They were too busy laughing and having fun.

Apparently full of happy beans, Balu picked her up and spun her in a circle. "I can't wait to tell my sister about our adventures."

"Your sister had a few of her own," Elyse reminded him between gasps for oxygen. "Yasmin was a bigger heroine than me."

"She's a pip," Balu crowed, tossing her into the air. "We're all pips today!"

Elyse laughed, the challenges of the past few months seeming to fly off her. They were well and safe and whatever the Creator's true nature, they owed the higher power a big debt of gratitude.

Today was a day for hope and joy.

"Ooh," one of the twins exclaimed. "Someone is getting a present!"

"Only if this idiot puts our consort down." Arcadius's crisp disapproval was unmistakable.

Still grinning, Balu set her on the floor. Elyse turned to find both Arcadius and Cade in front of her. Cade was holding up a large golden necklace composed of decorative hinged sections. Within each cleverly fitted piece, big cabochon rubies threw off flashes of crimson fire. To her amazement, the rubies weren't the largest gems. That honor belonged to the central pendant: a heart-shaped emerald with a golf ball's diameter. Elyse assumed the stone was an emerald anyway. The polished jewel was so clear it could have been crystal.

"Good Lord," she said. "Where did that come from?"

"We made it," Cade said. "Magically. From odds and ends Joseph had in his supply briefcase."

He lowered the neckpiece around her head. He had to be careful. The thing was ludicrously heavy. If he'd simply dropped it, he might have injured her. Too stunned to speak, she tipped up the glittering green centerpiece and gaped. This hardly looked like *odds and ends* to her. The ornate setting was beautiful—suitably ostentatious for a medieval emperor. She couldn't believe Cade and Arcadius had made it.

"If it's not to your taste, we can get you something else."

Cade's expression was uncertain. Elyse found her voice again. "It's exquisite." Her fingers stroked the huge emerald, now warming against her skin. "And overwhelming. Why are you giving it to me?"

"It's an engagement gift. Or have you forgotten you proposed to me?"

She had sort of done that, hadn't she?

"They're engaged!" Balu cried. "Hip hip hooray!"

She covered her burning cheeks as the other teenagers joined the cheer. Realizing she was pleased and not just embarrassed, Cade broke into a smile.

"*Now* you can dance with me," he said.

Elyse flung her arms around him.

His mode of dancing was a cross between a Cossack and a dervish. They whirled around so quickly she lost her breath.

"You're making her dizzy," Arcadius scolded.

"Fine," Cade laughed. "You take her for a while."

He bussed her cheek and passed her over.

"We will waltz," Arcadius announced. "That is a nice sedate human dance."

"Uh," Elyse said. "I'm afraid I don't know how."

Arcadius closed his eyes and focused, absorbing the technique from the metaphysical data soup. "Put your feet on my shoes. I'll take care of it."

He had the trick of it, no problem. With her feet on his, she did too.

Presto, change-o, I can waltz! she thought giddily. He and Cade made her feel that way about a lot of things. Though the steps didn't match the music, she enjoyed being swooped about. The feel of Arcadius's hand on her back was especially appealing.

"Fun?" he asked after a minute.

"Very," she confirmed.

"This is how humans dance at weddings."

"Sometimes. If they're fancy events."

He swooped her around some more. "You could be married twice, if you wanted. Once in each dimension."

"That might be interesting," she said absently. "I wouldn't mind seeing how djinn do things. You know, assuming two ceremonies isn't too much trouble."

"Djinn like parties." He cleared his throat. "I would request that my marriage to you happen in our world."

Elyse fell off his waltzing feet. Arcadius stopped dancing to steady her.

"You're proposing to me?"

"Why does this surprise you? I love you too. I wish to make a commitment."

"It's soon," she said. "We only just turned serious."

"Perhaps I'm not as . . . slow on the uptake as my double."

She laughed. "May I think about it?"

"As you wish," he said coolly.

"I'm not trying to insult you."

"I'm not taking insult," he assured her.

Well, she couldn't argue after he said that, not without pricking his pride more than she already had. He did seem all right, actually. His neck was only a little stiff as he nudged her feet back on his. Once they'd twirled around for another minute, he relaxed more. The air of enjoyment returned to his expression.

"I wonder how Joseph is doing," she mused aloud. "I hope he and Yasmin are okay."

"And Murat," Arcadius added. "We left our vizier overseeing many responsibilities."

"Murat *is* experienced."

"True," Arcadius agreed. "Perhaps today is not a day for worries."

This was so close to what she'd been thinking earlier that a zing of happiness went through her. In that moment, nothing seemed like it could go wrong.

Something had distracted Arcadius. "Well, well," he said as they made another stately turn. "From your mouth to the deity's ear."

He stopped and let her see what had caught his attention. Her heart jumped with surprised delight. As if her musing had summoned him, Joseph stood at the top of the landing stairs, watching their impromptu merrymaking with amazement. Her friend wore one the beautiful three-piece suits she remembered from before, the ones that made him look like he was Cade's butler.

Arcadius bent to speak in her ear. "He is outside the soundproofing. He doesn't know why those kids are flailing around like fools. Perhaps we should address that."

He took her hand and they walked to Joseph together. As they crossed the barrier of spelled Christmas lights, her ears popped and the club music disappeared.

"Joseph," she exclaimed, hugging him happily. "I'm so glad to see you again!"

He returned her tight embrace a little confusedly. The way he had to lean down reminded her he was almost as tall as the commanders.

"Sir," he blurted to Arcadius. "What *are* you wearing?"

"They're called 'sweats.' And this is a T-shirt."

"I know what they're—" Joseph pushed back from Elyse. "Never mind. I'm glad you're all right."

"We weren't expecting you so soon." Arcadius slung his arm around Elyse casually. "We defeated Mario. All of us together, including Elyse's dad. Leo banished him and Elyse's cousin to an ifrit island."

"Elyse's father . . ." Joseph glanced at her, wide-eyed. "What about the volcano?"

"He didn't die," she said. "He charmed the ifrit who lived behind it and escaped. By the way, those crazy dancing kids are the djinn Mario and Samir abducted. They're all okay."

"That's wonderful." Joseph tugged his waistcoat straighter. "You've been busy."

The way his gaze cut to Arcadius's encircling arm said he also meant romantically. Arcadius slapped him on the shoulder. The gesture was noticeably more familiar than the old him. "Best keep up, Joseph. Cade and she are engaged."

Joseph gave his head a little shake as if it were too full. Whether this was due to the news or the proud way Arcadius announced it, she couldn't tell. Elyse touched her new neckpiece self-consciously. Joseph hadn't noticed it. Maybe the gift didn't seem as conspicuous to him. Possibly, for a djinni, this was standard engagement jewelry.

Then again, knowing Arcadius and Cade's demanding standards, it was probably a tick better. That made her smile. She really did adore the crazy thing.

"Congratulations," he said, his manner a bit unsure. "I hope you'll be very happy. Cade is a lucky man."

Joseph was a self-controlled one. He didn't ask how the commanders' former goal to reunite played into the wedding plans.

"Is everything okay at home?" she asked. "The city? Murat?"

"Very well," Joseph said. "Thank you for your concern." He turned to address Arcadius. "Our people have held steady. You would be proud of them."

"Good," Arcadius said. "We appreciate you helping Murat steer the ship."

Elyse was pretty sure by *we* he meant him and Cade.

"What about Yasmin?" she inquired. "I'm surprised you didn't bring her with you."

"Why would I do that?" Joseph's startled reaction revealed he wasn't aware of the harem girl's crush on him. "Oh, you mean because of her brother. Yasmin will be grateful you rescued him. She was quite helpful, to tell the truth. She had the bright idea of recruiting some view café entrepreneurs to help recharge a portal. They finished their assignment quicker than our royal magic corp. That's why I'm here sooner than expected. Naturally, Yasmin stayed in the harem. Safe and sound, I should mention."

"We might need your help," Arcadius confided.

"Sir?"

"Apparently, you're a 'rock star' to these kids. I'm hoping you can convince them to return to our dimension without a fuss."

"They don't want to leave?"

Arcadius turned to watch them over his shoulder. "They've been having too much fun since escaping their ordeal. And they risked a lot to come here in the first place. Tempting though it might be to let them stay, I think they're too young not to get into trouble."

"I'd be happy to speak to them," Joseph said. "I assume I can offer them improved conditions?"

"Absolutely." Arcadius rubbed his chin. "They'll need someone to talk to, I imagine. They've been through a lot, and I don't just mean their abduction. Perhaps we should ask Iksander's mother to spearhead an initiative, to address the challenges our youth face. It seems like an issue a female would have a feeling for."

"Perhaps another woman could head it up," Elyse suggested delicately. "The sultana is already overseeing your soup kitchens. She can't be the only female in the Glorious City endowed with intelligence and caring."

Arcadius regarded her with a smidgen of suspicion.

"I'm being practical," she said. "Half your population is still statues. It seems to me the solution to your manpower problem is to ask your women to step up."

"Temporarily," he said.

"You could see how it works out: if the women like the new responsibilities, and if the results are positive. Those kids think fleeing to New York is the solution. Maybe it's not. Maybe real happiness requires seeing their own city change."

Arcadius crossed his arms. Despite his formidable presence, matching wits with him was fun. Because she knew he'd heard her, she smiled without speaking.

"We're not you," he huffed. "Our culture is different."

"Certainly," she agreed.

Arcadius let out a sigh. If he intended to debate her further, Cade joining them forestalled it.

"Joseph," he exclaimed, giving his friend a backslapping hug. "I didn't know you'd arrived. Why are you standing here on the stairs? We should talk in Elyse's apartment."

Cade led them in, but to her amusement, both he and Arcadius decided to play host. They offered their supposed underling food and drink . . . and then they prepared it. There was a bit of elbow bumping as the men everyone jumped to obey found their way around her kitchen. The jostling didn't matter. In the end, their faithful servant had a grilled BLT and a steaming cup of Darjeeling.

This struck her as more of a sign of change than if they'd cooked her a ten-course meal.

"Would you like milk?" Arcadius offered, seeming not to realize he'd done anything out of the ordinary. "I believe Elyse has some."

Joseph shut his gaping mouth. "Thank you, no. This is perfect."

He took a bite of sandwich, chewed, then gave up on holding his tongue. "What happened to you two?"

"We decided to work together," Arcadius said.

"It made sense," Cade added. "Plus, we're both in love with Elyse."

"I don't mean that. Or maybe I do." He cocked his head and examined them. "Your energy is different."

"We didn't do anything to that," Arcadius said. "We've decided not to recombine. We've grown too used to being separate. Also, Elyse likes us as we are."

Joseph leaned back in his chair. "Actually, I meant your energy is *more*."

"More?" Cade said.

"Is that possible?" Arcadius asked.

"It must be," Joseph said. "Your auras are virtually the same size. And they're both brighter than before."

"Hm," Arcadius said. "Perhaps that spell Elyse cut off in the middle reapportioned our shared essence more evenly."

Joseph shook his head firmly. "That's not what I'm seeing. You each look as if you have a whole spirit. If I hadn't seen you doubled with my own eyes, I'd think you were ordinary twins. I doubt I could combine you now no matter what spell I tried."

"I *knew* it," Elyse burst out. "I mean, I didn't know-know it, but I had a feeling."

"Not that I'm sorry," Arcadius said, "but how could that happen?"

"Love," Elyse said, the answer suddenly obvious to her. She colored when the men looked at her but continued explaining. "Not just loving me. You've both risked life and limb for others. You put your city and those kids and even each other ahead of yourselves individually. I might not be as good as you at believing, but all those things must have the power to make a spirit grow."

Cade smiled. "You don't sound as if you're having trouble believing now."

"No," Arcadius agreed thoughtfully. "You could almost be a djinni."

Elyse hunched her shoulders in embarrassment.

"It's nothing to be ashamed of," Cade said. "Faith makes life sweeter."

She almost warned him not to expect her to magically turn doubt free, but that didn't seem important. She couldn't deny her life was sweet, or that she'd learned to believe a lot of things she hadn't trusted in before. She felt stronger than ever: in her heart, in her spirit, even in how she saw herself in the mirror. She *was* brave enough to love both her men equally. The reward for all of them was more than worth the risk.

"Yes," she said.

"Yes?" Cade repeated, his brows rising.

"Yes, I'll marry both of you. One here and one in your city."

Cade turned to his double. "You asked her?"

"I asked her," Arcadius confirmed. He was grinning already but as Cade confronted him, his expression turned mischievous. "I thought one of us ought to do the deed the right way around."

"She *liked* asking me," Cade retorted. "She's a modern human female."

"I liked *both* ways," she asserted.

"Good," Cade said.

"Excellent," Arcadius chimed.

"Oh, brother," Joseph finished with an eye roll. "You two are lucky Elyse doesn't mind having her hands full."

They made her laugh in the best possible way. As she wrapped her arms around her belly to let her amusement out, she knew precisely what perfect faith felt like.

How could she not with her wonderful commanders to inspire her?

# # #

ABOUT THE AUTHOR

EMMA Holly is the award winning, *USA Today* bestselling author of more than thirty romantic books, featuring shapeshifters, demons, faeries and just plain extraordinary ordinary folks. She loves the hot stuff, both to read and to write!

If you'd like to discover what else she's written, please visit her website at http://www.emmaholly.com.

Emma runs monthly contests and sends out newsletters that often include coupons for ebooks. To receive them, go to her contest page.

Thanks so much for reading this book! If you enjoyed it, please consider leaving a review.

ELYSE Solomon hasn't had it easy. She lost her dad and her husband under suspicious circumstances, and her relatives know more than they're admitting about both deaths. Then a mysterious stranger with a briefcase full of cash moves into the basement of her New York brownstone. Arcadius is gorgeous, exquisitely polite, and sophisticated, but nothing about him adds up —that is, until Elyse discovers her sexy tenant is a genie desperate to save his people from a deadly curse. With so much heartache behind her, can Elyse find the courage to help the man who might be her true soul mate?

"One of my absolute favorite authors! . . . Mystery with some awesome romance!!! And an ending that has you begging for more!"
—Chelle's Book Report

"FANTASTIC! [T]his may be the best thing she has written to date . . . the first in an epic tale of romantic fantasy."—**InMyHumbleOpinion**

available in ebook and print

WEREWOLF cop Adam Santini is sworn to protect and serve all the supes in Resurrection, NY—including unsuspecting human Talents who wander in from Outside.

Telekinetic Ari is hot on the trail of a mysterious crime boss who wants to exploit her gift for his own evil ends, a mission that puts her on a collision course with the hottest cop in the RPD.

Adam wants the crime boss too, but mostly he wants Ari. She seems to be the mate he's been yearning for all his life, though getting a former street kid into bed with the Law could be his toughest case to date.

"*Hidden Talents* is the perfect package of supes, romance, mystery and HEA!"—**Paperback Dolls**

available in ebook and print

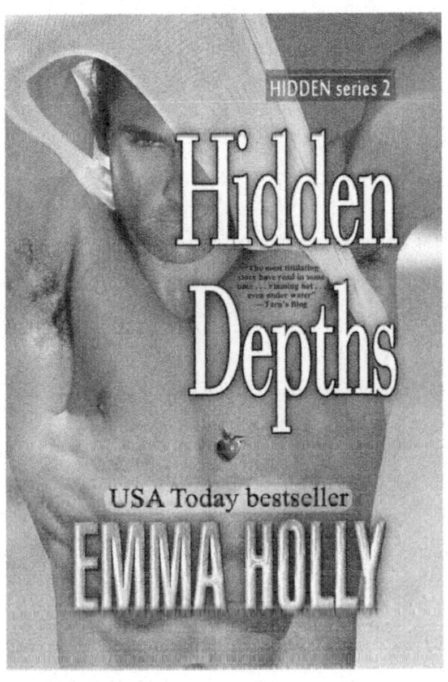

JAMES and Olivia Forster have been happily married for many years. A harmless kink here or there spices up their love life, but they can't imagine the kinks they'll encounter while sneaking off to their beach house for a long hot weekend.

Anso Vitul has ruled the wereseals for one short month. He hardly needs his authority questioned because he's going crazy from mating heat. Worried for him, Anso's best friend and male lover Ty offers to help him find the human mate his genes are seeking.

To Ty's amazement, Anso's quest leads him claim not one partner but a pair. Ty would object, except he too finds the Forsters hopelessly attractive.

"The most captivating and titillating story I have read in some time . . . Flaming hot . . . even under water"—**Tara's Blog**

available in ebook and print

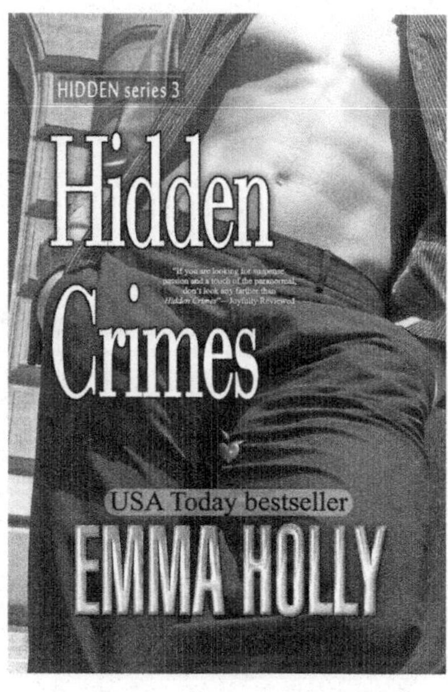

CATS and dogs shouldn't fall in love. Like any wolf, detective Nate Rivera knows this. He can't help it if the tigress he's been trading quips with at the supermarket is the most alluring woman he's ever met—sassy too, which suits him down to his designer boots.

Evina Mohajit is aware their flirtation can't lead to more. Still, she relishes trading banter with the hot werewolf. This hardworking single mom hasn't felt so female since her twins' baby daddy left to start his new family. Plus, as a station chief in Resurrection's Fire Department, she understands the demands of a dangerous job.

Their will-they-or-won't-they tango could go on forever if it weren't for the mortal peril the city's shifter children fall into. To save them, Nate and Evina must team up, a choice that ignites the sparks smoldering between them . . .

"Weaving the police procedural with her inventive love scenes [made] this book one I could not put down."—**The Romance Reviews**

available in ebook and print

DO you believe in dragons? Werewolf cop Rick Lupone would say no . . . until a dying faerie tells him the fate of his city depends on him. If he can't protect a mysterious woman in peril, everything may be lost. The only discovery more shocking is that the woman he's meant to save is his high school crush, Cass Maycee.

Half fae Cass didn't earn her Snow White nickname by chance. All her life, her refusal to abuse fae glamour kept men like Rick at arm's length. Now something new is waking up inside her, a secret heritage her pureblood father kept her in the dark about. Letting it out might kill her, but keeping it hidden is no longer an option. The dragons' ancient enemies are moving. If they find the prize before Rick and Cass, the supe-friendly city of Resurrection just might go up in flames.

"[*Hidden Dragons*] kept me completely enthralled . . . sexy & erotic"
—Platinum Reviews

available in ebook and print

SEXY fireman Chris Savoy has been closeted all his life. He's a weretiger in Resurrection, and no shifters are more macho than that city's. Due to a terrible tragedy in his past, Chris resigned himself to hiding what he is—a resolve that's threatened the night he lays eyes on cute gay werecop Tony Lupone.

Tony might be a wolf, but he wakes longings Chris finds difficult to deny. When a threat to the city throws these heroes together, not giving in seems impossible. Following their hearts, however, means risking everything . . .

"I've visited Emma Holly's magical fantasy city of Resurrection, New York, before and have enjoyed the other *Hidden* stories that take place there. They're all very imaginative and compelling, and absolutely scorching hot. *Hidden Passions* continues in that vein, with characters that are sympathetic and likeable, and storylines that keep me returning for more."
—joysann, **Publisher's Weekly Blog**

available in ebook and print

SELF-made billionaires Zane and Trey have been a club of two since they were eighteen. They've done everything together: play football, fall in love, even get smacked around by their dads. The only thing they haven't tried is seducing the same woman. When they set their sights on sexy chef Rebecca, these bad boys just might have met their match!

"This book is a mesmerizing, beautiful and oh-my-gods-hot work of art!"
—**BittenByLove** 5-hearts review

available in ebook and print